Sarah's Valley

By

Sharon R. Mierke

Copyright 2012 Sharon Mierke

ISBN 9780987956804

This book is dedicated:

To four important people in my life:

Wendy, Melissa, Tracy and Kurtis.

A special thank you to Alvin for editing, publishing and cover design.

Sarah's Valley

It was a 1929 Model A Ford, my pa's pride and joy (or, so he'd led me to believe). 'Course, I knew it was being held together with twine and fencing wire. That's why when it came to a dead-halt, refusing to climb a hill that appeared to mount right straight up to heaven, I wasn't one bit surprised. The surprising part came after no matter how many wires I shook and unplugged and plugged back in, Old Betsy'd just decided to give up the ghost. No amount of cajoling or threatening could get her engine to turn over. I'd coasted down one mountain of a hill, stalled on a rickety old wooden bridge at the bottom and that seemed to be as far as I was going to get.

"No wonder Pa was so quick to hand you off on me," I muttered. "Made out like he was lettin' go of his best friend."

I crawled out from under and hit my head on the bumper.

"Damned tarnation. Now what am I goin' to do?" I struggled to stand up, still holding my head, and swung my foot back, giving the tire a good healthy kick. One thing for sure, it hurt me more than it did Betsy.

"That ain't goin' to get you nowhere, son."

I swung around, nearly tripping over my own two feet.

"Where'd you come from, mister?" I gasped.

He laughed. Well, it seemed to me that's what it was, in a throaty sort of way. I'd never seen such an old man in my whole life. He must've been tall at one time because now he was bent with age and I still had to look up at him. I swear his tan hide-skin shirt and pants with its shiny knees and elbows were probably just as ancient. Leastways, they smelled as ancient. Not that you've seen everything there is to see in this world by the time you've reached sixteen but I'd seen my share of old folks. Besides my granny and grandpa, that is. This one looked about the same age as Moses did in that book Ma'd given me about stories in the Bible. He was holding onto a staff, 'xactly as Moses was, too. Not only that, he had long white hair and a beard that reached almost to his belt buckle.

"You ain't Moses, are you?" (In truth, I knew he couldn't be Moses but I seemed to ask before thinking.)

Ma always told me that if I didn't know something, I should ask. Never be shy about askin', that's what she'd said. Otherwise, she said, you'll go through life pretendin' to know everything when really deep down, you'll be stupid and scared. Well, I never wanted to end up stupid and scared so I always made sure to ask questions whenever I could. It irritated Pa to no end but he couldn't say much, considerin' Ma was now buried out in the backyard, right beside my grandma and a baby brother I never knew.

"No, son, I ain't Moses. Or Abraham, for that matter."

"Well, who are you? How'd you sneak up on me like that?"

He chuckled. "Maybe if you hadn't been so busy cussing at this old car, you would have heard me."

I could feel my cheeks burning. Of course, he was right. If I'd been payin' attention like I should and not going off like some wild animal, I would have heard him creepin' up on me.

"Why're you kicking the heck out of this thing anyway?" He stood away from the car and looked it over as if he'd never seen an old Model A before in his life.

"Maybe you noticed, mister, it ain't 'xactly takin' me up this hill like it should."

He glanced at me out of the corner of his eye. His eyes were so narrow that his bushy eyebrows almost swallowed them up.

"You figure if you kick the tires and cuss, it will start?"

I shook my head. "Naw, it makes me feel better, that's all." I glanced down at my worn leather boot. "Well, it don't make my foot feel any better and that's for sure."

The old man cackled. If I was wantin' some sympathy, it wasn't going to come from his direction. He shuffled over to the car and checked out a dent on the back fender.

"Why don't you have a horse? You'd be up that hill and long gone by now."

Just the mention of a horse made my eyes water. Pa might have claimed to give me his prized possession but it had been a two-way exchange. I'd left behind Sugar, the finest little mare you could ever find. And, why'd I leave her to take the car? So's those people, strangers to me, would think I was a 'somebody' as I drove into their yard. Pa said that nobody takes a horse anymore and we didn't want them folks to think we were dirt poor. Which, in actuality, we were.

I'd dreamed about whippin' into that rancher's yard in my car every day for the past three months - ever since I'd received the letter saying they'd be happy to have me in their employment. Said they were looking for a strong young man who knew lots about mendin' fences and runnin' a steam engine. And, that was me. Now all I had to do was make sure I made it to Swift Current, Saskatchewan, by next Tuesday.

Something inside of me wanted to stay with Pa but we both knew there was no future for a young man growin' up in northern Saskatchewan, what with the Depression and all. Pa and Grandpa had cleared as much land by hand as they could but there was barely enough area for growin' to keep food on the table. Someday, Pa said, when he and Grandpa were both probably in their graves, I could come back and make it into a real farm. Until then, however, I needed to get out, see some of the world and earn some money. 'Course, Pa said that if I happened to have any extra coins jinglin' in my jean's pocket, I might be happy to send a bit his way.

"Right now, mister, I wish I did have a horse. You know anything about cars?"

The old man shook his head. "I know they're not too reliable." He grinned, showing off his toothless gums.

"Where'd you come from anyway?" I asked. "You live round here?"

The old man pointed out towards the hills. "That's my home."

As far as I could see, there wasn't anything that even came close to resembling a home. I'd been in such a gall darn hurry to get through this valley with its mountain-like hills that I hadn't taken the time to survey my surroundings.

There was a narrow lazy-movin' river running under the worn-out bridge. It wasn't high but it might have been in normal years. The water looked brownish, warm and uninviting, even in the heat. There hadn't been enough rain in the past couple of years to fill a teacup. The whole country was sufferin'. Burnt-out brown grass covered the high hills that cradled the river below. There were few trees on the riverbank and the ones that grew there looked straggly and lifeless.

"This ain't much of a place to live," I said. Not that I wanted to hurt the old fellow's feelings, it's just that after living all my life in the north, this barren treeless landscape took some getting used to. Pa'd warned me about it. Said that's why he'd kept travelin' north; couldn't stand lookin' out the kitchen window and seein' nothin' but flat land and tumbleweeds bouncing along with the wind.

The old man grunted. "It's my home." He bent over, capped his eyes with both hands and looked in the window.

"You ever see a Model A before?" I asked. Not that it was anything to brag about. Most of the cars I'd met or that had passed me along the way were a lot newer.

He shook his head.

"You never saw a car before?" I asked, in wonderment.

He looked at me with his toothless grin. "Never saw a car so old."

"Oh, well, I'm only sixteen, you know." I could feel my face getting hot. "I've got a job waitin' for me in Swift Current. After I earn some money, I'll buy a new car."

The old man was silent for a moment. My grandpa would've said that he was contemplatin'. That was grandpa's biggest word so he tried to use it as much as he could. I didn't mind except when it meant that supper might be late.

"So, how are you going to get to Swift Current?" He reached up and stroked his beard. "Are you going to walk?" He held out his hand. "Perhaps, you'll be wantin' my cane?"

I wished that I'd have had a smart answer but after all, even though I was trying to act like an adult, I really wasn't one yet. Although I'd never admit this to Pa but sometimes I wished Ma were there to give me a hand. She used to read a lot. Even Pa said that she'd had a real quick mind. I think all the hard work just plum wore her body right out.

I guess the old fellow could see I was about to break into tears so he didn't want to embarrass me any further.

"Come on. No point standing out here burning up in the sun. You et anything today?"

I nodded. I didn't want to admit that my sandwiches were all gone. I would have still had some too except I'd gone and left the windows open last night whilst I slept by the side of the road. Some critter had climbed in and taken off with my food. Probably a chipmunk, I figure, since I'd heard them chattering away before I went to sleep. Pa'd given me a jar of homemade canned peaches and that'd been my only food for the day. The jar of milk had gone sour so I'd had to pour that out. I put my hands in my pocket to feel my purse. There was money in there for gas and some food. Pa said I'd be able to find a restaurant in Regina or Moose Jaw if need be.

Pa'd also given me a talking-to about strangers and how they'd just as soon steal your money as look at you, so I didn't tell the old man what was in my pocket.

"You think you could et again?"

I nodded. My stomach was terrible empty and it crossed my mind that, instead of food, I might have to spend that money on a bus ticket to Swift Current. That is, if there were any such thing as a bus in this god-forsaken land.

"Come on then."

I took one last look at Betsy.

He shook his head. "You don't have to worry; nobody's going to be driving that old relic anywhere."

He started down a narrow path that ran parallel to the river. I almost had to run to keep up. As far as I could see, there were no houses anywhere - only hot dry dirt under my feet and a hot dry wind in my face. If I could have slowed down, I would have taken out my pocket watch to check the time. The old man, however, was walking so fast and his dirty old moccasins were stirring up so much dust that I didn't dare stop. That's all I'd need to tell Pa: a man who looked like Moses led me out into the wilderness and I got lost - that's why I never made it to Swift Current, Pa.

It seemed like we'd walked for an eternity. The sun was just touching the top of one of those tall hills and I was wonderin' why on God's green earth I'd ever agreed to follow this man. I'd have been better off hitchhiking, making my way to the main highway; the highway that Pa said would eventually take me to my destination.

I was thinking all these thoughts and wonderin' if I shouldn't discreetly turn around and go back to the car when suddenly, the old fellow made a quick turn to the left. I stopped right in my tracks and stared. There, snuggled between two large grass-

covered mounds and built right into the hill, was a small log cabin, its roof covered with tall yellow prairie grass. There was a miniature square window on each side of the wooden slab door. About ten feet in front of the cabin was a fire pit with a black kettle suspended over the dead coals.

Off to the right, not far from the house, was a grey unpainted outhouse with a bit of lean to it. It looked as if someone had planted wild rose bushes around it but the flowers were finished and the branches dipped over with rosehips. Behind, there must've been some sort of cave in the side of the hill with a large wooden door covering the opening.

The old man turned towards me, a smile on his face.

"Here we are," he said. He pointed towards a flat stone that was close to the fire pit. "There, you sit. I'll put some coffee on." He hesitated. "You old enough to drink coffee or you want milk?"

"Coffee's fine."

The toothless grin again. "Good. I don't have any milk."

I watched as he made the fire and hung a blackened coffee pot over it. Out came a cast iron pan and before I knew it, there was bacon and potatoes frying. Nothing had ever smelled so good.

And, nothing had ever tasted so good. Without realizing it, I'd finished off three helpings and two cups of the blackest, thickest coffee I'd ever drank. This coffee put Pa's and Grandpa's to shame. Not that I'd ever tell them.

"So, mister, I really want to thank you for the grub." I stood up. "I guess I'd best be gettin' along now. I figure I'll sleep in the car tonight and hitchhike to the main road tomorrow."

The old fellow scraped off the plates and tossed the coffee grounds into the fire.

He smiled. "No need. I got some coverings. Lots of room here under the stars. There's a fellow I know goes into Regina every Saturday morning. You'll get a ride with him." He shrugged. "Maybe he can get your Model A running."

"Well, I really appreciate this. I sure do." I grinned and rubbed my belly. "Have to admit I don't feel much like walkin'." I sat back down again and looked down the hill at the slow moving river. "This river got a name?"

He nodded. "They call it the Qu'Appelle."

"That's a funny name. What language is that?"

"French."

"Oh."

We both sat and stared out at the water and the hills. It was a lonely place, yet somehow beautiful. In a strange way, I felt comfortable sitting with this relic of a man.

"What's your name, son?"

"Patrick Smithson. What's yours?"

"Oh, I've been called a few names over the years."

"Why's that? Doesn't everyone just have the name that they're born with?"

"Some do, some don't."

"Well then, what was the one that suited you the best?"

"You mean like the one I'd like engraved on my headstone?"

That was a thought that hadn't crossed my mind but I guess when you're sort of starin' death in the face every day, you might be thinkin' that way.

I nodded.

We were sitting in shadow now. The sun was behind one of those hills and the light from the fire flickered across his face. There must have been over a hundred wrinkles on that face. And, that was just from his cheeks up to his forehead.

"I guess that would have been Winnipesaukee."

I stared at him. "You mean you're an Indian?"

He grinned at me. "You've never seen an Indian before?"

I shook my head. "I thought Indians were red. I mean, that's what you're called, right? Redskins. How come you got light skin and white hair?"

He laughed. "My skin's light because my mother was English, just like you. My hair's white because I'm old."

"How old are you?"

"Almost a hundred."

"I never met anyone that old before. How come you live here all alone? Where's your family?"

He kept staring out across the water. For a brief moment, a sad look crossed over his face but I might have been wrong. I ain't exactly a professional when it comes to facial expressions.

"If your momma were English, then you're not a real Indian."

"No, son. I'm not a white man and I'm not an Indian."

He reached down and threw another branch on the fire. Sparks flew up.

"What does your name mean? Don't all Indian names have meaning?"

"There is no meaning to my name. It's only a name. You ask a lot of questions."

"I reckon I do. My ma told me that's the only way to learn."

He nodded. "Your ma's right."

I didn't have the heart to tell him that she wasn't with us anymore.

"I suppose there's lots of stories about your livin' in this here valley, Mr. Winnipesaukee. Seeing's I notice you don't have much for neighbours."

He shook his head. "That could make for mighty long stories, Mr. Smithson."

"Are they too long for tellin' in one night?"

"They might be."

"I'd be obliged if you'd share some of them. Seems like when folks are sittin' round a fire, someone should be storytellin'."

"Well, I reckon that's true. And the older one gets, the more stories he hears and the more there are to tell."

I slid off the rock and moved closer to the fire. One reason being I was getting a mighty sore behind. There was plenty of heat comin' from those coals so I slipped off my cotton jacket and put it under me. I sat forward, Indian-style and waited. For several seconds, the old man stared up at the quarter-moon that was inching its way into the still-light eastern sky. I imagine he was gatherin' his thoughts together.

Softly, he said, "To me, this isn't the Qu'Appelle Valley; this is Sarah's Valley."

"Who's Sarah?" I asked.

"Someone who lived a long time ago." He paused. There were no sounds to disturb us. I could hear the faint murmur of the river and the soft rustling of tall grass shifting in the breeze. Somewhere down the river, a lonely loon called out. No one answered.

(The following story is told by me, Patrick Smithson, about twenty years later. It's written as best as I can remember. Some parts might be missing and some parts might be a bit embellished.)

Chapter One

Benjamin Lawdry thought the bombing and shooting must be over. It had to stop sometime, didn't it? How many people were left to kill? Twice now, however, he'd been mistaken, so he stayed in his hiding place, not daring to move; hardly daring to breathe. His body ached with cold. Its icy damp fingers penetrated his very being. If only he could stretch out his arms or legs. He held his breath as hot salty tears ran down his cheeks each time the pain shot through his left thigh. He had no idea how serious the wound was and he hadn't enough nerve to look at it. His tattered soiled clothing smelled of smoke, gunpowder and dried blood. The stench from his own vomit filled his nostrils and he could feel its wet stickiness on the side of his face.

He wished his injury was in his head instead of his leg. Perhaps then, he wouldn't remember anything. If he didn't control his thoughts, he would go insane. Nevertheless, his mind kept racing back, racing back - like a nightmare that refused to end. His mother's and sister's screams would haunt him until he died. He squeezed his eyes shut until they hurt but that wasn't enough to drown out their cries. Was that soon to be his destiny? When the soldiers returned, would they find him huddled behind the old shed and fill him full of bullet holes? Would Captain Mowatt and his army murder a young boy? Of course, they would. Look what they'd done to the town now. Why bother leaving a useless boy alive?

No one believed Mowatt would destroy Falmouth in the first place. Why would he? Falmouth was proving to be an important port.

Well, everyone was wrong. All the townsfolk, including his own father. The five vessels sitting in the harbour were not bringing supplies; they were loaded with bombs, carcasses, howitzers and cannons. First, there had been the message for the people of Falmouth: everyone had two hours to evacuate. If they didn't comply, Mowatt and his men would burn the village to the ground. No one believed it would happen. He was a friend, a trading partner. They extended the time to eight, the next morning.Ha! The British were toying with them. His father had laughed. Mowatt wasn't a fool; he would never destroy such a prosperous young village.

Besides, his father had been in the same room with Mowatt the night Samuel Thompson's men captured him and took him to Marston's Tavern. They'd released him, however; later, sending a letter of apology. There was no way Mowatt would come back for revenge. Surely, he wouldn't. Nonetheless, he had returned. The proud citizens refused to give up their arms and leave. It was their land and they would defend it to the death, if need be. Never would they give in to the British. At twenty minutes before ten the next morning, the red flag appeared on the Canceaux's masthead. Thus began an eight-hour naval bombardment.

The Lawdry home in Munjoy's Hill became a rubble of ashes in less than two hours. There were three bodies inside, burned beyond recognition. Not until the last minute did Franklin Lawdry accept this as reality. By then, it was too late. There was only enough time to shove his thirteen-year-old son outside and tell him to run for his life. His last thoughts as he struggled to reach his wife and daughter through the thick, putrid smoke were of that son. He prayed for God to watch over him.

His father had yelled at him to run and not look back. Nevertheless, he had, only for a moment. All he remembered seeing was his father's back as he ran through the flames that engulfed their home. And, the screams. He heard the screams. The screams coming from the upstairs bedroom, the room Father said would be safe for his wife and daughter. Safe, it was true, from the soldiers. Not from the ravaging fire. No one would ever come out of that house alive. Why would his father risk his life, going back into that burning inferno? Even though still a boy, almost a man, he realized that his father could never live with himself if he didn't try to save the only two women in his life. A carcass had then burst in front of him, eating up the ground with bright red flames. A sharp piece of metal pierced his thigh. He gasped and grabbed his upper leg, blood oozing through his fingers. Blindly, he ran, through the ground fire, running until exhausted and trembling with pain, he collapsed behind the shed.

Why hadn't he stayed? Why obey his father at this time? The time when he was really needed? Perhaps, with the two of them working together, they could have rescued the women. His mother was the dearest woman in the world; how could he survive without his mother's love? How could he breathe without her? His sister, Regina, betrothed to Abraham Westerly. A fine young gentleman, who worked in his father's dry goods store. Abraham had agreed to stay at the store to keep looters out. If there had been any looters, they would all be dead by now.

Why had he obeyed today when just the day before, his father had asked him make a delivery and instead, he'd run off to play with his friend? Why be obedient this time? He would rather have died with everyone else. Maybe he would die. Maybe God would see to it.

These were his last thoughts as a heavy darkness, like a great iron door clanging shut, released him from his pain and thoughts. He did not awaken until dawn.

The air was cool against his face. A soft rain was falling. Where was he? Why was he here? He listened. All was silent except for the sound of rainwater dripping methodically off the corner of the shed roof to the ground. Drip. Drip. Drip. Yesterday's horrors returned. But, where was the sound of gunfire, the shouts of the soldiers and the cries of the people? Why was everything so quiet? So deathly quiet. He didn't move. Was the silence just a ruse?

Slowly, he lifted his head to look around. Straight in front of him was a long hedge, still a rich green while the trees behind it were already starting to show signs of autumn. To one side, there was a white picket fence. Beyond he could see smoke rising from a smouldering house. Even from his hiding spot, he could hear the rain sizzle as it dropped on to the hot cinders. The fetid smell in the air made his stomach churn. Fortunately, he did not comprehend its source.

He tried to straighten his injured leg but could move it only a few inches. The pain was so severe, it made him light headed. He closed his eyes and waited for the sensation to pass.

Yesterday's events came rushing back to him, filling his mind like grain being poured into a barrel, unable to control, running down, overflowing and spilling out. Could so much have really happened in one day? The ships in the harbour. The canons pointed straight at Falmouth. The citizens trying to make peace but stubbornly refusing to give up their guns. The shower of bombs and carcasses from the canons. The soldiers coming on to land, throwing torches into houses, shooting and killing. The noise. Deafening noise. Gun smoke burning eyes and nostrils. The wind shifting. The fire spreading. Thick smoke hanging over everything, choking everyone. The chaos as families struggled to leave but not willing to leave behind some of their belongings. The foolishness of it all. The horses and oxen bolting with each boom of a canon. How could something like this have happened? The screams. His own screams; his mother's and his sister's.

A loud moan filled the air. The sound of an animal caught in a trap. It pierced his ears yet he didn't realize that it came from own lips.

Leaves on the ground rustled and footsteps approaching grew louder. He didn't hear.

"Well, now. Look what I've found."

The voice brought him back. The moaning ceased. Benjamin's heart pounded. If this were one of Mowatt's soldiers, it would make no difference; he couldn't run anymore. His swelling leg, pinched against his pant leg, burned as if it were on fire. He closed his eyes and waited. For what, he did not know. Perhaps, a bullet to the head to relieve him of all his misery.

"Say," the voice said. "Ain't you Franklin Lawdry's boy?"

Benjamin opened his eyes. An old man, his face black from smoke and dirt, bent down beside him.

He patted Benjamin on the shoulder.

"You hurt bad, son?"

Benjamin nodded. "It's my leg, sir. Feels like it's on fire."

"Don't worry. We'll look after it for you. Me and my wife come back to look round after the fighting was over. Do you know where your folks are?"

Benjamin nodded.

"Want that I should take you to them?"

He shook his head, fighting back tears. "They're all dead, sir. All of them. They were burned up in our house. My father went back inside." A loud sob escaped his lips. "He couldn't reach them. I knew he couldn't." He looked up. "He knew he couldn't but he went anyway. I'm the only one that got away."

The old man removed his tattered hat and clutched it with both hands. "Sorry to hear about that. Your pa was a good man. I heerd talk about him. Made me sad to see his store burnt to the ground. Never knew he'd lost his life too."

He cleared his throat and replaced his hat.

"Guess we'd best see to that leg of yours now. What's your name, son?"

"Benjamin."

He smiled. "I go by the name of Joe Latkin and my wife's is Margaret."

He took Benjamin's hand in his and gave it a gentle shake.

"Well, Benjamin Lawdry, you're sure welcome to stay with the wife and me as long as you've a mind to. I could use some help with buildin' some kind of shelter. Winter's coming soon. Can't pay you anything. All's I can hope is that we find enough food to eat."

Thus began Benjamin Lawdry's life with Joe and Margaret Latkin. It lasted for nearly five years. It was a hard life but they treated Benjamin like their own son, a son they'd never been able to conceive. Margaret died from some type of fever. The Indians claimed it was cholera but no one knew for sure. Benjamin heard that it had completely wiped out one Indian village. Three days later, Joe broke his neck while felling a tree.

Benjamin stayed in the small makeshift home for several months before travelling west. There had been work in Falmouth. Most of the buildings were either burned to the ground or blown apart, but the cleanup meant hard labour with little pay. He'd worked on the docks some days, helping to rebuild the damaged ships. Mostly, he wanted to leave because every day he thought of his family. Some days he would walk to where his house once stood and sit for hours, staring at the ruins. He'd sorted through the ashes, searching for some kind of keepsake, but there was nothing. Joe Latkin had looked through the first time. Whether he'd come across any bodies and buried them, Benjamin never knew.

After burying the Latkins, there was nothing more for him in Falmouth. He moved west towards the White Mountains. After a year of trapping and living off the land, he joined a tribe of Abenaki Indians. He settled in with a small tribe close to Sebago Lake. Sebago meant 'great stretch of water.' And, that it was, being eight miles wide and eleven miles long. The Indians planted corn, beans and squash. They hunted, fished and gathered wild foods. Benjamin learned the Algonquin language. When winter came, they moved closer inland and covered their wigwams with hides and bark. In 1784, he chose Black Swan for a wife. It was a good life.

However, the slow easy way of the Abenaki was not to last. The British wanted them removed from the fertile plains of the rivers. The Iroquois wanted them destroyed. The French pressured them to join in fighting against the English. The Abenaki wanted nothing more than to dwell in their small villages, live each day as it came and in time, if the crops suffered or the hunting became scarce, to move on.

The English and the French pushed against them. Instead of engaging in a struggle, the Abenaki simply separated into smaller groups and disappeared into the night. Sometimes they set up a new camp; other times, they would regroup and counterattack. Whatever the older men decided, Benjamin obeyed. Except for his fair complexion, he looked like any other warrior.

In 1786, Benjamin became father to White Wolf. As he held the infant to his breast, for the first time since his mother and father had perished, he thought about the future. What did he want for the squirming infant in his arms? Life could not make any promises. That he had learned.

The Abenaki grew weary of running from the English and the Iroquois. They slowly migrated towards Canada. Benjamin, Black Swan and White Wolf went with them. The year was 1789.

The tribe pulled out when the leaves were turning red and gold. The autumn winds were still warm and navigating birds filled the sky, preparing for their long winter trips. The Abenaki were not as well prepared.

There were times Benjamin felt impatient with the carefree ways of his Indian people but Black Swan would never leave her family. Since Benjamin had no family, he stayed - because of her and his son. He knew, however, that some day he would have to take his son away. What would happen if the English or the French eradicated the Abenaki from the land? The land that didn't belong to them any more. They no longer had a homeland or Ndakinna. It didn't belong to the Iroquois either, but the English were not quite so eager to go up against them. The Iroquois would not melt into the night like the Abenaki; they would fight, pillage and burn. The Abenaki might call themselves alnanbal but sometimes Ben didn't think of them as real men. When they did fight, the young bucks went wild; the elders had no control.

The first winter was harsh; many of the very young and old perished, either starving or freezing to death. Benjamin spent days searching the land for food. His only concern was for Black Swan and White Wolf. Usually, he found only small rabbits or sometimes, after making a hole in the thick ice of a lake, he would catch a fish. As the winter stretched out, they had to walk farther and farther for their firewood. By March, the small cluster of wigwams was sitting out in the open and the crisp sharp winds forced everyone inside.

The band moved on when the ice on the nearby lake started to melt. They needed to find fresh hunting grounds. Not only that, the Iroquois were inching up towards them and they didn't have enough braves to fight. Benjamin was anxious to leave. He knew that if the Iroquois did attack, they could easily kill every man, woman and child in the village.

They walked northeast for two months. The land grew rich with trees, rivers and lakes. The hunting was good. The Abenaki had found their new home. No matter what Benjamin said, the tribe would not keep moving. They had everything they needed, why would they leave? When or if the enemy closed in on them, then they would move.

The following year, in the spring, Black Swan gave birth to a daughter. She was a tiny baby. Benjamin was afraid she would not live. He called her Autumn Flower because the flowers that bloom in the fall do not last long. He was right; Autumn Flower died before the summer heat arrived.

With the loss of his daughter, Benjamin lost his desire to move to his own people, the white. He settled into his Indian life, not worrying or caring too much about the future. White Wolf was his only joy. It wasn't until his son was nearly ten that Benjamin realized it was necessary to teach the boy English.

And, this he did. Day after day, hour after hour. Black Swan grew anxious. She was afraid her husband and son would abandon

her and her people. There was, however, a greater concern. The
Iroquois kept advancing. Each day one or two young braves would
not return from hunting. The women hid in their tepees until their
men returned. No day went by without weeping and wailing.

Then, suddenly, in the night, the Abenaki slipped away.
Benjamin awoke before the sun. He was alone. White Wolf and
Black Swan were not beside him. He pushed aside the skins that
covered the tepee's door and went outside. The camp was empty. It
was as if everyone had disappeared off the earth, including his wife
and son. Benjamin Lawdry was now more than thirty years of age
but the pain was no less than what he had felt back in 1775 when
he was a boy of thirteen. For months, he lived as a madman, barely
existing.

It was nearly two years before Benjamin located that Abenaki
tribe. The familiar wigwams were nestled beside a small lake,
bordering Lower Canada. For two days, Benjamin waited and
watched.

Finally, on the third day, he spotted Black Swan. She emerged
from a tent with a man. It was obvious that she had taken a new
husband. But where was his son? His heart ached. By the third day,
Benjamin had maneuvered his way to the other side of the camp. A
group of young warriors made their way down to the water,
laughing and shoving. Only one had fair skin. It was White Wolf.
His heart sang. He knew, however, that no one would simply hand
the boy over to him. As soon as he stepped into that camp, an
arrow would pierce his heart. He bided his time.

Several days later, the moment arrived. White Wolf walked into
the woods alone to relieve himself. He stood only a few feet away
from his father, who was hiding in the deep brush.

"White Wolf," Benjamin whispered, in English.

The boy did not move.

"It is me, your father."

The boy shook his head. "No," he said, in the Algonquin
language. "My father is dead."

Benjamin emerged from the brush. It was all he could do not to
crush his son to his heart but he knew that was not the Indian way.

"See," he whispered. "I am alive."

The boy stared. "But," he said, in halting English, "my mother
said that you were sick and we must leave you behind. She said

you had the fever and it would spread to the tribe." He shuddered. "I cried for you for so long, my father."

Benjamin shook his head. "No, I was not sick. She was afraid that I would take you to the white people, that is all."

The boy's eyes filled with tears. Benjamin walked closer. White Wolf rushed into his father's embrace. The two clung to each other.

White Wolf knew he could not have both his father and his mother. He would have to choose. Two nights later, when the clouds covered over the moon, he joined his English father.

Benjamin changed his son's name to William.

Therefore, it was that, in the year 1800, William and Benjamin Lawdry entered into Canada. William was now fourteen years old.

Winnipesaukee stopped talking. I looked over at him. The dying embers cast flickering red streaks across his lined face. His eyes were closed. I watched for a moment to see if his chest was rising and falling. Yes, it was. The old part-white man and part-Indian was still alive. I waited. Perhaps, the story was finished. If so, it wasn't much of a story. Leastways, not one that had to be told before one's death I wouldn't think. Not that he wasn't a great storyteller; Ma always said the Indians knew how to tell a tale.

Suddenly, his hand reached down, picked up a log and threw it on the fire. Sparks shot up and disappeared. The night air was getting chilly. I wrapped the smelly old blanket around me a little tighter. The ground was hard and the rolled up shirt wasn't much of a pillow. Now I was wishing I'd brought my feather pillow from the car.

The old man didn't say a word. He opened his eyes and stared up at the night sky.

"That's it?" I said. "What's all that got to do with this here valley being named Sarah?"

"You are an impatient young man," he said. "If you are to become a brave warrior, you must learn how to wait."

"Me? A brave warrior?" I laughed. "I'll never be a warrior. Only Indians are warriors."

"Ah, that is where you are wrong. We are all warriors in this land. A warrior fights for what is right, for the truth."

Maybe I couldn't remember everything that my mother'd taught me but one thing I knew for sure: If you live by the sword, you'll die by the sword. Even Pa, who'd been in many a squabble in his youth, had agreed with that. 'Course, I reckon sometimes that Pa agreed with Ma when down in his heart, he wasn't quite as agreeable.

"You sayin' everybody should be walkin' round with guns?" I asked.

He smiled. "A good warrior," he said, "never has to carry a weapon. The truth speaks for itself; you do not force anyone to accept what is truth."

"Did you ever carry one?"

He nodded. "Sometimes I was not a good warrior."

He lowered his head onto his chest and closed his eyes. He crossed his arms over his beard. Once again, silence.

It isn't that I don't appreciate quiet times. Leastways, when it's time to sleep. In fact, many's the time, I wouldn't have minded having a weapon, a real one, that is, to use on our old bull when he started getting romantic notions in the middle of the night.

Lord knows I tried to be quiet and wait but a man can take only so much silence.

"So, mister," I asked, "is there any more to this story? Not that it isn't interestin' to learn about that Mowatt person and everything. And, the young boy goin' with the Abenaki and all. That, however, was a long time ago. What's that got to do with you and this here valley?"

The old eyes pierced through the bushy eyebrows. He sighed.

"That is what a story is, son. Do you think that life began only after you were born?"

I raised myself up on one arm.

"Oh, no, Mr. Winnipesaukee. No, sirree. I've been listenin' to my grandpa enough to know that. He surely does go way back, 'specially when he's talkin' 'bout the good old days."

He laughed, in his gravely sort of way and said, "Sometimes when us old folk talk about the good old days, they really weren't all that good."

"So, why do you talk so much about them?"

"I guess we hope that by our telling, you young bucks will learn something."

"Well," I said, "when are you going to tell me?"
"As soon as you stop talking and start listening," he said.

Chapter Two

William and his father worked their way into Canada and up to Quebec. They settled in with the Nemaska people for a while by Lake Mistissini. Here they learned the way of the Cree during the summer while hunting at Nitchequon and Neoshweskaau, the Cree's hunting grounds. Benjamin taught William all that he could remember from his few years of schooling but soon realized it was not enough. The world was changing. In the fall, they travelled down to Montreal. William had a choice: he could enter either the Protestant or the Catholic school. He chose the Protestant.

In the next two years, he learned to read, cipher and hate the Roman Catholic Church. He also grew to despise the so-called faithful Christians who hated the Jews and used young Indian and black boys as slaves. One cold spring day, he watched in horror as the police dragged two women into the street. The men stripped the women to their waists before administering twenty-five lashes to their bare backs. It was at times like this that he thought back to his life as an Abenaki and he wondered if there was such a thing as true happiness in anyone's world.

Benjamin Lawdry died as his parents before him. He'd left his son, William, in the care of a Metis couple, Magedeline and Francois Versailles, while he spent the winter trapping in Upper Canada. His small airtight heater overheated, exploded and he died in the flames.

In 1812, William Lawdry moved to York. On August 16th, he joined six thousand Indians in an attack to capture Fort Detroit. The next spring the Americans seized York, looting and burning. William stayed with the Indians, not only to preserve his life, but because he felt more comfortable with them than the whites.

William met a young Indian girl in 1815. The following year another Benjamin Lawdry was born. It appeared, however, that William was not meant to live a long satisfying life. In 1818, he died on the Young Phoenix. It was the first recorded Long Point shipwreck. His frightened young wife disappeared, abandoning Benjamin on an English family's doorstep.

Therefore, the second Benjamin Lawdry grew up to be an Englishman. He attended an English school and learned cabinet making. By all accounts, he was very good at his trade. He and his family moved to the Ottawa area.

Benjamin fell in love and married Elizabeth Cummings in 1835. Elizabeth was from Portland, Maine, once known as Falmouth. The following year, they left Canada and returned to Portland. They had two children: Sarah and Franklin. Sarah was born in 1836 and Frank, in 1838.

"Aw," I said. "Now we must be getting to the part about Sarah. Who was she, Mr. Winnipesaukee?"

The old timer settled down into the bear rug (at least, it appeared to be bear) that he'd wrapped himself in, and closed his eyes. I waited. Finally, I got up and threw a couple of the biggest logs I could find, on the fire. If this was the end of the story, I wanted to warm up before I went to sleep and if the story was going to continue, I still wanted to warm up. It was amazing how the breeze could change so quickly from to being too hot to feelin' downright cool. That ol' quarter moon was high above us now, and as white as one of those flour sacks after Momma had bleached it. It cast such a light that the river shone pure silver and the prairie grass stood tall like white wheat, ready to harvest. It truly was a wondrous sight and probably one my mother could have described in poetry. In some ways, I appeared to take more after my pa, at least, in the poetry writing department.

I pulled out my pocket watch and faced it towards the fire. It was almost eleven. My eyelids were getting heavy and it seemed that either my storyteller had decided to leave off until morning or this was the end of his tale. 'Course, Momma's words have a way of always coming back to me, "Be patient with your grandparents, Patrick. They are old. Never forget that they have probably forgotten more than what you think you know."

Therefore, I kept quiet. Winnipesaukee's eyes were closed so I shut mine, too. I was just drifting off, dreamin' about travellin' down that big highway to Regina when the sound of his voice brought me back to reality.

He spoke softly but his voice sounded loud and rumbling in the night's dense silence.

Chapter Three

Portland was a thriving hub of activity when Benjamin Lawdry and his wife, Elizabeth arrived in 1836. The city and port had not only survived Captain Mowatt's attack but Indians had invaded twice and burned most of it to the ground. Benjamin, however, was a bright, optimistic young businessman and Elizabeth, a staunch believer in progress and the preservation of family and nation. It wasn't long before their cabinetry factory on Fore Street had to be expanded. Within three years, they were the proud owners of a fashionable home in Bramhall. The two children, Sarah and Frank, attended the finest schools.

Because Benjamin's stepparents were English, they never elaborated on his true identity. Although adopted, he always carried his true name: Lawdry. In Canada, both the Indians and the whites looked down on half-breeds. Just saying the word left a bad taste in one's mouth. Of course, Benjamin was actually more Indian than white but he was not aware of this.

He was also not aware that somewhere, deep within him, the spirit of the Abenaki raged. Elizabeth acknowledged the fact that her husband was sometimes restless although she never understood the reason. Nor did she realize how deep his disquieting thoughts went. She had, as some might describe, a more delicate constitution. Any slight apprehension would send her to her bed for several days. It never entered her mind that her husband might be discontented.

Not until one warm spring day in 1851.

Elizabeth was entertaining a group of society ladies that morning. Their maid was in the midst of serving a new flavoured coffee from South America when her husband flung open the sitting room French doors. His face was flushed and his black eyes, flashing.

"Elizabeth," he announced. "I've sold the factory. There's a wagon train leaving in three weeks and we'll be with it. We're moving west to California."

The silence in the room was broken only by the sound of shattering china as each of the ladies' teacups hit the floor and the thud as Elizabeth Lawdry's body joined them.

Elizabeth's friends had departed as quickly as possible, almost tripping over each other's long skirts. Most were gasping, weeping and fanning themselves as their young men helped them into the waiting carriages. The nervous horses stomped their feet and the groomsmen snickered. The Portland women didn't usually provide them with such entertainment.

Benjamin quickly summoned the family physician and he hastened to the house. A half hour later he left, carrying his little black bag in his hand and shaking his head. Miss Elizabeth spent the next three days in her bedroom. She did not speak to anyone. The children spent most of their time sitting on the floor outside her door, waiting and wondering what their destiny might be. Would Father be travelling west alone? Not that they would think of ever leaving Mother behind but surely she couldn't expect them to give up on such an adventure! The more they talked about it, the more convinced they became that the West was calling them.

"But how will we get Mother to come?" Frank asked.

Sarah shook her head. For once, it seemed she didn't have an answer. Finally, she said, "We must pray about it. Didn't Mother read to us in the Bible that if you wanted something, you must keep asking?"

"I thought Jesus said to keep knocking. Is that the same thing?"

Sarah shrugged. "Well, it wouldn't hurt to pray anyway. After all," she said, with great authority, "we may have to pray for a home, if Father truly sold this one."

Therefore, while daughter and son were giving thought to what they might say in their prayers, their father ate, slept and fretted in his study. He knew Elizabeth might be upset with his plans initially but he hadn't counted on such a drastic reaction. How many years did it take to understand one's wife? She seemed to have enjoyed the journey from Canada to Portland so much. Wouldn't she enjoy the journey to a virgin land even more? How exciting it was going to be! Why must she be so unpredictable? Had he not read the signs correctly? Could it have been that she just wanted to leave the cold uncivilized country of Canada for the slightly warmer climate and bustling life of the American city?

In hindsight, he realized that it would have been wiser to wait until the family was alone before bursting out with the news. That had been his initial plan but when he walked in the house and saw those beautiful blue eyes looking up at him with such love and trust in them, he couldn't help himself. Oh, what a fool he'd been.

Each day seemed to stretch out longer than the one before. Everyone tiptoed from room to room.

Sarah, who was tall and dark like her father, took everything in stride. She was the only family member who understood her father's dreams. How many times they had sat up on Bramhall's Hill looking out to sea. How many times their eyes had strayed instead to the scene behind them, to the west. The mountain range beckoned them.

"Wouldn't it be wonderful to find out what's beyond those mountains?" she had said, repeatedly. "Why must we live all our life here in Portland?"

Her father had always answered, "Someday, Sarah, my love, someday we will travel beyond the mountains."

"And where will we go, Father?" Her black eyes shone with excitement as her long raven black hair fanned out into the wind. "Will we go to California? There's gold there. Did you know?"

Benjamin would laugh and say, "So, you and I will go to the gold fields? And, what will we do with your brother and mother?"

Sarah could never answer because she saw only the two of them: father and daughter.

On the fourth morning, Elizabeth allowed her husband to enter their bedroom. The children crept up the stairs to their spot by the door. The servants stopped everything that they'd been doing and waited in silence. Elizabeth's voice carried quite nicely throughout most of the house.

"Are you out of your mind, Benjamin Lawdry?' she screamed. "Why, in heaven's name, would we move out west? We have everything here. I'm happy. The children are happy. What's the matter with you? Why aren't *you* happy? Business has never been so good. At least, that's what you claim. Or," she paused. "Is there something that you're not telling me?" Her skin turned chalky and her hands shook. "What are you not telling me? Have we lost everything? What have you done? Have you started running to the gambling houses?"

Before he could say anything, Elizabeth fell to the floor, weeping and beating the rug with her small dainty fists. He knelt down beside her.

"Darling," he said, lifting her up by the shoulders and holding her limp body against his chest. "Of course, I'm not going to the gambling houses." He patted her back as he nuzzled his face into her soft blond hair. "It's just that I've received this wonderful offer. A man from England got off the boat yesterday. He took a tour around Portland. He saw our house and immediately fell in love with it." He drew back, forcing her to look at him. "I've been to the bank. We have enough money to pay off our mortgage and to cover the cost for the wagon train. Mack Kenny has agreed to take over the lease for the factory and buy all my wood. Our trip is completely paid for."

She revived; anger being the wonderful catalyst that it is.

"Our trip?"

The children moved away from the door and down the hallway. They had no idea their sweet soft spoken mother could yell so vociferously.

"You mean *you* can pay for *your* trip. I refuse to be dragged off into some no man's land. And, you will not take my children. The children will stay here with me. I'm sure that friends and family will be happy to look after us. When you have come to your senses again, Benjamin Lawdry, and have no doubt lost all our money, then I'm sure you'll remember us and come back home."

After this outburst, Elizabeth appeared to have run out of steam. The voices became muffled. The children tiptoed back to the door and the staff slowly made their way to the bottom of the stairs, each with one ear facing the upstairs landing. The Lawdry's were one of the finest folks to work for in Portland but the staff was quite sure that cooks, maids and butlers wouldn't be accompanying them out west. They stood and listened with heavy hearts.

Two hours later, Benjamin opened the door and came out. By this time, the cook, the two maids and the carriage driver were sprawled on the floor at the bottom of the stairs, cursing their master for putting their mistress through such torture. They were, however, confident that everything would be fine; the family would sit down to a strong cup of English tea and they would all laugh over such a foolish notion. If someone were buying this house, perhaps, the new home would be even finer than this one. Cook was already deciding what demands she would make for her new kitchen.

Frank tried to stay awake but after an hour, he stretched out on the carpet and fell asleep. Sarah sat with her ear to the door, her eyes closed and a slight smile on her lips. When she heard her father's steps approaching, she jabbed her brother in the ribs with her fist.

"Wha…?"

"Get up, Frank," she said. "We're going to California!"

Chapter Four

Frank never did find out what had transpired in his parent's bedroom that day. His father never revealed what he said, how he said it or what he did to win over his mother. He came out of the room, pale but smiling. As he walked past his children, who were still sitting on the floor by the door, he patted each on the head. Frank's mother emerged hours later, her eyes red and her face flushed from crying but with a very determined look. She held a piece of paper in her hand. It was a list of her demands.

Still clinging to a thread of fast fading pride, she insisted that they could not throw their staff out into the streets. It was up to Benjamin to see to it that they kept their positions. If the new owners did not agree to this, she would not go west. She insisted on having an extra wagon for her clothes, the children's clothes and some furniture, including her mother's baby grand piano. Sarah and Frank would resume their music lessons as soon as the family settled in. There would be no concessions. And, settled they would be, in an established city or town. They would not live in the wilderness, in the middle of nowhere, worrying every day that bears or Indians might eat them alive.

"But, Mother," Frank said. "Indians don't eat people."

The family had gathered in Father's study to discuss the plans for the future.

She narrowed her eyes. "And, how would you know, Frank? You are but a boy and know nothing about the Wild West."

"But, surely, they don't eat people, do they, Father? Don't they just cut their scalps off?"

Sarah poked him and whispered, "Shut up."

His mother started fanning herself with the paper.

Her eyes filled with tears. "See, Benjamin. Even a thirteen year old child knows the dangers."

"But, I'm not a child. I'll be fourteen soon."

"Of course, you will, darling." She reached up and patted his head.

Frank was already a good two inches taller than his mother was. Even though Sarah was two years older, he could look straight into her black eyes. If only he could trade her dark eyes for his blue. It didn't seem right that the son should look so much like his fair mother and the daughter like the father. At least, he was going to be tall. That was his one consolation.

"Is there anything else, Elizabeth?" his father asked.

"Yes, there is. If I die on this little *trip*, as you call it, you must return home with my body. I want to be buried in a normal cemetery where I know my bones won't be dug up and eaten by wild beasts. And, in that case, you must promise me that you will keep the children here. Do you promise?"

Benjamin nodded. What point was there in arguing?

He smiled. "I promise."

Sarah, who had been uncharacteristically silent, said, "You know that no such thing is going to happen, Mother. But, surely, if something dreadful did happen, you would allow us to make up our own minds."

Elizabeth looked over at her daughter. If Benjamin hadn't been English, she would swear that Sarah, with her coal black hair and eyes, was Indian. She wasn't like any of the other young girls her age. While the others were sitting and learning to do crocheting and needlepoint, Sarah would be out wandering the hills, searching for wild berries and watching the geese fly overhead. How often her husband had rocked her in his arms as she despaired over her daughter's fate. Don't worry, he said, Sarah would settle down someday. Nevertheless, he worried: Was Sarah like him, cursed with a restless nature? Would the walls of the house push in on her, as it did on him? Did the moon call out to her at night? Would she sit by the hour beside a brook, listening to it sing? When she held a small dying bird in her hand, could she feel some of her life slipping away, too?

"Are you telling me, Sarah, that if I were killed by some wild animal or human, you would still want to return to that place?"

Sarah thought for a moment.

"Yes, Mother, I think that I might. We would put up a wooden headstone there so I could look at it and say, here is where I lost my dear mother. She was the most wonderful mother in the world. It would be a sacred place. Then, I could never forget you."

Elizabeth gave her husband a look of despair.

"Well, Sarah, we're not going to discuss this anymore. Nothing is going to happen to any of us." He then looked at his wife and reassured her, "And, if something does happen to you, my love, we will bring you home to Portland. I will keep the children here, even if it means locking them in a cellar until the day that I die."

This wasn't exactly the reassurance Elizabeth had been looking for.

Even Elizabeth had to admit that as the day grew closer, she started to feel the excitement, too. Perhaps, it was watching Benjamin and the children. She had never seen them so happy.

Somehow, what the neighbours thought didn't bother her as much as it had at the beginning. She grew tired of the women who were continually dropping in to let her know how sorry they felt for her. Instead of weeping with them, she started to tell them how thrilling it was going to be to settle into a new land. How proud she was of her brave husband who was willing to give up his business to obey the call from the government of the United States of America to 'go west, young man, go west.' They were proud to call themselves true Americans. The servants who had been moping around the house feeling sorry for themselves began to respond to the excitement. Frank remembered those last few days as some of the happiest of his life.

The wagon train pulled out of Portland before dawn. There were twenty-two wagons. Michael O'Leary, a short wide Irishman with a ruddy complexion and a voice that carried almost the length of the entire wagon train, was the Wagon Master. He sat on a roan that resembled a farmer's workhorse but had the speed of a hound. It didn't take long for people to realize that the two worked as one. By the end of the second day, the travellers learned something else about their trail boss; he could drink Irish whiskey like most men could gulp down water from a stream on a blistering hot day. Unfortunately, his mood never improved with the amount of whiskey he consumed.

O'Leary wasn't particularly pleased with Benjamin Lawdry bringing three wagons. Especially, when one was filled with, what he termed, 'a hell of a lot of prissy nonsense.'

"You hold this wagon train up, Lawdry, and the first thing that goes is that fancy piano, you hearin' me now? If that wagon filled with nonsensical stuff can't keep up, it gits left by the wayside. I ain't telling you twice."

"I'm sure he wouldn't mind if it were packed with crates of whiskey," Elizabeth whispered, when she was sure O'Leary was out of earshot.

He also wasn't pleased that Frank and Sarah were in charge of one of the wagons.

"I ain't doing any babysitting here, Lawdry. If these kids can't handle this wagon, you're off the train. You got that? We don't slow down for anyone."

Benjamin, in spite of his enthusiasm, hadn't managed to convince anyone besides his one groomsman, Teddy Neal, to accompany them. He had no idea what he would have done for a third driver if Teddy hadn't agreed to come. Some of the men who hired out as drivers were, as Elizabeth would have said, a bit on the unsavoury side, to say the least. Most of them carried firearms, hidden under their filthy jackets, and had knives strapped to various body limbs. They arrived in Portland with a wagon train and then waited to see if anyone traveling west would hire them. While they waited, they drank, gambled and slept wherever they dropped.

Benjamin purchased two oxen, eight mules, three wagons and two riding horses. The children were in charge of the second wagon and the oxen. It would be easier for them to handle two animals than four. Not only that, the oxen weren't quite as stubborn as the mules were. At least, in theory. Teddy drove the third wagon with the horses tied behind.

It didn't take long before Sarah could handle Molly and Petunia. For Frank, it wasn't as easy.

"Dumb brainless animals," he'd say as the oxen ambled off in the opposite direction. No matter how hard he pulled on the reins, they appeared to be oblivious of him. "Why can't Sarah and I drive the mules?" he'd asked.

"Because," his father said, "they've more a mind of their own. If they take off on you, you'll never control them. Don't worry, once we're on the trail, those two will just follow the wagon in front."

In private, however, he warned Sarah never to let Frank handle the wagon on his own, at least, not until he learned how.

After a couple of days on the trail, Benjamin began to realize that his son would have to stop driving. Twice, the oxen had wandered off while Frank was on the reins and Sarah had crawled inside to rest.

O'Leary had bellowed from somewhere down the trail, "Get that wagon back in line."

Frank was adamant. "They do it on purpose, Dad. As soon as I pick up the reins, they look at each other and take off. It's a big joke, that's all it is."

Sarah was almost beginning to believe him. As soon as she snapped the reins, the two old oxen lumbered ahead, never glancing to either side.

"All right," his father said. "Sarah, you drive and Frank, you feed and water them whenever we stop."

"But, Benjamin," Elizabeth protested, "Sarah will get so burned from the sun. Please, try and convince her to use the parasol."

Sarah, however, had no intention of sitting up in the wagon like a lady, holding a parasol. She needed both hands. Besides, she loved the sun on her skin. With each passing day, her skin grew darker and darker. Frank, on the other hand, became redder and redder.

"Maybe you should hold the parasol," Sarah teased.

It took several days for the wagon train to slip into its routine. When it came to arranging the camp spots, delegating the workload and barking out orders, O'Leary was definitely the Master. When it came to the meals, he willingly handed that over to his chuck wagon driver, William T. Black.

William was an old grey-haired Negro, who'd been a slave for many years. No one knew how many; it was impossible to imagine his age. There were stripes along his arms from whippings and he walked with a limp. No one knew if legally he was free but no one on the train cared except, perhaps, for Travis McNally. Mr. McNally believed that only the English and the Irish should inhabit the United States of America. It was common knowledge that he hated the French, the Blacks, the Coloureds and the American Indian. He made his opinions known to all. As he expounded on his beliefs around the campfire, Old William stood beside the blackened cast iron Dutch oven and ladled out the beans. If he heard anything at all, it didn't show. He'd lived a lifetime in the white man's shadow; he couldn't change now. There was a five-inch pink scar carved along the side of his black face. He never spoke except to yell out, "Come and git it."

It didn't take long for parents to learn that the quickest way to force a lazy boy to work was to threaten to send Old William after him.

They soon discovered something else about their silent disfigured cook; he never cooked anything except bacon and beans for breakfast and bacon and beans for supper. This, along with baking soda biscuits and steaming black coffee. Each family brought their own dried fruit, tea or molasses. Or, whatever food they fancied that would not spoil in the heat.

At the nooning, which O'Leary kept strictly to two hours, most folks rested in the shade. The animals were watered and allowed to graze. If there happened to be a stream nearby, some of the men would try to catch some fish. On the fourth day, a deer wandered too close so they had venison that evening. Everyone had to admit that Old William had the ability to cook something besides bacon and beans.

The women cleaned up after each meal.

"Guess," Frank said, "slaves don't wash dishes."

"Hush," Sarah said. "He's not a slave anymore. You want O'Leary to make you wash them? Besides," she said, "that's about the only time all the women get to visit. I think Momma is enjoying it."

She was right. It was the only time that Elizabeth could truly say she was having a good time. Not that she minded sitting for hours beside her husband. It was just that usually she was either bouncing around and not able to carry on a conversation or else she was hanging on to the sides of the wagon trying to keep from falling out. Even with all the pillows that the family owned, plus one of Teddy's, stuffed under, beside and behind her, at the end of the day, her back and neck still hurt.

Benjamin had teased her. "I'll make a tough pioneer woman out of you yet." Elizabeth had her doubts. As they bumped along the hardened ruts day after day, she would close her eyes and dream of silk and lace.

Night time wasn't much better. The wagons were narrow and cramped. She had measured to make sure her small piano would fit. Each one was exactly four feet wide and just under twelve feet long. At night, Benjamin crawled underneath and slept on the ground to give her more space. Still, Elizabeth had trouble sleeping. It wasn't so much the straw mattress her husband placed over the wooden boxes that made sleeping difficult, it was the sounds in the night that disturbed her: the leaves and branches rustling as an animal crept close by, the wind whistling and whining through the trees, the low moans and high screeches of the night birds. Although the nights were warm, she shivered and longed for her featherbed back in Portland - the soft featherbed that someone else was now enjoying.

Frank, like his mother, spent the night in the wagon. He, too, worried about the strange sounds. His biggest worry, however, was the oxen, the horses and the mules. Because he didn't do any of the driving now, he still had to pull his fair share. He understood that. After all, he'd been the one to brag about his age. Also, even though he was two years younger, he couldn't let Sarah do most of the work. She amazed him; she never tired. If he'd protested, she would gladly have taken over all his work to feed and tether all the animals. Frank didn't mind the horses. In fact, he loved horses. Even the mules showed him respect when it came to getting their food and water. It was those two bloody oxen that drove him crazy. It's true that they were big and strong but they were as dumb as a stone. Why was he so afraid of them?

Sarah, on the other hand, crawled under the wagon and fell asleep instantly. She tried to stay awake so that she could listen to the wind and look up at the stars but she couldn't keep her eyes open. Each day was another exciting day of adventure.

They enjoyed warm dry spring days for the first week.

"The weather's been cooperating up to now," Benjamin said, during the nooning. "We're making better time than what I expected." He looked up at the menacing clouds in the west. "If only it would last."

Teddy, who was sitting on his haunches beside him, nodded and said, "Maybe they'll keep moving to the south. Think we should batten everything down just in case?"

Benjamin stood up and stretched. "Yeah, we better. Looks like others are having the same thoughts."

Although there was an hour left for resting, the camp soon became a hub of activity.

Elizabeth, who had been resting inside, poked her head out.

"What's happening, Benjamin? Why are we pulling out early?"

"We're not. There's some black clouds coming our way so we're getting prepared in case it rains."

Before the rain, the wind came. It whipped through. Anything that wasn't stored inside or tied down, flew through the air. The youngsters, who had taken shelter inside their wagon, could hear trees branches ripping from the trunks and old rotting trees, uprooting. The howling wind was even louder than the flapping canvass. Somewhere, farther up the trail, they could hear a woman's screams.

For two long hours, Sarah and Frank huddled in the wagon. Frank looked out the back to try and see how his parents were faring but the rain was so dense he could hardly see the wagon behind. After the first hour, the canvas might as well have been one of his mother's silk sheets for all the good it did. Water dripped inside and tiny rivers streaked down the sides until everything was soaked. He and Sarah pulled wet quilts over their heads and waited.

The rain stopped as suddenly as it had begun. Within minutes, the sun was out. The children scrambled onto the driver's seat. The sun was shining as if it had never ceased for a moment of its life. The leaves and tall grass glistened. The air was fresh and the breeze, soft and caressing. They gazed at the campsite in astonishment.

The slow moving narrow stream that ran by the wagons on the far side of the circle was now a wide raging river, flooding its banks. They could see three of the wagons on their sides almost completely covered with water. The only part showing was a piece of canvas. As they watched, the wagons slowly started moving with the current.

Sarah started to climb down. "Someone has to save those wagons," she said.

Before her foot hit the ground, her father was beside the wagon.

"You kids stay right where you are," he said. "I don't want you leaving the wagon."

"But, Mother? Is she all right?"

"Yes, Sarah, your mother's fine. Teddy's fine. Teddy and I will go and see what we can do. You two, stay right here. I don't want to have to be worrying where you are."

"Sarah, look!" Frank pointed through the gap made by the downed wagons. "There's a horse. He's just floating on the water. Why doesn't he get out?"

Sarah put her arm around her younger brother.

"He's drowned, Frank."

Frank shuddered. He felt secure in Sarah's embrace. It wasn't often his sister hugged him.

Later that day, the children learned how overwhelming the storm's devastation was. Their father kept them busy all afternoon pulling out blankets and trying to dry as much as possible. Elizabeth had never worked so hard in her life. It wasn't that she couldn't have fluffed out her own sheets back in Portland, but it had been the maid's job. When Frank saw his mother struggling with the sopping wet bedclothes, he walked over and helped.

"We'll be on our way soon, Mother."

His mother nodded and smiled. Frank thought she looked very pale. He noticed that her hands shook as she worked.

"The only problem is, Frank, where do we put these things? Everything is wet."

Sarah walked over. "I know what we need," she said. "We need a proper cup of tea. Don't you agree?"

Elizabeth laughed. "I doubt there's one dry thing in this whole wagon train that would burn."

Teddy walked over just as Elizabeth spoke those words.

"You're right, Ma'am." he said. "Not even a piano."

Elizabeth's face turned ashen. "What are you saying, Teddy?"

Teddy took off his hat and held it in his hands.

"Just that, Mrs. Lawdry. I'm afraid everything in my wagon is soaked."

"Oh no," she shrieked and ran off in the direction of the third wagon. The three followed.

They waited outside as they heard her throwing things inside the wagon. It wasn't clear what she was tossing until a wet book with swollen pages flew out the opening. Next came a loud wail. Frank could only surmise that she was undoubtedly draped over the piano, crying and wishing she were anywhere but in this wet unyielding desolate land. At that moment, he felt the same.

Benjamin arrived then. A grim look on his face.

"What's wrong with Elizabeth?" he asked Teddy.

"It's the piano, sir. I'm afraid that it's ruined."

Benjamin walked over to the opening. "Elizabeth," he said. "Come out right now and stop making a fool of yourself. The whole camp can hear you."

His wife emerged. Her eyes were red and she held a handkerchief to her nose.

"My piano is ruined," she screamed. "You promised me the piano and now it's gone forever."

Benjamin answered in a quiet controlled voice.

"Tell Mathew Peters that your piano is ruined. I'm sure he'll feel sorry for you."

"Why are you saying this to me, Ben? Why are you looking at me like that?"

"Because Mr. Peters lost his wife, two children, his wagons and his livestock today." His eyes blazed. "If you must cry over a piano, do it quietly." With that, he turned and walked away.

From that day onward, Frank noticed a change in his mother. She was never a person who gave way to fits of laughter at any time but now she rarely smiled. Sometimes when he spoke to her, she didn't answer. It was as if she didn't hear anyone anymore. Once when he came round the corner of her wagon at noontime, he found her sitting on the ground with one of her silk shawls draped over her head. She was staring up into the sky and softly singing but there were tears rolling down her cheeks. He called to her but she didn't hear or see him so he left.

Seven days after the devastation from the flood, they arrived at a small outpost. Sarah reassured Frank that this would rejuvenate their mother. Everyone could dry the still-damp bedding, which was beginning to smell musty. They could open all the flaps and give the wagons a good airing-out and the families would be able to rest up. William T. Black would be able to stock up on dry flour and a fresh supply of beans and bacon.

Mr. Peters did not travel any further with them. He waited for the next train going east to return to Portland. There could be no burial because there were no bodies. The fierce river current had pulled the wagons over and had swept the family into the swelling river. Several men from the train spent the next few days following the river and watching the banks but they found nothing.

Chapter Five

There was much anticipation as they neared the outpost. Sarah heard the women talking about it after the evening meal. She took her mother's place cleaning up the supper dishes. Elizabeth ate her meal, or rather picked at her food, in the wagon. For the first couple of days, Frank sat with her, urging her to eat. His father needed to sit with the men. Every evening, they sat around the fire discussing the next day's journey and their trail boss would apportion out the assignments. There was no way he could sit and coddle his wife. When Frank wasn't able to persuade his mother to eat, Sarah took her turn.

"Mother," she said, trying to sound excited. "In only a few more days we'll be at the outpost. Aren't you looking forward to getting everything dried out and cleaned up? And, can you even imagine eating food that William T hasn't cooked?" She laughed. "Everyone says that's the best reason for stopping."

"He didn't have to do it, Sarah."

"Didn't have to do what, momma?" She already knew to what her mother was referring.

"The piano. There was no need to take an axe to it."

"It wasn't any good anymore, you know that."

Her mother looked at her. "But, he didn't have to destroy it. He could have left it under one of the trees. Perhaps, it would have dried out and someone else would have taken it."
Sarah picked up a biscuit and handed it to her mother. "Here, eat this."

"He did it just to hurt me, Sarah. Your father was angry and he wanted to hurt me."

Sarah shook her head. "No, he didn't do it to hurt you. There was no dry wood. William T. needed wood to make hot coffee and cook the beans. Everyone needed a hot meal, momma. You remember; we were so cold and wet."

"But if the wood was dry, the piano would have been fine. He destroyed it to hurt me."

"It was the keys that were ruined," Sarah explained for the hundredth time. "And, remember all the water that got under the lid? All the strings inside were soaking wet. You would never have

played it again. Father explained it to you; as soon as it started to
dry, the bands would all break."

There were tears in her mother's eyes. "I never would have come
on this trip if I'd known my piano would be chopped up for fire
wood."

Sarah sighed. "It wasn't Papa's fault. He left it in the wagon for
as long as he could. Mr. O'Leary made him do it, momma.
Everyone was expected to contribute something. We couldn't hang
on to sentimental things."

Elizabeth stared at her daughter.

"Is that what you think? That I made your father bring the piano
for sentimental reasons?"

Sarah lowered her eyes.

"Well, Sarah, one day when you're grown up and find yourself
all alone in this world, you may yearn for that little piano. When
you tire of listening to the birds in the trees because you do not
have a roof over your head, you might wish you could sit in a
lovely sitting room and touch those keys. You may think that it's a
great adventure to run wild like the beasts of the field but we are
not animals, Sarah. You are a fine English lady and you should
never forget that." She placed the biscuit back on the plate. "It was
a mistake agreeing to come with your father but I did, so I must
make the best of it." She laid her hand on Sarah's arm. "That is
something else a true lady does; we try to make the best of our
circumstances. That means that I will stop mourning for my piano.
I should be ashamed. I could have lost my children."

Frank wasn't sure exactly what everyone was expecting when
they pulled into the outpost. He was positive, however, that most in
the wagon train were disappointed, especially the women. No
wonder O'Leary hadn't said anything and of course, old William
T. never talked anyway. He didn't mind the black cook anymore.
Maybe he didn't talk much but he was a dependable man to have
on the train. Most folks thought he wasn't good for much more
than cooking beans but Frank had watched when all the men were
looking for the drowning victims. William T. searched harder than
anyone else did.

Once when they were alone, Frank had asked, "You got any

family, William T.?"

The Negro replied, "No mo', Frankie. I don' got no mo' fam-lee."

"What happened to them?"

He shrugged. "Los' them a long time go."

"Were they slaves, too?"

The old man laughed. "Ev-ryone's a slave, son."

"I'm not a slave."

"Oh, you wait an' see."

Frank tried to make him elaborate but that was all that William T. was saying.

He was waiting with dread to see his mother's reaction. For the past couple of days and for reasons unknown, her whole attitude about the trip seemed to be changing. Instead of staying in the back of the wagon and moping all day, she sat on the hard wooden seat beside his father again. She was back with the women cleaning up after supper. Did that mean that the crisis was over? He was sure that he would never understand women.

The outpost that had sounded like an oasis in the desert was nothing but a dilapidated log building sitting on a barren stretch of prairie. Behind it, there was a small corral with a couple of mangy horses hanging their heads over the top pole. The winds blew strong, causing some of the loose tins on the roof to flip up and then bang back down.

Even Sarah was a bit taken aback.

"You mean this is it?" she'd asked her father. The wagons had pulled into their usual circle. Even though there hadn't been any word of irate Indians in the area, they automatically drew their wagons into a circular formation every night. It gave them a feeling of security. The large fire that they kept burning all night usually frightened away wild animals lurking in the area.

Benjamin tried to be as positive as possible. He was still trying to understand his wife's sudden personality change; he hoped he wouldn't have an upset daughter now.

"Guess so." He took off his hat and wiped the sweat from his brow. "At least, we can get some supplies here." He smiled and pulled on one of his daughter's long braids.

The wind was so strong some days that Sarah had started braiding her hair. At least, she didn't have to keep sweeping it away from her eyes and out of her mouth now. The first day that she had tried it, her mother had stared at her. "I swear, Sarah, you look exactly like a young Indian maiden." Sarah wasn't sure if this was a compliment or not, but she took it as one. How wonderful to be an Indian maiden, free to roam the earth and not to have a care in the world!

There was wooden sign nailed above the door with the words *Supplies and Trading Post* burned into it. Even Frank, who took pride in his lack of proficiency in the English language, couldn't help but comment to his sister that the s's and the p's were backwards. Flattened tin cans covered the roof and a thin trail of smoke drifted up from a blackened tin smoke stack. There were two small square windows on both sides of the building. Other than the smoke and the two nags in the corral, there was no sign of life.

The men followed O'Leary into the store. The women and children waited. Frank was told to mind their livestock. He didn't particularly like being lumped into the same category as the women and children but he wasn't big enough to argue with O'Leary.

Frank did notice something though and he whispered it to Sarah.

"Mr. O'Leary has a gun," he said.

"Of course, he has. Everyone on the wagon train has one."

"No, I don't mean a rifle; I mean a pistol. I saw him take it out of his saddle bag and shove it into his waistband."

Sarah's eyebrows went up. "Really?"

"Think he's expecting trouble?"

She shook her head. "If he were, I'm sure he'd tell the others. Probably only a precaution. You never know who's sneaking around in these woods. We're a long way from civilization now, Frank."

Frank nodded. "William T. was saying that soon we'll be camping beside a lake that's as big as an ocean. He says that there might be Indians camping there too. We'll know when we get close if they're friendly or not."

"William T. tells you all this?"

"Yep. He's been helping me with the oxen. One day they started wandering off on me and he came and helped. He's showing me a few tricks to keep those two old girls in line."

"Tricks? Like what?"

"Like jerking the bit down towards the ground and only going after Petunia. If I can lead her, Molly will follow. If I grab Molly first, Petunia couldn't care less and it gives her more time to wander off."

"You've made friends with a very strange man, Frank."

"I like old William T."

Sarah shook her head and laughed. "I imagine you're the only one, besides O'Leary, that does."

The men were inside the store for almost an hour. Elizabeth was getting anxious. All anxiety vanished, however, when the women heard them returning, talking loudly and laughing. Most of them had purchased what they wanted: tobacco and whiskey.

"Okay, ladies." O'Leary shouted. "I'll take you in so you can look around. This ain't much of a place for women but there might be something there that you fancy. After that, we'll let William T. fill up with supplies." He glanced round at the group. "You, young Lawdry boy, you want to give William T. a hand?"

"Yes, sir." Frank grinned. He glanced over at the black cook. There was a twinkle in his eye, too.

Benjamin watched the old man and young boy walk away: one bent over and limping; the other, walking tall and measuring each step to coincide with his partner's step. He looked over at Sarah. "Now, did you ever see any two more opposite than that?"

Sarah laughed. "He's almost as white as William T. is black, isn't he?"

"And that old black man has seen more suffering in his lifetime than I hope your brother ever has to see."

He looked over at his daughter. "Your mother is right, you know."

Sarah smiled. "About what, Papa?"

"You look more like an Indian princess every day. All you need is a buckskin dress."

Sarah's eyes shone. "Oh, wouldn't that be wonderful? I would trade this long skirt of mine for a buckskin dress any day. They say that the leather is so soft to the touch. Someone said that it feels just like butter."

He reached over and pulled her braid. "Your papa will see what he can do."

"Really? Do you think that Mother would mind?"

He winked. "Maybe we won't tell her until after we've made the purchase. We'll have to find some friendly Indians to trade with first."

Even though the trading post wasn't exactly what most of the travellers had been hoping for, it still gave them a break from routine. Elizabeth was happy to rest her back and stretch her legs. It was sunny and hot so the women spread their blankets and mattresses out on the grass. There was a well on one side of the building so the men carried over pails of water for washing clothes and bodies.

"Thank heavens," Elizabeth said. "We're all starting to smell rather rank. I hope that it isn't too far to the next stop."

Her mood improved so much after she washed her hair, Benjamin said, "If I'd have known this was all it took, I would have been busy heating up water along the trail."

"Bear that in mind," she answered, with a demure smile.

That night, as Sarah stretched out under her wagon, she noticed that her father, instead of sleeping on the ground as usual, climbed into his wagon. All was right with Mother and Father. It was one less worry for her.

At five the next morning, after a hurried breakfast, O'Leary yelled, "Wagons ho!" and the homesteaders started off with renewed energy.

The old man stopped talking again. It's strange how his voice droned on and on but it never lulled me to sleep. In fact, I felt myself becomin' quite attached to this girl, Sarah, who looked like an Indian maiden. Not that I thought too much about girls. Pa said that I had lots of time for things like that. Besides, he told me, if you rush too fast, you could end up with a life of misery. Said that it's better to be lonely sometimes than to live with a cantankerous woman.

I didn't know if the old fellow was too tired to keep telling his story or not. I figured that if he'd worn himself out, I'd just go on thinking about this mysterious maiden until I fell asleep. Course, if he wanted to keep talkin', that was okay by me, too. I reached over and threw another piece of wood on the fire. By morning, he'd have to find more firewood, that's for sure. Takin' for granted he was going to fill me up with a big breakfast, that is.

Winnipesaukee was lying there looking up at the stars with a smile on his wrinkled old face. I put my arms behind my head and stared up at the night sky too. There ain't nothing in the world that quite matches the majesty of the starry heavens.

"There's got to be a God up there who made all that." That's what my momma used to say. Pa, he'd just grunt. Seemed to me that he really wanted to believe but something made him hesitate. Ma told me once that he'd heard too much about the Great War and that he found it hard to have faith anymore. Me? I seemed to flit from one belief to the other. Sure was hard to imagine that no one at all made those stars that were staring down at me though.

So, I looked up at the moon and the stars and thought about the young girl, Sarah, and wondered if she had ever been here. Was that why Winnipesaukee called this Sarah's Valley? No, his Sarah was on her way to California.

The old half-white man and half-Indian cleared his throat. It appeared that the story telling was not over yet. I shut my eyes and listened.

Chapter Six

The members of the wagon train began their journey westward with renewed energy. The tragic loss was behind them. The sun shone. Everything damp was now dry. They had replenished their food supply and felt blessed to be alive.

If any were not aware of how blessed they really were, Joseph Forester, a self-proclaimed pastor, reminded them of it every evening. At the first camp, after leaving Portland, Brother Forester (as he liked to be called), insisted on saying a prayer before eating the evening meal. O'Leary wasn't too keen on it but the womenfolk insisted. If they were to be travelling through country inhabited by the godless, they might need Divine protection. As the days and weeks went by, Forester's prayers got longer and louder. When he started on about hellfire and damnation, Benjamin informed Elizabeth that he didn't want their children exposed to that heresy. It appeared that there were a few other dissidents in the crowd too because more families were rushing in to take their plates and then escape to the wagons before the good Brother could begin his ten minute supplication. Finally, when he was down to four followers, O'Leary informed him that the prayers were over. If folks wanted to pray, they could do it inside their wagon. Moreover, they had to do it quietly.

Martha Forester, his wife, was a mousy little thing who stayed close to her husband and their one daughter. She stayed close to her daughter because, Sarah was sure, if she didn't, Rebecca would have been running after every man in the camp, young or old. She'd started out for Teddy Neal's wagon one night but got only about half way before her father grabbed her and turned her around.

Elizabeth confided in Benjamin that perhaps if Joseph Forester's wife and daughter were exemplary, he would have more credibility. Benjamin just shook his head.

"There's more spirituality in one of those trees over there than in that man," he said.

"You shouldn't talk like that, Benjamin."

Frank had overheard their conversation. The next day in the

wagon, he asked Sarah about it.

"Why'd God allow those people to drown?" he wanted to know. "Why should we pray when He's not listening anyway?"

"Shush." Sarah warned. "Don't you ever let Mother hear you talk like that."

"But it's true."

Sarah leaned forward and snapped the reins. They were driving through tall lush grass and it took all her strength to keep the oxen on course.

"No, it isn't. God hears prayers. It isn't His fault if we camped too close to the river. Even Indians know enough not to camp close by a river."

"So it's not God's fault at all?"

"Of course, not. He gave us brains; we should use them."

"But what about Brother Forester? Doesn't He answer his prayers? He sure yells them loud enough."

"Believe me, Frank; He doesn't listen to Brother Forester."

Frank glanced at his sister. Her lips were set in a straight line.

"How do you know? Ma says that he's a man of God, even if he is a bit irritating."

"He's no man of God."

Sarah always spoke her mind but it wasn't often that she would say something directly against her mother.

"Did Dad tell you that?"

She shook her head. "No. I know it, that's all."

"How do you know it, Sarah?"

"Never mind."

She didn't say another word and Frank knew enough not to question her any further.

Many wagon trains and travelers had ridden over this part of the trail. At least, in the late spring and summer months. In the winter, three or four foot snowdrifts would cover the road. The ruts were deep, however, and the oxen were moving even slower than usual. Or, as Frank said, they were closer to standing still than moving at all.

"At this rate, we'll never get to California," he moaned.

Chapter Seven

The land became more and more fertile, the closer they got to the
Great Lake. The wagons were forced to move with caution,
veering to the right and then to the left, through forests of giant elm
and oak trees. Frank and Sarah sat in silence, hypnotized by the
creak and jingle of the oxen's traces and the constant hum of black
flies and bees. The warm sunlight flickered through the trees and
rested on their faces. The oxen moved so leisurely but with such
deliberate steps, one wondered if they remembered that they were
pulling a heavy wagon. They looked neither to the right or to the
left, just plodded on, one step after another.

At the first clearing, the wagons drew into a circle for the noon
meal and rest. Everyone was relaxed. The trip had gone well since
their stop at the trading post.

"Sarah, look at this." Frank yelled, as he raced back to the
wagon. He'd tethered the horses a few hundred feet away from the
camp where the grass had appeared taller and greener.

Teddy had laughed at him. "The grass is always greener from far
away, my lad. Wait til you get there. It's no different than here."
He'd given Frank a poke in the ribs and teased, "Watch out for the
Indians now."

Frank had not only discovered that the grass was much greener;
he discovered a small ripple of water running through what
appeared to be a long man-made ditch. While the horses enjoyed
wandering back and forth from the soft sweet grass to the fresh
flowing water, Frank explored. His discovery shocked him.

"What is it?" she asked. Frank was always coming up with
something. Maybe she was just getting older but sometimes she
didn't have the patience for her younger brother anymore.She was
sure that he'd shown her every species of frogs and snakes that
existed in all America. Instead of feigning interest in his latest find,
she would much prefer to slip a nap into her noon stop.

"Look!" Frank gasped. He held up a human skull, parched white
by time and the elements. Even then, the hollowed out eye sockets
stared out and the teeth pulled back into a gruesome grin.

Sarah stared. "Where did you find that?"

Frank pointed to the ditch and the horses. "Over there."
"All right. Don't show Mother. Let's go and see what else we can find."

The site exposed several skulls along with other human bones. There were pottery fragments and flint arrowheads. In no time, they'd created a small pile.

"What are you two up to?"

It was O'Leary. He stood at the top of the ditch, staring down at them, his arms across his chest.

Frank was so excited about the find that he forgot his fear of the wagon master for a moment.

He held up a small skull for the big man to see. It was obviously the skull of a small child.

"Look," Frank said. "There's lots of skulls and bones down here. Look at the pile we made." He pointed to the mound. The heads faced different directions; the unseeing eyes seemed to be gaping at the world as if seeing it for the first time; the mouths grinned with secreted humour. They looked grotesque.

O'Leary's face changed from red to purple.

"You stupid kids. You've dug up an Indian burial ground. Get out of there right now." He turned and bellowed towards the wagons. "Lawdry, get those damn kids of yours out of there before we have every redskin in the country after us."

No one had to yell at them twice. They grabbed the horses and scrambled up the ditch.

"But how were we to know?" Frank asked Sarah, after they'd started back on the trail. "Why didn't O'Leary warn us or something?"

"They forget that we come from a civilized part of the country. But, like Pa said, we should have known, Frank. Or, we should have at least gone and told someone. It's our fault if the Indians come after us."

Frank's face paled. "You think they will?"

Sarah shrugged. "They don't attack unless they feel there's a reason, Frank. Something like this might upset them."

O'Leary was moving the train faster than usual. Even the oxen seemed to sense there was an urgency and picked up their pace. That night the men took extra precautions. Instead of only one man taking a turn at watch, there were two. Benjamin told Sarah that was the way it had to be for the next week. After all, it wouldn't take much effort for any upset Indians to find the wagon train.

The week passed by, however, without incident and the group began to relax. They finally arrived at the shores of the Great Lake.

"This is as big as the ocean, Pa," Sarah said. They stood together on the rocky shore, starring out at the seemingly endless body of water.

Benjamin laughed. "It looks like it, doesn't it? They tell me it's only a lake though. Did you know there is more than one?"

Sarah nodded. "I know. We learned about them in school. Does it make you homesick for the ocean, Pa?"

Her father paused for a second. He shook his head and smiled. "No, I'm looking forward to seeing the West, Sarah." He put his arm around her. "I want my family to see all the country, from one ocean to the other. Life is too short to limit yourself. There's so much to learn out there. Never stop learning, my daughter."

Instead of helping with the supper dishes, Elizabeth went directly to bed.

"It's nothing," she said to her husband. "Just a touch of queasiness. I'll be all right by morning."

Sarah slept soundly through the night and heard nothing. Frank, however, was a light sleeper. He heard his mother moaning and vomiting through most of the night. In the morning, she looked pale and shaky. She didn't eat any breakfast and stayed in the wagon.

Before noon, Benjamin asked Frank to run up ahead to the front of the wagon train.

"Tell O'Leary that I need him," he said.

"What's wrong, Pa?"

Benjamin's face was pale; his eyes, worried.

"I think we may have to stop for awhile. Your mother can't take the jostling."

If Benjamin had thought that the wagon master would stop a whole wagon train for one sick woman, he was mistaken.

"You want to stay back and let your woman rest, that's up to you, Lawdry. I don't hold up a whole wagon train for one person. It's easy to follow our trail. If you can't catch up, you know we'll be in Syracuse for a two-night stay. That's about a week's drive from here."

With that, he turned his horse around and galloped towards the front of the line, yelling, "Wagons, ho!"

Benjamin moved two of his wagons into the shade but insisted that Teddy stay with the rest.

"Don't worry," he said. "We'll meet up with you soon. No point in all of us sitting here."

Teddy moved into line but didn't look too happy about it.

The two youngsters sat in the shade of an ancient oak tree while their father tended to their mother. Once in awhile they could hear her quietly moaning.

"What do you think's the matter with her, Sarah?" Frank asked. They had been sitting there for what seemed to Frank to be hours and hours. He was not only bored but his stomach was empty too.

Sarah shrugged. "I hope it isn't something like smallpox or the influenza."

Before Frank could question her about her reasoning, their father opened the canvas and stepped down. He held an armful of bedding and some of Elizabeth's clothing.

The children stared, their hearts pounding.

The white cotton sheets and light blue flowered dress were drenched in blood.

Chapter Eight

The clouds rolled above them, dark and menacing. The father, son and daughter worked feverously to finish the grave before the rain came. There was no time for more weeping. If they didn't meet up with the wagon train, who knew what perils awaited them. A simple broken axle could be devastating.

"What about the promise, Pa?"

Benjamin looked across at his son. He had wrapped Elizabeth in her favourite quilt, the one her mother had given them as a wedding gift, and had laid her in the shallow grave. He wished the grave were deeper but the ground was too hard; the clumps of dirt held together by many tree roots. Sarah had chosen the spot, under a tall pine tree. It was a restful place. The hardest part would be covering her body with the cold dark earth. This was where her life would end. Here, in the middle of nowhere. Here, where there was no one to mourn her but her own small family. No friends, no neighbours, no relatives. Here, where perhaps even he would never return. However, he was not only burying his wife. There, in the bloodied bedclothes, buried in another hole, another life had been lost. Because of one life, another had died. Benjamin did not mourn the bloody mass that he buried; he cursed it. He cursed himself.

"What promise, son?"

"Remember, you promised Mother that you would take her back to Portland if she died."

Tears welled up in Benjamin's eyes. He'd made a promise that he could never keep. A promise that he had never dreamed he'd have to consider. A vow made to get what he wanted.

"I'm sorry, Frank. I'll have to break my promise to your mother. We could never travel all that way back by ourselves. We have to catch up with the wagon train as soon as we can."

Frank fought back the tears. "But you promised. You told her that you'd take her home. I don't want my mother buried out here with all the wild animals. And, the Indians. I don't want her out here with those savages. You know she's afraid of them." He picked up a clump of dirt and threw it at his father. "If it wasn't for you, we'd be home right now. Home in Portland and my mother would be alive. You killed my mother." Tears streamed down his face. "I hate you."

He picked up another piece of dirt but dropped it and ran off into the woods.

"Frank, stop!" Sarah screamed. She started to run after him.

Benjamin reached out and stopped her.

"No, let him go. He needs to be alone. He'll come back when he's ready. I don't blame him for being angry. It is my fault that your mother is dead." He reached out and touched her cheek. "Why don't you make the marker that you told her you would? You know, the one that would make this a special sacred place."

Sarah smiled at her father and nodded.

"You do that, Sarah, while I cover over your mother."

Sarah searched in the wagon until she found a wooden tray that had belonged to her grandmother. She used a sharp knife to carve out her mother's name and the date. As she was doing this, she listened to the sound of her father's shovel. She tried to remember what her last words to her mother had been. She couldn't remember. They hadn't been anything significant, that she knew. But then, she hadn't known that in a few hours she would be motherless, had she? If only she'd known....

Benjamin nailed the marker onto a stake and hammered it into the ground at the head of the grave.

"When Frank returns," he said, "we'll say a few words over the grave."

The sun was starting to dip into the west. Benjamin started a fire. Sarah went to check on the animals. In one way, she wanted to stay close to her mother for a while longer; in another way, she wanted to get as far away from this place as she could. Perhaps, she would just imagine that her mother had decided to return home. That was all; she wasn't dead. She would be waiting for her if Sarah ever decided to return to Portland.

There wasn't much to eat. Benjamin managed to find some dried fruit and a tin box filled with peanuts. Sarah dug out a coffee pot and found a packet of coffee stuffed inside. That was another reason Benjamin wanted to catch up to the others - William T. Black had a chuck wagon full of supplies.

Sarah and her father sat by the fire, waiting for Frank to return. It was now dark. The clouds had passed over. There had been a few sprinkles of rain but that was all. The moon and stars shone down upon them.

Frank did not return.

"Should we go out and look for him?" Sarah asked.

Her father shook his head. "No. He'll come back when it's the right time for him."

"What if he's hurt or a wild animal got him?"

"No, he'll come back." Benjamin couldn't accept anything like that happening.

They waited all the next day. Sarah couldn't look her father in the eye. What if Frank didn't return? What if he were so angry that he kept running into the woods? Running blindly? What if he were lost? Or, dead?

Benjamin had insisted that Sarah sleep in one of the wagons but she couldn't sleep the next night. She just knew something terrible had happened to her brother. How could her father have let him go like that? What kind of a father lets something like that happen? Her anger gave way to tears. She cried into her pillow until there were no tears left. She laid there, her body and mind spent.

She didn't know when her father slept. It seemed that he moved round all night. Once she heard him moving through the trees, and she wondered if he was searching for Frank.

Sometime towards morning, she fell into a deep sleep. She awoke to the sound of voices. Her hand clutched the blanket to her heart. Who was out there?

"Sarah," her father called. "It's time to get up. We have a long drive today."

She climbed outside. There was Frank, helping his father hitch up the oxen.

She rushed over to him.

"Frank," she yelled, "where have you been? I was worried sick about you."

"Now, Sarah," her father said, "leave your brother alone. I told you that he'd come back when he was ready. Now, let's get moving."

Whatever animosity there had been between father and son had disappeared. Her father had been right; Frank needed to grieve in his own way. When, she wondered, would Father do his mourning? When they reached California?

Before they pulled out, the three stood at their mother's grave. Benjamin bowed his head and repeated the Lord's prayer. Each said goodbye in their hearts, in their own way.

It took three days to catch up with the wagon train. It was late afternoon when they caught a glimpse of the wagons. Instead of moving, as they should be, however, they were still in a circle formation. Sarah pulled to a stop and waited for her father to drive up beside her.

"What do you make of that?" she asked. Obviously, something was not right. There was no way O'Leary would let them stay in one place this long.

"Maybe they're waiting for us," Frank suggested.

"Are you kidding? He wouldn't wait for his own mother." Sarah said that and then regretted it. She glanced at Frank out of the corner of her eye but he hadn't seemed to notice.

"It doesn't look good, kids. Let's pull the teams into the brush over there, out of sight. I'll go closer and check it out. You two stay right here."

The animals were quite content to get out of the heat. Frank climbed onto his father's wagon and Sarah stayed with the oxen.

"What do you think is wrong?" Frank asked, after his father left.

"I don't know. Maybe everyone is sick."

"Do you think that they have the same thing that Mother had?"

Sarah shook her head. "No. Our mother wasn't sick."

Frank stared at her. "Why would you say such a thing, Sarah? Of course, she was sick. She was so sick, she died."

Sarah swallowed. She would not cry.

"She wasn't sick that way, Frank. She was going to have a baby and they both died."

Frank stared at his sister.

"Did Father tell you that?"

She shook her head. "No. I just know, that's all."

"Because of all the blood?"

She nodded.

Neither of them spoke again until they heard their father returning several hours later. He was running towards them carrying his rifle. Sarah suddenly realized how much her father had aged in the past couple of days. His black hair hung down to his shoulders as before but his face was lined and his dark eyes looked lifeless. His skin was almost black from the sun.

"What's the matter?" she asked. "Why isn't the wagon train moving?"

Benjamin placed his rifle against the wagon wheel. He sighed and looked over at his son.

"I'm afraid there's been some more bad news," he said.

"What?" Frank asked. Somehow, he knew by the way his father was looking that it was going to concern him.

"William T. Black was murdered last night."

"The old black cook was murdered?" I sat up and looked over at the old storyteller. "Why would anyone want to kill an old man like that? He never bothered with anybody, did he?"

I have to admit that my mind was starting to drift away but this brought me right back to my senses. There was something strange about Winnipesauke's way of relating this tale. If anyone else had talked on and on in such a quiet expressionless way, I'd have been snoring after ten minutes. But, here I was, over an hour later, still intrigued. Mostly, as he talked, I dreamed that I was the young man, Frank. Imagine finding an Indians' burial ground! All I'd ever managed to dig up were a few arrowheads out in the pasture. And, even then, Grandpa said they were only stones that looked like arrowheads. My granddad had a way of taking the pleasure out of life. Pa said it was because he'd had a hard life, leaving home at thirteen to grow up on his own. Seemed to me, he should have found a bit of happiness by now though. Ma said he was just plain crusty.

Perhaps, I should have kept quiet and left the old man to go on with his story. I believe I may have disrupted his thoughts because he just lay there, covered in that smelly rug and stretched out on the ground with his arms folded on his chest. His eyes were open and he was staring straight up into the night sky. A feeling of shame swept over me so I lowered myself down to the ground again and covered up. Now if he decided to quit talking, I had no one to blame but myself.

We stayed like that for what seemed an eternity. Then, once again, his soft monotone voice filled the silent night.

"No," he said, in almost a whisper. "William T. Black did not

deserve to die."

Chapter Nine

Frank couldn't believe what he'd heard. Lots of folks hated the black people. But, to kill Old William? He never even spoke to anyone so how could he get into trouble? Moreover, hadn't he searched the hardest, looking for the Peters' children? A raging anger rushed through his body.

"Why, Pa?" he shouted. "Why would someone kill that old slave?" Tears sprang up into his eyes. "I'll kill the person who did this. I'll kill him." He pounded the wooden seat beside him with his fists. "Why did we ever come on this trip? I hate it here." Tears rolled down his face. "I want to go home. I want to go home with my mother." With that final outburst, he doubled over sobbing, his head on his knees.

Benjamin jumped up into the wagon and crushed his son to his chest. Sarah sat silently in her wagon and watched. Her heart was troubled. Life in the West was not going to be easy for Frank. If only her mother hadn't had to die.

"Son," Benjamin said, "they have already caught the person who did this."

Frank looked up; his face was blotchy and tear-stained. "They did? Who did it, Pa? Who did such a horrid thing?"

Benjamin looked over at Sarah and then back to Frank.

"It was Joseph Forester. Apparently, they caught him standing over William T. with the knife in his hand."

"The preacher? The preacher killed Old William?" Frank couldn't believe what he'd heard. "Why? Why would he do it, Pa?"

Benjamin sighed and leaned back. What kind of a turn had life taken? Why did his son have to cope with so much so quickly?

"His daughter says that William T. was trying to pull her into the bush and her father stopped him. They're having a court case about it now."

Sarah suddenly sat up straight. "What do you mean, they're having a court case?"

"Well, when something happens on a wagon train, something serious like this, and there's no judge close by, the wagon master holds court and tries the accused. If the person is found guilty, he's punished."

"So, if Forester is found guilty, what will happen to him?"

Benjamin closed his eyes and answered. "The rope is already hanging over a branch."

Sarah gasped. "They're going to hang him?"

Frank spoke up. He was calmer now. "She's lying. That Rebecca is lying."

His father looked at him. "Why do you say that, son?"

"Because I know that William T. wouldn't touch that white girl. I know that for sure."

"I think he's right, Pa," Sarah interjected. "There was some other reason for that old Negro to go after Forester."

Benjamin sat for a moment, thinking.

"You two want to go into camp to see what's going on?"

They both nodded.

They pulled the wagons in beside Teddy Neal. Benjamin went over and spoke with him for several minutes before returning to the children.

"Does Teddy know about Mother?" Sarah asked.

Benjamin nodded. "I talked to him the first time I came." He took out his handkerchief and wiped the sweat from his face and neck. It took a few moments before he could speak again. "He's very upset about it, Sarah." He paused and shook his head. "I had no idea he'd take it so hard. He thinks that he should have stayed with us. Says that he'll never leave us again for the rest of the trip."

Sarah smiled. "Well, that does make me feel a little better. I think he'll be good for Frank, Pa. He needs someone to talk to, besides family."

"Perhaps." He didn't speak for several seconds. "But, what about you, Sarah? Do you need someone to talk to?"

"No, I'm all right."

Her father pulled her close.

"You know I'm not good at some things."

"I know. Me, too." She smiled up at him. "We're not too good with emotional things, are we? But, it doesn't mean that we don't have lots of feelings deep down inside. Sometimes, I think too many. It's just hard to bring them out."

Benjamin gazed down at his daughter. She wasn't such a child anymore. She was becoming a young woman.

Loud shouting, mixed with cursing, interrupted their conversation. It seemed to be coming from the direction of the chuck wagon. They both walked towards it. Frank and Teddy followed.

Joseph Forester stood facing the crowd. His hair hung down, partly over his face, wet with his perspiration. He rolled his eyes from side to side. The front of his shirt was covered with William T.'s blood. Red blood, like everyone else's. Everyone in the wagon train was there to watch. Parents told the children to stay in the wagons but all of them sat perched on the benches, straining to hear; their eyes filled with a strange mixture of anticipation and terror. Frank wondered what O'Leary would do. Forester deserved hanging. Charged, however, for murdering a black man? Most people wouldn't even call that murder. It was the same as shooting an Indian in the back. They would argue that Forester was a family man and William T. was only a slave with no rights at all.

"Look at me, my brothers," Forester shouted. "Do I look like a killer? I am a man of God. I believe in God's command, 'Thou shalt not kill.'" He clutched his blood stained hands to his chest. "Believe me, I would never have done this horrific deed if my daughter's innocence was not in danger." He glared at his audience, his eyes wild and bulging. "What man here would not have done the very same thing?" He shook his fists at them. "Answer me! Which one of you would stand by and watch his own daughter being ravaged by the devil himself?" His eyes searched the crowd. "Answer me!" he screeched.

Suddenly everyone was talking at once.

"All right," O'Leary shouted over the yelling of the crowd. "That's all you have to say, Forester? This is your defence?"

"I swear on the Bible, it is the truth." He pulled out a gold cross necklace from under his shirt and held it to his lips. He lips moved in silent prayer.

O'Leary looked over the crowd.

"Are there no witnesses at all?" He franticly scanned the group.

The crowd grew silent.

"Surely," he said, his voice raised, "if Forester's daughter was being attacked, someone must have heard her scream." Still, no one spoke.

"Rebecca," he shouted. "Come up here."

"She can't," her father said. "This has been too difficult for her. Why do you need her? You can see what I've done. I've killed a Negro. Punish me, if you will."

"Shut up, Forester."

O'Leary spoke to one of the men in the front row. "Go and get his daughter. We are not going to condemn a man of rape until it's proven."

"But he's dead," Forester screamed. "What difference does it make now?" He spread out his arms. "See! I have confessed. You have no need of my daughter."

"I'm going to tell you one last time to shut up, Forester. If you say one more word, you will be thrown into the wagon and you'll stay there until the rope tightens around your neck."

The crowd gasped. They saw the rope that O'Leary had thrown over the tree branch; however, no one thought anyone would swing from it. After all, who would hang for killing a black slave? Would their wagon master change the rules because he was William T.'s friend?

"Now," he shouted again. "Bring that young woman out here."

Rebecca Forester picked her way slowly through the crowd. She had been listening to the proceedings from inside the wagon and didn't need anyone to summon her. The crowd stood mute and watched. She swung her hips as she walked and curled her lips into a leering grin. Rebecca had never had so much attention.

She stood in front of O'Leary.

"What do you want me to say?" she said. "That the old man didn't come after me? That I went out looking for him?" She laughed and swung her head so that her long chestnut brown hair slid seductively over her face.

"I want to know why you didn't scream."

"Now why would I do that and wake up all these kind people? And, why would I have to do that when my dear poppa was right close there with a big knife in his hand?"

Joseph Forester's face turned red.

Rebecca glared at her father. "Weren't you, daddy? You sure wouldn't let that mean old man take advantage of your little virgin daughter, now would you?"

"Shut up, Rebecca."

Someone in the audience spoke up. "Okay, O'Leary, maybe we don't have much sympathy for these folks. But, personally, I say, let Forester go. It's obvious that he was protecting his daughter. We might not think that she needs protecting but he was within his rights. The old cook deserved what he got."

There was a chorus of agreement. Some were already wandering back to their wagons, anxious to get on the trail. They had wasted enough time. Most felt that if it had been any other Negro and not O'Leary's friend, they'd have left hours before.

Suddenly, there was a quivering voice from the back.

"Stop. This is all wrong. Old William was not after Rebecca."

Everyone turned. A young girl of perhaps, thirteen or fourteen, stepped forward. Her mother gasped and ran towards her.

"Katherine," she cried. "No, please. I told you to stay in the wagon. Don't say anything."

O'Leary walked to meet her.

"What do you have to say, Katherine?"

The young girl's face was pale. Her eyes were red from crying. Her parents stood behind her, looking tired and worried. Her mother kept wringing her handkerchief in her hands.

She pointed to Jacob Forester. "It was Mr. Forester who was after me, not William T. after Rebecca. William T. came out to help me and he got himself killed."

The few people who had remained, stared at the young girl.

"Why didn't you come forward before?" O'Leary asked.

She looked down at the ground. "My ma and pa said that it would shame me. They said that everyone knew Mr. Forester had killed William T. anyway. It really didn't matter the reason." She looked up at the wagon master. "But, it does matter. I can't have people thinking bad of Old William. Even if he is dead." Tears ran down her cheeks. "He tried so hard to get Mr. Forester off of me." She sobbed. "He was a good man, Mr. O'Leary."

"That's a lie! That's a lie!" Forester yelled. "I never touched that little girl. What kind of a monster do you think I am? I could never do such a thing. I'm a man of God. All of you know that."

Before Benjamin could make a move, Sarah walked up and stood in front of Mr. Forester.

"Of course, you could," she said. "Remember when you tried to put your hand down the front of my dress, Brother Forester?"

The colour left the preacher's face.

"Is that true?" O'Leary asked.

"It's a lie."

"Why would a young woman lie about such a thing?" O'Leary yelled. "They are the ones who are feeling ashamed, Forester. They feel ashamed because of your wickedness. You should rot in hell."

O'Leary looked over the crowd that had collected again.

"Is there anyone here who thinks that Jacob Forester should not hang from a tree until he is dead?"

No one spoke.

"Good," O'Leary said. "Let's get on with it."

Chapter Ten

"You mean nobody is going to bury him, Pa?"

Benjamin shook his head. "It appears to me that he doesn't even deserve a burying, Sarah."

"What will happen to him? You know, to his body?"

"I imagine the wild animals will make a meal out of it."

He didn't have to see her shudder; he could feel it. At least, O'Leary had made sure that the old Negro slave received a proper burial.

They were already several miles away from the execution site. It had taken six strong men to hold the preacher down but eventually they had subdued him enough to hoist him on to a saddle. The loop was already around his neck. O'Leary slapped the horse on his backside with a whip. The horse reared and raced off. Forester dangled from the tree, his body jerking and his legs twisting until all life was gone. There were very few bystanders. The court showcasing had proved more interesting than the actual punishment. No one wanted to know any of the details of Brother Forester's sins. When Sarah Lawdry had stepped forward to add credibility to the young girl's accusations, Mr. Forester's future had been determined. His wife and daughter quietly returned to their wagon. They stayed to themselves until everyone was ready to leave but when O'Leary moved the train out, the women were not with it. Sarah felt sorry for the mother. Where would she go? Back to Portland? Everyone knew the dangers of travelling alone but no amount of coaxing could sway them. It didn't take a vivid imagination to know that the daughter would run off with the first available man.

For the next three days, the wagons moved slowly without incident. However, a heavy sombreness hung over everyone, even the youngsters.

The train now camped outside a small cluster of makeshift homes. No one had given the hamlet a name yet. It consisted of eight either completed or in the process of being completed, log or clapboard houses. The homes were scattered randomly along the narrow rut-filled dirt road that would someday be their main street. That is, if the inhabitants could make a living and attract newcomers. The land surrounding the area was rich and fertile. There was a lake nearby with clear water and at any given time, a person could sit and watch the fish jump. Yes, the folks who were working so hard to finish building their homes, were optimistic for the future.

"Yes, sir, this will be a booming town in no time," Izzy Goldstein, one of the founding fathers, said. "We got the wagon trains comin' through on a r'glar basis now. By next month, we'll have a real name and the U.S. mail will be delivered right to our doors."

Benjamin looked over at the dejected collection of unpainted and half-built one room shacks, the roofs covered with dirty grey canvas from their abandoned wagons instead of fresh new shingles. Behind several of them, he could see women and children bent over, trying to rip up the hard black soil to plant seeds. It was already late for planting and no one realized how early the fall frosts could arrive. He thought about his own home back in Portland, the modern conveniences, and the loyal servants who sang and laughed as they went about their daily chores. He thought about Elizabeth insisting that her maid air out their bedclothes every morning, how the morning coffee must be brewed just so or she would have it thrown out, how she insisted that every Friday she and Benjamin must attend some function, preferably charitable, to promote their business. She knew the importance of being 'seen.'

What madness had over-powered him? Even in his wildest imagination, how could he have thought his family could cope with something like this?

This was, without doubt, his future - barely surviving somewhere (he had no idea where) in a tiny insect and rodent infested shanty and slaving from morning until night to put food on his table. His wife had died because of his foolishness. A depraved monster molested his daughter. He glanced at Frank. The young lad had perhaps suffered the most; he'd lost not only his beloved mother but that same depraved monster murdered his Negro friend. Benjamin's once happy carefree son was now quiet and withdrawn. There was a troubled look in his eyes even when his lips were smiling. It was not easy to admit but perhaps, it was time to turn around and go back to Portland. How much more hardship could they handle?

"So," Benjamin asked, "what do you plan on calling your town?"

"Some of the folks suggested it should be named after me. After all," he said, after clearing his throat, "I was the one who built the first house here." He pointed to the farthest house, the only one with a roof not made of cloth. "That's mine there. Plan on bringin' in some shingles and buildin' supplies for the folks soon. Made a deal with some contractors back in Portland. They should be arrivin' any day now."

"They're coming in from Portland?"

"Yup. A whole wagon train of supplies." He squinted at Benjamin. "You thinkin' of maybe settlin' down here yourself?"

Benjamin shook his head.

"No. I was thinking more along the lines of travelling back to Portland with them."

"You know, Lawdry, I can't refund any of your money."

O'Leary was busy brushing down his horse when Benjamin approached him.

"I understand that."

The wagon master stopped for a moment and looked at him.

"You sure this is what you should do?"

"What do you mean?"

O'Leary returned to his brushing. "I mean, what will your kids think if you run back home?"

Benjamin felt the hair on the back of his neck bristle.

"You're saying that I'm a coward for wanting to take my children back home?"

O'Leary kept brushing. "No, I'm saying that it might be hard on your kids, that's all. How will you be treated when you get back?" He stopped brushing and straightened up. "Will your wife's family view you as a failure? That's what I'm saying, Benjamin. Did you not think of that?"

No, Benjamin hadn't thought of that. His main concern was to get them back into civilization. The thought that his friends or family would view him as a failure hadn't occurred to him. To return with his two distraught children and without his wife could cause some problems. How would Elizabeth's relatives feel about him? Especially, the ones who had protested their leaving with such vehemence.

"I didn't. I didn't think of that at all."

"What about the kids? Do they want to go back?"

Benjamin flushed. "I haven't talked to them yet. Sometimes a parent has to make the decision for the children, O'Leary."

O'Leary grinned.

"Sure, I know that. Maybe you hadn't noticed that your kids aren't such children anymore." He went back to brushing.

The train master could be irritating at times but Benjamin had to admit that he made sense. There was no way that he could force his children to return to Portland if they didn't want to. If they did, however, he'd have to be honest with them about the reaction they might encounter there.

He walked slowly back to the wagons. From a distance, he could see Sarah bent over the washboard, scrubbing clothes. She'd braided her raven hair into a single braid that reached the middle of her back. She worked steadily; when one garment was clean, she dipped it into the scalding water one last time, pulled it out, threw it into a washtub filled with cold water, wrung it and draped it over any unmovable object that she could find.

Frank was returning from the lake with the animals. The two oxen were walking meekly beside him; the mules and horses, following. Benjamin had to smile. Whatever animosity had existed between his son and those oxen had vanished.

Benjamin realized that O'Leary was right; his innocent children were growing up quickly. He would leave the decision to return to Portland up to them.

"What do you mean, go back to Portland?" Frank asked. "Why would we want to go back? Do you want to, Pa?"

Benjamin looked across the fire at his son. The three of them, along with Teddy Neal, sat around a small fire in front of the wagon. It was a warm evening. They were relaxing before settling down for the night. In the distance, they could hear laughter and an occasional shout. Most of the men had gathered at Izzy's house for the evening. He'd managed to obtain a crate of whiskey from one of the trains going through and was now sharing it with his new friends. Not that he was freely sharing it but O'Leary, for one, was ready to dole out almost anything for a bottle. His supply was getting low and when he had to ration his booze, Michael O'Leary was not a happy person. Losing his cook and friend, William T. Black, didn't help matters. The more he thought about the murder, the more he drank.

Travis McNally hadn't joined the boisterous crowd either. Not that he wasn't yearning for a good drink of whisky; he refused to buy it from a Jew.

Benjamin glanced round at the others. "I want to find out how each of you feels. We've gone through some terrible times and I want to know if you want to keep going, that's all. This isn't about me now; it's about you and how you feel."

He turned his attention to Teddy. "What about you? I know you didn't bargain for this. Would you prefer to return to Portland?"

Teddy swirled the last bit of coffee around in his cup. It took several seconds before he looked up to speak, a slight touch of Ireland still on his tongue.

"I don't know what your plans are, Mr. Lawdry, but as I said before, I'll stick with you in any decision that you make. If you feel it's too hard on the children, I'll be happy to turn round and go back."

Sarah spoke up. "Is this what it's about, Pa? You think that it's too hard on us?"

"Well, I was thinking that, Sarah. You've had a lot to deal with so far and I can't guarantee that everything will go smoothly from here on in."

Sara smiled. "We know that, don't we, Frank?"

Frank nodded. "What would we ever do if we went back to Portland? You sold the store, Pa. We don't even have a house there now. I'd rather keep going and build a new one in California. I know Ma won't be there but she wouldn't be in Portland either. I think it would be more lonely without her there." He turned to his sister. "We want to travel the Santa Fe trail, don't we?"

Sarah nodded. "And then from the Santa Fe, we can travel right across into California. We looked it up on a map before we left home, Pa. Once we hit Independence, it will be easy going."

Teddy grinned. "Yeah," he said, "it's just getting to Independence that's the kicker."

They laughed. Sarah refilled the coffee cups. Somewhere at the other edge of town, they could hear yelling and shouting.

"Now, that sounds like a good old-fashioned fistfight," Teddy said. "Guess that Irish whiskey might be too much for some."

By the sudden applause, it appeared that one of the opponents must have been either knocked down or out.

"Let's hope that it isn't O'Leary," Benjamin said. "I want to get an early start.

At five a.m., the call went out for breakfast. The sun was just starting to show itself over the horizon. One of the men, Rodger Blackburn, took over the chuck wagon duties. He wasn't as good as the former cook but no one complained. Mostly, because no one else wanted to be coerced into it. Sarah hurriedly struggled into her clean but still slightly damp clothes. She could smell the coffee brewing and bacon frying. Today's breakfast would be especially good but as the days went by, supplies would become scantier and the meals would reflect that. By the time they reached the next town or outpost, everyone would be delirious for a change of menu. At least now they had stocked up on some dried foods. Mr. Goldstein knew exactly what the travellers needed and most had purchased a few things from him. He assured them that if they ever came back the same way, he would have more than double the supplies.

No one stood round drinking coffee and chatting. The breakfast lined moved quickly and efficiently.

"Okay, everybody, let's be ready to move out in an hour." O'Leary stood by the chuck wagon, his plate in hand. If he'd been up all night, fighting and drinking, it didn't show. He repeated his request several times before shoving his empty plate towards one of the women. Everyone started to gulp down their food because they knew that once O'Leary was up on his horse, he would harass them until they were in their wagons.

While Blackburn was busy shoving the last of the utensils into the wagon, Travis McNally rushed over.

"Rodger," he begged. "Could you just give me a slab of bread or something?"

"Sorry, Travis. You get here when I'm serving. I don't make any exceptions. No reason you can't be here with the rest of them." He looked up from his work. "What in blazes happened to you?"

Travis McNally pulled his hat down. Even then, he couldn't hide his black eye, which was quickly swelling shut.

Blackburn grinned. "That's some way to start the morning. Who gave you that shiner anyway? Or, did you walk into the corner of your wagon?" His grin broadened. "Or, maybe your lovely wife was upset with you. Was that it?"

"Just be quiet, will you?"

"Well, can't see how you're going to keep that a secret. It's looking good compared to what it will be like tomorrow. You gonna tell me who popped you or do I have to ask around?"

"No, don't ask anybody. I'll tell you. Just keep quiet about it." He reached up, touched his eye and flinched. "It was that Jew, that's who it was."

Blackburn's eyes got bigger. "Izzy Goldstein gave you that shiner this morning? What the heck did you do to rile him up?"

"Nothing. I did nothing."

"No way, McNally. You wouldn't even talk to him yesterday. What's going on here?"

Before McNally could answer, the call went out, "Wagons ho!" and he rushed to his wagon. Blackburn slammed the gate shut and climbed up. O'Leary didn't mind if the chuck wagon trailed behind as long as the meals were on time so he sat and watched as each wagon lumbered past. McNally's wagon was second from the end. He grinned and waved his hat but the man with the black eye didn't respond.

Everyone was relieved that the day was so uneventful. They made good time and camped for the night by a bluff of trees. The animals drank from a nearby stream and there was fresh water for coffee. The only interruption that evening was a loud discussion between Michael O'Leary and Travis McNally. It wasn't long and soon everyone found out the cause of the black eye. It appeared that McNally wouldn't buy whisky from a Jew but it wasn't beneath his dignity to steal from a Jew. O'Leary let the matter drop. He seemed to think that the humiliation of it all was punishment enough. After all, McNally was almost six feet tall and the little Jew was only five foot five. In addition, he ended up with a whopper of a black eye and no whiskey.

Chapter Eleven

A week went by. The sun shone. The breeze was cool. It seemed the miles were just melting away. Everyone on the wagon train knew that they had made the right decision, in spite of the tragedies they'd encountered. Frank was beginning to take an interest in life again. He spoke often of his mother but he was beginning to focus on pleasant memories and the bitterness was slowly dissipating.

Sarah was as calm and steady as she had always been. Benjamin watched in wonderment as she methodically went about her daily chores, a small secretive smile on her lips. It was impossible to tell if she was enjoying them or not. At times, it seemed that her mind was somewhere in a faraway place. A place, that he was certain was peaceful and serene; a place where she could wander alone, as free as the small yellow finches that flitted from tree to tree. He'd sat motionless one evening until one had landed only inches away. Elizabeth had never had the patience to sit for so long. Sarah, he knew, would wait for hours just to watch a baby robin fly from its nest. Frank wasn't interested in birds at all.

On the eighth day, the scenery changed. They spent most of the morning climbing a ridge and the rest of the day, slowly moving their way down into a valley. The valley wasn't wide but the terrain was rugged. No matter how many wagon wheels rolled over it, the ground was rocky and unyielding.

"Anybody live round here?" Frank asked O'Leary.

The evening meal was over. Ever since the old cook had died, the wagon master made it a habit of visiting each family before darkness set in. There was a sadness about him now that made him appear more vulnerable. Frank and Sarah weren't afraid of him anymore. In fact, they had started looking forward to the few minutes that he spent with them.

O'Leary stood with a cup of coffee in his hand, laced with a few drops of whiskey to be sure, and leaned against the side of the wagon. He shoved his hat to the back of his head.

"Not many live out this way, Frank. This is the start of the Blue Ridge Mountains. They run south from here, all the way down through the Carolina's and into Georgia. Could be some Indian tribes but not many whites."

"What kind of Indians?"

"Mmm. Might be some Cherokee left. This used to be called The Cherokee Mountains way back in the seventeen hundred's."

"Think we might run into some?"

The big man laughed. "Well, you can be sure we won't meet them on the trail. If you look hard enough maybe you'll spot a few peering at you through the trees."

Frank's eyes got bigger. "You really think so?"

O'Leary threw his coffee grounds into the bush. "You never know," he said, and wandered off to the next wagon.

"Did you hear that, Pa? We could meet some real Indians."

Teddy looked over at Benjamin. "And, let's hope they're nice friendly ones."

Benjamin stood up and stretched. The sun was starting to set. They would need their sleep; the trail ahead led up another ridge that looked more rugged than the first one that they'd crossed.

He walked over and tousled his son's hair. "If we do meet some Indians, I'm sure we won't have to worry. All those glorified cowboy-Indian stories come from books and someone's imagination, son."

"But, Pa," Sarah said. "You know there've been wars with the Indians. They attacked and burned Portland down two or three times."

"That was long ago. They don't attack people in this day and age. They're civilized now."

Teddy started towards his wagon. "I sure do hope you're right, Mr. Lawdry," he called back. When he reached the back of his wagon, he turned. "Sometimes, it's the whites that aren't too civilized, you know."

Benjamin laughed. "Okay, Teddy, you've put the fear of God in us now. There better not be an all-out Indian war or my word won't be worth much."

All of them laughed and went their separate ways. Sarah climbed under her wagon. She'd made her bed hours before because she knew that the instant her head hit the pillow, she'd be asleep. Frank climbed into the wagon. Every time he went inside, he thought about his mother. Sometimes, his body literally ached for her. There was no one to hug him now. Sarah was like his father. They didn't do things like that. That was what he missed the most - his mother's touch and the soft scent of her lilac toilet water. Even after travelling all day in the sun, she still smelled good.

Another young man lay awake at night thinking about Elizabeth Lawdry too. Tears would roll down his face and he would bury his face in his pillow. Would he ever be able to forget those soft blue eyes? The touch of her hand as she reached over to console him or talk to him? Why had she married a man who was so distant and cold? Someone who didn't understand her like he did? Not that he didn't have a great respect for Benjamin Lawdry. He did.

He would never forget the day that he'd approached her. What a fool he'd been! How could he have mistaken her kindness for something more? And, in true Elizabeth fashion, she'd let him down so gently. Why had he taken advantage of the situation? That, he would never understand. She'd been so shocked and hurt. He remembered her eyes after the kiss. The kiss that had shocked him too. Afterwards, she'd treated him as a child. That was almost more painful. If only it could be kept secret. She thought that it was. Teddy knew otherwise. Someone had seen them.

Chapter Twelve

The western side of the ridge was much more taxing. The wagons heaved from side to side, groaning and creaking. Water splashed out of the barrels that were attached to the sides of the wagons. The horses reared and the mules balked at every step. The oxen lumbered on, unflappable. There was no convenient place for the nooning, so the caravans kept moving. O'Leary promised an early stop at the bottom of the last ravine. No one minded; everyone wanted to get back down on level ground again.

By early afternoon, the sun disappeared and the sky turned dark with ominous clouds. The wagon train pushed on. No one wanted to navigate the wagons over the rugged terrain when it was wet and slippery.

Frank sat beside his sister, hanging on to the side to save his life. Sarah leaned back, pulling the reins taut against her chest and pressing her feet against floorboards for support. Her lips were set in a firm line of determination. Each downward jolt threatened to send them both careening off into the deep ravine or being crushed against the rugged rock formations.

"Think we'll get out of here before this storm breaks, Sarah?"

Before she could answer, there was a deafening clap of thunder, seconds later a flash of lighting and the first large raindrops began to pelt down. Within minutes, the two were soaked. Water bounced off the backs of the oxen and sprayed into the air. Frank crawled into the wagon and brought out a couple of grey army blankets. He draped one over Sarah and one over himself.

"I can't see two feet in front of us. How will we be able to keep up with the others?"

Sarah never took her eyes off the backs of the oxen. "We'll have to trust the animals, that's all." The wagon started to skid.

"Sarah," Frank screamed. "Watch out!"

At that moment, the wheel scraped along the side of a jutting rock. The ground was so slippery that instead of righting itself, the whole wagon slid further against the rock. One by one, the spokes splintered and smashed apart. Slowly, the wagon shifted to the right and the front side went down with a crash, the wheel breaking lose and rolling away into the haze. With a loud bang, the axle slammed against the side of the jagged rock and stayed there. Sarah grabbed Frank before he flew through the air. They landed together in a heap in the corner, hanging on to the wagon and to each other. The oxen stood still.

"What are we going to do?" Frank wanted to know. "Where's Pa? Where is anybody?" He tried to straighten out and peer round the side. "I can't see a thing; it's raining too heavy."

Besides the rain pouring down, there was mist rising up from the ground. It was almost impossible to see the heads of the oxen.

Sarah started to move on to the seat. The left front and back wheels were sitting a foot or more off the ground.

"There's nothing that you or I can do. We'll have to sit here and wait for Pa. He can't be that far behind us."

"Do you think that maybe we got off the trail? If we did, Sarah, dad would never see us in this rain."

"Well, someone somewhere along the trail will find us, I'm sure. I think we should get off the wagon and sit under it. At least, then we'll be drier."

Frank nodded. Water was running down his face and dripping off the end of his nose.

"Can't we go inside the wagon?"

Sarah shook her head. "What if we moved and the whole wagon started moving? I think we better stay out of it."

The two painstakingly climbed out. With each creak and groan, they were sure the axle would give way but the wagon didn't budge from its awkward position. They crawled underneath. Here they had protection from the rain but not the icy dampness. It penetrated through the wet blankets while the two clung to each other, shivering. The hours went by; darkness descended like an evil black tent. The rain didn't let up.

"We have to unhitch the oxen." Sarah's voice shook with the cold. "You know you can't trust them. If they decide to take off on us, the wagon might rip apart. Besides, in a few minutes it will be too dark to see."

"But where is everyone? Why hasn't our father come for us?"

"I don't know." She shrugged. "I imagine it would be too dangerous to try climbing back up, Frank. Maybe some of the others have had trouble too."

"Pa would still come to look for us."

"I doubt he can see anything in this downpour." Sarah touched her brother's arm. "Don't worry. Someone will find us soon. If not right away, they'll come when the rain stops." She crawled out and then looked back. "Come on, chicken. Are you afraid of a little rain?"

Frank grinned. "If you call this a little, I'd hate to think what a lot would be."

Laughing, they held onto the side of the wagon and made their way to the front. The rocky ground was sloped and so slippery that they had to stop and test the ground beneath with each small step. The oxen hadn't budged. Rain poured down their bent-over heads and ran in streams to the ground. Frank was sure that if the whole world collapsed, those two old oxen wouldn't move a muscle.

It was no easy task to remove the harnesses. Both children slid under the oxen's bellies several times before they managed to free them. The animals stood still for a few minutes before ambling off into the dark.

"Shouldn't we try and tether them?" Frank wanted to know.

"They won't wander very far. It's too hard for them to walk on this slick rock. I think they'll just find a patch of grass and stay there."

"I doubt that there's a patch of grass anywhere around here."

Sarah laughed. "Well, if there is, you can be sure that those two will find it." She grabbed his arm as she started sliding. "Let's get back under the wagon. I'll bring out some dry blankets and clothes for us. I think there's some beef jerky back there too. I'm famished."

"Why can't we stay inside the wagon now?"

"We can try."

The wagon was at such a slant, however, that they decided it was safer to go back underneath. The inside was such a mess and it was so dark, it was almost impossible to find anything. Finally, in desperation, they grabbed anything that might help keep them warm. Frank searched with his hands through wooden boxes until he found a cloth sack filled with raisins.

They huddled together in the dark, covered with clothes and blankets and ate the raisins as slowly as they could. It took several hours before they stopped shivering and fell asleep. Sarah woke up in the night. The rain had stopped. She looked out from under the wagon and saw a black sky filled with stars. The wet leaves on the few trees that were growing up through the rocks, sparkled in the moonlight. Where was everyone? Why hadn't someone stopped to help them? Where had Teddy and their father disappeared to?

The sun was already in the sky when she awoke again. Frank lay cocooned in his blanket with their father's overcoat on top, fast asleep beside her. She lay there for a while, listening. Other than the songs of unfamiliar birds, the constant croak of frogs and the buzz of what sounded like millions of insects, the air was silent. Once or twice, she thought she heard one of the oxen snorting some distance away. What she didn't hear was the hum of voices and the noise of a wagon train preparing for its day's journey. Surely, they couldn't have travelled that much further in that blinding rainstorm. The sounds on a mountain, especially early in the still morning, travel for miles.

"Frank," she said, shaking his arm. "Wake up."

Her younger brother opened one eye. "Do I have to? I'm so tired. Can't we just sleep a little longer?" He closed his eye.

She shook him again. "No. Wake up. We have to find the others. They must be waiting for us at the bottom of the mountain."

Frank pulled his arms out and stretched. "I guess so. All I can say, Sarah, is that Pa had better not be on his way to California without us."

"Oh, you're silly. You know Pa will be there. He would never leave us on our own. We must have drifted off the main trail when it was raining so hard and the others kept going and didn't even see us. Come on. Let's get moving. We're going to have to walk, you know."

Frank groaned and muttered, "I hope it isn't too far."

"Do you think we should carry some things with us?"

They stood looking at the deep ravine that stretched out before them. It was amazing that the wagon hadn't hit that rock and gone hurtling down the mountain. If Sarah had been able to see the dangerous path, she would have pulled over and waited out the storm. Now, they were going to have to leave a wagon with one smashed wheel, and probably a broken axle, and climb down on foot to find the others. The question was would her father want to climb all the way back up to mend the wagon and then try to drive it back down the rugged mountainside? Would O'Leary be willing to wait for them? That, she doubted. Even now, she was sure, he would be extremely upset with her. Hadn't he warned her father about having children driving the wagon?

"Why?" Frank wondered. "Don't we have to come back up anyway?"

"I wonder if O'Leary will let Pa come back. He won't want to hold up the train." She looked around. "We're a long way up, Frank. They must be miles and miles away."

"We better take a few things with us then. I mean, we might get hungry before we reach the bottom, don't you think?"

She nodded and climbed into the wagon. A few minutes later, she backed out, clutching several items under her arm.

"Here," she said, holding out the tin that held their matches and a small gunnysack filled with dried fruit, beans and a small container of coffee. Frank grabbed them out of her hand. She turned round and went back in. When she reappeared, she had a couple of pillowcases stuffed with some clothing and a few toiletries. She'd found her mother's silver hairbrush and hand mirror and wrapped them with a towel. Perhaps no one considered them essentials but she didn't want to take the chance that they might get broken or lost. Whenever she would look at them, she would remember her mother sitting at her dressing table in Portland, brushing out her long blond hair.

"We'd better take Pa's axe, Sarah. And, what about the small cooking pot?"

Sarah looked at her brother. "I'm sure we won't need that. After all, we'll be eating with the rest. There's lots of pots in the chuck wagon, isn't there?"

Frank's eyes filled with tears. "What if we never meet up with them? What if it's just you and me?"

Sarah walked over and tousled her brother's sun-bleached hair. "You know that's not going to happen." She grabbed both of his arms and stared into his eyes. "Our father would never leave us. Never." She gave his arms a shake and let go. "But," she smiled. "I'll put the pot in the sack anyway."

They each hoisted a full pillow case over one shoulder and started the slow descent down the mountain. One false step and it could mean disaster. They used their one free hand to hold on to each other or to grab rocks or shrubs for support.

"If I start to slide, Frank, make sure you let go of me."

"I will never let go of you. If you slide down the mountain, I'll go with you."

"That's plain silly and you know it. How would Pa feel with both of us gone, not even knowing what happened to us?"

Frank was silent. He couldn't imagine life without Sarah. No one else could die. His heart still ached for his mother and often times before he fell asleep at night, he thought about the old Negro, William T. Even though he'd turned his head quickly when his father had warned him not to look, Frank would always remember the preacher swinging from the tree. He knew that he deserved to die; after all, wasn't it the preacher himself who said it had to be an eye for an eye? Still, he didn't like to think about dying. Not even if it were an animal. Sarah, on the other hand, not only loved the meat, she loved the hunt. He could see it in her eyes; the smile on her lips when the bullet hit its target. He shivered. How could someone love wildlife so much and yet kill with such ease?

"Are you all right, Frank?"

He nodded.

"Well," she said, "you can start to relax now; I think the next stretch will be easier."

"Why can't we see the wagon trail?"

They stopped and looked around. Now that it was easier walking, they could take the time to check out the terrain.

Sarah shook her head. "I don't know. Surely, we couldn't have gotten that far off course. I wonder if the rain hasn't washed out all the tracks?" She pointed to the south. "Let's move this way. The ground seems more level over there."

They struggled over rock mounds and around short straggly bushes until they came to what looked like a flat washed-out trail. Except for one thing - it must have been almost a half mile wide.

Frank gasped. "Sarah," he said, pointing up the mountain, "Look!"

Sarah, who had been following, stopped. The two stared with open mouths. Far in the distance and high above, it looked as if a giant hand had swooped down and scooped out half the mountain. The peak still jutted out, precariously upon nothing. It resembled a gigantic mouth that had opened up and vomited out its insides.

Silently, the two looked in the opposite direction - down the mountain. Their eyes followed the wide stream of yellowish claylike mud that now covered the ground.

"It's like a volcano erupted, isn't it, Sarah?"

"It's a mudslide. All that rain washed the mountain down."

Without speaking, they started down the incline, careful to stay away from the soft mud that still appeared to be alive.

The forest line was ahead of them. Before reaching it, they could see where the mudslide had made a path right through. Here and there, the tops of tall old pine trees poked out from the clay and boulders, some the size of small houses, lay tossed in various places.

"Sarah," Frank called out as his sister started running. "Sarah, wait. This is why they couldn't come to us. They couldn't get back up the mountain. They're camped up ahead. We'll find them. We'll find them." Tears ran down his face. "They made it through this. They did. I know they did." The last few words were lost in a sob.

He saw his sister throw her sack down and then fall to the ground herself. She was pulling at something. Something sticking out of the mud. What was wrong with her? Why didn't she keep walking? They needed to keep moving. They had to find the wagon train.

"Stay back," she screamed. "Don't come any closer."

Frank paid her no heed. He ran up to her and stared down at the object in her hand.

"Sarah," he whispered. "What is it?"

He fell to his knees. Bile erupted into his throat. Tears ran down their faces. Their world had ended.

There, sticking out of the mud was part of a human arm; its hand raised to the heavens as if begging someone for help. The deep heavy mountain clay covered over the rest of the body.

The old man stopped. There was a catch in his voice as if he himself were right there; right there, where two youngsters suddenly realized that their pa was buried somewhere under all that mountain clay. Suddenly, I felt a lump comin' up into my throat. Could I even imagine finding my pa that way? I suppose I might wonder and worry a bit after settlin' myself into that ranch in Swift Current but I'd never have to worry about no mountain cavin' in on him and Grandpa, that's for certain. The worst that could probably happen would be losin' a finger or hand in that old thrashin' machine. Ma had worried herself sick over that. Specially when Pa'd got his wedding ring caught one time. That was the last time he ever wore that ring again and Ma didn't mind one bit. Said if it meant savin' his hand, that was jus' fine with her. Pa teased her a lot about all the girls chasin' after him, thinking he was single again but Ma said that was okay with her too. Said it would serve them right, getting hooked up with an old coot like him. Those were the days that I really missed.

I'd learned by now not to get all concerned when Mr. Winnipesaukee stopped talking. I knew that he was seein' the whole picture in his mind. I was, too. It made my heart sad, thinking about all those folks who'd died back when times were so tough. I wanted to ask him how two young people, younger than me, could live all on their own. Where would they go? How could they live without supplies or who could protect them from the Indians or worse yet, highway men? Grandpa'd told me once that that's what the bad guys were called back then. They'd rob decent innocent folks who were travellin' to their new homesteads. Usually, those people would be carryin' money to buy seed for their first crops or for purchasing a good milk cow or a breedin' bull. Yes, sir, those two children had lots to worry about.

The minutes ticked by. I turned my head. I didn't want the old fellow to think that I'd fallen asleep. No, it was surely a story that wouldn't cause slumber.

He hadn't succumbed either. His eyes were open and he was staring up at the heavens. I took a better look and could see that his cheeks were wet. 'Course, it could have been from the mist that was risin' off the river. I could feel its soft touch on my face, too. The water on my cheeks wasn't from that, however. I was thinkin' about those children and feelin' their pain. I wiped my face with the old blanket. The tears were gone but there was a great sadness inside of me.

Just when I thought I couldn't stand the sorrow within me for one second more, the storyteller began to speak.

Chapter Thirteen

Frank fell to his knees. He stared at the arm with its hand and outspread fingers.

"Who is it?" he gasped.

Sarah shook her head. "I don't know," she whispered. "I just know that it's not our pa's."

Frank looked up the mountain at the mudslide.

"Don't you think that anyone survived? Isn't there a chance that someone was able to get away?" He reached up and wiped his tears with his sleeve. "Couldn't Pa be somewhere farther down the mountain?"

Sarah sighed. "No, Frank. I'm sure that the whole train is buried under here. Horses, wagons and all. The mountain collapsed during the rain. They wouldn't have known what was happening. And, even if they did, there was no way to escape." She stood up and followed his eyes up towards the overhanging peak. It could have been five or more miles away. It was difficult to judge the distance. "It would have caved in so quickly. Once the mudslide started, there was no turning back. It would've hit them from behind. I imagine it was over as fast as it started."

She walked over to a pine tree and sat beneath it. Frank sat beside her. They cried softly together, each with their own thoughts and memories. When there were no more tears to shed, they stood up. There was nothing to discuss. They were no longer the children who had ridden out of Portland; they were rapidly hardening to the ways of the wilderness. Was there any choice? Without a word, they were aware of the responsibilities that lay ahead of them. No one was there to tell them what to do or how to do it. They were on their own.

"We'll have to go back up the mountain, Frank. We have to find the oxen and bring them down."

"What will we do with two oxen? We don't have a wagon any more."

"We might need to sell them. We have no money, Frank."

"There was some money in the wagon."

"There was? Why didn't you tell me?"

Frank shrugged. "I thought that Pa would be going back up and he might not want me touching it. It's hidden under the floor boards."

Sarah smiled. "That's okay. You did the right thing." She started back up the rugged path. "Hurry, we don't want to be up here any longer than we have to."

Frank hesitated.

"What's the matter, Frank? You don't have to worry about another mudslide. I'm certain there won't be another one until the next rainstorm. Or, maybe never."

"It's not that, Sarah. It's just that I feel like we're leaving our father here all alone. Shouldn't we do something for him?"

"We will. When we come back down, we'll make up a marker so that others will know what happened here." She walked over and hugged her brother. "Don't worry. Our father and this wagon train will never be forgotten."

"What about the arm?"

"We'll cover it over and say a few words for everyone."

The two started up the steep incline. "Of course, you never know, Sarah. Maybe we will come across some at the bottom, farther down the trail. They could've kept going to make sure they were far from the slide. They might be waiting for us. Or, maybe Pa's alive and he thinks we're dead. Have you thought of that?"

Sarah reached over and grabbed his hand. "You're right; you never know. In that case, we'd better hurry."

It was late afternoon before they reached the wagon. They found only one of the oxen. Molly, the more timid animal, had stayed close to the wagon.

"Where do you think Petunia is?" Frank wondered.

"I hate to think it but I have a feeling she might have fallen down the ravine. Oxen aren't that steady on their feet."

"Hmmm." Frank said. "I can't count the times that I wished that old ox would have fallen over a cliff. Now I wish she was with us." His eyes welled with tears. "We've lost everyone, Sarah, even stubborn old Petunia."

Sarah was tying Molly to the wagon. "No, we haven't. We still have each other. Nothing is going to separate us."

"If something happens to you, Sarah, my life will be over."

"No, it won't. You will keep going and you will make a good life for yourself. Remember that. You must never give up. Promise me."

He looked over at his sister. She stood tall and proud. Her black hair shone in the sun and her dark eyes implored him. She did not look away until he'd promised. Sarah was like that. A promise made with her was something sacred. He shuddered to think that he might break such a vow.

They went through everything in the wagon. Sarah stripped off her dirty dress and put on a pair of her father's pants and a shirt. She tied a piece of twine around her waist to hold everything together.

"Here, Frank, put this on." Sarah shoved one of her father's felt hats into his hand.

"But that was Pa's church hat," he protested.

"That's all right. You need something to keep the sun off your face."

Within a half hour, they were ready to start their downward trek again. This time, however, it was much slower travelling. Molly would have preferred to stay where she was.

"We have to move carefully, Frank. If Molly falls and breaks a leg, I don't know what we'd do."

"We'd have to shoot her, that's a fact." Frank walked on one side of the animal, holding the bridle while Sarah held onto it on the other side.

"I know that. The question is - with what? We don't have Pa's rifle."

Frank grinned. "No, but we do have his pistol."

Sarah stopped, jerking Molly's head back. She faced her brother.

"What are you talking about? Pa never owned a pistol."

Frank shrugged. "Maybe not but someone did. When I was getting the money, I ripped up another board and came across this." He lifted his shirt and pulled a handgun out of his waistband.

Sarah stared at her brother. "And when had you planned on sharing this with me? After you accidentally shot yourself in the foot?"

Frank's face coloured. "I guess I just wanted to be able to look after you, Sarah. You're a girl; I should be taking care of you."

"Well, never mind." She smiled. "You do look after me. We look after each other."

They started moving again.

"But don't ever tell me that you have to look after me because I'm a girl, Frank. Understand?"

Sarah didn't see him nod but she knew he wouldn't bring up that subject again. She was relieved, however, to know that they did have a weapon. They could only hope it was in working order. It wasn't her father's so it could have been under those boards for a long time. How did they know if the money even belonged to him?

After several minutes of walking, she asked, "Are there bullets in it?"

"I don't know. There was a box of bullets with it and I took that, too."

"Good."

They walked the rest of the way in silence. The only sound echoing in the quiet mountain air was Molly's huffing and snorting. As if she knew something wasn't right, the closer they got to the mudslide, the more agitated the old ox became. The two of them led her farther down the trail before tying her to a tree and then they walked back, back to where an unknown number slept in their burial ground, covered over by half a mountain.

It wasn't easy returning. In the back of their minds, they were praying that their father was not buried under all the rubble but deep in their hearts, they knew he was. Where else could he be? The mental picture was almost too much to bear.

They stood for a moment and stared up towards the source of the disaster. The mud surface had already hardened from the heat of the day's sun. It flowed out like a woman's brown skirt over the earth. There was no sign that horses or wagons had ever passed through the area. The only sign of any life buried under the hard mass was the one arm.

"I wish we'd never seen that arm."

"I know," Sarah said, in a quiet voice. "Then, we could keep searching. We would always believe that Pa was just around the next corner."

Frank nodded. "We would never have given up looking for him, would we?"

She shook her head. "No, we would have never given up."

It wasn't easy covering over the uplifted arm. They couldn't dig up much of the clay so they covered it with branches first and then searched for soft mulch from beneath the trees.

"Sarah, either the wind or the rain is going to remove this."

Sarah, who was also becoming discouraged, said, "I know. It won't be long and an animal will find it, anyway. Let's leave it and get started on the marker." She looked out towards the west. "It will be dark soon. We're going to have to camp here for the night."

"Here?" Frank's face turned pale.

"Down the trail a ways." She grabbed his hand. "Come on. Let's get Molly and get a fire going. We haven't eaten all day."

Frank followed his sister. As much as he wanted to be as far away from the mudslide as he could, something inside of him did not want to leave. It was the same feeling he'd had when they left his mother behind.

They found a sheltered area within a circle of trees a short ways off the trail. No one had camped there before because it was small and most folks travelled in larger groups. Frank gathered wood and started the fire while Sarah worked on the marker. He found enough rainwater in the rock crevasses for drinking and for making coffee.

"We've only dried fruit and jerky, Sarah. There's flour but I don't know how to make biscuits."

Sarah smiled. "That's okay. You'll learn. At least, we'll have some hot coffee to drink. It smells wonderful."

Frank, who thought that he'd never be able to eat again because of his overwhelming sadness, bit off a chunk of jerky and started chewing.

"Just because Ma and Pa aren't here, doesn't mean that we shouldn't say a prayer before we eat, Frank."

Frank stared at her, his mouth full. He swallowed before speaking.

"What are we going to pray for, Sarah? What do we have to thank God for? That we have lost both of our parents? That we are all alone in this world and have no home? What, Sarah? What are you going to gives thanks for?"

Sarah was silent for several seconds. Then, she bowed her head.

"Thank you, Lord, for giving my brother, Frank, and me a chance to live. Thank you for the food that we are now eating. Thank you for bringing out the sunshine today. Thank you for sparing Molly for us. We will now need your help and guidance as we travel to our new home in California. We ask all this in the name of your Son. Amen.

Chapter Fourteen

The threesome continued travelling down the same trail that the
wagon train would have taken. The path, flattened by past wagon
wheels, stretched out for miles before them. Between the narrow
wagon lines, the grass grew two feet tall, a mixture of fresh green
and dried gold. Ancient spruce and pine trees hugged them on both
sides. On the third day, they came upon a blackened, barren open
field, the remains of a lightning strike. The smell still lingered. The
storm was responsible for more than a mudslide.

Molly was the one who set the pace. She plodded on, never
hurrying, never stopping. If the lush green grass was an
enticement, she never showed it. When the sun started to go down,
she stopped at the first watering hole and refused to walk any
further.

After bringing her back up from a river one evening, Frank said,
"It's as if she's been here before. She seems to know every camp
spot there is."

"She could, you know. I have no idea where Pa got her."

Frank settled down to enjoy a piece of his sister's fried bread. He
didn't say anything anymore about her praying. It seemed to bring
Sarah peace and that was the most important thing. As for Frank, it
would be a long time before he would ever ask God for help again.

By the fifth day, their meagre food supply had diminished.

"What will we eat, Sarah? We can't walk all day just by drinking
water and eating wild berries."

It was already hot and barely mid-morning. The days were
getting shorter but the sun still shone high above. There hadn't
been a cloud in the sky since the rainstorm. They could feel the
warm earth through the thick soles of their shoes and with each
step, they left behind small puffs of dust. For several days, they
had followed O'Leary's example by stopping and resting at noon.
In the beginning, there seemed to be a rush to get somewhere but
as the days went by and they met no one on the trail, their pace
slowed. They had no idea what trials, be they light or difficult, (but
they were aware that there would be both) lie ahead of them so
they were in no hurry to get there.

"When we get to the next town, Frank, we'll have to send a

telegram to Portland. We'd better let Aunt Bessy know about Mother and Father."

Frank nodded. "You think that someone might come and get us?"

"No, but I think that if we don't have enough money, someone might send us some so that we could go back home."

They walked along in silence.

"Do you want to go back to Portland, Sarah?"

Sarah looked over the tall grass at her brother. "What do you mean? What choice do we have? We're all alone, Frank."

"I thought that you prayed for God to help us get to California."

"Franklin Lawdry, I thought you never listened to my prayers."

"Well, I do listen. I might not believe, but I do listen." He grinned at his sister. "So, what is it, Sis? Do we go on to California or do we go back to Portland?"

"I think the question is, which life would we prefer? If we go back to Portland, we will have to live with Mother's relatives. None of them was too fond of Pa, you know. They will never let us forget that our father killed our mother and then died himself and left two orphans behind. Is that something that we want to live with? Or, do we want to take the chance and make our way west? We have no idea what awaits us. It will be very hard going. We'll have to learn to depend on just ourselves. There will be no one to help us. This is not an easy decision to make, Frank."

They continued walking for a time.

"I think, Sarah." Frank stopped walking and looked over at his sister. "That I would like to go to California. We've come a long ways already. I can't bear to travel back over those places where our parents are buried. Let's do what Pa started out to do."

Sarah nodded.

"All right. Our first step will be to find a trading post or something. This trail must lead to one."

They reached the top of a high hill. The trees had faded away behind them and an open field of dry dead grass stretched out for miles in front of them in all directions. They stood still and gazed about. There was nothing but dull yellow hay for as far as the eye could see. From the heavens, there was nothing but the sun beating down on them.

"This is going to be awful hot walking, Sarah." Frank pulled his hat further down over his forehead.

"I know. I wish I could see the end of it."

"Doesn't look like there's any water for miles around, does it?" Sarah looked worried.

"There's enough for us for a least a couple of days if we only use it for drinking but it will be rough on Molly."

Frank looked fondly at Molly, who had been standing behind him, waiting patiently for the next move. As she waited, she chewed contentedly on a mouthful of dry grass.

He looked out into the distance again. Suddenly, he raised his arm and pointed.

"See over there, Sarah. I think I see a bluff of trees. There might be a town there. Or, at least, some water."

Sarah held her hand above her eyes and squinted. "There is something over there, I guess. It's a long ways off. It might take a couple of days to reach it."

"Molly should be okay for that long, shouldn't she? I'll share my water with her."

"Okay. There's no point in standing here. We have to move ahead anyway. Let's go."

They trudged on for several hours before stopping.

"Sarah, let's just lie down in the grass and rest a bit. It's so tall; it will give us a little shade."

It did give them shade but without even a hint of breeze, the air was dead and stifling. Frank told Sarah that it reminded him of the times he'd stood beside the cook as she opened the oven door to bring out a batch of freshly baked cookies.

"It isn't one bit cooler here than right in that oven. Except there's no cookie smell. That's the only difference."

Sarah laughed. "Well, don't start dreaming about those cookies because it might be a long time before we enjoy something like that."

Frank didn't need to be reminded.

It wasn't long, however, and both of them fell into a deep sleep.

Molly's loud bellowing suddenly filled the air. It wasn't her usual low bawl; it was a high-pitched squeal. The two children frantically jumped to their feet, forgetting for the moment where they were.

"What's the matter?" Frank yelled. "What's going on?"

Sarah looked as bewildered as he did. Molly was now stamping her feet and bellowing louder. Before they could grab her bridle, she gave one last squeal and started running down the trail. The pillowcases filled with supplies bouncing up and down on her back.

"Molly," Sarah yelled. "Stop. Whoa."

Molly, however, did not intend to slow down. She kept up her awkward gallop.

"The stupid old thing probably saw a snake or something." Sarah watched as the animal grew smaller in the distance. She sighed. "It's going to take all day to catch her now. Stupid old thing!"

Frank grabbed Sarah's arm. "It wasn't a snake. Look, Sarah." He pointed. "Let's get out of here!"

Sarah looked. To the south of them, the sky was billowing with fast-moving grey clouds.

"It's a storm heading this way," she said.

"No," Frank screamed. "Look along the ground." His eyes were wide with terror.

There was a bright red line running along the ground. In the few moments that they stood mesmerized, they could see it moving closer, eating up everything in its way.

"Fire!" Sarah screamed. "It's a grass fire. Come on!"

They started running after Molly. Would all three be able to outrun the fast moving flames? Could any of them outrun it?

Frank ran as he had never run before. All he could hear was each foot as it hit the ground and his heart banging in his chest. Even with his long legs, Sarah kept pace with him. His lungs felt like they would burst.

It wasn't long before another sound reached their ears. It was the fire crackling as it swept across the land. He heard it before he felt its heat. Neither of them turned to look.

"Frank," Sarah screamed. Just as she uttered his name, he saw her fly headfirst to the ground. She lay sprawled on the narrow path, her one foot still lodged in a gopher hole.

Frank bent down to help her up.

"Come on. Get up. The fire's getting closer." He started to pull her arm. "Sarah, you have to hurry."

Perspiration covered Sarah's face and pain filled her eyes. She grimaced with each pull. Frank moved down to her foot.

"Here," he said, in a gentler tone. "Let me get your foot out for you."

He touched her ankle and she screamed.

"No." She grabbed his arm. "My ankle's broken. I can't go on any further." Her face was changing quickly from red to chalky white. "You have to keep moving. I'm going to pass out soon. Go, Frank. Get out of here. Try to save yourself."

Frank started to cry. "No, I'm not leaving you. I'll carry you." He tried pulling her up by her arms but she screamed out again in pain.

"Frank, please, just go. Remember, you promised me that you would. Now, go."

She tried pushing him away but instead fell unconscious into his arms.

"No, Sarah. I will never leave you." He sobbed as he held his sister in his arms.

He heard the fire getting closer as it tore its way across the earth. Already the smoke burned his eyes and the inside of his nose and he felt the heat, so hot he thought his clothes would melt off his back. Just before everything went black, he heard his father calling. He felt his strong arms lifting him.

"Father," he whispered. "I knew that you would come for us."

Chapter Fifteen

Before he saw or heard anything, before he opened his eyes or
spoke, he remembered the smell. At first, it was a puzzle. Where
had he smelled something like this before? He lie motionless, his
brain working hard, trying to collect his thoughts.

His thoughts returned slowly and jumbled. The fire! Someone
had picked him up and carried him away. Or, had it been a dream?
No, for if it had been a dream, he would now be dead. But, he
wasn't. Or, was he? Everything was so confusing. And, Sarah.
Where was Sarah? Had Father rescued her too? Father! He had
almost forgotten who his saviour was.

He bolted upright, his heart racing.

"Pa," he yelled. "Pa, where are you?"

Only silence filled the room. Silence and darkness. And, a smell.

Frank looked around but couldn't see anything. He had to be in
some sort of shelter. A place protected from the fire. But, where?
The fright and panic subsided and calmness set in. His breathing
returned to normal and his mind cleared. The cool air made his
throat feel better.

It must now be night time, not only because of the darkness but
also, because of the silence. He held his breath and listened. There
were only the sounds of the night - the soft rustling of the wind, a
cricket chirping somewhere close by, the mournful call of some
night bird. Somewhere, not far off, he thought that a wolf or
coyote called out. That meant they were out of the grassland and
into trees again. But, where was everyone and where was Sarah?
Had she died in the flames? Tears came to his eyes but he refused
to submit to them. Someone had rescued him. He'd thought that it
was his father but if it had been, his father would be by his side.
No, that had been only a dream. Whoever had saved his life had
brought him to this safe place. Everyone here must be asleep. He
would not call out and wake them.

As his eyes grew more accustomed to the darkness, he began to
make out certain forms. He realized that high above him there was
a small opening and from it, a dim shaft of moonlight drifted down
into the room. Now he could see the outline of an opening in front
of him. It was a tent flap. He touched the covering that someone

had placed beside him. It was a deer skin. He lifted it to smell it. His mind flooded with memories.

This rug did not belong to a white man. The white mans' furs had a different smell. This belonged to an Indian. Frank knew this from the days he'd spent in his father's store. Many times, members of the Norridgewock tribe came in to trade. They liked the wooden cabinets and chests that his father made. His father always laughed and said, "Where are you going to put this? Your wigwams are too small." They would only grunt and answer, "How many furs for this one?" His father was happy to get the furs but he would always lay them out in the sun for several days before he'd sell them.

"Why do they smell like that?" Frank had asked.

"They smell like the Indian," his father had said. "They smell like the smoke from their campfire and like the Indians themselves."

"They smell differently than us?"

His father had nodded. "They don't go in for fancy soaps and shampoos with perfume like the white man does."

"How does he get clean then?"

His father had smiled. "He's as clean as the outdoors. He washes in the streams and dries his hair in the wind."

Sarah, who had been listening, said, "That's how I'd like to be, Pa."

Her father had laughed and said, "That doesn't surprise me one bit. You might find it hard to convince your mother that you don't need a bar of soap though."

Yes, that was a good memory. That was all he would have now. But what about his sister? Would he have only memories of her too? If there were only one man who had come down that trail, he couldn't have picked up both of them, especially Sarah with her broken ankle. Had he left her there to die?

He lay back down and closed his eyes. The tears rolled down the sides of his face and into his ears. He made no effort to wipe them away. It seemed that he was always crying lately. Sarah cried too but she didn't carry her sorrow with her afterwards. Not like he did. He wore it like a millstone around his neck. She'd cried when Mother died and she was devastated when Father was killed but when the tears dried, she stood up and carried on. Why could he not be like that?

He was not afraid of the Indians. If they had saved his life, they wouldn't hurt him. He knew that. Besides, his father had tried to inculcate a respect for the red man in Frank and Sarah's hearts. "They are human beings just like us," he'd tell them. Father would have thought nothing of bringing them home to give them a good meal once in awhile. Sometimes, when their crops had not produced well, they would come into town, looking gaunt and destitute. The mere mention of it to his mother, however, had sent her into a frenzy.

"You will never bring those savages into this house, Benjamin Lawdry. What would our friends think? You have your business associates and a family to consider." She'd started waving her handkerchief in front of her face. "You are positively making me swoon. I swear you do this simply to upset me." Father had grabbed her before she collapsed and he'd never brought the subject up again. Frank wasn't sure if he'd wanted them in the house either but later Sarah had said that it would have been worth it just to see the look on some people's faces. Like, Aunt Bessy, for instance.

Frank fell back to sleep. The last thing on his mind was a picture of his great-aunt, Bessy, walking into the parlour and seeing an Indian sitting with his father, sipping tea in one of his mother's fancy tea cups from China.

The next time he awoke, it was daylight. Sunshine streamed in through the opening high above. He was in a tepee made from animal hide. He closed his eyes again. What was the custom among the Indians? Should he stay where he was until someone came for him? He was sure this was not the Norridgewock tribe that lived near Portland. What tribe was it and how did they view the white man? Had they rescued him only to make him into slave? Or, worse. Would they torture him before burning him alive on a stake?

Before he opened his eyes again, he thought he heard something like a soft sigh. Perhaps, it was the wind. He sat up. An old wrinkled squaw sat in the corner watching him. He stared at her and she stared back. At that moment, he realized that she had been there all night long. She had been waiting for him to wake up.

"Do you know where my sister is?" he asked.

Her eyes were blank.

"Do you know English?"

This time she grunted, slowly unbent her thin emancipated body and opened the flap. She stood back and waited for him to go out.

Frank got up slowly, having no idea what he would be facing on the other side of that tent flap. When he stood up, he towered over the frail woman.

The first thing that struck him as he walked into the bright sunshine was the silence. This did not sound like Indian campgrounds. There were no laughing children, no yapping dogs, no women sitting in the sunshine, weaving baskets or doing bead work. His father had spoken about those things. Here, there was only emptiness and silence. There were only two other tents pitched close by. Frank followed the elderly bent over woman. She shuffled along until she stood in front of one of the tepees. She opened the flap, pointed inside and grunted. He went in.

There was his sister, lying on the hard ground. She was on her back with a rolled-up jacket under her head for a pillow.

"Sarah," he cried out. "You're alive."

He fell down on the floor beside her. Her eyes were closed. She did not open them. Someone had cut her pant leg and wrapped something around her ankle, right up to her knee. A strong sweet scent filled the tent. A young Indian brave sat cross-legged beside her. He probably wasn't much older than Sarah was but his eyes had the worried look of an old man. He wore white man's clothes: cotton pants and a long-sleeved shirt but they were dirty and torn. His long black hair hung in two braids down his chest. Instead of the beaded moccasins that Indians usually wore, he wore oxfords, tied with string and grey with dust.

"Sarah," he shouted again. "Sarah, wake up!" He shook her arm.

"She will not wake up yet," the Indian said. He spoke in a low flat voice as if not wanting to disturb the sleeping girl.

Frank looked up.

"Why? What have you done to her?" Anger rose inside him, erupting like a raging river, spilling its banks. "If you hurt her, I'll kill you," he screamed. He shoved his fist over his sister's prostrate body, ready to punch the man in the face. The Indian grabbed his wrist in midair and held it. His eyes burned.

"Who is this woman to you?"

"She's my sister." He tried to pull his arm away but the Indian held it tight. Tears sprang into his eyes. "She's the only family that I have." The brave let his arm go and Frank's head dropped to Sarah's chest. He sobbed loudly while the Indian sat still and watched, never saying a word.

In the years that followed, Frank often wondered about his blind reaction. If the man sitting across from him had been white, would he have felt such sudden rage? How could he have forgotten so quickly that these people saved his sister's life?

Over an hour passed without anyone moving. Frank's sobs came and went. As long as he could feel Sarah's chest rhythmically beating, he was not going to move. If she stopped breathing, he would die, too. He would ask the stone-faced Indian to shove his sharp hunting knife right into his chest. There would be no life without Sarah.

Whether the Indian stayed with them, Frank would never know. He finally fell into an exhausted sleep. Many hours later, he felt Sarah move and then moan.

"Frank," she said, "get off of me. I can hardly breathe."

Frank sat up with a start. The young brave was there and the old woman who'd brought Frank to the tent. Neither spoke. There was no emotion in their eyes. That the young woman had woken up seemed no surprise to them.

"Are you all right?" Frank asked. "You've been asleep for hours."

She tried to sit up but the old woman leaned over, grunted and pushed her back down.

The man said, "You must lie still for awhile more. Your ankle is healing. It will be better soon."

Sarah looked around, noticing, for the first time, where she was.

"Are you the one who rescued us from the fire?" she asked, addressing the man.

He nodded. "Yes, my father and I. The fire was coming very close. You would have died soon."

"Where did you come from? We didn't see anyone else on the trail."

"We followed you for several days. We had been hunting in the mountains."

Sarah looked away from his gaze. "Everyone in our wagon train perished in a mudslide. Frank and I are the only ones left."

"Yes, we saw."

She looked up at him. "You were behind us all the time?"

"Yes."

"Where is the fire now? Can it come here?"

He shook his head. "No, it will not reach us. We are on the other side of a small lake. The wind has driven the flames far to the south again."

Sarah turned to her brother.

"Have you thanked this man already for saving our lives, Frank?"

Frank felt his cheeks turning red.

"There is no need," the Indian said.

"Of course, there is. We owe our lives to you." She closed her eyes for a moment, reliving the nightmare. "It must have been very difficult for you to lift us up onto your horses." Her eyes filled with tears. "To even care enough to do this for us." She couldn't continue.

"You do not think that an Indian would save a white person?"

It was Sarah's turn to blush.

"No, no. That's not what I mean. I just meant that it's not everyone who would risk their life for someone else, no matter what colour his skin is."

"Your name is Sarah?" He turned to Frank. "And, you are Frank?"

They both nodded.

"What is your name?" Sarah asked.

"My name is Levi." He turned to the old woman. "This is my grandmother. She does not know any English. You can call her Awasosqua. Bear Woman. Or, sometimes we call her Old Squaw."

"How do you know English so well, Levi?" Sarah asked.

"The Jesuits taught me English and French." There was a hint of pride in his voice. "Do you know French?"

Sarah shook her head.

He sighed. "Now we have had to come here to get away from the French."

"Why? What will they do to you?"

"The French want us only if we will fight the English and the Iroquois with them or if we will join their church. The English want us out of the country. We have been travelling west so that they will not find us."

"What tribe are you?"

"We are the Abenaki. Have you heard of us?"

Sarah nodded. "Why are you here? Aren't you a long ways from your land?"

"Yes. We were on our way north but the English stopped us from entering Canada. We will wait for awhile and then try again."

"Why won't they let you into Canada?"

"Because they think that the Abenaki are fighting with the French."

"Are you?"

"We fight with no one. It is only the white men who hate each other."

Frank spoke up. He was beginning to relax now, knowing that neither he nor his sister was in any danger. "But," he said, "where is everyone? There are only three tents here."

"We will be moving tomorrow to our camp. Your sister's ankle will be stronger by then."

Sarah suddenly became aware of her injury and without thinking tried to move her foot. She winced with pain.

"Why aren't you with the others?" Frank asked.

"My father and I have been staying here while we hunted for food. Our people have not planted crops and the hunting has not been good. There is meat in the mountains but the rain came so we had to return. We have been away for many days. Our families will be hungry."

Frank looked over at the grandmother. "Why would you bring someone so old with you? Wouldn't she be a burden to you?"

Levi turned to his grandmother and spoke to her in the Algonquin language. She threw her head back and cackled. Frank saw that she had very few teeth. Wrinkles lined her dark sallow skin and one long white braid hung down the middle of her back. One might assume that she was ready to die from old age but her bright black eyes flashed with mischief like that of a young maiden. She made a reply to Levi and burst into laughter again. She was still chuckling as she got up and shuffled out.

"Did I say something funny?" Frank wanted to know.

"Yes, to my grandmother that is humorous. How can she be a

burden when she is the one who has the most wisdom?"

Levi turned his attention to Sarah.

"My grandmother is going to bring you something to eat now." He looked at Frank. "Are you hungry too, my young friend?"

Sarah caught the twinkle in his eye.

Frank nodded. He couldn't remember the last time he'd had anything in his stomach. At this point, it didn't matter what the old woman would bring, he would eat it.

Levi got up and went out.

Frank grabbed Sarah's hand.

"Are you really going to be okay?" he asked. "We can't stay here, Sarah. As soon as you can walk, we'll leave."

"I know. Don't worry; I'll be all right." Her voice shook.

"You'll be better after you eat. I know you will. If we can leave soon, we'll probably be able to find Molly. Don't you think?"

Sarah slowly raised her other hand and placed it over his.

"Frank," she whispered. "Please, don't worry. These people are looking after us."

"But, they're Indians," he whispered. "Why would they want to help us? Maybe they think we have money or something."

Sarah shook her head and closed her eyes. Tears stung Frank's eyes because he felt ashamed.

They stayed in silence until the grandmother came into the tent. She held a wooden bowl in one hand and an old battered spoon in the other. Quietly, she slipped down beside Sarah. Frank watched as she carefully placed the bowl on the ground and then gently lifted Sarah's head. Sarah opened her eyes. She looked at the old woman and smiled. With no hesitation, she opened her mouth for Levi's grandmother to spoon in the steaming liquid. The old woman didn't rush. She waited patiently for Sarah to swallow each mouthful and then rest before she poured in the next one.

Levi appeared at the tent entrance.

"Come," he said to Frank. Frank stood up, his head touching the side of the tepee. Sarah did not look at him. He went outside.

It was now late afternoon. There was a fire burning within a circle of large stones. Within the circle was a smaller circle of stones and on these there was a large cast iron pot. Steam rose up from it but that was all. Frank couldn't smell meat, like stew or perhaps, a nice chunk of venison simmering in its own juices.

It didn't take long for Frank to find out what the delicacy in the pot was: it was wild onions, mushrooms and garlic with dandelion greens, simmering in water. Levi dipped a birch bark bowl into the soup, filled it and handed it to him. There was no spoon. He lifted it to his lips and drank as he saw his companion doing. It was the most delicious meal that he had eaten since the loss of the wagon train. Perhaps, for the first time in his life, Frank came to appreciate the simple act of human kindness. It would mould his life for the years to come in ways he could never imagine.

Thus began life with the Abenaki Indians.

The old man had been speaking for such a long time that now when he stopped, for the first time, I became aware of the silence. It just ain't in my nature to lull round in bed or lie there dreamin' but for some unknown reason, I sort of took delight in the quietness of it all. The moon was starting its way towards the western sky and before long, the sun would be peekin' its head up in the east. I should have been tryin' to force my eyes to stay open but there didn't seem to be a bit of sleep in my body. It wasn't that Mr. Winnipesaukee was a vibrant storyteller. Far from it. My grandpa, with his eyes afire and his arms waving, had him beat all to heck. There was something about his voice, however, that drew you like a magnet. It reminded me of our cat, Tom, watchin' a sunbeam; you knew he was too lazy to try catchin' it but it kept him alert for hours. He couldn't take his eyes off it. That's how I was - hypnotized, like an old barnyard cat.

Maybe he was waitin' for all his words to make an impression on my brain. And, they were. I could see myself livin' right there with those Indians. In fact, they'd made such an impression that I was thinking how mighty tasty onion, mushroom, garlic and dandelion soup would taste. Now, that's really stretchin' it for a growing sixteen year old boy.

'Course, I was thinking about other things too. For instance, how I'd found myself in a similar situation. Not that all my family'd been killed but here I was all alone in the world. Not even havin' a sister with me. I was settin' out all on my own too. I'd started out feelin' pretty cocky when I left home but already I'd lost my food to varmints, had Pa's car break down and now, here I was, sittin' with a stranger listening to an all-nighter story when I

should have been getting my sleep and worryin' about how I was goin' to get to Swift Current. Oh yes, I was feeling a lot like Frank Lawdry at this point.

Just as I was about to go into a worryin' fret, the old timer's voice started up again and I was back at the Indian camp.

Chapter Sixteen

True to his word, the next morning they started their journey to the main campground. Levi's father knew some English but he chose not to speak often, not even in his native tongue. He was a quiet solemn man. His mother, Levi's grandmother, Awasosqua, chatted non-stop, never expecting to get a reply from anyone. After conversing with no one in particular for about twenty minutes, she would burst into laughter. Frank made sure to stay as far away from her as he could.

Sometime during the evening or early morning while the youngsters slept, someone had constructed a travois to transport Sarah. By the time Frank was up, it was already rigged up to one of the horses. There were two long poles tied to each side of the saddle while the ends dragged along the ground. Hides were placed over the poles, forming a sort of hammock in between. There was a soft bear rug on the top. Before Frank could protest, Levi had picked Sarah up and carried her outside. He laid her gently on the bear rug.

Their breakfast consisted of hard bread cooked over the fire and some kind of root tea. No one spoke while they ate. There was nothing tasty about it but it filled an emptiness in the stomach.

Frank sat off by himself to eat and before he'd finished, the men had disassembled the tents. The old woman placed the neatly folded pile of hides at the bottom of the travois below Sarah's feet. She tied three pots together with a leather rope and hung them over the horse's neck. The larger iron pot banged the animal's chest with each step. Either the horse had not enough interest to protest or there was just no life left in her. She was a mangy looking black mare who walked with her head bowed almost to the ground.

"Don't you ever brush your horses?" Frank asked Levi. All of them, even the younger ones that the men rode, looked neglected.

Levi turned to look at him. "Why would we brush our horses? Do they worry about how they look?"

Instead of standing and watching everyone work, Frank had decided to approach Levi to see what he could do. Somehow, he felt he must prove he was a young man who did more than sit and cry.

"No, they don't care how they look but wouldn't it make them feel good?"

Levi grunted. "There are much more important things to worry about than trying to make our horses feel good about themselves."

"I think it's good to take care of things, especially your animals."

"Perhaps that's because the white man has too much time on his hands. The red man is too busy looking for food for his people."

It took Frank many years before he came to realize that he would never win an argument with an Indian.

"Here," Levi said, handing Frank a dinted tin pail. "There's a creek beyond those trees. Bring up some water to douse the fire."

Frank gladly picked up the pail and headed for the creek. It wasn't much of a creek; it was so shallow that when he laid the pail in the water only a dribble went in. He ended up making three trips with a half-filled pail of water and mud.

He hadn't talked to Sarah; she was still upset with him. Whenever he started to approach her, she closed her eyes. He would stand and wait but her eyes wouldn't open. The old squaw continued to cluck and fuss over her. Didn't she understand that he'd undergone a traumatic experience also?

Tears stung his eyes but he refused to give in to them. He was sick of crying like a woman. In fact, he was worse than a woman. This day, he made a vow. Franklin Benjamin Lawdry was finished with crying. He was no longer a boy; he was a man.

Frank did not break this oath until many years later. By then he'd learned being a man had nothing to do with crying.

The small band was ready to leave. Old Squaw jumped up on her mare as spry as a young girl. Levi's father beckoned Frank.

"Come," he said. He stood and waited by his horse. Black Thundercloud was about the same height as Frank was. Although he was only in his late thirties (Frank learned later that most of the men were married at fourteen), he had deep lines on his face. His straight black hair hung down to his shoulders. He wore Indian garb; his pants and shirt made from deer hide, worn shiny with time. Around his neck, he'd tied a bright red handkerchief. He had beaded moccasins on his feet. He smelled of smoke, soiled leather and sweat.

Black Thundercloud held his hands together by the horse's belly, making a step for Frank to mount. Once he was up, the Indian grabbed the mane and sprang up behind him, barely touching him. This was a feat that Frank tried to imitate for years afterwards but was never able to master, although his sister did.

They rode without saddles. Each horse carried a hide from the tent on its back and over it was a bright multicoloured blanket. They rode slowly, picking their way through the forest. Frank and Black Thundercloud took the lead. Levi rode behind them with the travois while the old grandmother took up the rear. Sometimes she kept up, other times she would stop and wander into the forest, emerging victoriously with some type of herb or medicinal plant. The others paid no heed. They rode in silence, slouched over with their heads bobbing with each step that their horses took.

Once Frank's anxiety subsided, he began to listen to the sounds of the forest. His mind wandered back to the past but he knew it wasn't healthy to dwell on it. It had happened. He wondered about the men whom he was riding with. Their stories would undoubtedly be much more distressing. It's true he had lost his parents but at least he could recall a good life. His family hadn't been constantly scrounging for food. He'd known the pleasures of having maids and servants. These men would never understand anything like that. They lived no better than the animals in the forest.

Now and then, a bird's frantic call or the rustle of foliage as some small animal scurried away broke the silence. Each horse would stop and munch on some grass whenever it was hungry and the riders never interfered. Before long Frank too, began to slouch, moving slowly with his horse's rhythm. There was the slight touch of Black Thundercloud's legs against his but other than that, he would have never known that he was sharing the horse with another man. The hours slipped away. They stopped once by a slow moving river. Everyone had a drink. Levi took water to Sarah. Frank watched. It should have been his job. No one spoke about having something to eat but surely, their stomachs were aching for food. He worried that Sarah might pass out from hunger. Or, that he would. The slow moving procession kept pushing forward, however, until the sun was almost down.

He was nearly lulled to sleep when suddenly his horse jerked and started walking at a faster pace. It surprised him that there was that much life left in it. The horse was trotting by the time they reached an opening in the forest. Frank saw a small Indian village spread out in front of him.

He didn't count but it looked like a dozen or more dome shaped wigwams scattered about in a circular shape. In the centre, there was a large fire pit with a fire burning. Several pots were sitting on rocks with steam drifting up from them. To his right, beyond the last wigwam, he could see what appeared to be a hastily put together corral made with long spindly poplar trees. Bark still covered the poles. Short branches stuck out in various directions with dead leaves clinging to them. It housed at least ten horses and a couple of skinny cows.

As the entourage drew closer, people began to approach from all directions. Wide-eyed children wearing nothing more over their brown bodies than loincloths made from deerskins appeared out of nowhere. They formed a line in front of the adults. All of them, never taking their eyes off Frank, the tall young man with shoulder length blond hair. Blond hair, now bleached white from the sun. His skin was no longer burnt but had tanned to a light brown. He would never have skin as dark as Sarah or his father but the sore redness was gone. The children stared as if seeing a god. Frank, in his ignorance, thought they were rude and undisciplined.

Suddenly, everyone was talking at once. No one spoke in English. Several men about the same age as Levi's father pushed their way through the crowd. They raised their voices and waved their arms. Whatever they were saying, it was obvious they were angry. If they noticed Frank and Sarah, it didn't show. At first, Frank thought they were upset that Levi had brought two white people home with him but soon it became apparent that the problem was food. Levi and his father had no meat. They had gone on a hunting trip and had returned empty handed, except for bringing back two more mouths to feed.

"Kwe-yoh. Kwe-yoh. Chi ba gi guat."

Although Frank and Sarah had no idea what they were saying, they knew by the tone that it was not anything good.

Although there was little food, the women prepared a small bowl for each of the five. They sat round the fire. Levi and Black Thundercloud talked with four other men as they ate. The talk was solemn; there was no cheerful bantering. There were no smiles. Two of the men had carried Sarah over to the fire on the travois.

She sat up to eat. Her colour was returning.

The children became quiet with the arrival of the white strangers. They couldn't take their eyes off Frank. If he turned and stared back at them, they ran off into the woods and disappeared. A few minutes later, they would return silently, their eyes wide with wonderment.

Later that evening, when at last sharing a tent with Sarah, he said, "Did you see how they stood and stared at me? If I'd been so rude, Mother would have cuffed me. They are just like animals in many ways."

"Frank, they're only children. My goodness, I don't think that you are in any position to judge them," she said. "After all, we do owe our lives to them."

"You don't have to continually remind me of that. I'm only saying that it's best that we watch out for ourselves, that's all. I don't think we can totally trust them."

Sarah was lying on a bed made of branches covered with skins. She had taken a few steps earlier and found that her ankle was getting stronger. Soon after arriving, the old woman had gently removed the bandage, which was not a bandage at all but strong wide leaves that she'd plucked from a plant by the creek. Before wrapping the ankle, she had plastered something that looked like black mud on the swelling. Whatever it was, it was working; the swelling was gone and there was no more pain.

Frank's bed was a couple of feet away. The wigwam was large. Freshly bent poplar and willow branches made up the frame. Their strong fresh woody scent filled the air. There were many different types of hides stretched over the frame, making it look like a patchwork quilt. An opening at the top allowed smoke to escape and some light to come in. A deerskin covered the doorway.

Sarah sighed. She felt, for the first time in many days, protected and content. The escape from the fire had been overwhelming. Almost too much to bear. She remembered the flames, the smoke and the pain in her ankle. That was all that she could remember. Her next memory was Levi. The young Indian man dressed in white man's clothes. She had drifted in and out of consciousness but she remembered the feel of his strong arms as his horse raced away from the raging fire. She felt his strong body crushing her and although she had no idea who he was or where he came from, she knew that she was out of harm's way.

"You do realize, Frank Lawdry, that Levi has more education than either you or me, don't you?"

"Then why is he here?"

"Because, I imagine, this is where he wants to be. This is his home and these are his people."

Frank came to accept another fact of life: he could never win an argument with his sister.

Days drifted by. Weeks drifted by, and soon those days and weeks had drifted into three months. Sarah and Frank talked about the day that they would leave, the day that they would set out for California but somehow nothing ever materialized. Levi would pick out their horses but then, one would go lame. Or, he would change his mind; there was a better one for Frank but it had to be broken in. They would have to wait. By the time the horses were chosen and ready to travel, it was time for the fall festival. Every October, there was a feast with great celebrating. No one wanted them to leave. After the festival, the weather was getting too cold. They needed Frank to help them prepare for winter.

"Sarah, do you realize that we are going to be here for the whole winter? Do you see how they have tricked us?"

"They haven't tricked us. It is their way, that's all. They want us to stay so they make up excuses. What difference does it make? At least here, we have food and shelter. We have forever to get to California."

Frank stared at his sister. She had changed. Every day, he watched as she worked with the Indian women. She had already mastered the Algonquin language while he still struggled with it. He saw no purpose in learning it. Where would he ever speak it again? There were no Abenaki where they were going. There weren't even any Algonquin. Those were the eastern tribes. He and Sarah were travelling west. Besides, if he did need to have something translated, there was always Levi.

That was another sore spot with Frank. Levi.

"What do you and Levi have to talk about all the time, Sarah?"

She was busy weaving a large basket to store whatever foodstuffs they could find for the winter.

"What do you mean, 'all the time?' I'm not talking to Levi all the time."

"Well, you sure talk with him a lot. More than with me."

She looked up from her work and smiled. "He is my best friend. If it weren't for him, I would be dead."

"Haven't you said 'thank you' enough times now?"

She laughed. "I don't think there are enough times, Frank. By the way, do you know how to say 'thank you' in Abenaki?"

"No. Why should I?"

"It might be nice to say it to the women when they bring your food to you or to Jedodiah when he lets you ride his horse. Or, what about old Yellow Moon when she fusses over you because she thinks that you're sick? And, what about the children when they make little gifts for you because they believe you are some sort of prince? "

Frank sat down beside his sister. Why was he continually fighting within himself? No one had ever treated him so well, yet something held him back. Why could he not accept the Abenaki as Sarah had?

"All right. You win. How do you say 'thank you' in Abenaki?"

"It is *Wliwni.*"

"That's it?"

"You could say, *Wliwni, nidoba.*"

"What does that mean?"

"It means 'thank you, friend.'"

"Okay, I'll do it."

Sarah smiled. "*Wli gen.*"

"That's enough, Sarah. One word at a time, please."

He could hear her soft laughter as he walked away and he knew that she was happy with him.

The autumn leaves were now beginning to drop from the trees and the wind had an icy touch. It was time to prepare for the winter. The women began to line the wigwams with layers of hides. Every day the men went hunting. Some days they would return with elk or moose and there would be great celebrating. They needed more though. They wanted to find the buffalo. The buffalo filled their western brothers' stomachs with food. However, the buffalo was not good only for food; the hides covered wigwams and kept out the cold winter winds. Only one hide would provide warm coats for at least two big men. The leftovers would be used for shields and bedding. The hair, for thread. This is what they had heard. If only they could find a herd before the white man did.

It was common knowledge among the Indians what the white man did to the buffalo. He would go in with his powerful rifles and slaughter hundreds at a time. The hides were removed and the carcasses left to rot in the sun.

The men sat around the campfire every night, planning the hunt. They would be gone for many days. The search wouldn't end until they found the buffalo. Otherwise, the tribe might not make it through the winter.

"Sarah," Frank burst into the tent. "Levi says that I can go on the big hunt. Look!" He held up an old army rifle. "He says that I can have this."

Sarah looked at the old gun. Levi's father had probably traded valuable furs for it. Furs that would be double its value or more. It upset her that the Indians were so naïve when it came to dealing with the white man. It upset her that the whites were so unethical when dealing with the Indians.

She managed to say, "Just don't shoot yourself in the foot, brother."

There was a bitter north wind that morning. The sky threatened to snow. No one in the band, including Sarah and Frank, knew anything about late fall blizzards. In the east, there was snow, sometimes mountains of it, but not until December or January. The hunting party rose before daylight. The women were up. The fire was burning. There was coffee for the men, coffee Levi had brought for his mother. Cholera claimed her life before she could taste the white mans' drink.

Sarah remembered the day that Levi had told her about his mother.

"Did anyone else die?" she'd asked.

"Yes," he said. "Many in the village died. That was before we came to this place. We once had over thirty wigwams. Now we have only thirteen here."

"Did you lose any more of your family?"

"Yes. My wife and baby son died also."

"I'm sorry," she'd whispered.

The hunting party brought out their horses and mounted. Steam poured from the horses' nostrils and from the men's mouths as they talked. The women stood clustered together, wrapped in blankets. Only two men turned to look back. Both looked at the same woman.

Chapter Seventeen

In later years, two things stood out in Frank's mind concerning the hunt: one was the cold, the bone-chilling cold. The other was the killing. He knew they needed the food; their lives depended upon it but he would never get used to the killing. Never get used to the blood.

They were gone for only four hours when the blizzard struck. For miles, they trudged along, barely seeing the back end of the horse in front. The cold wind stung their faces and penetrated through their clothing. Ice crystals formed on their eyelashes and facial hair. The drifts became deeper with each passing minute. The horses stumbled and snorted, sending out clouds of vapour. There was one thing for which to be thankful - they rode bareback. The heat from their horses probably kept them from freezing to death. Frank bent over, wrapped his arms around his horse's neck and buried his face in the mane.

Running Wolf, one of the prominent village elders, was in the lead. It was he who'd had the vision. The vision of the buffalo running across the western plains toward the White Mountains - thousands of them, just waiting for the Abenaki. Everyone in the village was excited about it. It had been a long time since anyone had seen a vision.

"If they believe so much in visions, why don't they find out where the buffalo are before we start out?" Frank had asked Sarah the night before they left.

"They never question the spirits," was all that Sarah said.

After battling the storm in the open for many hours, a thick bluff of oak trees appeared suddenly before them. They worked their way between the trees until they were out of the severe wind. The men dismounted and began breaking off tree branches. They dug out a wide hole in the snow and started a fire. Levi brought out a pot and brewed a strong pot of coffee. Although they were out of the wind, the air was biting cold but at least the snow wasn't blowing in their faces. The warmth from the fire and the hot coffee put everyone in a good mood.

One of the men shouted, *"Notlokangan. Notlokangan."*

Soon, the men were telling stories about days gone by. Frank picked up a few words here and there that he recognized but the laughter was so contagious that even when he didn't understand what they were saying, he laughed with the rest of them.

The trees protected them from the north wind, the heat from the fire almost burned their faces, their bellies were full, and the stories were good. The hours slipped away. No one worried about the future, not even Frank.

The blizzard lasted for two more days. The men realized that it would be foolish to wander through the blinding snow so they set up camp where they were. Although the frozen oak branches didn't bend like the poplar or willow, they were able to create a makeshift shelter from branches covered with hide. Frank cleared away patches of snow so the horses would have an easier time finding food. There wasn't much growth beneath the trees but the Indian horses seemed content to eat almost anything.

Levi had given Frank an Appaloosa to ride and he grew to love the little mare. The men would laugh at him when he patted her nose and talked to her or rubbed her down with straw after a ride. At first, it bothered him but after awhile he understood that they meant nothing bad. They enjoyed making fun of each other, too.

"How can they make fun of someone when they fall off a horse?" Frank had asked Levi one day.

Levi had grinned and said, "Better to laugh than to cry, my friend."

After the blizzard, the sun shone. The temperature rose and drops of water began dripping off the trees. Suddenly, it seemed more like spring than fall. The small hunting party packed up, in good spirits, ready to find the buffalo.

They travelled for two more days before coming to the plains. This, they knew, was where the buffalo roamed. On the second evening, they were camped at the bottom of a grassy knoll with a narrow stream trickling through. It was cooler again but there was no sign of snow. Dead grass covered the hills. They finished their one meal for the day - three tasty rabbits shared among the eight men. They drank the last of Levi's coffee. After a couple of stories, the men wrapped themselves in their deerskin blankets and fell asleep.

The sun was only a faint gleam in the eastern sky when Frank opened his eyes. He rolled over on his back and listened. Was the pounding a sound or was it the ground moving beneath him?

"Levi," he yelled. The men were slowly starting to sit up and look around. "What is it, Levi? What's making the ground move?"

Levi felt the ground with his hand and shook his head. The thundering grew louder.

Dazed, they jumped up. Was the earth breaking up beneath their feet?

"Look at the sky," Frank yelled. The sky towards the east was bright with the rising sun but to the northwest, it was almost black. The blackness was quickly rolling in towards them, coming closer and closer.

"Kwe-yoh. Kwe-yoh," the men shouted. *"Kita! Kita!"* They grabbed their rifles.

Each second, it seemed, the sound grew louder and the air became thicker with dust. They all stood, stunned, unsure of what to do. Frank's heart pounded. Should they start running in the other direction? He felt sick to his stomach. It was hard to breathe. He pulled his jacket up over his nose and mouth. What was going to happen to them? All he could think of was the mudslide; the mudslide that covered over his father, snuffing out his life. Surely, this could not be the same. There was no rain; there were no mountains. There was only the wind blowing dirt into their faces and the sound of approaching doom. Then, through the dust he could see something black rising up over the hills. It was like a wildfire rushing over the land, devouring and killing everything in its path.

Two of the men started to shout and wave their arms, motioning for the others to follow. Their words were drowned out in the pandemonium. They ran towards the river. Frank and the others raced after them.

Some years the river was high and fast-flowing but now it was shallow. Over the years, an overhang had formed along the bank and now all of them huddled under that narrow hollowed-out ledge. It was certainly no guarantee of safety but there was no other shelter.

"The horses," he screamed in Levi's ear. "The horses."

Levi shook his head; he couldn't hear him. Frank tried to shield his eyes with his hand and peer through the dust. The horses were gone. They'd broken their ropes. He knew they would be miles away by now. Would he ever see Elizabeth, his little Appaloosa again? At least, she would be safe.

He closed his eyes for a moment and when he opened them, there was no light at all. Frank felt as if someone had thrust a blanket over his head and pulled it tight. He opened his mouth to catch his breath but started choking. Hundreds of hooves suddenly pounded above him and plunged over the embankment before coming to a deafening crash no more than a ten feet in front of him. One animal after another pushed and stumbled against each other, racing blindly over the riverbank. Some fell and were trampled.

He wedged his body as close to the wall of dirt as he could and cradled his head with his arms. Levi wrapped his arms around him and buried his own face against Frank's back.

It had been only twenty minutes but it felt like a lifetime to the men trapped under the dirt ledge. Slowly, the ear-splitting thundering subsided, rumbling off into the distance. The dust drifted away and settled back down to earth. All of them stayed under the ledge. No one dared to move. Finally, Levi unwrapped his arms. Frank struggled to stand up. A layer of dirt covered his face, hair, and clothing. His eyes and throat burned. He stamped his feet and slapped his clothes. One man ran to the river to splash water into his eyes. The water, however, was so muddy it brought no relief.

It was then that Frank noticed not everyone was standing.

"Levi," he yelled. "Look! Two of the men are hurt."

Levi turned, at the same time trying to blink some of the dust from his eyes. His black eyes widened as he stared at the two men, their grotesquely twisted bodies pounded into the earth.

He grabbed Frank's arm and said, "Don't look, my friend. This is not for you to see."

It was too late. As Frank stared, he saw not only the two hunters whose sightless eyes stared back at him; he saw his own father, crushed to death under layers and layers of clay. He saw his mother's grave, dug somewhere along a lonely pioneer trail. Not much farther away, an old Negro slave lay buried under the cold hard ground and above it, a body swung from a tree limb.

Without warning, his stomach heaved and he bent over to vomit.

It was a nightmarish sight. The embankment had given way and the buffalo had trampled the men. Their mangled bodies lie still with no sign of life. Ezra, one of Levi's uncles, took off his jacket and placed it over one of the dead; Levi took off his and covered the other man's face. What was left of it.

No one spoke for several minutes. Frank sat down and put his head between his hands. He wished Sarah were with him.

"We will bury them where they died," Standing Tall said.

No one spoke as they used their rifles and hands to dig away the sand and clay. Sweat ran down Frank's back and dripped off his forehead. The more he thought about the men, the faster he worked. He prayed that someday those images would be removed from his mind. When both graves were deep enough, Frank sat off by himself. Silently and solemnly, they buried their dead. On top of each grave, Levi placed the man's rifle. The four elders sat beside the graves and began to sing the death dirge. The song echoed mournfully over the barren land, sending shivers down Frank's spine. Levi walked over and sat beside him.

"Does the song have any meaning?" he asked.

Levi nodded. "It helps to send their spirit to the other world."

"How can that help?"

"It is just their way, that is all."

Frank watched and listened. One of the rifles that lay on top of the grave was smashed beyond repair but the other one was so much better than his was. He wondered if the gods would mind if he exchanged them.

"They will need those rifles to protect themselves in the next world," Levi said, reading the white boy's mind. "That is what the Indian believe."

"Do you believe that?"

Levi shrugged. "The white man tells me the Indian is wrong but I do not see much difference. Both say there is an Afterlife. One calls it Heaven; the other calls it, the Happy Hunting Ground. I have not made up my mind what I believe."

Frank looked over at the men. They sat beside the mounds of dirt, their arms stretched up towards the heavens as they sang; their eyes, glazed over and unseeing.

"Me, neither," he said.

Off in the distance, they could see the cloud of dust made by the stampeding buffalo growing smaller. Soon, it would disappear.

"Will we still go after them?" Frank asked. "We don't have our horses anymore."

"We will go," Levi said. "We cannot go back home without food for the winter."

Without saying a word, the four men stood up, picked up their rifles, and started walking in the direction of the buffalo. Frank and Levi followed. They walked in silence. Their leader, the visionary, was not with them anymore. He who had the vision to hunt the buffalo had been killed by the buffalo.

I was beginning to wonder if Mr. Winnipesaukee wasn't tryin' to teach me some sort of lesson. I mean, here I was kickin' the heck out of my old car and worrin' about getting to this fancy ranch job whilst those poor Indians were stranded out in the middle of nowhere with nothin' but the clothes on their back. That was Ma's way of teachin' me things; every story she told had some sort of meaning and every story seemed to be about a young man my age. 'Course, the difference was that Ma's tales didn't go on quite as long as this old fellow's did.

I'm afraid that for the next few minutes, my mind did some wanderin'. It always happens when I start to think about my mother. I'd started to when Winnipesaukee said that Frank had named his mare Elizabeth. I'd been a mind to name Sugar after my ma too but Grandpa thought it might upset Pa, so I didn't.

It wasn't too long and I could hear the old man snoring. Well, I didn't blame him at all; after all, he'd been goin' on for at least, a couple of hours already. I knew he hadn't come to the finale but I supposed that he'd start up again in the morning. Or, maybe by then, he'd be worn out from talkin' and that would be the end of it.

I was jus' startin' to imagine myself in Frank's place and wonderin' what I would do when I heard a loud snort, a clearing of the throat and the voice started up again.

Chapter Eighteen

Frank didn't think they would ever see the buffalo again. He was tired. So tired that it was an effort to place one foot in front of the other. His arms ached from digging and there was a gash along one side of his neck, filled with dirt and dried blood. Dust literally penetrated every stitch of clothing and it was starting to rub against him. If only the men would stop so that he could shake out his clothes. Nevertheless, they kept walking. Far ahead of them, the cloud of dust had begun to dissipate so they were sure the buffalo had come to a stop. Frank thought that it meant the herd was completely out of sight.

"Levi," he said, as he walked alongside of him. "We're so far away from the camp, how will we get home?"

"Don't worry, we'll get home."

"But, we have no horses. How will we carry the meat back even if we do find the buffalo?"

Levi was just as tired and dirty as Frank.

"Why does the white man always worry and complain about everything?"

They trudged along the rest of the way in silence. As the sun was going down, they settled into a small dip in the flat land. There was no water. They could see scattered bluffs of trees in the distance but the exhausted men could go no farther. Frank went to gather buffalo chips for the fire. Ezra left the group and came back with a jackrabbit the size of a small dog.

Everyone's mood improved after eating. No one mentioned there was no water to drink. They had no blankets so they stretched out on the grass. The moon rose in the sky, turning the night into an eerie 'spirit' world. Frank's last thought was of his sister. Would he ever see her again? It seemed that he had just closed his eyes and someone was poking him to get up. In the east, the sky was pink.

There was little talk; there was nothing to eat, nothing to drink. The air was crisp. Each man picked up his rifle and started the long walk south towards the buffalo. There was no dust to follow, only the memory of it.

After walking several hours, they spied a clump of willow trees in the distance. The trees surrounded a small tired-looking slough. Green slime covered the water and it smelled fetid. The ridge cut out by the water in good years was now about ten feet from the water line.

Frank didn't care how warm or unpleasant the water tasted, he rushed down to take a drink.

"Stop," Levi yelled. "That will make you sick."

"I can't go another minute without water. Is it better to die or be sick?"

The older men chuckled.

"Come," Ezra said. "This is *mgoakw*. Swamp. We will build a fire and boil the water first."

Frank looked around. "What will we boil water in? We have nothing."

The men talked amongst themselves in Abenaki. He wasn't sure what they were saying but he did understand *Piz wat*. It meant 'good for nothing' and he knew they were talking about him.

While one of the men built the fire, the others took their rifles and went to hunt for food. Frank sat in the shade - hungry, thirsty, tired and frustrated. Did they think that he was so stupid, he didn't know they had no pots for boiling water? Maybe the gods were going to supply one, like the gods supplied the buffalo? He heard two shots in the distance. They were getting low on shells. Levi said that someone would have to make a trip to the white mans' post to buy some soon. The Abenaki would trade their many buffalo hides for the shells. Aw, another undertaking for the gods, it would seem.

The men returned with one rabbit and a snake.

"We will boil our water before we begin skinning our dinner," Black Hawk announced.

From the hide skin bags where they kept their matches and shells, each man produced his tin cup. Sheepishly, Frank brought his out. The men roared with laughter.

"Why didn't they just tell me we would boil the water in our cups?" he said to Levi later. "Why did they try to make me look like a fool?"

Levi smiled. "There is nothing wrong in looking like a fool, when you are being one."

The men ate and then lay down for a rest.

"I thought we were in a hurry to find the buffalo," Frank whispered to Levi.

"In an hour, we will have more energy. The men have spent many years hunting; they know what is best."

When the hour was up, Levi had to nudge Frank to wake him up.

They walked the rest of the day without seeing the buffalo. It wasn't until the third day that they came upon them. Frank stared out across the prairie. The men were standing on a hill and down in the valley, they saw what looked to be a thousand buffalo. The animals covered the land as far as the eye could see. One had to look closely to notice if even one was moving. No wonder this was such easy kill for the white man.

They made their way cautiously down the hill. The herd was still over a mile away. The men discussed their course of action. When they were finished, they exclaimed, "*Kwe-yoh! Wli, wli.*"

Levi explained how the hunt would go. Frank had to know so that he wouldn't interfere with the elders.

"We will stay at this end of the herd. The wind is right so they won't catch our scent. Standing Tall will tell you which animal is yours to kill. Do not shoot at any others."

They spread out, slowly inching their way towards the herd. The buffalo continued eating. They appeared blind and deaf. When they were several feet away, each man went down on one knee and aimed his rifle at his assigned animal. All six shots echoed simultaneously. Six buffalo dropped to the ground. The ones standing nearby simply moved away. There was no stampede.

"Levi," Frank shouted. "I shot mine. Look at that! One shot and I got him!"

Levi laughed. "One of these days, my friend, you will have to try hitting a moving target."

In the excitement, however, Frank didn't realize that two other shots rang out. Not until Levi grabbed his arm and ran, half-dragging him towards one of the dead buffalo. They hunkered down behind the big animal while more shots whizzed over their heads.

Besides the six buffalo, there were also two dead Abenaki.

Chapter Nineteen

Standing Tall and Black Hawk were also pinned behind a dead buffalo. They had lifted their rifles and were returning the fire.

"Who's out there?" Frank screamed. His heart pounded. He wiped the sweat from his face with his sleeve. His mouth tasted dry and sour from fear. He was sure that any minute one of the bullets would penetrate right through the buffalo and lodge in his brain. "Why are they shooting at us? Why are they trying to kill us?"

Levi shook his head. "I have no idea. It's white men, that I know. Maybe they don't want us taking the buffalo."

"There's hundreds of buffalo here. Who's going to miss six of them?"

Levi shrugged. "Maybe they just want to kill the Indian; maybe they don't want the buffalo."

With that, he calmly shoved a bullet into his rifle, quickly raised it over the back of the animal, fired and slid back down.

"Can you see who's there?"

"No." He started inserting another bullet. Frank did the same.

Levi smiled at the young white man with the white blonde hair and said, "All right, my friend, on the count of three, let's go together. I'll take the one farthest on the left; you take the one next. Understand?"

Frank nodded. This was his war now too. They stood up together with their rifles raised.

The Indian hunting party had been an easy target but now the man hunters were the open targets.

Two shots rang out as one. Frank saw two men crumble to the ground before he and Levi slid down. There was no answering shot. They reached for another bullet and waited. There was silence. They glanced over at the other two across from them.

Standing Tall shouted something to Levi. Levi answered.

"What did he say?" Frank asked.

"He thinks the enemy is dead. He and Black Hawk will check. We are to cover them." He cocked his rifle.

Black Hawk lifted his rifle and shot. There was no reply.

"It could be a trick," Frank said. "They could be waiting for us to walk up."

"Black Hawk will be careful. He has hunt men before. Come, stand up; we will shoot at the first movement."

Frank stood beside Levi. He could see five men lying prostrate on the ground, their chests covered in bright red blood. Suddenly, an arm moved. He raised his rifle and pulled the trigger. The body jumped from the bullet's impact and the arm fell down.

Frank broke out in a cold sweat. He turned away from the gory scene.

Levi put his hand on Frank's shoulder. "You did good, my friend."

"I never shot a man before."

"Neither did I."

Frank walked a few feet away, fell to his knees and vomited.

The two older Abenaki went about their work methodically. They had to gut and bleed the animals before the meat turned bad. They were not going to leave them to rot and kill six more. Frank did his share of the work but kept his eyes away from the dead bodies. He would never understand the Indians. They should be mourning the dead but, instead, they were thinking of the living.

Levi and Frank stayed to cut and pack the meat while the older men left to bury their Abenaki brothers.

"Do you want to help, Levi?" Frank asked. "Both your uncles are dead."

Levi shook his head. "No," he said. "I can do more good helping you."

Standing Tall and Black Hawk sent up their wailing dirge as they dug the graves. Even then, the buffalo didn't run off. Only now and again did they lift their heads as if listening to the wild Indian song.

As nightfall drew closer, they built a fire and set chunks of buffalo meat on the hot rocks to cook. Standing Tall brought in the outlaws' horses. There were five fine looking horses and one pack-mule.

Black Hawk said, "Frank, you search through the white men's saddle bags. See if there is anything that we can use."

"I don't know if I can do that."

"Why? They are dead."

Frank could feel his face burning. "I know. It just doesn't seem right somehow."

Standing Tall looked at him, the fire reflecting in his black eyes. "They are dead because they killed two of my brothers." His eyes burned with anger. "Does that seem right to you?"

Frank shook his head. "No, it's not right. I'll look."

He removed the saddles and saddle bags. All the while, he talked to the horses. After taking off their bridles, he tethered them. He wished there was water nearby but it was too dark to search now. In the morning, he would water them. They were strong healthy animals and he wanted to keep them that way. The Abenaki needed horses. Now they had transportation for the buffalo meat.

Dark clouds had drifted in from the west throughout the early evening so the night sky was black. The air turned cold. They could hear thunder rumbling in the distance. Their campfire burned bright with buffalo chips. The men sat silently around the fire. The buffalo meat had restored their strength but not their spirit. Their hunting party had been cut in half. Four Abenaki braves were buried in the earth. Five white men lay sprawled on the ground beyond them, waiting for the vultures to come for their feast.

"Aren't we going to bury them?" Frank asked Levi.

"If it were the other way around, would the white man bury the red man?"

"I would. No matter how much I hated them, I would bury them."

Levi smiled as he stared into the fire. "You would not have killed in the first place." Light flickered across his face, revealing lines of sadness. He looked at Frank. "Not unless you had to; not unless you were fighting for a friend. Then, you would kill."

Frank thought about that for a moment. He remembered the hatred he'd felt for that preacher on the wagon train but could he have killed him? The thought had never crossed his mind. Could he have killed if he'd caught him molesting his sister or someone else? No, he would never have considered it. Perhaps now he would.

"You're the same, Levi."

"Yes, we are brothers."

"I heard once that for you to be a brother to the Indian, you must cut yourself and mix the blood together. Is that true?"

Levi laughed. "Where do you get such wild ideas about the red man? No, Frank, we do not have to mix our blood. There is more to being a brother than blood."

"You're very wise, Levi. I hope that someday, I'll be like you."

"If I have wisdom, it comes from the white man and the Indian. Believe me, my brother, there is evil with both. There are fools with both. Learn the good from each. That is my advice to you."

They left before dawn. Instead of retracing their steps, they travelled east instead of north.

"Just in case we come upon some of the white men's friends," Levi explained. "This way we might get a day's head start on them."

"I can't see these guys having any friends, can you?"

"If any white man sees five of his own dead and two Indian graves close by, suddenly they will become their friends."

"Why didn't we bury the bodies? No one would know that anyone had even been killed then."

"The elders would not want to touch the bodies. We do not know what spirit world they have gone to. It's best not to interfere."

"Maybe they're just dead. Have you ever thought of that, Levi?"

Levi shrugged. "Even the white man believes in an afterlife."

"I don't."

"Perhaps, my brother, you are right."

By noon, the clouds had moved to the south and the sun beat down, hot and unrelenting. It seemed strange that just days before they had struggled through a blizzard. They travelled east for two days and then swung to the north. There was now plenty of grass and water. The trees gave shelter from the heat. The men talked and laughed as they made their way home. What was there to be sad about? They had food, hides and fresh horses. The warriors who had lost their lives were somewhere in the Happy Hunting Ground. There was no reason to weep for them.

They spent the evenings sitting around the fire, telling tales or gambling with pebbles. Frank was slowly learning some of the Abenaki language. He thought that Levi might get tired of always having to translate everything for him. After all, Sarah had already mastered it. She worked and laughed with the women at the camp as if she'd lived there all her life.

"My brother," Levi said. "The men are pleased with you. They say that you will make a great warrior someday."

Frank didn't say anything. Someday when he and Sarah were settled in California perhaps they would laugh about it. Imagine Frank Lawdry being an Indian warrior!

Chapter Twenty

On the third day travelling north, the wind changed. They faced it now. It stung their faces and cut through their thin shirts. The men searched the saddle bags for warmer clothes. By evening, the snow began to fall. They wrapped up in whatever they could find to keep warm and used the saddles for a protection from the wind and for a pillow.

Frank woke up to a white snowy world. The fire was already roaring and breakfast was cooking. He was happy to smell coffee boiling and salted pork frying. It might not be a typical Abenaki breakfast but the men were all enjoying it - thanks to the dead white men.

They spent the next several days battling the snowdrifts. The horses struggled through, steam pouring from their nostrils. Most of the time the men walked, leading and coaxing the horses on. If Frank thought the oxen were stubborn, he soon changed his mind. Petunia was a lamb compared to this pack mule. By the end of each day, Frank was more worn out from yanking and whipping that animal than from struggling through the snow himself. He fell asleep each night cursing every mule that was ever born.

Black Hawk, who watched Frank struggle to bring the mule into the shelter of the trees, laughed and said, *"Ktchiawassak."*

Everyone laughed. Levi explained, "That's the word for The Great Beast. It has a long nose and curly teeth."

Frank looked over at the mule. The name fit. "That's his name then. Ktchiawassak. I think I'll call him Wassak for short."

The wind abated but the temperature plummeted. Their breath hung in the air. Every few minutes they would bang their hands together and slap their chests to keep from freezing. The Indian men removed their saddles and threw them into the brush.

"Levi, we can't just leave these saddles here. They're good saddles. Back home yours are old and ready to throw out." He looked at the three saddles. "I won't throw mine away."

"Suit yourself. We're going to ride bareback to stay warm. The horse's body will keep us from freezing. There is one saddle left on the spare horse. You can have that one when we get back."

Frank shook his head. "No. I'll keep mine. You can have the other one when we get back."

The men mounted, wrapped their arms around the horse's neck and put their faces into the mane. Frank sat in the saddle, bending down with the horn poking into his stomach. The leather was hard and cold. If he could walk, he would keep warmer but the snow was too deep. The only positive thing was that Wassak didn't cause any trouble. Frank wrapped the mule's rope around the saddle horn with plenty of slack and left the stubborn animal to fend for himself. Wassak must have realized that if he didn't keep moving, he would freeze to death.

After three hours, they stopped and made a fire. The sky was heavy with dark clouds. It looked like another blizzard was on the way.

"How far are we from home now, do you think?" Frank asked Levi.

"We will be home in two more days. Just to the east of here is where the grassfire was. We will stick to the trees. In the open, we could not survive."

Frank stayed with his saddle until the next afternoon. He couldn't stand the cold any longer. The saddle came off. He threw it under the boughs of an old evergreen tree, vowing to return in the spring to retrieve it.

That evening, the men were quiet. The struggle through the snow and the frigid temperatures was taking its toll. Frank dug out some more coffee from the one remaining saddle bag. He had tried to stuff in as much as he could from his saddle bag into this one. He found some beef jerky and a tin of chewing tobacco. The two older men's eyes lit up when they saw the tobacco and Frank was glad that he hadn't thrown it out. There was something else that he had kept but he wasn't sure why. Perhaps, he felt that it would warm them up when the cold got unbearable. It seemed that way now. A wind had come up and peering through the trees, Frank could see the snow beginning to swirl and drift. Although there were no leaves on the trees, they still provided a windbreak and there were enough scattered spruce and pine to stop the winds from getting at them. Frank dreaded the morning when they would have to once again leave this protection and face the elements. If it hadn't been for Sarah, he would have stayed where he was. If he froze, so be it.

The men were already nodding off by the fire when Frank brought out the small flask of whiskey.

"Do you think we should have some of this?" he asked. "I kept it because I thought it might warm us up."

"*Ockoby! Ockoby!*" The men's eyes suddenly came to life.

Frank looked at Levi.

"Whiskey. That's what he's saying." He took the flask from Frank's hand. "I hope you know what you're doing, my brother." He got up and poured some whiskey into Standing Tall and Black Hawk's tin cups.

"*Wliwni. Wliwni.*" They grinned and held up their cups to Frank.

"You're welcome," he said, happy that he had done something that pleased them.

Levi poured some for himself and for Frank. It was the first time Frank had ever tasted anything stronger than his mother's raspberry wine. The liquid poured down his throat, burning and making him choke. The men roared.

With each swallow, the liquor went down a little easier. Frank knew one thing: no one drank it for the good taste. It was the most vile thing he'd ever put into his stomach. It did accomplish one thing though - he was definitely starting to warm up. In fact, it wasn't long before he had to unbutton his shirt. The others were doing the same. Standing Tall started to sing. By the time the flask was empty, all four were doing the sun dance around the fire.

Frank woke up hours later. The fire was out; it was dark and there was no sound. Except for the wind howling through the trees.

Without raising his head or moving a muscle, he called out, "Levi?" Even the sound of his own voice made his head hurt. It echoed through the night air only to come back and pound in his ears.

There was only silence.

He had never been so cold. Nor had he ever felt so sick. Before he could get up and move towards the few lingering embers of the campfire, he was violently ill. His burning insides felt like they were encased in layers of ice. He moved his hands up to rub his arms but there was no feeling in either one. He vomited again. His vision became blurred but he knew where the fire should be and crawled through the snow on his stomach towards the ashes. All he knew was that he had to get warm. If he didn't, he would die. Without moving his head, he reached over and threw some branches down on the few live cinders. Nothing happened. He moved his head closer and tried to blow. With each breath, a pain shot between his eyes. He tried again. This time the embers started to glow a little brighter. He closed his eyes and blew as hard as he could. Ashes flew into the air, sparks sprayed out and the branch caught fire. As the flames crackled and grew higher, Frank threw on more branches. After a few minutes, the heat became so intense that he had to roll back a couple of feet. He slowly sat up and held his hands out towards the heat. It wasn't until then that he started to look around for the others. The light from the fire now cast a yellowy glow over the camp. One of the horses snorted and softly whinnied. To his right, Frank could see someone sprawled in the snow.

"Levi," he called. There was no movement. Frank crawled over.

"Levi," he shouted again. There was no response. Frank touched the man's face. Now that he was getting some life back in his hands, he could feel Levi's skin. It was ice-cold. He began to shake him.

"Levi," he screamed. "Don't you dare die on me." He grabbed the Indian by his shirt and started to lift and drag him towards the fire. Twice he became so dizzy, he had to drop him and wait until his head cleared. He laid him as close to the fire as he dared and then tried to stand up. For a moment, everything whirled but he kept standing. Now he spied the other two men. Both of them were sprawled on their backs in the snow, naked. There was a look of tranquility frozen on their faces. Frank had no idea how much time had passed.

He started to walk towards them but didn't realize that his feet were still like chunks of ice. He took two steps and fell. After that, he crawled. Black Hawk was the nearest. On his hands and knees, he dragged him towards the fire. When he had placed him close to Levi, he crawled to Standing Tall. Neither man responded to his voice or his shakings. Both men were thin and weighed less than Frank did.

He added more wood. The flames leapt up. There was a pot beside him so he filled it with snow and placed it on the fire. The snow sizzled as it melted. While Frank waited for the water to get hot, he rubbed down the bodies with snow and then tried to cover them as best he could.

"*Kita. Kita,*" he yelled in their ears. He wasn't sure of the exact meaning of the word but he knew everyone used it when they wanted someone to listen.

He was so sure all three were dead and was wishing he himself were dead when someone groaned. Frank looked over at the frozen lifeless bodies. Could one of them still be alive? Perhaps, he was only imaging it. No. Standing Tall groaned again.

He opened his eyes, stared at the fire, and then at Frank. Although his eyes were open, he was not seeing.

"Standing Tall," Frank shouted. "It's me. It's Frank."

Still, he stared with no sign of comprehension.

"Who are you?" Frank yelled. "What is your name? *Awanigia? Awnaigia?*"

He grabbed hold of the man's shirt and began to shake him.

"Who are you? *Awanigia?*"

Slowly, ever so slowly, like a candle getting brighter, Standing Tall's eyes cleared.

He looked at Frank and smiled. "Standing Tall," he said. "That is my name."

"Yes," Frank shouted. "Yes, that's who you are."

"Did you forget my name?"

Frank grabbed and hugged him. "You're alive, Standing Tall. You're alive."

The older Indian man said, "I know I'm alive." He looked down at the other two who hadn't moved since Frank had dragged them there. "But what about these? *Chi ba gi no guat.*"

"I know. It doesn't look good."

He threw more wood on the fire. The water was boiling.

"Here," he said, handing Standing Tall a cup of hot water.

Frank crawled over to the coats that they had abandoned in their drunken stupor. He draped one around the Indian's back and threw the others over the lifeless bodies on the ground.

Standing Tall sat in front of the fire, staring into the flames, with the tin cup cradled in his hands. He looked as if he'd been sitting there all night.

Frank pulled his own coat on. What had possessed him to take it off in the first place? How could whiskey have such a hold on someone? To feel hot when in fact the air was frigid?

He made his way to Levi. Before this, he hadn't seen any sign of life. Now, he could see Levi's chest heaving up and down. Perhaps, he'd been too confused himself. He bent over his friend. No, not his friend. His brother.

"Levi." He put his mouth up to his ear. "Levi. Do you hear me?"

A look of irritation crossed the Indian's face.

"Levi." Frank spoke louder. "Are you all right?"

"Go away," Levi groaned. "Leave me alone. I'm dying."

Frank started to laugh. It felt good to laugh. Levi was alive. But, there was still Black Hawk. This time, instead of yelling in his ear, Frank simply put his hand on his chest. He felt it go up and down. The man was alive. He tucked the coat closer to his body and left him. He threw more logs on the fire, checked Levi once again and then lay down in front of the fire.

Ah! Winnipesaukee was beginning to sound like my mother again. And, it's not like I don't appreciate such wise counsel. Pa and Grandpa had told me about the evils of liquor but somehow it never came across quite as strong as Ma's advice. I always had the feelin' that even though the two cursed it, they still enjoyed it. They did their downright best to scare me with tales of corruption and immoral deeds but somehow it always ended up soundin' more like an adventure than somethin' condemned by God. Maybe it was the twinkle in their eyes that gave them away. Now with Ma, that was a different story. She knew 'xactly what would be the end for drunkards and it was no paradise, that's for sure.

The old man had stopped talkin' again and I was sort of glad for the rest. Somehow, it was takin' a toll on me, all this listenin'. I put my hands behind my head and gazed up at the stars. One thing I do grant him, he was one heck of a story teller. Right now, however, I had to stop and think about all the things that had been happenin'. Somehow, I got the distinct feelin' that Frank was startin' to become more of an Indian than he realized. Maybe I was too. I'd never ever heard a story by an Indian - not even a half-Indian, half-white man person. Right at this moment, I would have happily left this life and gone off to live with the Abenaki. Or, was it Sarah? That girl was playin' on my mind.

I guess I must have drifted off to sleep for awhile. The next thing I heard was Mr. Winnipesaukee clearing his throat.

Chapter Twenty One

The morning that the little hunting band straggled into camp was gloomy and dark with low grey clouds. The temperature was warmer but it was little consolation to the worn out men. They were barely aware of their surroundings.

Frank saw Sarah running towards them but that was all he saw. He fell to the ground and didn't wake up for the next twenty-four hours. When he did, he had no idea where he was. All he knew was that at last, he was warm and his sister was beside him, gently pouring warm broth down his throat.

"It's all right, Frank. You're back home." She put the cup down and held him close. "This is the last time I ever let you go off without me." She began to rock him in her arms. "We will never be apart again."

Frank opened his eyes. He could see the tears running down her cheeks. He tried to smile and touch her cheek but fell back to sleep before he could move his lips or his arm.

On the second day, he discovered that he was not the only one whom his sister was caring for. Levi was resting on the other side of the wigwam. He would wake up to the sound of Sarah's soft voice, only to realize that she was speaking, not to him, but to his Indian brother.

"Sarah," he called out. "Could you bring me something to eat? I'm so hungry."

"I just gave you something. Why is it that you need me every time that I'm helping Levi?"

"Why do you sound so impatient? You're my sister. Levi has his own sisters to wait on him."

Sarah bent down closer. "No, he doesn't have his sisters anymore, Frank. Both of them, Annabella and Shining Star, died while you were away. Others died, too. It was cold and we had little to eat. I've heard from Standing Tall and Black Hawk how difficult it was for you but it was not easy for us either. If you hadn't come with food, the whole village might never have made it until spring. We are all lucky to be alive. You and me."

Frank stared up at her.

"I killed a man, Sarah."

Sarah nodded. "Yes, I know."

"I might have killed another man too. I don't know."

She held him close and stroked his long blond hair. He wasn't her little brother anymore. In the weeks he'd been away, he had grown into a man. She wished that she could protect him from all evil but she couldn't do that. This was untamed land and the men who conquered it were the same.

"It will pass," she said. "Someday, you won't think about it anymore."

But Sarah knew that it would not pass. He would never forget. Would she forget? Could she forget the three white men who rode into the camp? The three who took their food, the little that they had, and the two rifles? How thankful she was that Moon Dog, the old man, had hidden the one good rifle. Could she ever forget the ugly tall man with long black hair and a beard who'd tried to pull her into one of the tents and when he gave up trying to fight with her, grabbed one of the young girls? She was only thirteen. Would she ever forget the shocked look on his face as she came in behind him, held up the rifle and fired? No, she would never forget. She would never forget how calm she was as she turned the gun on the other two men and forced them to get on their horses. How calm she had been as she fired shots over their heads and watched as they galloped off into the woods. For three nights, she'd kept a lookout, so sure they would return. John John and Broken Horse, the only men left in the village who could carry the dead man, removed the body. Sarah didn't know where they took it or what they did with it and she didn't ask. No, she could never forget. She did know that when Frank was better, she would have to tell him. Better she, than someone else.

If only her father were still beside her. She could see him, gazing at her with that little smile on his lips and amusement in his eyes. They were two of the same. She could never have lived her life in Portland, so content with nothing. Nothing but food, clothing and shelter. Nothing but climbing some social ladder. A ladder that climbed to nowhere. No, here was where there was life. Life and death. Each day was a struggle. Each day you knew you were alive because you had to fight for it. Sarah Lawdry would never host dainty little tea parties in the parlour. Especially not now. Not after she had killed a man.

It wasn't that she'd forgotten her mother. There was a part of Elizabeth there, too. It's just that it was mostly hidden. Sometimes when she awoke in the middle of the night, Sarah could hear the sound of her mother's piano. It calmed her and she fell back to sleep.

Spring arrived early that year. That was good because Sarah was sure they couldn't hang on much longer. By March, they were down to one meal a day. As soon as the last storm of the season was over, the men went in search of food. The sun was shining and the snow was beginning to melt. The buffalo meat had lasted for most of the winter. The women brought the frozen hides outside and stretched them in the sun. It wasn't long before the children were playing outside. The girls had their dolls made from corn stalks or cattails and the boys, their small bows, slings and spears. The women sat by the fire, gossiping or playing Little Pines. Joy and laughter filled the camp. No one mentioned the hard winter or the invasion by the white men. Everyone showed great admiration for the two white people who now seemed so much a part of their community.

The snow had all but disappeared before Frank brought up the subject.

"When do you think we should be on our way?" he asked one morning before breakfast. A group of men had gone hunting and they left Frank behind to cut wood. It was not a job he enjoyed. Like some of the other younger men, he thought that it was a woman's job.

Sarah, who was sitting in front of the wigwam, humming as she mended one of Levi's shirts, asked, "Be on our way where, Frank?"

Frank stared at her. He reached over and poked her arm. "Wake up, Sarah. You know exactly where I mean. Isn't it time that we left?"

Sarah looked uncomfortable. "I don't know. There isn't really any rush."

"I doubt that we would call this 'rushing.' I mean, we did say that we would go to California. You know, like Pa wanted. Don't you still want to go? Surely, you don't want to keep living here, do you?"

It wasn't easy to tell when Sarah was blushing because of her dark skin but he knew that she was now.

She pulled the buffalo hair through the cloth. Levi's clothes couldn't be mended many more times. There were almost more patches than cloth now.

"Frank, there is something that I've been meaning to tell you." She laid the cloth down and looked at him. "It's about me and Levi."

Frank stared at her. How could she do this to him?

She covered his hand with hers. "He would like me to be his wife."

Frank yanked his hand away. "How did you answer? Did you tell him that we're leaving? Did you tell him that we're going to California? That you would never let me go out on my own? Did you, Sarah?"

"Of course, I told him that I'd have to talk to you first. It is up to you, Frank. If you want to leave, I'll go with you. I told you that I would never let you go off by yourself again and I meant it."

Frank jumped up and walked away. Sarah called after him but he didn't look back. He grabbed his axe and headed out to the woods. She had no right to do this to him. She had no right to force him to make this decision. He'd seen the way the two of them looked at each other. He just never thought that Sarah would consider marrying an Indian. Was this the kind of life that she wanted? It wasn't that he didn't approve of Levi. Levi was the bravest, most knowledgeable man he'd ever known. Next to his father, that is. But, he didn't fit into the white mans' life. Did his sister really believe that she could be an Abenaki? Perhaps, it was a novelty now but someday that would wear off and reality would set in. He chopped and cut down trees until the blisters on his hands started bleeding. The sun was going down.

He knew what he had to do. Did he really have a choice? Sarah was his life. Maybe he wasn't as concerned about living with the Abenaki as he was losing his sister to Levi.

Chapter Twenty Two

The wedding took place three weeks later.

The marriage pole was up. Any who disapproved of the marriage could hit it with a stick to show their displeasure. Frank didn't go near it.

Everyone in the camp dressed in his or her best garments. Some had metal pendants draped around their necks and wore peaked caps. Others chose western clothing - the women in bright red and orange silks and the men in mismatched pants and shirts, clean but wrinkled. Sarah and Levi appeared in soft beaded buckskin. Both of them had their hair pulled back into one long braid. The bride carried some wild flowers that one of the children had picked for her.

Levi stood with four men on the north side; Sarah stood with four women on the south side of the gathering. All of them faced the *Sag8mo*, the Elder Man and Elder Woman in the centre, who performed the ceremony. The Elders faced the east.

Frank stayed by his wigwam. He watched as the Elders approached both groups. They would be inquiring about the marriage: what were their intentions? Did both clans agree? It would be only a formality. Sarah wasn't part of a clan.

When the pipe ceremony and prayers began, Frank went into his tent and stretched out on his bed. Sarah wouldn't notice if he was there or not. He heard the singing and could hear some of the words spoken. There was laughter and then silence. That, he knew was the exchange of food baskets. Sarah had explained it to him. He told her it was foolishness. The women's group brings a basket filled with vegetables. Levi gives an empty basket to Sarah. Sarah fills it and takes it.

"What's the point?" he'd asked her.

She'd smiled and said, "It's tradition, Frank. I think it's beautiful."

"You realize most of the things you say lately are silly, Sarah."

She'd raised her eyebrows. "No, I didn't realize that."

"Well, it's true. You never talk to me anymore; you just sit and hum with a foolish grin on your face."

She had laughed but it was true. She spent more time with Levi and the women. Frank spent more and more time by himself. Most of it with the horses. Even Standing Tall had to admire how shiny their coats were.

"You are turning them into a bunch of squaws," he said.

There was a sudden shout and laughter as some of the crowd pulled down the marriage pole and threw it into the fire. That meant everyone approved of the marriage.

He heard the Man Elder say in a loud strong voice, "Creator, you have heard their sacred words of marriage. We ask for your blessing upon Sarah and Levi that they keep their marriage union and grow in love and goodness together that their lodge may be filled with your blessing and peace forever. *Kchi Oliwni.* May the peace of the Creator be with you always."

Frank fell asleep to the sounds of singing and laughter.

In August, six Abenaki men rode into the village.

From a half mile away, the villagers heard their shouts. *"Kuai! Kuai!."*

Five of them wore white mans' clothing. The apparent leader was an elderly man riding bareback on a black horse. His pants and a shirt were made from soft deer hide and covered with beadwork. Two long white braids hung down his chest.

Men, women and children came running. Some of the women clapped their hands as they ran. A boisterous mixture of Abenaki and English filled the air.

"Kuai! Paakuin8gwzian, t8ni k'doll8wzin?"

"Hello. I am very well and you?"

"N'w8wl8wzi nia achi, wliwni ni."

"I am well too, thank you."

Everyone was shaking everyone's hand. Frank had no idea who the old man was but it was obvious he had a place of honour. As royalty might do, he waited to one side while each male villager came up to introduce himself. They smiled shyly at him and waited for his hand to come up first.

When the group rode in, Levi and Frank were working on one of the wigwams, replacing the old hide with the buffalo hide.

"Who's that?" Frank asked Levi. "Is he like the Grand Chief or something?"

Up to now, in the village, there was no chief. The older men handled all the issues. Lately, there had been a dispute among the men. Some thought it was time for the group to head east and travel back up towards Canada. The English, who had been on their tail, had probably forgotten about them by now. Besides that, the winters were too harsh. Many of their old friends and family were back in Maine and Quebec. Others, including Levi, argued against it.

"Why" asked Levi, "do you decide to pick up and move now? It's late summer. The hunting is still good here. We can start preparing for winter now. It's not the time to move. In the spring, we can consider it."

"Does Sarah want to leave?" Frank asked, when they were alone.

Levi shrugged. "I don't want to approach her with the subject right now."

Frank laughed. "Ah, the great warrior has fallen."

Levi turned his head but not before Frank saw the pink in his cheeks. Sarah did have a way with her. Now she had two men at her disposal.

Frank and Levi stood back and watched the procession.

"No, he isn't a Grand Chief, Frank, although he has almost as much honour. That is Wougwses. It means Fox. He is so old, he doesn't remember the date when he was born. There is no other man in our tribe as old."

"How do you know that?"

Levi grinned and poked Frank's arm. "Because he's our hero. You know, he's like George Washington. You see, we have our heroes too; the ones who fight the white man and wear many scalps on their belt." He poked Frank again. "Let's hope that he's not looking for a beautiful yellow scalp, hey?"

"Ha! He will think that I'm a god like the children do. You don't scare me, brother-in-law."

They both laughed. Frank couldn't imagine an Abenaki scalping a white man.

Levi put down the piece of hide that he was holding. "Let's go and welcome him. He'll think that we are rude."

"I don't understand. Why would he come? How did he know that your village was here?"

Levi laughed. "There is one thing about the Abenaki. Everyone is a gossip. By now, most of the tribes probably know that I have left the English school so they will keep travelling until they find us. We are far from *Ndakina,* our homeland. They will try to talk us into going east with them. Wait and see."

Frank walked beside Levi. "You mean they would keep coming west until they found you?"

"Of course. We are all family." He stopped and placed his hand on Frank's shoulder. "You know what you did for your sister? You gave up your own happiness for her happiness. The Abenaki would do the same. They have travelled all this way to make sure that everything is all right. Now we will have a big celebration. Wait and see."

Levi hadn't exaggerated when he said there would be a feast. Wougwses was given the place of honour. The children who at first had been shy, crept closer and soon were huddled around him, their eyes bright with excitement. The old man sat in silence facing the fire, his legs and arms crossed in front of him.

The men talked of many things, asking Wougwses' advice. He answered each question in a soft gentle voice, never rushing. If the younger men learned nothing else, they learned patience. It was later during the evening that Levi went up to him.

"Oh, Wougwses," he said, in Abenaki. "I would like you to meet my new wife." He drew Sarah closer.

The old man looked up. He held his hand up to Sarah. "Sit beside me," he said.

Sarah sat down. Wougwses stared at her until finally she lowered her eyes and said quietly to Levi. "What does he want from me, Levi?"

"Shh. Wait. He will speak."

The old man continued to stare. The women moved about, picking up their sleeping children and carrying them off to bed. Some of the men drifted away, collecting in small groups, smoking and quietly talking. Every now and then, there would be an outburst of laughter. Wougwses never took his eyes off Sarah. Frank sat across from them. The fire was dying down now but there was enough glow to light up the old face. Frank saw lines and wrinkles etched into tired weather beaten skin.

Five minutes passed. Sarah could feel tears stinging her eyes. If only he'd look away but he didn't.

"You are Abenaki," he said, in English. The words came so suddenly out of nowhere, it seemed, that Sarah was startled.

"No," she said, thinking that he was not pleased with Levi marrying a white woman. "No, I am English."

"No. You are Abenaki," he repeated.

Levi leaned over. "Wougwses, Great Father, my wife, Sarah, is a white woman. She and her brother, Frank, have lived with us for many months now. Frank stood beside me and fought the white men who shot at us. He also killed the buffalo. Sarah is the one who saved the young girl, Morning Star, when other white men came while we were hunting. They are our family but they are not Abenaki."

The old man smiled. He reached over and touched Sarah's hand. "You are Abenaki."

Sarah smiled at him. "Thank you," she said, for it was truly a compliment.

He continued, "Your great-grandfather was Benjamin Lawdry."

Sarah's mouth dropped open. "That is our father's name. Benjamin Lawdry. How would you know that?"

Wougwses stared across the fire at Frank. "This is your brother but he does not look like a Lawdry."

Frank found his voice. "No, it's true. I look like my mother. Sarah looks like our father. But, sir, his name was Benjamin Lawdry. Not our great-grandfather - our father."

"Your great-grandfather, Benjamin, was married to Black Swan in 1784. They had two children but one died. The baby girl, Autumn Flower, died. Their son, White Wolfe, lived and he became your grandfather. You, Sarah," he took her hand in his, "look like Black Swan."

Frank stood up. "But how do you know this? No one ever told us this story."

"That is because I am the only one who knows. Your father would not know it."

"I don't believe that. If this were true, he would have said something. He never said, never, that he was an Indian."

"Frank," Sarah said, "sit down and listen. Wougwses must have a reason for believing this."

"What?" Frank said. "Just because you happen to look like

someone?"

Sarah glared at him. "Someone who was married to a man who had the same last name as us. That couldn't be a coincidence, could it?"

Frank kept quiet but everything the old man was saying was ridiculous. There was no way that his father was an Indian. There was no way.

She turned to Wougwses. "Tell us what you know and how you know it. Please."

Wougwses was silent for a few minutes. Some of the others had gathered around the fire again. They sat and waited.

"We were camped near Lake Sebago the year that young Benjamin joined our tribe. He was an orphan. In 1786, Benjamin married Black Swan. Two years later they had a boy. They called him White Wolfe."

Frank stood up again. "You're telling me that you were living there when this Benjamin Lawdry joined your tribe?"

"Yes, Frank." Sarah glowered at him. "That's what he's saying. Now sit down and listen."

Sarah looked at Wougwses. "Tell us. You said that I looked just like Black Swan. Do you remember her that well."

"Yes," he said. "She was my youngest daughter."

I leaned on my elbow to look over at the old man. He was grinning as he looked up at the stars. Seemed to me, he thought that the gods had played a good joke on Frank.

"You mean that in all actuality, those two children were real Indians?"

Winnipesaukee laughed. It was sort of a gurgle but nonetheless, quite infectious so I laughed along with him.

"You'd know if you'd been paying attention," he said.

Well, I reckon he was right but he'd have to admit it was an unusually long story and when it gets into the wee hours of the morning, it's not exactly that easy to keep names and dates that clear in a person's mind.

"Yes sir," is all I said. "I'll be more attentive from now on."

I got up, stretched and picked up some more wood to throw on the fire.

"You want me to make us some coffee?" I asked.

He shook his head. "That'll keep us awake all night."

"We pretty much are already," I answered.

"Reckon you're right. You go ahead, son. I'll rest my eyes for a few minutes."

That was what my ma always said, especially when her body was fadin' away - 'rest my eyes.' I knew whenever she said it, she'd be fast asleep within minutes. Before I'd spooned the coffee grounds into the pot, Winnipesaukee was snorin'.

I let him sleep for as long as I could. I knew that if I didn't wake him up, he'd sleep until morning. I also figured he'd be pretty darn upset with me if I didn't let him finish up his story so as soon as the coffee had boiled and I'd poured it into the cups, I went over and shook him awake.

"Here you are," I said, trying to act as if I'd knowed that he was ready to open his eyes.

Embarrassed that I'd had to wake him, he grunted, grabbed the cup and sat up.

"Should be good," he said. "Took long enough to brew it."

That was one thing I had trouble understandin': my grandpa was the same way and I was beginnin' to see my pa turnin' that way too. The older they got, the less patience they had. Shouldn't it be the other way round? There's nothin' as irritatin' as an impatient old man. Or, woman for that matter, I guess. Grandpa used to grumble about Grandma once in awhile but Pa would always intercede and tell him not to talk about the dead. Unless, it was good, of course.

"So," I asked. "What did Frank think about all that? Was he happy to be related to Wougwses?"

The old man took another swallow of coffee and with a grin on his face, started up the story again.

Chapter Twenty Three

"I don't believe it. I'm not an Indian." That was all Frank could say. He rushed into his tent and Sarah followed. She grabbed his arm and swung him around.

"Why, Frank? What's the matter with being an Indian? Do you think that being white is better?"

He shook his head. "No." That was what he wanted to believe. "I mean, I don't know. Sarah." He looked at her with pleading eyes. "I'm sorry. Try to understand. I don't hate the Abenaki. It's good living here but it's like this is your world. I don't fit in. Levi is like a brother to me but he isn't like a real brother. I'm English, Sarah. English, like my mother."

There were tears in his sister's eyes. "I'm sorry too, Frank. To me, it's like finally knowing who I am." She smiled through the tears. "Remember how I used to climb the hills back in Portland and Mother would be so upset with me? How hard she tried to make me into a lady? And you, Frank, you were always the little gentleman." She reached up and touched his blond hair. "You still are. You, my brother, are a fine young English gentleman."

"And what will I do now? Where will I go? You'll stay here, won't you?"

"Of course, I will. I thought that was all settled."

"I'm sorry. Everything seems different now. I don't know why."

There was sadness in Sarah's eyes. "Levi is my husband. I could never leave him." She pulled him to her and held him close. She whispered in his ear, "Stay for awhile, Frank. Stay until next spring." She stood back and pleaded, "Please. It would mean so much to me."

"What difference does it make when I leave?" He smiled at her as he watched the tears run down her cheeks. She was so beautiful. Like an Indian princess. Her shiny black hair, pulled back from her face, showed off her high-cheeked bones and black eyes.

She smiled back. "Because," she said, "in the spring you are going to become an uncle. You can't leave before you see my baby."

Frank stared at her for a moment. "A what? You're going to have a baby?" His eyes widened. "You're sure, Sarah?

"Of course, I'm sure."

Frank continued to stare and not say anything.

"Aren't you happy for me? Aren't you happy for me and Levi?"

Frank shook his head, trying to clear his thoughts.

"Yes. Yes, I'm happy for you. It's just such a shock, that's all."

She grinned at him. "Now why would that be such a shock? I don't have to sit you down and tell you where babies come from, do I?"

Frank felt his face get warm. "No, it's only that it seems so final now."

"Final? What do you mean?"

"I mean, now you'll never leave and go to California with me, will you?"

"Frank, I wasn't going to go with you anyway. Unless, Levi wanted to go too."

"You promised that you would never let me go off by myself."

"I know. And, you know that if you had told me not to marry Levi, I wouldn't have. You know that."

"But now, you'll stick with the tribe, won't you?"

"Yes, this is my home now."

She turned and went out. Outside, everyone who was still awake had gathered round the fire. Wougwses was telling a story. Sarah saw Levi watching her. She went to him. He drew her close.

The visitors stayed with the village for ten days. Three families decided to travel east with them. Levi and the rest would not leave until spring. The evening before the entourage left, there was an Honour Dance for Wougwses. Everyone who knew him joined in. There was only one who stood off to himself. Frank. When the dance was over, Wougwses stood up and thanked the dancers.

The fall stretched out that year for so long the Abenaki thought there would be no snow at all. The harvest was good. The women had planted corn, beans and squash together on mounds. Corn towered into the sky with beans wrapped around the stalks and squash covered the ground for such a distance that if the frost hadn't come, it would have spread right into camp. Not only that, hidden in the bluffs of trees nearby, there was an abundance of wild garlic, horse radish, mushrooms and berries. Every day the men arrived back home with wild game. The successful hunter would send his children out to distribute meat to all the people in the village. He never took more for his own family. The leftovers were dried for the winter or kept over for the following days. No one went to bed with an empty stomach. There would be no need to hunt buffalo that year.

Frank hadn't mentioned leaving again and Sarah didn't bring the subject up. If Levi thought Frank was despondent, he didn't mention it. Everyone went about their day's activities without comment. That was the Indian way.

Three days went by before Sarah noticed that her brother was missing.

"Where can he be?" she cried, wringing her hands. "Levi, what has happened to him? He would have told me if he was going somewhere. Where could he have gone?"

They searched through the camp. No one had seen or talked to Frank in days. His wigwam hadn't been slept in. His rifle and hunting knife were gone, as was his favourite riding horse.

The following morning, Standing Tall, Levi and Black Hawk, went out to search for him. Sarah stayed in her tent. The women took turns coming in to bring her food and wild peppermint tea. She took turns being worried and angry. How could he be so thoughtless? Surely, if he intended to leave for California, he'd have the decency to say good-bye. Could he hate her so much?

On the evening of the second day, the men returned. One horse was dragging a travois behind. Frank lay on it; his face pale, his eyes closed. He had a horse blanket draped over him. His long blond hair hung limply over the sides of the poles. One of the women ran to get Sarah.

Sarah rushed out. Her black eyes shone for a moment. Then, she stopped and stared down at her brother.

"Is he alive?" she whispered. She could not go close until she knew.

Levi slid off his horse and went to Frank. He bent down and touched his forehead. "Barely," he said.

Sarah rushed over. She fell to the ground beside her brother. "Frank, Frank," she screamed in his ear. He heard nothing. "What's wrong with him? Has he been shot?"

Levi pulled her gently away. "He's sick, Sarah. We don't know what sickness he has. When we found him, he was delirious with fever."

"But where did you find him? Why didn't he come home when he knew he wasn't feeling good?"

"He was out where he set his traps. It looked like he decided to stay there when he took sick. There were signs of a fire but by the time we got there, it had been out for a long time. The nights are cold and he had only his horse blanket."

Sarah burst into tears. She wiped them with her hand. Her brother was so white and yet she could feel the heat from the fever. His face was wet.

"Bring him into his tent, Levi. I'll stay with him. I'll make him well."

Levi helped her to stand up.

"We'll put him in his tent but, Sarah, one of the other women will care for him. You have the baby to think about. What if it's a serious disease? You don't want to put yourself or the baby in danger."

She stared at him. "Levi, I will look after my brother. I am the only one that he has in this world. I'm strong and our baby will be strong." There was concern in his eyes. "Please, we'll be all right." She touched his face. "We'll be all right," she whispered.

Everyone in the village watched as Levi picked up his brother-in-law and carried him into the wigwam. Sarah followed. Already, Josephine, the one who collected herbs for medicine, was rushing to her home to find something to give to Frank. Another of the women, Chog Luskw, brought in a basin of cold water.

"Here," she said, in Abenaki, "try to bring down the temperature."

"*Wliwni,*" Sarah answered. She picked the cloth out of the water, wrung it and pressed it against Frank's forehead. Within seconds, it was hot again. She dipped it back into the cold water. After four times, the water was warm. Silently, Chog Luskw entered the tent, placed a new basin with cold water beside Sarah and took the other one away. This they did for the whole night. Before the sun was up, Levi came in.

"Sarah," he said. "I'll do this now. You and Chog Luskw must get some rest. If you get too tired, you will get sick too."

Sarah's eyes brimmed with tears. "I can't leave, Levi. He hasn't opened his eyes. Not once. I'm so afraid that he'll die if I leave him." Her hands shook as she lifted the cloth to his face.

"No," he said. "You are going to lie down now and rest."

Sarah started to shake her head but Levi lifted her up with his arm around her waist. He gently drew her over to a blanket on the other side of the tent. "See," he said. "You are right here. When Frank wakes up, I'll tell you."

She fell sobbing onto the blanket. Levi took a robe and covered her. "You must think about the baby," he said. "It isn't good to cry like this."

"The baby will be all right. It's my brother, Levi, it's my brother that we have to worry about. Please, stop talking about this baby."

He tightened his grip on her arm. "You forget that I have watched one of my sons die. I do not want to lose another."

Sarah watched as he turned his back to her and went back to Frank. She reached under the cover to feel the new life in her belly. How could she have forgotten Levi's past sorrow?

Chapter Twenty Four

For nearly a week, Frank tossed and rolled from side to side on his bed. The fever came and went. If he was lucid for several minutes at a time, all he could think about was his horse. He remembered tethering her. Was she getting enough to eat? Who was leading her down to the creek for water? If only old Josephine would stop pouring something down his throat. However, he was too weak to stop her. He tried to glare at her but all she did was yap away in Abenaki and pour more of her herbal concoction into his mouth. He'd never liked her. She talked too much and bossed him around too much. Why would someone whom he disliked so intensely, want to save his life? Or, was he dying? Was she trying to poison him? He wanted to push her hand away but found he could barely raise his own hand off the blanket.

A scream pierced through the air. Was it a real scream or just in his mind? He tried to raise himself up but as soon as he lifted his head, he became dizzy and fell back into his darkness. He remembered people in the tent; many people. Dark objects moving around behind the fire. The smoke. Sweet smelling smoke. It was supposed to drift up and go through the hole in the top of the wigwam. Why was it so hot and smoky? Why was Levi singing such a mournful dirge? Was it Levi? He opened his eyes. He had to know.

Someone had died. Was his Sarah dead? He yelled out. The black forms turned and stared at him. Old Josephine was there. He knew it was her. She was a witch. He hated her. She was ripping something away from his sister. It was a blanket. A blanket covered with blood. He remembered his mother dying. The bloody clothes. His insides turned cold and darkness came again. This time he welcomed it.

Time went by and Frank had no recollection of its passing. When finally he regained consciousness, silence filled the room. Silence and cold. He shivered. At last, he could think clearly; he knew who he was and where he was.

Where was the fire? It was winter; there had to be a fire. If not, he would freeze to death. He opened his eyes. Everything was dark. Far above, he could see the brightness of the night sky.

Everyone must be sleeping. Why would they not keep his fire burning?

"Sarah?" His voice sounded loud as it echoed in his ears. He called out again, "Sarah?"

No one answered. He listened. There was someone else in the room with him. He could hear breathing. Or, was it breathing? Sometimes it seemed to stop altogether; then, it would start up again. Shallow and raspy.

He managed to push back his cover. His hands shook. The air was biting cold. He knew that his fever had finally left him but he was weak. His eyes were adjusting. The room wasn't entirely black because a small amount of moonlight drifted down from the top of the wigwam. He leaned to the side, peering into the darkness, trying to see who was with him.

"Sarah?" There was no response.

There was only one thing to do: he had to get over to that person. If only he could walk. If only he could crawl. He wasn't sure if he could even do that. It had taken all his energy to turn onto his side.

Where was everyone? Why was he alone? It angered him to think that no one would keep the fire going. He tried calling out. Surely, someone would hear and come to bring hot broth.

"Levi," he shouted as loudly as he could. Perhaps, it had been only a whisper; he couldn't tell. If that were Sarah with him, where was her husband? Levi would never leave Sarah. Never.

Frank became aware of the sounds coming from outside. He was waiting to hear footsteps. All he heard, however, was the sound of the wind whistling through the trees. It was a bleak lonely sound.

It took so much of his energy to call out that he was forced to rest again. He was getting colder. Once again, he tried to lift his head off the pillow. This time, instead of falling back down when he got dizzy, he waited until it passed. Slowly, ever so slowly, he forced himself into a sitting position. Blackness swirled in front of his eyes.

He pulled the hide blanket off. His body jerked from the cold and he shivered. He got up on his knees and started crawling towards the body on the other side of the room. It was only eight feet away but it might as well have been a hundred. After moving about a foot, he broke out in a sweat. The room started to spin and everything went black.

He had no idea how long he lay sprawled on the cold earthen floor. When he did open his eyes, nothing had changed. It was still night. He was alone and he had never been so cold in his life. If only Josephine would think to check on him and bring some of her hot broth.

This time as he made his way across the floor, he stopped each time he felt faint and placed his forehead down on the cold ground. As he got closer to the body, the breathing stopped. He inched his way to the side. His eyes didn't want to focus so he reached over and touched the person's face.

"Sarah." Her name choked in his throat. "Sarah," he cried out. Although he couldn't hear her breathing anymore, her face was not cold like a dead person's; it was hot with fever. He placed his hand on her chest to feel it rise and fall but it didn't.

He waited for his tears but there weren't any. His life was nearly over anyway. If he didn't starve to death, he would freeze. Had the Abenaki left the two of them to die?

Carefully, he lifted the blanket and moved in beside his sister. He wrapped his arm around her and fell asleep.

"And that's it?" I asked when the old fellow stopped. "That's the end of your tale? Sarah and Frank die together somewhere out in the middle of nowhere? In some smelly old wigwam?" I sat up and faced Winnipesaukee. "Mister," I said. "That's a terrible story. If I'da known how sad this was going to be, I'd have told you to forget the whole thing. I wasn't planning on givin' up a good night's sleep, jus' to be all depressed for the rest of my life."

It was as if he hadn't heard a word that I'd said. He just lay there, staring straight up at the stars. One thing I knew for a certain; he wasn't going to give me an answer. I got up and threw some more wood on the fire.

"Maybe if Frank would have had some wood, he could have got that fire going and he would have made it," I said to no one in particular since I wasn't sure if anyone was even listenin'.

I'd finally got myself all comfortable and was hopin' to get the picture of two people dying together out of my mind when the voice started up again. Where does your story go when your main characters are both dead? It seemed that Winnipesaukee was about to tell me.

Chapter Twenty Five

It could have been the next morning or it could have been days
later, Frank had no idea. All he knew was that the sun was shining
in through the smoke hole. It wasn't, however, the light or the
freezing cold that had made him pry open his eyes; it was a sound.
At first, he had no idea what it was or where it came from. In his
weakened state, he had forgotten who was beside him. He closed
his eyes again and waited. Here, it came again. A low moan.

Sarah. Sarah was beside him. His eyes flew open. He rolled to
his side to face her.

"Sarah." He reached over and pulled her closer. "Sarah, can you
hear me?"

There was no response.

He reached up and felt her forehead. It wasn't as hot as before.
He could now hear her breathing. It was still shallow but it was
steady.

"It's going to be all right. We'll make it, Sarah." It had been so
long since he'd had the will to live. In fact, the will was suddenly
so strong, he felt light headed. Words spilled from his tongue; he
wasn't aware if they made sense or not.

"It's just the two of us again, Sis. We're alone. I don't know
where the rest are. They let the fire go out. Old Josephine kept
making me drink this awful potion. Remember her? I swear she's
as crazy as a bat. You'd have laughed, Sarah. I don't know where
she went to. Maybe I swore at her too many times. But, I know
Levi was here. I saw him. I heard him singing. I don't know where
he went. Maybe he's gone to get food for us." He watched her face
for any sign of life. Could she hear him? He hadn't meant to
ramble. "You have to wake up. Don't forget about the baby, Sarah.
Remember? You're going to have a baby. I'm going to be an
uncle. Levi is going to have a son. That's what he thinks. He's sure
he's going to have a son. Did you know that? I told him it would
serve him right if he had six daughters." Frank laughed. How long
had it been since he'd even felt like laughing? He laughed again
just to hear the sound. "You should have seen the look on his face!
It was hilarious." He began to stroke her hair. "Please, wake up.
You promised that you wouldn't leave me. You have to keep your

promise. You have to, Sarah. I love you."

He became aware of the bitter cold again. Every time he opened his mouth, he could see his breath. They could not survive without warmth. The wigwam had to be warm for Sarah. He searched the room but there was no wood piled up anywhere. Outside, trees surrounded the wigwams. Was he strong enough to go out and find firewood? He had to be. There was no choice. Otherwise, Sarah would die.

Without disturbing his sister, he crawled out from under the covering. Before moving away, he pulled it up higher under her chin and tucked it in beside her body. He touched her cheek. It was cool. If her fever was gone, she dare not get a chill.

He did not have energy enough to search for a coat so he crawled to his bed and pulled off a piece of buffalo hide. It took all the strength he had to lift it up over his shoulders. His moccasins were at the end of his bed. He tried pushing his bare feet into them but his hands were so stiff that he became exasperated. Finally, after several tries, he was able to pull them on but it was impossible to tie them. He wrapped the laces around his ankle as best he could. Before opening the flap of the wigwam, he banged his hands together, trying to get some feeling into them. If only he could remember where his mitts were. How was he going to get to the woods? All he could do was crawl. He turned back and took one last look at Sarah. Her skin was pallid.

He pulled the flap to the side. The sunlight was so bright, he had to stop and close his eyes for several seconds. The sun may have been shining but there was no warmth in it. The air was sharp with cold. His breath formed into a cloud in front of his face. He sat back and looked around. All he saw was white snow. Where were the other wigwams? Where was the common fire pit that was always burning? It was daytime. The village should have been alive. Where were the Abenaki? He looked out to the corral. It was empty. Everyone was gone.

It was not easy to grasp. Why would they leave? He didn't understand. There had to be a reason. No one would pull out and let two people die all alone. Especially, not Levi. Levi would never have left without Sarah.

It was then that he noticed the wood piled high along the front of the tent to his left. All he had to do was reach out for it. There was no need to go into the woods. Had someone left it there, knowing he might need it? Perhaps, believing there was a chance he and Sarah might live? He didn't know the answers and at the moment, he couldn't concern himself with it.

He dragged some of the wood inside, closing the deer hide door as fast as he could. The wood was there and the matches but his fingers didn't want to cooperate. It took almost an hour to get a fire going. When, at last, it seemed that it would keep burning and not fizzle out, he collapsed on his bed. He lay there watching the smoke drift up. Now and again, Sarah would sigh or moan. It worried him but it also told him that she was still alive. If he could just get warm, he would go to search for food. He had no idea what he could find out in the dead of winter. If all of the Indians were gone, they would have taken their food with them. Some of that food did not belong to them. They had obviously forgotten that he and Sarah had worked as hard at preserving the winter food supply as any of them. Right now, however, he was too tired to be angry or to be forgiving.

He was glad that the old woman had left her pans. When he could finally move his hands, he picked up a pot. There were several bags of herbs left behind too. His legs were still very shaky so he crawled to the door, leaned out and scooped some snow into the pan. In a matter of minutes, it was boiling. He removed it from the fire and dropped in some leaves from one of the bags. Frank had no idea what it was or how it tasted.

When it had cooled somewhat, he lifted the pot to his lips and took a drink. He felt the warmth of it move down his throat and into his stomach. After taking several swallows, he took it over to Sarah. The wigwam was warm now and soon he'd have to bring more wood in.

"Here, Sarah." He tried to gently lift her head. "You have to drink this." He parted her lips with the pot. Some of the hot liquid went into her mouth, some dribbled down her chin. "Sarah." He called her name again. Once again, he poured some of the tea into her mouth. This time, she swallowed. "Good girl. Good girl. Try a little more. Here." She swallowed again. After that, she went back into her sleep but her breathing was stronger and Frank knew that she would live.

For the next two days, he kept giving her the tea. It helped him to regain some of his strength back too. On the third morning, when Frank opened his eyes, Sarah was sitting up with her eyes open.

"Sarah, you're alive."

She nodded and smiled. "Did you think I was dead, little brother?"

He laughed. "I thought we both were."

They sat and looked at each other for several moments without talking. It seemed like they were strangers meeting for the first time.

"You were very sick, Frank. We didn't know what was wrong with you. Do you remember?"

Frank shook his head. "I can't recall much of anything. Mostly, all I remember is Josephine trying to make me drink horrible tasting tea." He laughed.

"After you got sick, some of the others did, too. Two of the old ones died and one of the little girls. We just buried them and then the snow and cold came. After that, I don't remember much myself."

"I thought I heard you screaming, Sarah." He looked over at her white face; so white now against her black hair. "Were you in pain or was I just crazy with the fever?"

Her eyes filled with tears. "No. You did hear me, Frank." She bent her head down and stared at her hands. "My babies are gone. They said that there were two of them. A boy and a girl. Now, there are none." Her tears dripped down onto her blanket.

Frank went to her and wrapped his arms around her frail body. She laid her head on his chest and sobbed. When she had no more strength left, he lowered her back down and covered her.

"Sleep for awhile, my Sarah," he whispered. "I'll find us some food."

He didn't have the heart to tell her that her people had abandoned her. That her own husband had forsaken her. And why? Was it because she had lost her babies?

While Sarah slept, Frank drank more of the tea and then put on his winter clothes. Although he was still weak, he could now walk without feeling faint or dizzy. It was another cold sunny day. He wasn't sure of what month it was. Perhaps, January. All he knew was that it had been a good fall. Good, that is, until the sickness hit.

Inside the wigwam, he'd felt stronger; once outside, he realized that he still had a long way to go to regaining his full strength. The cold air filled his lungs and it felt as if they would burst. His eyes burned from the sun's reflection on the snow. The snowdrifts were only about a foot deep in some areas but he barely had enough energy to put one foot in front of the other. How was he going to go out and hunt for food? He would die from exhaustion.

He would search one place first. That was the food cache. All he could do was hope that there would be something left behind.

He, Levi and Standing Tall had built the cache not far from the village. They'd dug it out of the side of a small hill. It was a perfect location. There were trees and bushes around so that anyone travelling close by would never notice it. Levi had constructed a wooden frame and door to keep wild animals out. Because it stayed cool in the summer, it was used the year round.

Under normal circumstances, Frank could have made it there in less than ten minutes, his long legs stretching out in front of him. The others, running to catch up. Now, it took almost an hour. By the time he reached it, his body was wet with perspiration. The door was half covered by the snow. He sank down and rested before trying to shovel it away with his hands. Even in his leather mitts, his hands were stiff with cold.

He crawled over and started to push the snow from the door. It was hard-packed and heavy. Finally, after what seemed like hours, he cleared enough so the door could open. By then, however, he had barely enough energy to stand. Slowly, by opening it enough to wedge his body in, he was able to lean against it and using all his body weight, it creaked open. Frank fell inside.

Frank hadn't realized how dark it would be inside. He'd forgotten that one of the women always came with them. It was the women who told them how they wanted everything organized. It was the women who always remembered to bring a torch for light. There was some light from the open door; enough for him to see that there was food. He walked deeper into the cave, his neck bent down so he wouldn't hit his head. There were baskets of dried beans and corn piled up against the walls; meat hung from the ceiling and there were tubs of dried fish on the shelves. Nothing was missing. The cache was filled with food. Why had the people from the village not taken it?

He fumbled round in the dark until he found an empty sack. In it he placed vegetables and chunks of venison. What he and Sarah needed was stew, rich stew to fill their shrunken stomachs and to give them the needed energy to survive the rest of the winter.

Frank knew that he could fill Sarah's empty stomach but her heart was another matter. There was only one man who might be able to do that and he had disappeared.

Sarah and Frank survived that cold lonely winter. Their health improved with each passing day. There was plenty of food in the cache and the wigwam was warm. A bond formed between them that would never be broken. Neither one knew what had happened to Levi or why the Abenaki had abandoned them. The subject was never discussed. Once in awhile Frank could see the pain in Sarah's eyes but he had no words with which to comfort her. Sometimes they would talk about leaving for California in the spring but somehow, it seemed foolish to plan ahead. Instead, they would take each day as it came.

One evening, as they sat by the fire, Sarah said, "You know what I wish I had, Frank?"

He grinned. "I don't know. Some books to read?"

"Well, besides that." She smiled. "You'll never guess but sometimes I wish I had a piano. Remember when Mother said that I would? I didn't believe her. But, wouldn't it be grand to sit together on a cold night like this and listen to some music?"

"Well, maybe if we close our eyes we'll be able to hear the sound of the wind. Doesn't that bring you joy?"

She laughed. "Now that proves you're an Abenaki, Frank."

Chapter Twenty Six

Spring seemed a long time in coming that year. There were many days when the wind blew so hard, they could do nothing but sit inside and hope the wigwam wouldn't lift off the ground. By the time the wood supply had disappeared, Frank was strong enough to go into the bush. He found an axe left behind under a tree. Most of the men never bothered to put their tools away; they left them wherever they finished for the day. He recalled how frustrated it would make him feel but now he was glad for it. Levi told him there was no point being upset. None of the tools rusted like the white mans' tools, so why worry.

Slowly, ever so slowly, the snow began to disappear. Under all that snow, there was green grass. The winds changed from the north to the south. Sarah took a wooden stool and placed it outside in front of the wigwam. There, she sat for hours, her eyes closed, soaking in the warmth of the sun. Each day her complexion improved and her body grew stronger.

One evening when it was warm enough to sit outside in front of the fire, she said, "It's time for us to move on, Frank."

It was a moment that Frank knew would come eventually but still one that he had been dreading. There was such a sad empty look in her eyes.

"Perhaps, if we wait a bit longer, Levi will return."

She shook her head. "No. He is gone forever."

"Why would he leave us like this, Sarah? I don't understand."

"There was a reason. Maybe we'll never know what it was but he wouldn't leave without one. That much I know."

"Where will we go?"

"West."

"How far west, Sarah?"

She looked across the fire at him. "It doesn't matter. We'll know the spot when we get there."

He nodded. "Tomorrow I'll start to get our supplies ready. It won't be easy without horses. Are you strong enough to walk?"

"Yes. We did it once before."

"But that was when Levi rescued us." It was out of his mouth before he thought about it. "I'm sorry, Sarah. That was cruel of me."

"Frank, we're not going to go through life pretending that Levi never existed. He was my husband. It would be wrong not to remember his good qualities."

Frank smiled. "Like remembering our parents, too." He looked up at the moon. "Who would have thought that we'd see so much death and heartache after we left Portland?"

"I suppose if we'd stayed there, we would be busy going to college now."

"How old are we anyway, Sarah? I don't even keep track anymore, do you?"

Sarah laughed. "Of course, I do. I don't know what the date is but I do know that this spring you'll be sixteen."

"I'm sixteen? You mean we've been gone for over two years now?"

"Yes. Sometimes it feels like so much longer. I'll be eighteen this fall."

He picked up a stick and poked at the fire. Sparks flew into the air. Somewhere in the darkness, a night owl gave a mournful call. The first black flies and moths were making an appearance, drawn in by the flames.

"Frank, I think tomorrow we should go out and look at the burial ground before we leave."

Frank's head jerked up. "Why would you want to do that? These are the people who deserted you, Sarah. Don't you think they're best forgotten?"

There were tears in her eyes. "I have to see if they buried my babies."

"I'm sorry. I never stop to think before I speak, do I?"

There was a tiny smile on her lips. "I understand you, Frank. It's all right."

The next morning, after breakfast, they walked to the burial ground. It wasn't far. It was on the other side of the narrow stream that had provided the villagers with water. Some of the men had placed rocks across the shallow water to make a pathway to the grounds. The little graveyard covered the side of the hill. It wasn't too close to the river for fear of spring flooding. On a sunny day, if you were fetching water from the stream, you could see the sun gleaming on some of the articles left on the graves. The graves tended to be facing different directions. If possible, they would bury the remains in the same position in which they'd died. If not, the body was placed in a foetal position, facing west.

Frank held Sarah's hand as they walked. He could feel her body begin to tremble when the burial ground came into sight. In spite of the warm day, her hand was cold. The river gurgled and murmured, sounding happy to be moving again. Buds were starting to form on the trees and small crocuses were poking their heads out of the ground. The air smelled sweet and fresh.

Sarah wore her Indian dress made from deerskin - her wedding dress. Frank remembered all the hours she'd spent sewing the beads on the shirt and along the skirt's hemline. It didn't seem right to wear it now but this time he'd kept quiet. There were things that she felt she had to do that he would no doubt never understand.

"Frank," she said, as they got closer, "look at all the new graves. These weren't here the last time that I came up." They stopped and stared. "So many must have died after we got sick."

Frank looked up and saw something that made his mouth turn dry. Before he could stop her, Sarah ripped her hand away, screaming as she ran, "No, no, no."

He ran after her, stumbling as he went. Why, oh why, did he let her come here? Could she handle any more tragedy? Could he? Or, was this better? Was it better knowing the truth?

"Levi, Levi," Sarah sobbed, as she fell on top of the grave. "Levi, why did you do this to me? Why did you leave me like this?"

Frank went to her and put his hand on her shoulders. "Sarah, I'm so sorry."

He went down on his knees and pulled her up. She buried her face in his chest. There was nothing he could say to bring her solace. All he could do was hold her until her weeping subsided.

Levi's rifle lay across the grave. Underneath it, neatly folded, was a deer hide suit. The one Sarah had asked him to wear on their wedding day.

Beside his grave, there were two small graves. So small, no one could have noticed them except for a tiny shirt held down with a rock. It was the shirt Sarah had made for her baby.

Frank walked away and sat down by the stream. There was nothing that he could say or do to take away any of Sarah's pain. At least, now she knew that Levi hadn't abandoned her. Now she could grieve for her husband and her children.

He waited for her. From high on the hill, Sarah's song broke the silence.

"*Ya ni go we ya. Ni go we ya. Ni go we.*"

The song of mourning. The death song.

Chapter Twenty Seven

For the next three days, they trudged through high grass, around small ponds and past thickly wooded areas. Snakes slithered away from them, flies swarmed around their heads and timid deer watched from the woods. Finally, they reached what they were looking for: a wagon trail. They knew there should be water close by and a place to camp for the night. If they were lucky, a wagon train might be passing through and if there were room, they could hitch a ride. Without a doubt, somewhere along the way, there would be a trading post or a settlement. Every day was warm and sunny, the air filled with the newness of spring. They travelled for two more days before it started to rain. It rained, on and off, for three days. Most of the time, they walked through the woods, trying to keep dry. On the third day, they started across a wide-open barren prairie. Even with all the rain, the grass was short and dead looking. No more than a half a mile into it, there was a cloudburst and they had to retreat to the trees. They were drenched through to their skin.

"Will we ever find dry kindling?" Sarah wondered, as she used a stick to poke at the ground, searching for anything that would burn. Frank stood and watched her for a moment. She moved slowly like an old woman.

"How are you feeling, Sarah?" he asked. "Is your fever back?"

She looked up. "No. I'm all right. Still a little weak, that's all. What about you?"

He laughed. "I guess I'm not in much better shape." He shrugged. "I don't know. Sometimes I don't think I'll ever feel really strong again."

"We will. Right now, we just need to get dry and warm. Look at all those pine cones under that tree." Her face lit up. "Finally, something dry that will burn."

They dozed beside the fire, listening to the rain pattering on the leaves above. Frank had made a canopy with branches to keep them somewhat dry. It was mid-afternoon but the sky was dark. There were no breaks in the clouds.

Sarah was asleep and Frank didn't see it until it was too late. He only caught sight of the last wagon as it disappeared into the rainy mist. He ran out to the road and yelled but he knew that it was futile. No one could hear him over the noise of the wagon wheels, the howling wind, and the heavy rain. He went back to the fire, water dripping off his hair, down his face and onto his wet clothing. Sarah was still sleeping. He didn't tell her about it. He threw more damp wood on the fire, hoping it would keep burning. It smoked and sputtered but did not go out. Frank shivered, wrapped a piece of buffalo hide around his shoulders, and wished they were in California. California, where the sun always shines. That's what his father had told him.

During the night, the rain stopped. The next morning the sun shone through the trees making the raindrops on the leaves glisten. The day started out hot and it didn't take long for the muddy road to become rock hard. They would walk for two hours and then rest by the winding river that was never more than a half mile away from the trail.

"How are you feeling?" Frank asked Sarah after they'd set up camp for the night. "Your face is so flushed. Do you think you might have a fever again?"

She smiled and shook her head. "No. I'm all right on the outside. It's the inside that refuses to heal."

"You're having pain?" Frank knew nothing about child bearing or how long it took for a woman's body to recover.

Her eyes filled with tears. "No. It's only the pain in my heart, Frank."

"I'm sorry. I didn't understand." He reached over and took her hand in his. "Will it heal with time? Like with Mother and Father?"

"I don't know."

"It isn't that I don't think about them anymore. You know what I mean, don't you, Sarah? I think about them often but it doesn't hurt so much anymore. Now it's sort of like looking at a photo. They look real but they don't talk to me."

She squeezed his hand and smiled. "I hope it will be like that for me, too."

They slept under the stars. Night sounds filled the air and Frank laid awake for a long time, wondering what was going to become of him and his sister.

By late afternoon the next day, they saw a building in the distance.

"What do you think that is, Sarah?"

As soon as it came into view, they stopped and stood staring. It had been a long time since they'd been close to any white civilization.

Frank laughed. "I almost forgot what a house looks like. Not that this is anything that we'd ever see back in Maine, that's for sure."

Sarah shielded her eyes. "It must be some kind of trading post. I don't see any other buildings, do you?"

Frank shook his head. They were low on supplies now. Although Frank had caught a fish for supper for the past three nights, they couldn't count on that for the rest of their journey.

"We need to buy food, Sarah, but how can we without any money?"

"We'll see if they'll trade for some of our hides." She looked over at him. "Isn't that why you've been carrying all of them?"

Frank blushed. It was true; he walked almost bent over with a load of furs and hides on his back. When the nights were cold, he would carefully remove one and cover Sarah. When she asked him why he didn't take one, he always said that he was warm enough. She would see him shivering though and thought that he was very foolish. Finally, after insisting that if he didn't cover himself, she would, he relented and with great care, pulled out one of the buffalo hides. The hides were old but Frank knew that someone would buy them to make a coat.

He nodded. "I guess I could take one in first to see what I could get for it."

"That would make sense, brother."

As they got closer, they could see that it was an old log outpost. It looked dilapidated and abandoned. The only sign of life was the three horses tied up to the hitching post. Their heads drooped almost to the ground and white lather dripped from their bodies. There was a water trough under the post but they had either already had their fill or they were too worn out to bend further.

"I hope those horses were walked first before they watered them," Frank said. "Some idiots just don't care how they treat their animals."

Large pine and spruce trees surrounded three sides of the building. The front faced south. The wagon trail went right past the front door and then travelled on for as far as a person could see over the empty prairie. The river turned north but the trail kept going west.

"What do you think, Sarah? Do you think that maybe I should go in by myself?"

Sarah gave him a sharp look. "Of course not. We'll go in together. I'm sure there's nothing to be afraid of. Besides, we have to buy supplies. We have no choice."

"I wonder if it wouldn't be better if I said you were my wife? We could say that our horses bolted and ran off with our wagon and supplies. What do you think?"

"Well, we better think of something fast; the door's opening."

He grabbed her hand and pulled her forward. "Okay, that's our story." They started to walk towards the building.

The man standing on the step raised his head, shoved his hat to the back of his head, and stared. He blinked several times and then squinted as if trying to remove an apparition. In one hand, he held a half-empty bottle of whiskey. He was a short but heavy barrel-chested man with shoulder length black hair and a matching beard. It appeared that the two spindly bowed legs, planted far apart, kept his body from falling over. Even from where they stood, they could see greasy perspiration on his forehead and nose. He wore a filthy red checked shirt with the sleeves rolled up to the elbows revealing large hairy forearms and there were dirty moccasins on his feet. There was a wild look in his eyes as he lifted the bottle up, took a swig, and stared at them again.

Frank called out, "Howdy, mister."

The drunk's eyes bulged. He slapped his thigh with one hand, raised his bottle high and bellowed, "Ya hoo!" He staggered backwards a few steps, banged up against the door and cursed. The horses raised their heads and nervously pulled on their reins.

"Am I seein' things or what? Lookee what we got here," he yelled. "I'll be damned if we ain't got some comp'ny. Hey, there, li'l lady, come on and join the party. Don' you be shy now." He threw his head back and laughed but this time he lost his balance and fell forward, off the step, and on to his knees in the dirt. The bottle rolled out of his reach, slopping out whiskey as it went. The big man crawled after it and grabbed it just before the last few swallows spilled out. He tipped it up and guzzled it down. Slowly, he tried getting up. Sarah and Frank stood without moving.

"Ya see what you made me do?" he shouted as he tried to yank his pistol out from his waistband.

"He's going to kill us," Sarah whispered.

Frank let go of her hand.

"Nobody's going to kill us," he said.

The exact moment that the gun came out of the waistband, the door opened and another man walked out onto the step. He was a tall thin man with watery blue eyes and dull yellow hair down to his shoulders. His clothes hung loosely on his body. There was a gun belt around his waist.

"Moses," he yelled. "What in blazes are you up to? Put your gun down. You'll shoot yourself." He looked at Frank and Sarah and grinned. His teeth matched his hair, dull yellow with one top one missing. "Don't mind him; he's just an old drunk if there ever was one. Couldn't shoot his way out of a barrel, that smelly old coot. Now," he said, as he placed his hands on his hips just above his gun belt and looked the newcomers up and down, "what have we got here? You two lost your way or something? Missed the wagon train, did you?" He winked at Sarah. "Bet you two were rolling in the hay someplace and didn't even know they left without you." He roared. "Seems that's happened to me a couple of times, if I do say so myself." He looked over at the man named Moses and said, "Bet you haven't seen a pretty little lady like this in a long time, have you?" His eyes travelled over Sarah's body. "No, sir. Can't say that I have either. Don't get too many women stopping by."

Moses' interest turned from his empty bottle to Sarah. His black eyes quickly filled with drunken lust. He ran his tongue over his lips.

"I ain't seen one like this in a long time, Tom. Too long, I'd say."

Sarah looked to the ground so he couldn't see the repulsion in her eyes. Frank saw her body stiffen.

"I'm Frank Lawdry," he said, " and this is my wife, Sarah. If this is a trading post, we'd like to get some supplies. We have some furs and hides to trade. You see, we lost our wagon and horses back away and when the wagon train went by, we were too far off the road to catch them."

Both men gawked at them.

"This is a trading post, isn't it?" he asked. "Don't the wagon trains stop here?"

"Why, yes sir. This is some sort of trading post, fellow. Hope you realize we were just joshing with your wife. Most of the Indian women who come through here travelling with a white man, well, excuse me for saying this, ma'am, but they usually aren't the marrying type, if you know what I mean."

Sarah didn't look up.

"Could we get those supplies now, mister?"

"Sure, you can, son. You and your missus come on in." He turned to Moses. "You get out of here and let these good folks get their supplies now. Go on. Go out into the bush and sleep it off. You're so drunk, the flies won't even come near." He waved his arms as if chasing a dog off the premises. "Go on, get!"

Moses stumbled along the side of the building, making his way to the back. Before Sarah reached the steps, she could hear him retching. A cold dread settled over her. She did not trust these two men. There were three horses at the post. Where was the third man?

Sarah followed Frank inside. He kept the pile of hides tucked under his arm. She carried their meagre supplies in a backpack that she'd made from soft deer hide. She'd exchanged her cotton clothing for the traditional Indian dress as soon as she'd married Levi. Most of the Abenaki women preferred cotton and bright silks but not Sarah.

A blue haze of tobacco smoke filled the dim musty room. The windows were so grimy that very little light made its way inside. Besides the tobacco, the room smelled of whiskey, sour sweat and the faint tinge of rancid bacon grease. Sarah stood behind Frank and looked around. She could see several barrels along the wall. These undoubtedly held flour, dried beans or peas and perhaps, coffee and tea. The shelves in front of them were almost bare except for a stack of men's overalls and a few boxes of ammunition. It looked as if someone had carelessly tossed several old pistols into one corner. Along the west wall, a long narrow table served as a counter. Behind it was a shelf holding a dozen or more bottles of whiskey, most half-filled or almost empty, and several dirty glasses sitting upside down. Three crudely constructed tables filled the centre of the room, each surrounded by three wooden chairs. There were cans on the table for ashes and cans on the floor for spit.

In the far corner there was a door opening to a room at the back. It was covered with a piece of cloth so stained it was impossible to tell the colour. Sarah could hear someone moving back there. She kept her eye on the door.

"Now, you show me what you got, young fellow. I'm sure we can make a real good deal." Tom stood at the door leading to the back room and faced them. "Or, maybe you and the missus would like a drink first." He winked at Sarah. "I hear Indian women really go for the fire water."

Sarah felt a chill run through her body again.

"Listen, mister," Frank said. "All we want are some food supplies. That's all. I don't think my wife appreciates your comments." He moved closer to Sarah.

Tom laughed. "Sure, sure."

Frank placed the hides on the floor, carefully peeled off the top hide and held it up. "How about some flour and coffee for this one?"

"That don't look like much to me. What more do you have?"

Frank looked up at him. "Listen," he said. "This supply has to last the trip so I can't give much. I'm not asking for much either - just some food to get us through to the next stop where we can catch up with a wagon train." He looked over at Sarah. "My wife here can't carry too much. She lost our babies a few months back and she's still a bit weak."

"Hey, anything I can do to help a nice young couple out. You set your hide on the counter there and help yourself. I'll be in the kitchen, whipping up some grub. I take it you could use something in your stomachs about now, right?" He grinned at Sarah. "Now, I know it ain't like your homemade cooking but it'll make you feel better. When you're finished gathering up your supplies, just sit down at one of these tables and I'll bring it out." He pulled the curtain aside and turned back. "You might think about staying the night. I hear there's some highwaymen travelling down this trail. It sure ain't safe for the two of you to be out there all by yourselves." With that, he disappeared into the back room. They could hear him talking to someone but they were speaking too low to make out the words. Suddenly, there was a burst of laughter.

"Frank, let's hurry and get out of here," Sarah whispered. "I don't trust that man one bit."

Frank nodded. "Grab that sack over there and put some flour and beans in it. We can sort the beans out afterwards." He threw the hide on the counter. There was an empty glass jar on the counter; he grabbed it and dipped it into the barrel of coffee.

They shoved everything into Sarah's knapsack. Frank picked up the rest of his hides and they hurried out the door.

"Where do we go, Frank?"

There seemed to be only two choices: one was back into the woods and the other, the prairie trail going west. If they went west, there would be no shelter at all. They would be right out in the open. Could they take the chance that these men would leave them alone?

"Come on, Sarah, let's go north." He grabbed her hand and pulled her towards the side of the cabin. "We can go up through the woods behind the trading post."

"But we'll be getting further away from the trail."

He glanced back at her. "But we'll be alive."

Without looking back, they took off running. They didn't stop until they were deep into the woods and the cabin was out of sight.

"I think my heart is going to bounce right out of my body," Sarah said with her hand over her chest. She gave Frank a weak smile. "But, I don't think we should stop. It won't take them long to figure out where we went."

"I doubt they'll try to find us now. Why would they?"

"Frank, do you honestly think that they're the ones who run the trading post?"

He raised his brows. "Well, I suppose so."

"Frank, that Tom didn't even care how many supplies we took. If he were the proprietor, he would have been counting his costs. Why would their horses be sitting outside all sweaty if they were looking after the post? If you ask me, they're the highwaymen."

He turned and looked back over their trail. It would be easy for the men to follow them.

"Where do you think the owner is?"

Sarah shrugged. "It would be foolish to think that he went with the wagon train. He'd stay at his post waiting for the next train."

"You think maybe they killed him?"

"Could easy have. They both had guns."

Frank nodded. "You're probably right. Can you walk some more?"

Sarah smiled. "When it means my life, I can walk. No matter what."

It was not as easy to walk now. The undergrowth was dense and often they had to stop to pick their way through brush and fallen trees. Very little sun had filtered through the trees when it was shining but now that it was setting, the forest was already dark.

"I think we should find a place to sleep, Sarah. They won't be able to track us down in the dark anyway."

Sarah nodded. She had very little energy left.

"There," she said, pointing. "Let's sleep under that spruce tree."

The tree was old and its bottom branches slopped down, covering a large area but high enough off the ground to form a cavernous shelter. They crawled underneath. The ground was soft with dried up cones and needles. Neither spoke. They closed their eyes and slept.

"Well, look what we have here. Seems our guests didn't like our hospitality. Look it here, Moses. What do you think of this? Think we ought to teach this nice young couple some manners?"

Sarah opened her eyes. It was morning. The two men from the trading post stood facing the tree. Tom was holding a rifle. They were both grinning.

"Yes, sir. I surely do think you ought to teach them a lesson, Tom. I think I ought to teach that purty li'l Indian girl a lesson. Maybe after I'm finished with her, she won't even want that white headed guy again." He threw back his head and roared.

Sarah looked at Frank. His eyes were closed. She poked him with her foot but he didn't wake up.

Tom pointed his rifle at Frank. "You come on out of here now, girl. If you wake up that husband of yours, I'll put a bullet right between his eyes."

She stared at his vacant eyes and knew he meant what he said.

"I'll come," she said. Before she could get all the way out from under the tree, Tom reached over and grabbed her hair. He dragged her along the ground until they were about six feet away. Sarah lay at his feet.

"Whoopee! Now ain't we gonna have fun with you," Moses shouted.

No one saw any movement. No one heard a sound. The gunshots echoed through the silent forest like the boom of thunder after a silent lightning flash.

Sarah, her heart pounding, raised her head and watched in horror as the man in front of her fell to the ground, his chest covered in blood. Seconds later, the second man flew backwards, most of his face blown away. Sarah clutched her chest and looked around. Frank lay on the ground, under the tree branch. There was a buffalo hide over his arm and under it, a smoking rifle.

She crawled to him. They held on to each other and Sarah wept.

"It's all right. It's over." He kissed the top of her head. "I had no choice. We're safe now."

"The gun," she whispered. She raised her eyes and looked at him. "How could you, Frank? How could you steal Levi's gun from his grave?"

As soon as the old man started talkin' about those two men at the tradin' post, I'd decided to sit up. Right from the start, I knew they'd be trouble. Soon as I hear someone has watery blue eyes and a tooth missin', I reckon that spells trouble with a capital T.

I looked at Winnipesaukee. He was starin' out into the night as if he was seein' it all himself. I didn't notice until after I'd thrown a few logs on the fire that there were tears rollin' down his cheeks.

"You feel like you want to take a break?" I asked. "Maybe you'd like another cup of coffee? It's about as thick as molasses now after boilin' away on the coals."

Winnipesaukee laughed and nodded. I liked it when he laughed because when his face broke into hundreds of wrinkles, his eyes disappeared. I couldn't even imagine how many wrinkles there were under that beard. Then, with the firelight shinin' on him, he looked like some old dried up prune. 'Course, I'd never have shared that observance with him.

I filled up two cups with the blackest thickest coffee I'd ever poured and handed one to the old man. He sat up, holding his coffee in one hand, and stared into the fire. I sat up too. We both sat in silence, starin' at the fire, for what seemed forever. I would say probably more like five minutes. I don't know why I expected him to keep talkin' during his break; after all, I was the one who'd suggested it.

"So," I said, "Frank took Levi's gun. That makes sense to me. Good thing he did too because it sure saved a lot of heartache. I was really startin' to worry about that girl, Sarah."

Winnipesaukee continued staring into the fire.

"Don't you think it was a good thing? I mean, it seems kind of pointless to leave a perfectly good gun on top of a grave."

It seemed that I wasn't goin' to get any comment on that so I just kept quiet and waited for the rest of the story. It began after he'd drained the last drop of coffee down his throat.

It was a story worth waiting for.

Chapter Twenty Eight

"I did what I felt I had to do."

That was all Frank said.

He picked up his furs and tucked them under one arm. There was no need to drape them over the rifle anymore.

"There's one more man in that house. For sure he heard the gunshots and when his friends don't return, he'll come looking." He stood and waited for Sarah to get up. "We can't waste any time. Get your knapsack."

They travelled north west. The brush was thick and the going was slow. Even with long sleeves to protect their arms, sharp branches poked through to their skin. Most of the time they covered their faces with their hands, trying to keep protruding limbs from poking out an eye. They dared not move out into the open. In fact, they had no idea where there was an opening or if there was one. The river was their guide. There was no sign of human life anywhere. The first night they found another large evergreen tree and slept under the boughs. The only food they ate all day was wild berries. That, along with plenty of cold fresh water from the river to drink. Their stomachs ached for food but they couldn't take a chance and light a fire.

Sarah was quiet all day. Frank knew that the sight of Levi's gun was upsetting to her but he held on to it. He would not apologize. There was no way that he was going to let a good gun rust out on top of a grave. What would Levi have wanted? A weapon going to waste or one that would save his wife's life? There was no question in Frank's mind as to what the answer would be. Besides, if Levi had gone to some spirit world, as the Abenaki believed, of what use was a gun? It made no sense. If Sarah wanted to believe that, that was fine. He would protect her in this life.

On the second day, they came to a part of the river that was narrower and shallower so they crossed over. It was almost dark by the time they stopped for the day. There was no sign of anyone following them. Several times during the day, they would stop and listen but it was always quiet, only the soothing sounds of the forest. Again, they made a cold camp. Sarah had picked up wild garlic and mushrooms along the way. They washed them and ate them.

Finally, the forest thinned out and by noon the next day, they were on grassy land. This was not like the open prairie where Frank had killed the buffalo or the land south of the trading post; this was beautiful green hilly land with bluffs of trees here and there.

They stood on a hill and looked out.

"Look, Sarah." Frank pointed towards something farther to the north. "That looks like smoke, don't you think?"

"It does. Do you think it might be a homestead? Or, do you think it's an Indian village?"

He picked up the furs. "I guess we might as well go and see. We won't get there until tomorrow some time anyway. It's farther than what we think."

That evening, they camped by the river. Frank caught a couple of fish that they skewered and cooked over a fire. Sarah smashed the coffee beans with a rock and made a pot of coffee. They settled back and watched the flames until they flickered and died. The scent of spring flowers and the calls of mating birds filled the air. The river gurgled contentedly as it tumbled over the rocks.

"Sarah," Frank said. "I'm sorry that I didn't tell you about Levi's gun. It's just that I didn't think you'd let me bring it and I knew we had to have one. This country is too raw and wild to wander round without a weapon." He watched her face, hoping for any sign of reconciliation.

Finally, she looked at him. Her eyes were filled with tears but also, affection.

"Brother, what am I to say? You're now a man. You make your own decisions. I probably would have stopped you from taking it." She blinked her tears away. "A very sentimental choice on my part. It was a good thing you kept it hidden. Levi's gun saved me. Saved me from something worse than death. And you, for they would have killed you." She smiled as the tears now spilled down her cheeks. "Perhaps that was why the rifle was left there. It was meant for you."

For the first time in days, Frank relaxed. It was as if a heavy weight fell from his shoulders. Sarah's approval meant more to him than he realized.

"Where do you think we should settle, Sarah?" It was dark now but the moon cast a white silvery glow over the land.

"It sounds strange to hear you say that. California is so far off, isn't it? Almost like a dream."

"I think that it was Papa's dream but perhaps, not ours. We were children when we left home; we didn't even have any dreams. It seems like a lifetime ago. Do you sometimes wish we could go back and start all over again?"

Sarah laughed softly. "I can't even think like that. There's too much that I'd like to be different."

"There were some good times though, weren't there? Remember how much trouble those old mules gave me?"

They laughed.

"I didn't realize that you thought of that as being a good time. It seems to me, I heard you cussing out there in the bush an awful lot, Frank Lawdry."

"Yeah, but somehow, I can't help wonder where old Molly ended up."

"Maybe she just kept going to California, Frank."

They lay quietly for a while, each with their own thoughts.

"This is beautiful land, Sarah. Maybe we should see if we can't build a homestead out here."

"Don't you need money to buy land? Or, do you think the government has started giving it away for free?" she asked, in a teasing voice.

Frank stared up at the moon for several seconds. "Maybe we could build a log house somewhere in these woods. By the time anyone from the government finds us, we'll have some money saved from trapping and we could pay for the land." He looked over at her. "Don't you like the countryside here?"

"It's very nice. But, I don't know, somehow it doesn't feel like home. I guess we're still too close to that trading post. Right now, I'd like to be a million miles away."

"You want to keep going north?"

"I think we should check out the smoke we saw. It would be good to know where we are, find out if there's a settlement close by."

"Maybe I could get some work in a mill or something. You could teach school, Sarah. If we had some money saved up, we could start out again and look for a place. Where would you like to live?" He looked across at her. Her black hair shone silver in the moonlight. "Should we travel to the mountains? Or, would you like the flat prairie where we could stick our rifle out the window and get ourselves a buffalo?"

She laughed. Her laughter always reminded him of his mother.

"Your tastes are always so extreme." She grinned, showing an even row of white teeth. "I would love to live in a valley, Frank. To me, the most beautiful place in the world would be cradled on all sides by high grassy hills and bluffs of trees. And, of course, there would be a river running right through. Wouldn't you like that?" Before waiting for a reply, she went on, "We would build a little log house right in those hills. It would be facing south so we could watch the river, the sunrise and the sunset every day." She paused and looked up at the starry heavens. Softly, she said, "That's where I would like to live, Frank."

"Then, that's what we'll do. We'll search for that place."

"We won't have to search, brother; we will know it when we see it."

With that, they each went to sleep, a smile playing on their lips. It felt good to have a dream.

The next afternoon they came upon the log cabin, nestled in among the trees. The only sign of life was the lazy grey smoke drifting up from the tin chimney. It was a square building with a window on each side of the door; each window framed on the inside with white lacy curtains. There were no steps; the door sat evenly with the ground. To the right, they could see a corral, its log fencing winding around skinny poplar trees and enclosing a small makeshift barn made from slabs. A rooster was perched on a wooden water trough that sat in front of the barn while several white chickens squawked and pecked the ground in front of him. A well-worn footpath connected the house to the corral gate. Three horses lifted their heads in unison and looked in their direction.

Sarah and Frank stood behind an old spruce tree, watched, and waited. They were going to be more cautious this time. The lace curtains might look innocent enough but the trading post had looked innocent also.

Suddenly, the door swung open, banging against the side of the house, and a plump woman with white hair pulled back tightly behind her head, raised a rifle and yelled, "Okay, you two varmints, come out from behind thet bush." She pulled the trigger and fired into the air. "Come out with your hands up."

Frank debated for a second too long about hanging on to his own rifle. The second bullet whizzed above their heads.

"Hold it, lady," he yelled. "We're coming out. Don't shoot."

The two shuffled out from behind the trees with their hands in the air.

"That's all that's with you?" she yelled from the doorway. "If'n you're lyin', you'll git your feet shot right out from under you."

"There's only the two of us," Sarah shouted. "Me and my brother."

"Oh glory be," the older woman said as she lowered her gun. "I coulda shot the both of you. What, in the name of heaven, are you two children doin' way out here anyway?"

"We're making our way west, ma'am," Frank answered. "And, we're not children."

"You surely don' look like no grownups to me. What's your names anyhow?"

"Frank and Sarah Lawdry. We're brother and sister, ma'am."

She squinted at them. "You surely don' look like no sister and brother either. You best not to be lyin' to me, boy. Somebody send you here from the trading post?"

"No, ma'am. We truly are brother and sister. Honest."

"How come you looks like an Indian?" She pointed at Sarah with the rifle butt.

"Actually, ma'am," Sarah said, "Frank and I are part English and part Abenaki. Frank takes after our mother and I look like my father."

The older woman grunted.

"Y'all can call me Maude," she shouted. She stood with her legs spread apart, holding the gun across her ample bosom. She was a weighty woman and the men's faded denim overalls she wore did nothing to enhance her shape. Under the overalls she wore a man's cotton shirt with the long sleeves cut off, one shorter than the other. It looked as if at one time it had been white but was now a dull grey. Her large breasts sagged down to meet up with her bulbous belly. She was barefoot. "Course, mor' 'an likely if I hadn't shot ya, those fellas over at the tradin' post woulda. Yer lucky to git through those woods alive. 'Specially, a young woman like you are." She nodded at Sarah.

"You wouldn't be referring to a couple of men called Moses and Tom, would you?" Frank asked.

Maude stared at them for a second. Her eyebrows went up and her mouth opened slightly. She blinked. "You know those two yahoos?"

"We had an encounter with them in the woods."

"An' you're still alive to tell the tale, young man?"

"More than I can say about them, ma'am."

Maude burst out laughing. The rifle bounced up and down in time with her stomach.

"Well, I'll be a son of a gun. Ain't that the end ta end all."

The woman shook her head and laid the rifle up against the house.

"Well, don' jest stan' with your mouths open and your hands in the air. Come on in."

With some trepidation, the two walked towards the house. Maude stood to one side by the open door. As they got closer, they both relaxed and their breathing returned to normal. Maude Henderson had one of the kindest faces that they'd encountered thus far in their travels. She had deep laugh lines that seemed to reach from the corners of her eyes to the corners of her lips. Her cheeks were round, pink and shiny; her twinkling eyes, as blue as azure skies.

The cabin consisted of one large room, crowded with dark furniture but still having the semblance of neatness. One side was designated as the bedroom; the other, the kitchen and eating area. A four-poster bed, shoved into one corner, filled almost half of it. A diamond patterned multi-coloured patchwork quilt covered it. Along the wall, at the end of the bed, was a massive mahogany bureau. The tip of its ornate mirror nearly touched the slanted ceiling. A silver comb, brush and hand mirror were laid out neatly on a crocheted doily. There were no windows along this wall but the sunlight shining in through the window facing the front made the room light and cheery.

The cook stove stood straight ahead of them, so close to the bed that the reservoir could substitute for a night table. The dining table was to their left, along the side wall, underneath a window. A stained and faded flowered cotton tablecloth was draped over it, with one end slightly higher than the other end. A pair of grimy glass salt and pepper shakers and a yellow chipped bowl filled with a mound of half-melted butter sat in the centre. A trunk piled high with a saddle, bridles and several horse blankets stood underneath the window facing the front yard. There were three pegs on the wall, each holding jackets and overalls.

The room was warm and filled with the scent of firewood, fresh bread and coffee.

"Wal, don' jest stan' there. You better sit down an' have a bite to eat. If'n I don' share this bread with someone, I'll be eatin' it all myself." She patted her belly. "An lord knows, I surely don' need any more stuffin' added."

She laughed and pulled out a chair for Sarah.

"You sit now, darlin'. You look plain tuckered out."

The two sat in silence, holding their breath, as they watched their host pick up a knife, hold the large loaf of hot bread to her bosom and slice through, stopping so close to her body that Frank was sure he was going to see one breast lopped off.

"It's not often I git visitors," she said, as she slapped six thick slices of bread on a platter and placed it on the table. She laughed again, a laugh that started in her throat and finished somewhere in that large lower abdomen. "In fact, I'd say, I never git them." Another roar. "So, I figure I'd best be usin' some of my fancy dishes. You young 'uns talk like you come from good stock. Where'd you say you was from?"

Frank spoke up. "We're originally from Portland, Maine, ma'am. Our folks started out with a wagon train a couple of years ago. We were on our way to California."

Maude lifted the flowered curtain covering a small cupboard beside the stove and brought out three china cups. She filled them with steaming coffee and placed them in front of Sarah and Frank. After pouring herself one, she pulled out the last chair and sat down.

"I take it you've had your share of troubles, have you?"

"Yes, ma'am. We lost our mother first; then, a mudslide buried the whole wagon train. That's when our pa died. Sarah and I were the only survivors."

Maude shook her head in sympathy. She picked up the plate.

"Here, now. You better eat up."

Sarah and Frank both reached for their second slice. Sarah couldn't remember ever eating bread that melted in her mouth like that.

"Do you live out here all by yourself?" she asked.

"Didn't start out that way, darlin'. I had me a good man but he went off to fetch supplies a year ago and he never come back."

Sarah lowered her head. "I'm sorry."

"Oh, that's okay. I do all right. At least, I did til those galoots killed Mr. McCracken and took over the trading post. They've caused me a bit of worry." She waved her arm around the room. "This here stuff ain't mine, case you was wonderin'. It was Mr. Henderson's first wife who had all this. She was a fancy lady, I reckon. Guess life was jus' too rough for her. She's buried out back."

"What do you think happened to your husband?" Sarah asked.

Maude shrugged. "First, I thought the Injuns had got him but that didn't make much sense, seein' as how he and the Injuns was good friends. No, I reckon it was some white highwaymen. Prob'ly kilt him and took his pelts 'fore he even got to the post. That's what I reckon."

"If you don't mind my asking, ma'am, how do you make a living out here?" Frank asked.

"Don' mind you askin' at all, son. And, you can drop the 'ma'am', if'n it's all right with you. Jus' call me Maude." She reached over to the stove, lifted the coffee pot and filled everyone's cups. "Mostly, I live off the land. Got me some chickens and a cow. Some winters is pretty rough but I manage. Used to sell my eggs and jams at the trading post whenever a wagon train was passin' through but that come to an end a couple of months ago." She drained her coffee. "You say you kilt two of them?"

Frank nodded. "We think there was a third man though."

"No need to worry 'bout thet third one. He's as yeller as they come. If'n you got the two bad uns, you can be sure ol' Tooley's headin' fer the hills right now." She laughed. "Yes, sir, thet feller's scared of his shadow."

Frank cleared his throat. "We were wondering, ma'am." He blushed. "I mean, Maude … if it would be all right if we spent a few days with you, just to rest up a bit. We'd be happy to help out with your chores."

"Young man, I'd be plumb tickled to death to have you young 'uns stay with me awhile. You're welcome to stay as long as you like. I ain't had a decent conversation with anyone for so long, I can't remember." She laughed. "Fact is, you might be wantin' to leave jus' to git away from all this jabberin' I do."

Sarah smiled. "I don't think so, Maude. It's been a long time since we've had anyone to talk with, too. Except for Tom and Moses, that is. And that kind of conversation we can do without."

"I hear you, darlin'."

She got up once more to bring over the coffee pot; after Frank and Sarah declined, she refilled hers.

"There's plenty of room here. Stay fer as long as you like."

Frank and Sarah insisted on sleeping in the barn.

"You're more'n welcome to sleep inside," Maude said. "Thet bed is big nuff for you and me, Sarah. Frank, you could sleep on the floor."

Sarah smiled. "We're not going to put you out, Maude. Besides, we're so used to sleeping out of doors, I doubt I could sleep in a bed now."

She couldn't imagine sharing a bed with the huge woman standing in front of her.

"Well, then, Sarah, you jest kick thet ol' cow out. She don' need to be in there anyhow." Maude cleared the top of her trunk and pulled out several quilts. "We'll make it right comfy in there for you. And, if it rains, y'all come right inside. I doubt that roof will keep the rain off. You hear now?"

"Yes, ma'am." Frank grinned.

They cleaned out the barn, brought in some fresh hay and made two beds in one corner. Frank brought up fresh water from the river for the animals and for Maude. Sarah disappeared into the woods and came back an hour later with fresh garlic and mushrooms.

"Well, I declare, I'm goin' to keep you two here as long as I can. Why, I ain't had fresh mushrooms for ages. Always too worried bout going into the woods and gittin' kilt by those awful men.

They'd shoot you in the back as sure as lookin' at you." Maude slapped Frank on the back. "I can't tell you how happy I am to hear thet you shot those two."

Before they fell asleep that night, Sarah said, "Maude sure has a way of making killing sound so good and natural, doesn't she?"

Frank smiled. "At least, it makes me feel better, Sarah. I hope and pray I never have to kill another man."

It was a warm night with a breeze. The sounds that came to them were comforting and reassuring. Once in awhile, one of the horses neighed softly, the chickens scratched, and the leaves on the poplar trees whispered.

The future looked promising. For the first time in a long time, they felt secure.

"I surely do hope the future was good. If anyone deserved something good, it was those two, wasn't it, Mr. Winnipesaukee?"

The old man nodded. There was a smile touchin' his lips and his eyes had a kind of dreamy look to them.

The moon hid suddenly behind a clump of clouds and the wind started playin' through the tall grass, makin' a swishy kind of sound. I'd been adding wood to the fire so now it crackled and sent sparks shootin' high up into the darkness. I could still feel the heat even though I'd moved when the flames got a little too close. This fire gave off more light than our old coal oil lamp back home.

Neither of us spoke for a while. I wasn't sure if this was the end of the tale or not. I must say I do like a story that has a happy ending. But, the thing was - is that where Sarah and Frank were going to spend the rest of their days? Livin' with a nice old woman out in the bush somewhere? Something else was botherin' me, too.

"Was that the last man that Frank ever killed?"

Winnipesaukee sighed.

"Frank never had the feel for killing," he said. "It takes a certain kind of man to kill, even to look a doe in the eye and shoot. Frank never had that in him; he should've lived his life in the city."

"What do you think he wanted to be? A cabinet maker like his pa?"

"No, Frank should have been a teacher maybe, or a banker."

I sat right up. "You're joshin' me, right? Frank - a school teacher?"

Now that was a sure way for me to lose respect for him. School teachin's for girls. Everyone knows that.

The old fellow laughed. He shaded his eyes with one hand and looked over at me. If there was ever a twinkle in someone's eye, it was right there in his.

"I reckon he would've liked to teach young strong minded boys like you," he said. "Don't tell me you don't have any schooling?"

I shrugged. Learnin' isn't something I'm right good at. At least, not learnin' out of some old books anyway. Pa says you learn the most from life itself. I guess if Ma were still alive, I might be still struggling to get out of sixth grade.

"I got some," I said. "Nuff to get by anyway."

He grunted. "You'd be best to save your money from this job you're going to and spend some time in college."

I didn't want to show any disrespect but goin' to college was about the last thing on my mind. Miss Trask, my fifth grade teacher, told me that I'd be doing good if I didn't end up in jail. That was after I'd decided her lunch box would make a good home for an orphan toad. How was I to know that when she opened the lid, it would jump out and right down the front of her dress. Even to this day, when I imagine her running out of the school and down the road screamin', I just can't stop laughin'. Her biggest problem was she didn't have a sense of humour. 'Course, Pa gave me a whuppin' for that one, too. But only after Ma made him and after he'd stopped laughin' himself. No, a college life wasn't for me.

"So, I was wonderin', what ever happened with the trading post? You know, the one where the owner was killed by those three bad guys? Seems to me, there would be a real need for something like that out there in the wilderness."

Winnipesaukee grunted. "That's part of my story, son. If you want me to finish before the sun comes up, you'll have to stop interrupting."

Chapter Twenty Nine

Every morning, the three of them rose with the sun and never ceased working until the sun went back down in the west.

"I don't know how you do it, Maude," Frank said, "living here, all on your own."

They'd had a particularly hard day of fencing in the burning sun and were sitting around the table, enjoying their second cup of coffee. The cabin was still warm but there was a cool breeze blowing in through the window. Fresh venison, new red potatoes from the garden and the first pick of peas filled their bellies. On top of that, Maude surprised them with canned raspberries and whipped cream for dessert.

Maude laughed. "Tell you truly, afore you came, I was almost ready to pack it in. Thet fence was gettin' the best of me. You young 'uns have given me a new lease on life and that's fer sure." She grinned and the creases from her eyes met the creases of her mouth. "Yes sir, if the fencin' didn't kill me, I figured thet Moses would sure as anything, put a plug in my back one day. Sure was tough, walking round, always looking behind. Yes, sir, you did me a mighty big favour, putting that fellow out of his own misery, Frank." She glanced at the plates on the table, all of them scraped clean. "And, you sure did us a favour, killing thet big buck this morning. I don't think I've ever seen such a good shot."

"I hope you don't think I enjoy doing all this killing, Maude."

Maude smiled, a thoughtful look on her face. "Lord no, you don't look like the type that enjoys the kill, Frank. There's some that get the thrill from it and there's some that do it cause they have to." She stood up and started gathering the dishes. "I reckon you know when it's the right time."

Three days later, they moved the horses and cows into the fresh pasture.

"Look at them," Maude said, "if they could sing, that's what they'd be doing."

They stood, leaning over the wire, watching Maude's animals as they munched the tall green grass.

"What do you think has happened to the trading post?" Frank

asked, as he picked up a blade of grass and chewed on it.

"If'n it's still there," Maude said. "You never know who could pass by, steal everything in sight, and then set a match to it. Maybe Indians even. They hate those trading posts. Unless the white men give them whiskey. Then, they keep coming back. Those dirty white men should be shot. Indians ain't no good when it comes to drinking whiskey. Fer some reason, they jest can't tolerate it."

"Do you think any wagon trains have passed through lately?" Frank asked.

"I reckon so. Unless, like you say, that mudslide closed off part of the trail. That case, there won't be quite so many. Imagine someone'll be workin' to open it again though. Lots of folks are headin' west now. Soon there won't be enough room to breathe. You wait an' see."

"You think we might go and see what's happened, Maude?"

"Be a right good idea, Frank. No point in everything goin' to waste if'n the place is deserted." She turned to look at him. "You thinkin' thet if there's signs of a wagon train, you might be wantin' to hitch up with it?"

Frank shrugged. "It's something to think about. Walking across the country isn't the easiest for Sarah."

Maude nodded. "Don't be rushin' on my account."

"I know, Maude."

The next morning, Frank hitched two of the horses up to a wagon. It was dawn and the air was crisp.

"How long can your animals be on their own, Maude?"

"No need to hurry. Thet one cow's calf is almost full grown but if I ain't milkin' her, thet calf will keep suckin'." She chuckled. "Some days there's hardly any milk left over fer me." She hoisted herself up into the wagon. "Better we make the most of the cool air. It's gonna be another scorcher, fer sure."

Sarah sat beside her and Frank settled down in the back. The wagon bounced and swayed as Maude followed an almost invisible trail, hidden underneath the tall prairie grass.

It was already late afternoon when they rounded a bluff of trees and saw the trading post.

"Well, at least, it's still standin'. Looks pretty desolate from here, don't it?"

Sarah nodded. Her heart was beginning to beat faster.

"You're sure we don't have to worry about that other man?"

Maude laughed. "Darlin', you don' have to give that yokel a second thought. Trust me, he's a weasel of a man."

He might be a weasel but Frank picked the rifle up off the floor and held it across his knees.

"Maybe we shouldn't pull right in front," he said. "What do you think? A coward is more than likely to shoot from inside."

"Yer right."

She swung the horses onto the path that led to the back where the corrals were and pulled up alongside of the building. They sat still for a moment and looked around.

"Seems nobody's here," Maude said. "Can't hear anything, can you?"

There was no sound except for the trees rustling and the occasional bird call.

Maude climbed down and reached up for her shotgun.

"Might jest as well go inside and see what's what. We can cook up a right good supper on that stove in there. You want to bring the grub in, Frank?"

Frank grabbed the two baskets that Maude had filled with bread, buns, canned meat, and vegetables. Enough food, he'd thought, to last for at least a week. By the time he'd collected them and managed to hang on to his rifle, the women were almost to the front of the store. He started to follow them but a movement in the woods caught his eye. Perhaps, the sound made him turn and look. He set one basket down, never taking his eyes off the spot where he was sure he'd seen something moving. Or, someone. He waited. Nothing. Suddenly, a grouse squawked and flew up from the brush.

"Oh man, I'm getting paranoid," he whispered. He picked up the basket and went to meet the women.

As he was rounding the corner, he saw Maude yank open the door and point the shotgun inside. He hoped that no innocent wanderer had sought shelter there. Maude was one of the kindest, gentlest persons he'd ever met, that is, after she got to know you, but he certainly wouldn't want to find himself looking down the butt end of her gun. He had no doubts that she might pull the trigger and then say, "Oh, oh."

The two women disappeared inside.

Frank entered. He glanced at Sarah. She was standing by the door, staring around the room. Maude was disappearing through the curtain into the back room.

"You all right, Sarah?"

She nodded. "Can't say that I wanted to come back here though." She looked around again. "Nothing seems to have changed, has it? That must mean that no one has been by here."

Suddenly, Maude yelled.

"Come on back here, you two."

Frank went first and pulled back the curtain. Maude was standing in front of the stove.

"Don't want to frighten you, but look at this." She pointed to a dark stain on the wooden floor. "Here's some more." There were splotches of dark red blood on the kitchen table. She bent her head down and examined it more closely. "Fresh, too."

Sarah's face went pale. "The third man. He didn't leave after all."

Maude shook her head. "Can't see that. I'd figure that fellow would've rode off soon as the trouble started. Scared of his own shadow, that scoundrel."

"I thought I saw some movement in the bushes when we were coming in," Frank said.

"You saw something and you never told us?" Sarah asked, her eyes rolling in his direction.

"I wasn't sure and then while I waited, a bird flew up." He looked over at Maude. "And that's probably all it was - a bird. Whoever's here must be hiding somewhere. Maybe some injured drifter who's more afraid of us than we are of him. He might even be gone by now."

"Let's hope yer right about that."

"Frank, it must be that other man. It has to be." Fear filled Sarah's eyes. "Maybe someone came and tried to kill him. What can we do? He could come in shooting anytime and kill us all."

"Well, there's only one thing to do," Maude said. "We gotta find this fellow." She started for the back door. "He ain't in the house and there's no horses in the corral so he's gotta be close by."

"There were three horses here before," Sarah said.

Maude nodded. "See? I tol' you. That Tooley's took off with all the horses. Whoever's here must have got lost or something.

Probably scared we're the owners." She opened the door and bellowed, "Hey! Whoever's out there, you can come on in. We ain't goin' to hurt you none."

Frank and Sarah both held their breath and waited for a couple of bullets to go whizzing over their heads.

There was only silence.

"Maybe come dark, I'll take a look in that barn."

"No, Maude." Frank smiled. "Maybe come dark, I'll take a look in that barn."

They fired up the stove and settled down to a good supper. Maude ate as if she hadn't a care in the world. Frank had a good appetite but sat upright and jumped up at every sound. Sarah picked at her food.

When darkness came, Frank slipped out the front door and crept quietly alongside the building. Instead of taking the path, he walked inside the line of trees and came up behind the barn. It was much the same as Maude's barn, slapped together with wooden slabs. He stood in the darkness, breathing slow and easy. Somewhere in the darkness, one of the horses snorted and stamped his foot. Clouds covered the moon and the air felt sultry, heavy with the promise of rain.

He almost missed it the first time. It sounded like a small animal, perhaps, injured or frightened. Then it came, again: a low moan, from inside the barn. The horses in the corral raised their heads, listening. Frank lifted his rifle and made his way cautiously to the door. When he reached it, he stopped and listened. All that he could hear was his heart pounding in his ears. Whoever was in there, moaned again.

"Okay, mister," he called out. "You're going to know I'm coming in because this door makes plenty of noise. I don't want to come in shooting. I know you're hurt already. Why don't you make things easy and just come out, all by yourself?"

There was no response.

"Listen, I don't know who you are and I don't care. Why don't you come into the house and Maude can fix up your wounds? You just have to tell me one thing: Is your name Tooley? Can you answer me that?"

In the night's stillness, he could hear soft raspy breathing but no one answered.

Slowly, ever so slowly, Frank placed the butt of his gun behind the one slab door and started to pry it open. He grimaced with every creak. One of the horses whinnied and stamped his feet. When the door was about one quarter way open, he gave it a push with the rifle butt and it flew back, hitting the side of the barn with a loud bang. Before the door hit the barn, Frank was inside, leaning against the wall. He tried to control his breathing but found himself gasping for air. The room was airless and filled with the scent of dried hay. His heartbeat was still out of control. He held the cocked gun out in front and waited; his finger was on the trigger.

It seemed an eternity but he knew enough of the Indian ways to be patient. The injured man may have passed out or he could be waiting just as he was, with a loaded rifle. He could out-wait any white man.

Time passed. Frank could hear him breathing but couldn't figure out where the man was hiding. It had to be in one of the horse stalls.

Fifteen minutes must have gone by before Frank heard a commotion outside. The horses shuffled, stomped, and then were quiet.

Before Frank could give a warning, Maude burst through the door, holding up a fiery torch in one hand and her shotgun in the other, ready to fire.

For a moment, he was speechless. Finally, he yelled, "Maude, look out, there's a man in here!"

She didn't seem to hear him; she just kept walking, a strange look on her face.

"Well, what have we got here?" she exclaimed and walked further into the barn.

Frank followed, trying to peer around her, to see what she was looking at.

"Well, land's sake. Would you look at this, Frank."

He moved out from behind her. She raised her torch so that the light shone into the one horse stall. There, huddled into the farthest corner, was a small creature. The eyes were closed and there was no movement.

"It looks like a little kid," Frank whispered. "Is he dead? Look at all the blood."

Maude moved closer.

"Stay back, Frank. I think he's passed out but I don't want to frighten him too much." She turned to him. "Here, hold the light. It's going to burn out soon and I want to get him out of here before it does."

She moved quickly over and scooped the child up in her arms.

"Okay," she said, "Let's get to the house before he wakes up."

Frank led the way through the darkness. Sarah stood waiting with the back door open.

"What on earth...?" she exclaimed.

Maude rushed past her and laid the unconscious child on the kitchen table. Sarah grabbed the pail of water from off the cupboard and quickly plunged one of Maude's tea towels into it. She wrung it out and gently started to wash the child's face. She could see the chest rising and falling, ever so faintly.

"Hard to tell what's dirt and what's blood, ain't it?" Maude said, as she started removing the shirt. "Here's where the wound is." She tore away the filthy shirt. Some of it stuck to the dried blood and the child moaned but didn't wake up.

"He must be only about nine or ten. Even for that, he's a bit small. What happened, do you think?" Frank asked Maude.

"I don't know," she murmured, as she leaned closer to check it out. "Wash that wound up, Sarah."

Sarah wrung the cloth out again and gently dabbed at the still open wound. Blood oozed out each time she pressed. She dipped the cloth into the water repeatedly, trying to wash away some of the caked-on blood. The water was turning brownish-red.

"It almost looks like a bullet wound, Maude," Sarah said. "But who would try to kill a child?"

Maude shook her head. "Let's hope he comes out of it soon. We won't know anything 'til then. See if you can get that a little cleaner. Maybe wash away some more of the dirt. Looks like he's been livin' out in the wild or something."

"Could be someone shot, thinking it was an animal," Frank said.

When Sarah was finished cleaning the wound, Maude took another towel, folded it and pressed it against the wound.

"You wanna rip off a little of your shirttail, Frank?" she asked. "I think we ought to bind this up tight to stop the bleeding."

Frank took off his shirt, found a sharp butcher knife in one of the cupboards drawers and cut a strip off from the bottom. Maude took it and wrapped it around the small chest. Already, there was blood showing through the folded towel.

Maude lifted the child into her arms.

"Let's put him in this back room," Sarah said. "There's a bed. It isn't clean but it will have to do."

Now all they could do was wait. They took turns through the night, sitting near the bed, listening to the quiet groans and animal-like sobs. Sarah sat in the hot stuffy room for most of the night, patiently wiping the feverish face and speaking in a low gentle voice.

"You'll be all right," she whispered. "Everything's going to be all right. We aren't going to hurt you. Frank, Maude, and I will look after you. You don't have to be afraid anymore." The child twitched and grimaced, the tiny thin lips opened, ready to scream but no sound came. "There, there. You'll be all right. Don't be afraid," Sarah said, as she held the frail body closer to hers.

With each silent cry, Sarah cried, too. Tears rolled down her face and dripped on to the child's hair. Blond hair, like Frank's. She thought of her own son and wondered whom he would have looked like. If he had lived. Would his hair be blond like his grandmother's and uncle's or black like his father's and grandfather's? How old would he be now? And, the little girl? There were two of them. Two babies. She couldn't remember how many days or weeks or months had passed by since she and Frank left the village. Time didn't matter anymore. Would it ever matter again?

Levi. If she closed her eyes, she saw him there, looking down at her. His eyes filled with love and concern. He'd called her name but she couldn't answer. The pain was so strong. She was so weak. He was strong but she was weak. And now, he was gone. He was dead; her babies were dead. She was alive. How could that be?

She pulled the injured child to her breast and rocked back and forth. The little heart beating against hers, told her there was still life there. Life and hope.

In early morning, it started to thunder and lightning. Rain banged on the tin roof. Sarah glanced out the dirty window. The barn was barely visible through the thick grey veil of rain.

Suddenly, the child moved and pulled away from her. Sarah looked down into deep blue eyes; eyes that were wild with terror.

Fear distorted the small face. Weak arms tried to push against Sarah.

"It's all right, little one," Sarah said. She tried pulling the child back against her but the small thin arms resisted still.

"I'm not going to hurt you. We're going to help you."

Sarah saw the terror and felt fear coursing through the small, trembling, thin body. She tried to pull the child back into her arms again but she couldn't. The child slipped to the floor and collapsed.

"Frank," she screamed. "Come and help."

Maude rushed into the room with Frank right behind. Maude picked the small form up and placed it on the bed again.

"Is he dead?"

"No, Sarah. He's passed out again, poor little fellow." Maude gently placed a raggedy quilt over the thin body. "He doesn't have an ounce of fat on him." She stood up. "I'm going to fix some broth. He's got to have something in his stomach. Frank, why don't you sit here with him? Sarah, you come back into the kitchen and stretch out on that bench. You could use some rest."

"No, Maude. I'd like to stay here."

"I know you'd like to, girl, but it ain't good for you to stay here too long. I see it in yer eyes. This ain't good for you."

" Maude's right, Sarah. I'll stay here. You need your rest." Frank pulled his sister close and held her. Her body was shaking. "You're not as strong as you think, sister." He moved back and smiled. "This is your little brother telling you what to do now."

Sarah smiled. "You'll tell me when he wakes up, Frank?"

Frank nodded.

"He's very frightened." She looked at Maude and then Frank again. "I'm so worried. Do you think that maybe…" She closed her eyes and when she opened them, they were filled with tears. "That maybe his mind is gone?"

Frank pulled her back into his arms and whispered into her ear. "Sarah, Sarah, why do you worry about something before you know the facts?" He held her at arm's length and looked into her eyes. "Please, don't concern yourself with that, okay? We'll meet that challenge when we have to face it. And, I'm sure he'll be fine. I'm almost as worried about you as I am about him." He reached out and pulled her braid. "You look a fright, you know."

Sarah's eyes welled with tears. She wasn't sure if it was Frank's tenderness or if, for one brief moment, an image of her father filled her mind. The way he used to reach out and pull her braid.

She smiled through her tears, nodded and went into the kitchen. It wasn't until she'd settled onto the bench and closed her eyes that she realized how tired she really was. Somewhere, far away, she heard screams but she couldn't open her eyes.

Winnipesaukee had talked for a long time without any breaks. His rattley old voice just droned on and on. But the story! I was beginning to wonder if he wasn't makin' this up as he went along. 'Course, if he was, he was doing a great job and I wasn't goin' to interrupt him. No, sirree.

"I was wonderin'," I said, as I watched the old man twist around to get himself more comfortable, "did that little boy really lose his mind? Imagine, someone shootin' a kid! I always thought I'd like to live back in them old days - you know, the cowboy and Indian days, but maybe they weren't so great after all. It surely sounds like an awful lot of work to me. I mean, just to get your food for the day woulda been a chore sometimes. Personally, I think Sarah and Frank should've stayed with old Maude for the rest of their lives. Is that what they did?"

Winnipesaukee laughed. "Well, I reckon if their only concern was their bellies, they might have. Maude's cooking was probably the best they'd et since they left their home in Portland. Sometimes, a person doesn't have much choice in life, however."

"You're telling me they had to keep movin' on?"

The old man sighed. "Like I say, sometimes a person doesn't have much choice."

I sat up and leaned forward. "So, where do you fit in here, Mr. Winnipesaukee? If these are your relatives, you must have met them somewheres along the way. Did you travel with them or is this a story that's been passed on and on?"

There was a pause.

"I reckon a lot of this story has been passed on and on, son." He looked up at me, squinting 'cause of the smoke from the smoldering fire, and said, "I doubt you'll remember much but one thing you can tell folks for sure; there was one old half-breed who kept you up all night, telling a tall tale." He smiled and his whole face filled up with wrinkles. "And who knows, maybe you'll learn

something from all this."

"Oh, I've already learned plenty," I said. After all, I didn't want him to feel that it was all for naught.

"What have you learned, son?"

Winnipesaukee picked up the last of the logs and threw them on the fire. For a few minutes, thick smoke billowed around them until a spark suddenly caught and burst into flames. All was quiet except for the wood crackling. Except for us, the whole world was asleep, even the slow moving river was silent.

"Well, one thing I learned was how important family is. Only thing, I don' have a brother or sister. There's only me, my pa and grandpa. I mean, I did have a brother but he was dead when he was born. Ma felt bad about that but she knew it weren't her fault." I stopped for a moment, remembering how Ma had cried so long over that. Then, I remembered someone else. "Guess Sarah felt just like my ma. Must be terrible carryin' that baby in your belly for all that time and then not havin' anything in the end."

Winnipesaukee stared into the flames.

"Son, I don't think it's something men can understand. Seems there's a need that women have." He shook his head. "Something you and I will never understand."

He stopped talkin' then and kept starin' into the fire. The minutes ticked by.

"'Course," I said, finally, "I learned other stuff, too."

He looked up and smiled. "And, what other things did you learn, my young Mr. Smithson?"

Now I had to come up with something. Seems I have a tendency to stick my foot in my mouth at times.

"Well, sir, for instance, I learned you can't trust just anyone. You know, like that preacher. And even the Abenaki."

"What do you mean, the Abenaki?"

"Well, look how they took off and left those two. Would you trust people like that?"

"I'd trust them with my life; that's how much I'd trust them."

"But they left Sarah and Frank. They left them to die."

"If they left them to die, why did they leave all the food and firewood?"

I shrugged. "I don't know. Why did they?"

"Because they were sick and dying themselves."

"So, why didn't they stay?"

"They were hoping to get back to their people. If the whole village were wiped out, no one would know."

"Do you think they got back?"

Winnipesaukee lay back on his bear rug and stared up at the starry heavens.

"No. No one ever got back home. They all died, one by one, on the trail."

"How do you know that? Maybe one or two made it."

He sighed. "No, the story was told; years later, an Abenaki elder traveled through the land, collecting the bones and he buried them."

"Where? Where did he bury them?"

"In the burial ground across the river from the Abenaki village."

"You mean where Levi and Sarah's babies were buried?"

I turned and looked over at the old man. His eyes were closed. The firelight brought out shadows in his gaunt face. It reminded me of dying so I turned away and looked up at the heavens.

"Yes," he whispered, "where the babies were buried. And, Levi."

"What about this boy they found?" I asked, wanting to change the subject.

Winnipesaukee laughed. "Aw, yes, the boy."

Chapter Thirty

"What are we going to do with him, Maude?" Frank yelled.

Frank held the child with one arm, trying to grab the flailing arms that hammered his face, with the other. Even through his shirt, he could feel the small wildly-pounding heartbeat. The high pitched screams pierced his eardrums. Just when he thought the fight was over, it would begin all over again. Arms and legs flew in every direction.

"Hold him tighter, Frank. Look, that wound is opening up again. Get a good grip. He'll tucker out soon. There's nothing to him; he's got to give up." She reached over, grabbed the small filthy feet that were kicking into the air and held them. "Did you ever see so much terror in anyone's eyes? I don't know if I want to even know what happened to this little thing."

Then, suddenly, with one last piercing scream, it was over.

"Oh, my god, is he dead, Maude?" Frank held the limp child in his arms.

Maude reached up and placed her hand over the small chest.

"I can't feel anything. Lay him down on the bed." She bent down and placed her ear over the child's nose and mouth. She shook her head. "Let me see if he has a pulse." Gently, she took the small hand and searched for a pulse. Again, she shook her head.

"He's dead, isn't he?" Frank sat down at the end of the bed. He looked up at the older woman. "What's wrong with this country? Will it ever become civilized? I don't think I can take anymore, Maude. I have to take Sarah back. I don't think she can handle any more death." He looked down and studied his hands, hands that only a couple of years ago were soft and delicate. And pink. He used to have pink skin. Now, they were calloused and dark brown from the sun. Once, they were an innocent young man's hands; now, they were blood-guilty hands.

He looked up, his eyes wet. "Maybe it's just me. I'm sick of the killing. I want out. I want to go back home."

Maude sighed. "It's not always like this." She walked over and put her hand on his shoulder. "Come on, I'll make us a cup of tea. We'll bury the lad later."

"That's what I mean. Here we have a young boy to bury and we don't know his name. We don't know if he has parents looking for him. He's just a nobody, Maude. That's not right. What do we even put on his marker?"

Maude smiled. "We'll think of something. Come."

Frank and Maude sat at the table, drinking their tea in silence. Sarah slept on the bench; her face was pale but her breathing was steady.

"I noticed how Sarah took to that child, Frank." She smiled. "She'd make a good mother. Some women are just naturally made that way. Me, I never took to young 'uns much." She looked at him with a twinkle in her eye. "I think I scare them with my voice and size."

Frank looked over at his sister and he was filled with tenderness for the sleeping Indian princess. That's what she truly was.

"It's different for Sarah, Maude. Right now, she should be holding her own babies." His eyes again filled with tears. Tears he'd vowed never to shed. He blinked and looked away. "She was married. Married to a man named Levi. They were expecting twins. Two babies. A boy and a girl. At least, that's what they found out when she lost them. Then, Levi died too. She lost everyone she loved." He looked down again at his hands. "Everyone but me, that is."

"I'm sorry. I figured she'd gone through something. Could see the sadness in her eyes all the time. But, she's got you. You're her light, Frank. You're the one who'll see she gets through everything and finds happiness."

He shook his head. "Seems we can't escape heartache. Sometimes, I think I cause her more worry than anything."

"So, what do you plan on doing?"

"I guess we'd best wait here at the trading post until a wagon train comes through and then we can ride back with them to the east coast. I think that's the best thing to do."

"Oh, you do, do you?" Sarah sat up. "Since when do you start making these decisions without consulting me, Frank Lawdry?"

"Sarah! I didn't know you were awake." Frank felt his face getting warm. "Well, I do think that's the best, don't you? Haven't we had enough of this wild country? Don't you think it's time to go back to civilization?"

Sarah swung her legs off the bench. "Frank, if everyone felt like you, the west would never become civilized. We're the ones who have to settle down and tame it. We're the ones who have to build homes and plant the fields of grain. We're the ones who have to build the schools and hospitals." She gazed around the room. "Where's the boy? Is he sleeping?"

"I'll make you a cup of tea, Sarah." Maude stood up and reached for the tea kettle.

Sarah looked at Frank. "What happened, Frank?"

"He died, Sarah. He just collapsed in my arms. We left him on the bed. I'll go out and dig a grave." He stood up and pushed his chair back. "I'm sorry. I know you wanted to help him but he was too weak. He probably lost too much blood."

Sarah got up and walked to the bedroom. Maude and Frank exchanged glances.

"It's okay," Maude said. "You go and I'll stay with your sister."

A few moments later, Sarah was back at the bedroom door.

"Maude," she said, "I think you made a mistake. The boy isn't dead. His pulse is faint but he's alive."

Maude rushed into the small room. Even before she reached the bedside, she could see the tiny chest moving slowly up and down.

She reached down and touched his forehead. It was warm.

"Well, I'll be darned. I was sure this little fellow was dead." She grinned. "Guess, for the time being, your brother can stop digging the grave." She put her arm around Sarah. "I'm saying, 'time being' because he's still got a long ways to go before he'll be healthy again. You do understand that, Sarah?"

Sarah looked down at the sleeping child.

"Yes, I know. I won't get my hopes up, Maude."

For the next three days, Sarah took care of the child: wiping the feverish head with a cold damp cloth, trying to pour water down the parched throat or simply sitting, holding the child close to her breast and rocking. On the fourth day, the fever broke. This time there was no fight left in the frail body. Gently, Sarah coaxed the child to swallow some broth.

"I think the next thing we'll have to do," Maude said, "is fill that old washtub outside with some water. All of us could use a bath. Especially, that little fellow." She looked over at Sarah. The two were now inseparable. The child clung to Sarah, never letting the young woman out of sight.

Sarah laughed. "We're beginning to smell like we did after a few days on the wagon train. There was no way O'Leary would have stopped to let us bathe, that's for sure."

Just the mention of the tough wagon master brought back too many memories for Frank. He went outside to bring in the washtub. Maude stoked up the fire and Frank filled the tub with water from the rain barrel.

Frank went out to care for the horses and told the women to call him when they'd finished bathing. He'd been gone about ten minutes when Sarah called from the backdoor.

"Frank, come here for minute."

He walked to the step and looked up at her. "What's the matter? Why are you grinning like that?"

"Because that little boy we thought was a boy, isn't one."

He stared at her. "What on earth, are you saying?"

She laughed. "He is a she. That's what I'm saying."

"You mean that little wild animal is really a girl?"

"That's what I'm saying."

Frank shook his head and started back to the horses. "Well, if that don't beat all," he said.

Chapter Thirty One

Each day, the child grew stronger. She gazed up at Sarah with her large blue eyes but she never spoke. If Sarah moved away quickly, the little girl raced after her, her eyes wide with fright. One morning, Sarah went to the outhouse in the backyard while the child slept. When she awoke to find her surrogate mother missing, she became so hysterical that Maude had to carry the screaming girl outside to Sarah.

They stayed at the outpost for almost two weeks, every day waiting to see if someone would come by searching for the little girl.

One morning, Frank announced, "I'm going to take one of the horses and scout around a bit. Maybe I'll find out what happened."

Sarah was sitting on the bench, brushing the girl's hair.

"Be careful, Frank. There might be highway men out there."

He nodded. "There might be a lot of things out there." He grinned. "Maybe there'll be a princess out there. One with long yellow hair. I'll rescue her from the fire breathing dragon and we'll live happily ever after." He raised his arm as if striking something with an imaginary sword. "What do you think of that, Daffy?"

Although the little girl never smiled, Frank saw a faint touch of amusement in her eyes.

Frank felt they should give the girl a name. Her hair reminded him of the daffodils his mother had planted in their garden in Portland.

"But, you shouldn't call her Daffy," Sarah protested. It seemed, however, that the girl found it amusing so the name stuck. At least, with Frank. The two women called her Daffodil.

Sarah started to worry when Frank didn't return for his evening meal.

"I think I'll just sit outside in the front and wait. He should've been here for his supper, Maude."

"He'll get here. Don't worry about Frank," Maude said. "You should know by now that he can look after himself."

"I can't help myself; he's all I have."

Maude smiled. "You're lucky to have someone."

"Oh, I'm so sorry. I was being very selfish, wasn't I?"

"I weren't thinking of myself; I was thinking of that one." She pointed to Daffodil. "She's the one who needs the lookin' after."

"I'll look after her." She held Daffodil's face in her hands and kissed her forehead. "You know that, don't you?"

"I believe I saw a smile on her face, Sarah."

Sarah looked up, tears in her eyes. "She's going to be all right. I just know it."

"Love can make everything all right. You take Daffodil and go sit out there and wait. I'll bring you out a cup of coffee. And, Daffodil, I'll bring you a thick slice of bread with honey on it. How would you like that?"

The little girl nodded.

"Well, I'll be," said Maude. "That's the first time she's spoken to me. I reckon she will be okay."

Sarah heard the horse's hoof beats before she saw the rider. It was dark now but the moon was bright. Daffodil slept beside her, her head on Sarah's lap. Sarah waited, her heart pounding. It had to be Frank. Why was he so late? Where could anyone ride in the dark anyway? Why hadn't he started for the trading post earlier?

A horse came into view. Sarah stood up, forgetting about the child. She heard a sound behind her and knew that Maude was standing just inside the door with her rifle cocked. Daffodil made a small cry and grabbed on to Sarah's skirt.

The horse and rider were outlined clearly in the moonlight.

"Maude," she said. "I'm sure that's Frank's horse but doesn't it look like there's someone with him?"

Maude stepped out and peered out towards the incoming rider.

"Yer right. That's Frank but there's somebody ridin' in back of him." She laughed. "You can hear that old nag of mine huffin' an' puffin' from here. That's what happens when you stand in the pasture all day long, doin' nothing."

Frank galloped up to the step and yanked back the reins. His horse snorted to a stop, spraying the air with sweat and foam.

"I brought back another visitor for you," he said. He let the reins drop to the ground, lifted his leg over the horse's neck and jumped off. The person riding bareback behind him also slid to the ground. It was too dark to make out if the form was male or female but Sarah could see that his passenger was almost as tall as Frank.

"Well, you two come inside, Frank," Maude said. "We kept the vittles warm for you and there's enough for an army. I'll walk that poor ol' nag of mine to cool her off. Sarah can take care of the food." She picked up the reins and started pulling the reluctant horse towards the dark road that ran in front of the trading post. "No," she muttered, "you ain't getting any water until you're all cooled off." She patted the horse's neck. "And, not until I've dried you off. That boy sure did run you, didn't he?"

The others walked into the store, Sarah leading the way with Daffodil hiding behind her skirt. The coal oil lamp sitting on the counter filled the room with a yellowy glow.

"We were starting to worry, Frank." Sarah laughed. She turned to face them. "Well, I started to worry. Maude said you could look after yourself. She's usually right. Now, tell me, who's your friend?"

The young man standing behind Frank could have been his twin. He had dirty blond hair that hung limply, touching his shoulders and even in the dimly lit room, she could see piercing blue eyes staring back at her. Both were tall and thin. The newcomer's eyes, however, although they might have been the same colour as her brother's were empty, without any emotion.

She smiled at him and held out her hand. "I'm Sarah. Well, maybe Frank already told you. Anyway, we're happy to have you."

The visitor made no move to shake her hand so she lowered it. She looked at Frank.

Frank shrugged. "This is Obadiah. I don't know too much about him." He smiled and gently patted the young man on the back. "But, I did promise him some good food so if it's not too much trouble, Sarah."

"Oh, no. Of course not." She gave them both a smile and turned towards the kitchen. Supper would be a very quiet meal. It crossed her mind that perhaps the Indians had cut out both Obadiah's and Daffodil's tongues. A slight shudder went through her body but then she dismissed the thought. Obviously, he'd told Frank his name.

Daffodil, who had been hiding her face in Sarah's skirt, glanced up when Sarah turned. She stared up at the young man standing beside Frank.

"Rosie," Obadiah whispered. He walked up to Daffodil and bent down. "Rosie, is that really you?"

She stared, her eyes wide.

"Rosie, it's you. It's you." Tears sprang up into the deep blue eyes and spilled down his cheeks. He went to his knees and gathered the trembling girl into his arms. They clung to each other; the young man sobbing, the child, staring out in silence.

"I didn't think I'd ever see you again." He held her at arm's length. "I can't believe this. I thought you were dead, Rosie." He crushed her to his chest again. "You were all I had left and I thought I'd lost you."

Sarah and Frank both stood watching, unable to say anything.

Finally, Frank spoke up. "I take it you two know each other?" He couldn't help but grin as he said it.

Obadiah wiped his cheeks with his sleeve. "This," he said, "is my little sister, Rosie."

"She hasn't said a word since we found her," Sarah said.

Obadiah gently caressed her face and hair.

"I don't blame her," he said. "I haven't felt like speaking until now either."

"Well," Sarah said, "let's go into the kitchen and I'll give you boys something to eat. Maude will be so pleased to meet you, Obadiah."

She smiled down at Rosie. "So, your name is Rosie. I guess Frank will have to stop calling you Daffy now, won't he?"

Rosie shook her head.

"I told you she liked that name, sis," Frank said. He reached over and pulled her braid. "And look at that, I almost got a smile out of her."

When Maude finally came in from attending to her horse, the three were sitting at the table, drinking coffee. Obadiah and Frank had pushed their empty plates back and Rosie sat curled on her brother's lap, sound asleep. She still hadn't spoken.

"I know she'll speak when she's ready," Sarah was saying.

Maude stood by the door and stared in amazement. "You gotta be family," she said. "Thank the Lord, you've found her. That little thing was so close to dying, it's a miracle she's breathin' today. Sarah's love and care gave her the will to live. That's for sure."

As soon as introductions were over, Maude said, "You're saying that she still hasn't talked?"

"No, but I know she will when she's ready," Sarah said. "This is a shock even seeing her brother again."

"It isn't I want to pry," Maude said, "but can you tell us what happened? It looked to us that some lowlife shot little Daffodil. Is that so?"

Obadiah's eyes filled with tears. He nodded. "She could have been. We got separated. There were bullets flying all over the place. I searched and searched for her after it was over. I figured the men had taken her." He started to rock back and forth, holding his sister's head close to his chest. Tears rolled down his face. "That was my biggest fear - that the men would take her with them."

"What men might that be?" Maude said. She poured herself a cup of coffee and sat down with them.

The young man sniffed and ran his sleeve under his nose. "I don't know who they were. Highwaymen, I reckon."

"How many?"

"Four."

"You see which direction they went?"

"I think they headed north."

She nodded. "That's good. Probably took the trail heading up to Chicago. I hear that's where most of them outlaws go." She took a swallow of coffee. "What happened to yer folks, son? I take it, you young 'uns weren't travelin' alone."

He shook his head. Without looking up, he said, "They shot them. When Pa heard the horses coming, he told Rosie and me to get behind the boulders. He told me I had to take care of Rosie. Ma hid in one of the wagons with a rifle. They took all the money Pa had and then went to look for Ma. As soon as the one man started to get into the wagon, Ma fired. She might have hit him in the arm or something. I heard him yell and cuss. The next thing, there was gunshots. Rosie, here, got scared I guess and took off running. One of the bullets must've hit her. I figured I'd be able to find her after the men left." He started to sob. "I thought that if I started running after her, they'd see us and shoot us both. Besides, I wanted to bury Ma and Pa before she could see them. When I was finished, I went looking for her. When I couldn't find her, I thought for sure, they'd taken her with them."

Maude pulled a big handkerchief from her overall pocket and

handed it to him. He wiped his face and blew his nose.

"I was waiting to die when Frank found me. There was nothing for me to live for." He looked at Frank. "Sorry, I put up such a fight. It made me mad that someone wanted to help me. If I could've killed you, I think I would have. You understand?"

Frank nodded. "Don't even think about it. I might've done the same thing. Good thing you were almost starved to death. Otherwise, I would've had quite a fight on my hands." He grinned at the young man. "Now you're filled up, you ready for some shuteye?"

Obadiah smiled for the first time and Sarah swore she had never seen anyone with eyes like that.

"Daffodil's been sleepin' with Sarah every night. I wonder if she might want to be with you tonight, Obadiah." Maude said. "There ain't much room in the house but I can fix up a spot in the barn, if'n that's okay with you?"

Obadiah nodded. "Mostly, I've been sleeping under the stars on the cold hard ground so a bed made of hay sounds mighty fine." He turned to Sarah. "I guess I'd best say 'thank you' for taking such good care of Rosie. I can't tell you how much I appreciate it."

"I'm just happy that you've found each other."

Obadiah blushed. "I hope you don't mind me asking: Frank says you're his sister but you look like you're Indian. I was thinking that maybe he was raised by Indians or you were raised by whites?"

Sarah threw her head back and laughed.

"No, we're really brother and sister. Our father was part Abenaki and our mother was English. Frank looks like our mother and I look like our father."

"Really? Our mother was part Ojibwa. Our father was Swedish. I know we don't look like we have much Indian blood in us."

"So, how old are you and your sister?" Maude asked.

"I'm going on seventeen; my sister, Rosie, is just turned nine."

Maude shook her head. "That's too young for you to be wanderin' out on your own. You got some special place to be headin' for?"

"We were on our way to my Aunt Esther's. My uncle got real sick so we were heading out to their place to settle in with them. They live way up in the Dakota Territory. Got themselves a nice piece of land. Pa figured that would be our place to live. We never did have much before. Just rented some land and raised a few cattle and pigs."

"When was your aunt expecting you to be there?" Frank asked.

"Well, we was hoping to get there in time for fall roundup. Figured it would take all spring and summer to cross the country."

Sarah looked over at her brother. "Just exactly what were you thinking, Frank?"

Frank shook his head. "I wasn't thinking of anything. But, you know as well as I do, these children can't travel all that way by themselves. We have to come up with some plan. Right, Maude?"

Maude stood and picked up the dishes and cups. "I know one thing: we're all tuckered out. Let's sleep on it. We'll figure something out in the morning."

Obadiah wrapped Rosie in a blanket and carried her out to the barn. Maude slept in the bed in the back room; Sarah, on the bench and Frank, on the floor.

After the lamps had been extinguished and Sarah could hear Maude's rather loud snoring, she whispered, "Frank, are you awake?"

"Yeah."

"You think we should take those two on to their aunt's place, don't you?"

"I don't see we have any choice. It's not as if we have any special place to go. That little girl needs a woman to look after her and, you know, she sure cares for you. If we can spend the winter in the Dakota Territory, maybe we'll know more where we want to settle down."

"You're right. We can't let those two go off on their own. Poor things. They're orphans like you and me, Frank."

"Yeah, except they do have family to go to. I'm sure if we take them there, those folks won't mind putting us up for the winter. I can do the outside work with Obadiah and you can help in the house. We'll earn our keep."

With that, the two fell asleep, content in knowing that, at last, they had a destination.

There was a bit of a night wind stirring up now and I pulled my

*blanket closer. My face was burnin' most of the time from the fire
and my backside was freezin'. I surely did enjoy listening to the old
codger though. Guess it sort of reminded me of my own grandpa.
'Course, my grandpa was like a youngster compared to old
Winnipesauke.*

*"You know," I said, when there was a brief lull, "I reckon, I
should be writin' some of this down. It's going to be awful hard to
remember everything, ain't it?"*

*The old man laughed. It reminded me of Old Man Schlouter back
home. He was this old German fellow who farmed a couple of
miles down the road from us. Pa said that when he laughed, he
sounded like an old tractor that needed a good oiling. Personally, I
liked it. It was a good honest sort of laugh. Like the person doing
it, really meant it. Ma said that it sounded like it started in his
heart and worked its way up through his mouth. Ma was always a
little more poetic about everything.*

"So, why do you want to remember all of this anyway?"

*"Well, I was lying here thinkin' of my grandpa and thinkin' that
this is the kind of story he really likes. He's old too, you know, and
he loves talkin' about the old days. I wish you could meet him
someday. You and him would have lots of stories to share."*

Old Winnipesaukee smiled. "I'm sure we would."

*It wasn't that I was feelin' all that sleepy but somehow this darn
old yawn crept up on me. I tried to hide it but the old fellow
noticed.*

*"Looks like I've tired you right out, son. I think this story might
just be too long to tell. Or, maybe I talk too much. Shouldn't have
gone back quite so far in history, I guess."*

*"No, no. I want to hear the rest of it. You can't stop now. Not
when there's two more orphans on their own. What happened to
them? Did they all get up into Dakota Territory?"*

*"Oh yes, they got up to Dakota Territory eventually. It later
became Montana. Of course, there were some obstacles along the
way."*

"You telling me there was more shootin'?"

*"Well, there wasn't any more shooting on the way to St. Louis.
That was their first stop. I guess to a youngster like you, the trip
there might have been a little on the boring side. There were no
outlaws, no wild Indians, and nary a highwayman to be found.*

Folks were kind and hospitable to those young travelers. Farmers put them up in their barns and sent them off with all the fresh eggs and meat they could carry. And, homemade bread. Those pioneer women sure knew how to cook. One rancher gave them each a horse to ride. Of course, they had to spend a couple of days rounding up cattle but they were happy to do that. Yessiree, those were very happy times for Frank and Sarah. Not that there weren't any misfortunes along the way. Seems there were always some of those."

"What about Obadiah and Rosie? I mean, they'd lost both their parents. That's not so easy to get over. I didn't say nothing before, but my ma died too. I remember how I felt. I thought for a while that there was no point in even livin'. I think that's how Rosie felt. Did that little girl ever start to talk?"

Chapter Thirty Two

Maude spent days getting those children ready for their trip. Not that anyone considered Frank and Sarah, or even Obadiah, for that matter, children. In Maude's eyes, however, they were. She fussed over them, washed and mended their clothes, sewed up a pair of overalls for Rosie and packed and repacked their gear.

"I swear," Frank said, "if I didn't know you better, Maude, I'd think you were trying to keep all of us here."

Maude looked up from her sewing. "And, I swear, son, if I could, I would." Warm tears filled her eyes. "It's goin' to be a mighty lonely life here after you're gone."

"Why don't you come with us? There's nothing holding you here, is there?"

Maude sighed. "I reckon I've given up on my husband ever comin' back but, for some reason, I'm jus' too tired to move on. I've got my little house, my animals and my garden." She looked up. "I figure there'll soon be someone takin' over the tradin' post. Word will get carried round. Then, before you know it, I'll be getting neighbours. Might even be a town springin' up before long."

Frank laughed. "And, you hope those neighbours will be good ones."

Maude joined him. "'Specially," she said, "when I don't have a crack shot like you to protect me."

She snapped her thread off and held the worn shirt she'd been mending out in front of her. After carefully scrutinizing each stitch, she folded it carefully.

"No," she said. "There's lots of good folk out there. You'll meet them, Frank. Jus' use your wits, that's all I say. My old man always said that if it looks too good to be true, there's probably a hitch to it. You work hard and you'll have grub on the table. Folks will hear that you're a good man. Be honest even if it means losin' a little. And true to yourself. That's important too. You can't get involved in somethin' you don't believe in."

Obadiah was sitting by the door, holding Rosie on his lap.

"And, that applies to you, too, Obadiah," she said. "You got responsibilities now with that little girl. You make sure you get her safe and sound up to those kinfolk of yours."

Obadiah nodded. "Yes, ma'am."

Two days later, the foursome was ready to leave.

"I wish you'd take one of the horses," Maude said.

"You need those horses more than we do," Sarah said, as she embraced her. "Besides, this way no one can fight over who gets to ride. Right, Rosie?"

The little girl smiled up at her. Her colour was returning and the haunted look was gone from her eyes. Sarah hoped she would soon start to talk again. Maude gathered her up in her arms and held her close for a few moments before setting her back down.

"You be a good little girl now, darlin'," she said, "and you stay close to Sarah. She'll take real good care of you."

Rosie smiled and nodded.

"All right. Y'all get goin' now. You're wasting time, standin' here talking with me. Before you know it, you'll have to drop everything and go do the milkin'."

Sarah rushed over to give her one last hug.

"We can't say how much you mean to us, Maude. We'll never forget you."

 Maude turned to walk back to her house but not before they saw the tears in each other's eyes.

They traveled on for a fortnight before stormy weather hit. There was a village in sight but the wind and rain came down in full force before they could reach it. Fortunately, they spied a small cave carved into the side of a high hill. The fierce wind battered their bodies as they slowly crawled up the steep grade. The ground was wet and slippery so every step was a challenge.

"You think there might be a bear or something in there?" Obadiah yelled up at Frank, who was taking the lead.

Frank turned and yelled back, "If there is, he better move out."

They had to push aside dead branches and prickly brambles before they could enter. The cave, if that's what one could call it, was a small area wedged between two large rocks. It was impossible for either he or Frank to stand up at its highest point. There wasn't much depth to it; there was just enough room for the four to sit down and to place their gear behind them. It was, however, a welcoming shelter from the storm.

For over an hour, they sat huddled together watching the violent storm unfold before them. Even though it was still early afternoon, the sky was dark and ominous. Trees bent over, almost parallel with the ground as the wind tore through the bluffs of oak and poplar trees on the hillside surrounding the cave. They listened to branches cracking and trees ripping from the earth and smashing to the ground.

The wind turned bitterly cold so they sat huddled together, wet and shivering.

Thunder rumbled so close that the hill itself shuddered and within seconds a bolt of lightning struck the tree closest to the cave. Sparks and flames flew up into the darkened sky as the wind tossed the treetop into the air as if it were nothing but a burnt out candle. The remaining trunk sizzled and smoked as the rain pounded against it. The putrid smell drifted into the cave.

Finally, the storm wore itself out. The wind ceased but the rain continued, constant and heavy.

"What can we do for a fire, Frank?" Sarah asked. "Rosie is so wet and cold. We need to dry out before we all get sick."

Frank stared out at the pouring rain.

"There is nothing even remotely dry enough to burn," he said. "And look at this rain - if this goes on all night, we won't be able to have a hot breakfast."

"Wait a minute," Obadiah said. "Maybe there's something in the cave that will burn."

"Like what?" Frank wanted to know.

"I don't know. I'll see what's at the back of the cave."

"It only goes back a few feet, Obadiah. I doubt there's anything that will burn."

Obadiah crawled to the back of the cave, lifted up their bags and felt along the floor.

"I think I've found something," he said. "At least, it will heat the cave up a bit."

He took his hat off and proceeded to scoop something into it.

"Here," he said, with a triumphant grin. "This will burn for awhile."

Sarah peered into this hat but could only make out something dark.

"What on earth is that?"

He grinned at her. "Probably bear dung. I'm glad the bear's not here but I'm glad he left something behind."

Frank shook his head. "Well, we can give it a try. I don't think it will burn for very long though."

"Trust me, it will," Obadiah said. "I believe there's lots more where this came from."

They all burst out laughing, even Rosie who had been shivering in Sarah's arms.

It took awhile but eventually they were able to get a small fire burning. Frank spent most of the time trying to wave the smoke back out the cave but it did give them some heat and light so that they were able to find some food in their bags. When their means of burning was finished, they curled up and slept from sheer exhaustion. The wind subsided during the night and they woke up to sunshine and a sparkling calm world.

The next day, about mid-afternoon, they neared the village. Along the side of the road, there was a wooden sign reading, 'Welcome to Sweet Haven.' The wood was new and the paint, fresh. They stood beside it and stared in disbelief.

"Have you ever seen anything like this?" Sarah gasped, as she gazed about. "There's not one house standing."

"Look." Obadiah pointed. "Someone's coming down the road. There must be people still living here."

A man was walking towards them, pushing a wheel barrow filled with a few household items. He stared, his eyes wild and unseeing. It was difficult to tell his age; he could have been twenty or fifty. His ripped and tattered clothing barely covered his body. Dried blood was caked to the side of this face.

"Mister," Frank called out. "What's happened here? Are you all right?"

The man's head jerked up and he let go of the wheel barrel.

He raised his eyes and hands to the sky. His voice shook. "A wind. A giant wind. It was a funnel that came from the sky. I couldn't see the top of it; it reached up to heaven. I've never heard such a sound. Everything flew through the air like leaves in a whirlwind. My wife and children. My mother and father. All gone." He turned and looked back at the wreckage. "How did I survive? Why? Why am I here and they're all gone?" He started to sob. "Every person is dead except me. Why?"

The four stared at him with no answer.

"What will you do now?" Sarah asked.

The man shook his head. "I have nowhere to go. I buried only one body - my mother's. I'm afraid to find the others." His shoulders shook as he suppressed a silent sob. "Will you do that for me? Will you bury the people? There are so many." He shook his head. "I can't do it."

Once again, his eyes glazed over and he started walking.

"Mister," Frank called out. "Wait and you can travel with us."

If the man heard, he took no notice.

Sarah had never seen such devastation. At least, in the mudslide, the people were buried; there was no need to search for bodies. Here, debris covered the ground. Smashed splintered boards, clothing, and furniture covered the street. It looked as if a giant foot had stepped on everything. Here and there, however, were bits of furniture standing whole and undamaged.

Then, there were the bodies; limbs twisted grotesquely with vacant eyes staring heavenward. Some were partially hidden under a portion of a roof; others, it seemed had been tossed in the air like rag dolls and then let drop. Somewhere at the end of the street, she could hear a dog barking. Other than that, there was only an eerie silence.

Sarah reached down and touched the top of Rosie's head. The little girl's eyes were wide with terror. Her small body trembled.

Sarah shuddered. Could a child suffer through all this and not be scarred for life? No wonder she didn't want to speak. Was this all there was to life? Sorrow and tragedy?

Frank was the first to take action.

"All right," he said. "Sarah, you take Rosie over to the edge of town and get a fire started. Pick up some of the wood along the way. The loose boards. If you find any food, take it. We'll camp here for the night. Obadiah and I will take care of the rest."

It was already dark and Sarah could still hear them shovelling and throwing boards onto a pile. Frank found a shovel in the rubble and used it to dig the graves. He brought other tools over to their camping spot. Obadiah built a large fire in the centre of the street. They worked into the night. Once Sarah looked up from her bed under a tree and in the fire's light, saw Frank standing beside the only remaining wall of a building, vomiting. She didn't know when they finished because when she awoke, they were both stretched out on the grass beside her, asleep.

They left the next morning, trying to keep their eyes away from the devastation. Sarah didn't ask any questions and neither Obadiah nor Frank offered any information. She didn't want to know how many bodies they had buried. How many were women; how many were children. It was better not to know.

"There's no point in leaving these here," Frank reasoned as he stood holding an axe in one hand and a large hunting knife in the other. "We can make use of them. These, too," he said, as he touched a couple of rifles on the ground, with his foot. Beside the guns, there was a frying pan and several cooking pots. There were also several packages of coffee, dried beans and beef jerky.

"I know. It just makes me kind of sad, that's all," Sarah said. "These folks had to travel so far and work so hard for this. Now, look, everything is finished."

Frank went down on his haunches and started packing one of the sacks. "Well, we can't bring them back to life, can we?" He looked up at his sister. "You do whatever you have to, to stay alive in this god-forsaken country."

"Frank, what are you trying to say?"

"I'm trying to say that anyone with an ounce of sense would never come out here. That's what I'm saying."

"You're saying Father was foolish bringing us west?"

"Of course, he was. He knew nothing about this land. Look what's happened to us thus far, Sarah. Look what's happened to Obadiah's folks, to this town. We've lost both our parents. You've lost a husband and children. I've killed men. You think that's all fine and dandy?"

Sarah straightened. "No, Frank. I don't. Certainly, if Father had known what the country was like, he would've stayed back in Portland, but he didn't. We wanted to go too, remember? Even Mother."

Frank stood up. "No, Sarah. Mother did not want to go. She had no choice. Her house was sold out from under her." He looked off into the distance. "Sometimes it's very hard for me to forgive him."

"To forgive your father? You have always felt this way?"

Frank looked down at the ground and dug the toe of his shoe into the dirt.

"It was a lark until Mother died. After that, a part of my life went out from me."

"Why didn't you tell me this?"

Frank shrugged. "For what purpose? Our life is already carved out for us. We can't go back; we don't want to stay here, so we have to keep moving. Do we have any choice, Sarah?"

Sarah, for the first time in a very long time, looked at her brother. Really looked at him. Why hadn't she noticed the change? Was she so wrapped up in herself that she couldn't see what was happening to him? Once, not that long ago, his eyes looked innocent and kind; now, they looked cold and suspicious. There were dark and puffy lines beneath them as if he hadn't slept in days. His long blond hair hung down his back in oily strings. The lips that could turn up into a smile so readily were set in a thin firm line. It came to her mind that if Frank were a stranger and she was meeting him for the first time, she would be cautious. He looked remote and at the same time, callous. Frontiersman's resilience had replaced his youthful gentlemanliness and mildness.

"There was someone who wanted Mother to stay back in Portland. Did you know that, Sarah?"

"Well, I'm sure there were a lot of people who did. She did have family there. And, friends. Mother had many friends. You know that, Frank."

"No, I mean someone who wanted her to leave Father."

Sarah stared at Frank. "What, on earth, are you talking about?"

"Teddy Neal. That's whom I'm talking about. I heard them talking in the parlour. He begged her to stay."

Sarah laughed. "Well, I'm sure he just meant to warn her. After all, he worked for Father for quite some time. He was like family, Frank."

Frank shook his head. "No. I heard him tell her how much he loved her and that if she left, he would die. He said he couldn't live without her."

"Oh, Frank, I'm sure you're exaggerating. You were just a child then."

"I might have been a child but I know that the kiss he gave her wasn't on her cheek."

Sarah was silent for a moment. "But, Frank," she said. "Mother chose to come West with Father."

Frank smiled. "Yes and so did Teddy Neal, didn't he?"

The foursome left the village ruins behind and trudged on. Frank and Obadiah went ahead, watching for small game they could kill for their next meal. Sarah walked in silence, her mind filled with thoughts about her mother and the young groomsman who had worked for them. It filled her with sadness because she knew her father knew nothing of it. Otherwise, Teddy would have never been on the wagon train. Her father would see to that. She realized how little she knew about her mother. Nothing, really. She was a child when her mother died. A wild Indian child. Why had her mother allowed Teddy to accompany them? Surely, she could have stopped him. Did she think that once they were out west, she could choose which man she wanted? No, she could never believe that about her own mother. Tears rolled, unchecked, down her cheeks.

"Sarah?" The voice was soft and quivering.

Sarah stopped. "Was that you, Rosie? Did you say something?"

The little girl nodded. There were tears in her eyes. "Have you stopped talking too, Sarah? Is it because you saw all those bad things? All those dead people? Is that why you stopped talking, like I did?"

Sarah went down on her knees and pulled Rosie into her arms. In the midst of all this sorrow, she had never heard such a sweet sound. At last, there was light in her dark world. Who would have ever told her that hearing a silent child speak again, could bring so much joy? She held Rosie out from her and wiped the tears from her own cheeks and then from the child's.

"You thought that I had stopped talking? Is that why you started?"

Rosie nodded. "I was so scared that you were never going to talk to me again."

She placed her hands around the small face. "No, I will never stop talking. Especially, to you, Rosie."

Somewhere, far off in the distance, I heard a loon call out. They made a lonely sound. In some ways, almost human. It echoed over the water and made a chill go up my spine. Pa and me'd heard them plenty a time when we went fishin' but, somehow, in this lonely place, it sounded a lot sadder. When me and Pa were together, there was only silence. We never talked while we fished. Actually, we never talked much at any time, I reckon. This was a new experience for me and that's for sure. Here I was, in a place I'd never been, listening to an old man I'd never met before.

He had a way of making me sad and happy all at the same time.

"Mr. Winnipesaukee, I gotta tell you, I was feeling mighty sorry for Sarah. You know, with her mom and all. Do you really think her mother was goin' to run off with that Teddy fellow?"

The old man thought for a moment. "No. At the time, Frank was too young to understand. As the years went by, he realized that the kiss she had shared with the young groomsman was only one-sided."

"You mean it's kind of like when you really like one of your teachers but she's too old for you?"

The old man cackled. "That's about it."

"But Rosie started to talk again. I was sure glad to hear that. So, one thing that was sad caused something good to happen."

"That's a good way of putting it."

"So, where'd they go after they left that village behind? Did they meet up with the man who'd lost all his family? Do you think that was a tornado that went through that place and destroyed everything?"

"Yes, that was a tornado. They did meet up with the man and he traveled with them to St. Louis."

"How long did it take for them to get there?"

"They reached St. Louis by late fall. It would have taken longer but they happened to meet up with a wagon train traveling in that direction. The wagon master was happy to find two extra men because there were some renegade Indians in the area."

"Was there a fight?"

"No, the train rolled into St. Louis one cool fall day. If I remember correctly, it was the year 1857. Or, thereabouts, anyway."

Chapter Thirty Three

Winter in St. Louis

Frank took turns driving with a man named Straight Shooter Smith. Everyone on the train called him Shooter. He was not only the oldest person; he was definitely the most colourful. He had a long torso and short bowed legs. Almost all of his teeth were missing and he never took his hat off because he didn't have a hair on his head. When he went over to visit with Sarah, which he seemed to do quite frequently, Sarah spent most of the time covering Rosie's ears so she wouldn't have to listen to the profanity.

"Can't you stop him from coming over here?" she asked Frank. "He's the most disgusting person I've ever met."

"Aw, Shooter isn't too bad. He sort of grows on you. You'll get used to him. Just keep Rosie in the wagon when you see him coming."

Sarah glared at him. "I shouldn't have to do that, Frank. That old man should know enough not to swear like that in front of a woman. Besides, he's half-deaf and talks so loud that everyone a mile away can hear him."

Frank laughed. "Yeah, he is kind of loud, isn't he?"

"And, he smells. How can you sit beside him all day and not get sick to your stomach?"

Frank grinned. "I have a secret." He pulled something out of his shirt pocket.

"What, on earth, is that?"

"It's an Indian amulet that some old squaw gave me one time."

"Are you saying that the charm protects you from Shooter's smell?"

He laughed again. "Only when I fill it with crushed garlic. See." He handed it to her so she could smell it.

Sarah jumped back.

"Good heavens, Frank, you two deserve each other. You smell worse than he does."

"Well, I figure, if we're getting a free ride to St. Louis, I have to put up with a few discomforts. Trust me, this smells better than Shooter. But, I'll tell you, it's worth it just to listen to some of his tales. He's going to help us get settled for the winter. St. Louis is a big city, Sarah. Bigger than Portland. He says he knows where Obadiah and I can get work for the winter at the docks. We'll need someone to show us the ropes."

"I don't mind him showing us the ropes but he better not get any ideas about me."

"Ideas about you?"

"That's what I said. I don't want him hanging around me or Rosie."

Frank shrugged. "He's just wanting to be friendly, that's all. He's old enough to be your grandfather."

"I know that and you know that, but Mr. Shooter might not. Tell him that the next time he tries to put his smelly arm around me, I'll shoot him."

"I'll make sure and tell him." He walked away but turned back, grinning. "You'd better start packing a gun, Missy."

Sarah didn't know what Frank told Shooter but whatever it was, it worked. Every time, he saw her, he turned around and went in the opposite direction.

It was a cold windy day and the sky threatened to snow, when they finally made their way to the Mississippi river. Beyond the river, lay a city so vast that most in the wagon train had to rein in their wagon and stare. It had been months for some, years for others, since they had seen more than twenty or thirty people together in one place. None had ever seen anything like this.

"Yessiree," Shooter said, as he turned his head to the side and spit a mouthful of tobacco juice onto the ground. "Woulda been better if'n we could've made it all the way to Independence but this'll do. This is a good place to winter. Lots of work here." He nudged Frank and winked. "Lots of nice French women." He cackled. "Ya'll be wantin' one of them to keep ya warm this winter."

Therefore, it was that Sarah tolerated Shooter for the next three weeks until he found a place for them to stay for the winter. Frank and Obadiah had no problem finding work, loading and unloading boats. Sarah and Rosie spent most of the day roaming the back streets picking up stray pieces of wood and coal to keep the small house they were renting warm. By the time their evening meal was finished, all four of them were ready to sleep for the night.

According to the locals, it was an extraordinarily mild winter. The Mississippi wasn't even frozen over solid. Sarah, however, found the wind sharp and cold as it penetrated her thin winter coat. She would have preferred to wear her Indian clothes but too many men pestered her when she did, so she stuck to an old cloth coat Maude had given her. She waited anxiously for spring so they could continue their trip to Montana. Rosie and Obadiah needed a real home and family.

One night, in late January, Frank and Obadiah didn't return home at their usual time. The hours ticked by. Sarah heated and reheated the stew. Finally, she fed Rosie and put her to bed.

"Where are Uncle Frank and Obadiah?" the child asked.

Sarah smiled. "They've probably had to work longer," she said. "There must have been lots of cargo to unload today." She hugged Rosie. "Don't worry, they'll be home soon."

It was past midnight before Sarah wrapped herself in a blanket and crawled in beside Rosie on the straw mattress. The men were still not home. What could she do? She had no idea where they might be. She couldn't wake up Rosie and wander around the docks at this hour. She went from worry to anger to worry. There were terrible things happening on the streets late at night. What if someone robbed them and beat them up? What if there'd been an accident at work? What if? What if? Her brain wouldn't stop.

Sometime in the night, she drifted off because suddenly she was startled out of her sleep by loud boisterous laughter. She sat up, clutching the blanket to her chest. Her heart pounded. The room was cold. A sickly yellow glow from the coal oil lamp in the kitchen filled the bedroom doorway. The stove lid clattered as someone stoked wood into it. Who was in the kitchen? She listened. There had to be more than two people out there. A woman spoke very quietly. Someone roared with laughter. Could that be Frank? No, it couldn't be. Frank was a quiet sombre man with a gentle laugh. He didn't laugh like an idiot.

"Now, we're all nice and cosy."

It was Frank's voice but the words were too loud. She heard a chair scrape and someone fell on the floor. More laughter. A woman's shrill laughter.

Sarah rose from the bed, draping a blanket around her. She inched towards the door but stayed in the darkness. There was no need to tread softly; no one in the other room would hear her anyway. As she surveyed the scene in front of her, she recoiled in disgust. Her lips pursed in anger.

There were two women in the kitchen with Frank and Obadiah. Sarah stared. She didn't have to use her imagination to know what kind of women these were. Their coats hung open, exposing tight fitting, bright gaudy-red dresses and their white breasts bulged over the plunging necklines. Their lips were painted bright red and their eyelids were black. Even from where Sarah stood, she could see the lines on their faces. They were prostitutes with lots of mileage behind them.

Frank held an almost empty whiskey bottle in one hand and his other arm was looped around the neck of one of the women. She laughed when his head fell down onto her bosom. Obadiah was trying to pick himself up off the floor. With each futile attempt, all of them would burst into drunken laughter.

Sarah moved closer to the door. Four faces turned toward her.

"What's the matter with you, Frank Lawdry?" She stood, glaring at her brother. "There is a young child here. Are you insane?"

Frank tried to focus but his eyes didn't cooperate. He shook his head, as if that would clear his mind. Spit rolled down his chin. Obadiah had succeeded in sitting up. He looked at Sarah, seeing her for the first time.

"Child?" he mumbled. "Wha' child?"

"Your sister, Obadiah. Your little sister. Do you want her to see you like this?"

Obadiah shook his head and grinned.

"Like this?" he slurred.

"You're drunk." She turned to her brother. "And you, Frank. You're the older; you should know better than take Obadiah drinking and then …" She could hardly bring herself to look at either woman. " …bring these women home with you."

"Who's there, Auntie Sarah?" Rosie called out.

Sarah rushed back to the bed.

"No one you want to meet, Rosie. Go back to sleep." She pulled the blanket over the girl. "It's late."

The kitchen had turned suddenly quiet. Sarah went back and stood in the doorway. By this time, both women were standing.

"Hey, you didn't tell us there was any kids here. I ain't doin' nothin' with no kids around." The one with the orange-red hair started towards the door. "An' don' think you're gettin' any of yer money back either."

The chubby blond woman followed, trying to button her coat as she walked. "Yer wasted our whole evening. We coulda' found ourselves some real men."

They walked out and slammed the door. Obadiah's eyes rolled back and he fell backwards on the floor. Frank turned to call the women back, got dizzy and just made it to the slop pail in time.

Sarah went into the kitchen and put another piece of wood in the stove.

"Sarah," Frank called. "Can you help? I'm dying."

She didn't answer. She stepped over Obadiah and went back to bed.

The snow had barely melted when they joined up with a large wagon train and began their long trip northward. It was the beginning of March, an early spring. There were, however, not four but five of them now.

Much to Sarah's chagrin, close to the end of winter, Frank began to spend most of his evenings roving from tavern to tavern. She knew there was nothing to keep him occupied in their small three room house. The winter days were short and the cold winter nights were long. At least, Obadiah knew enough to stay home. Many nights she heard Frank stumbling in but she wrapped the blanket around her ears and closed her mind as to what he might be doing.

Two days before the wagon train was to leave, Frank brought a young French woman to the house and announced that she was his wife. Her name was Marie LaLonde. She was a petit French girl with short black hair, snappy black eyes and a very limited English vocabulary.

They were already three days on the road before Sarah was able to get Frank alone.

"You've been avoiding me, Frank."

"I've been busy; you can see that." He started to walk away.

Sarah grabbed his arm. "We haven't talked since you came home with Marie. I want to know about her. When did you get married? Why didn't you tell me? I'm your sister. What's going on, Frank? We have never kept secrets like this before."

He shrugged. "So? We were children. Now, we're adults. You are free to do whatever you choose. Look for a husband; I won't stop you. I promised I would go up to the Dakota Territory with you and that's what I'll do. But my private life is my own. Marie will make a good wife."

"Perhaps, she should start by helping out right now. There's work to do and all she does is stay in your wagon. You take food to her like she's some kind of princess."

"I don't need to listen to this."

"I don't think you are married, Frank. I think she's one of the women you picked up at some tavern. She's not here to work; she's here for your pleasure."

There was only a brief second of silence before Frank's hand went into the air and landed on Sarah's cheek. She spun from the impact and landed on the ground.

Frank stared at his hand and then at his sister before turning away. Sarah watched him walk away through her tears.

She didn't see him or Marie for the rest of the day. The next morning his wagon was gone.

"That's all right, Sarah," Obadiah said. "I'll look after you. We'll make it to Aunt Esther's and you can live with us."

Rosie clung to Sarah. She knew that she could never abandon these children. At night, when everyone was asleep, she lay in her bed under the wagon, wondering if she would ever see her brother again. She watched the moon and remembered the nights she'd spent doing the same thing when her parents were still alive. It seemed like a lifetime ago.

I hadn't realized that tears were streamin' down my face until I looked over at the old man and saw that his cheeks were wet too. My heart was simply achin' for that girl, Sarah. How could Frank have been so hard hearted?

"What do you think got into that Frank?" I asked. "It just don't seem like him to turn on his sister like that."

Winnipesaukee gazed up at the heavens. His face looked so sad; I almost had the thought of runnin' over to put my arms around him.

But, then agin', I didn't exactly know him all that well and he might not be the type that goes for that sort of thing.

I decided to be quiet now and wait for an answer. I could see he was havin' a hard time tryin' to explain this.

Finally, he spoke. His voice was so quiet I had to really pay attention.

"Yes sir, that was a side of Frank that no one had ever seen before. I reckon even Frank didn't understand it. It was almost like the Devil himself got into him. And, maybe he did."

With that, he closed his eyes. I figured he must be goin' to sleep now. It was somewhat selfish on my part wantin' him to stay awake and finish his story. After all, I was a youngster and he was old and needin' his sleep.

I had almost drifted off when his voice started up again.

"You aren't wondering if Sarah ever got to Montana?" he asked.

I sat up.

"Well, yes sir, I was, but I was thinkin' maybe you wanted to get some sleep."

"Hmmph," he grunted. "I'll have forever to sleep soon. If you want to hear the end of my story, I'll tell it."

"I'd like that. I really would."

There was somethin' else I was a might curious about. "Do you know what Frank told Shooter so's he stayed away from Sarah?"

The old man's lips twitched. "Well, son, that's mostly for older folks to know but I reckon you'll be learning about it soon enough. It seems Frank may have mentioned something about Sarah having some sort of disease. You know, the type loose women might have."

I gasped. "Did Sarah know?"

"No, Sarah never found out about that."

"Well, sir, did Sarah ever see her brother again?"

Winnipesaukee smiled. "You'll have to be patient. This is my story so I have to tell it my way."

Chapter Thirty Four

Some of Sarah's soul left her that day; the day that she awoke to find her brother gone. Mindlessly, from sunrise to sunset, she struggled to toil harder; emotionally, she strove to love Rosie and Obadiah a little more but the emptiness remained. Each night she left the camp after everyone was asleep. She snuck past the dozing guards and walked in the moonlight. Some nights she would wander far away, stand gazing at the moon and in a low monotone voice, she would call out *Ya Ni Go We Ya Ni Go We YaNi Go We* - the dead song.

The land lay empty before them. The dozens of covered wagons lumbered on, rolling over ruts already formed by the steel rims of former travellers. The weather remained crisp and clear. Each morning there was fresh dew on the grass but the sun shone a little stronger.

A variety of characters made up the wagon train. Obadiah scrutinized each one. He took it upon himself to watch over Sarah as well as his sister, Rosie. The majority were families, hoping to find fertile farmland; the women looked thin and worn and the men, anxious. Most of them had one or two milking cows tied behind a wagon as well as a riding horse. Some brought crates filled with chickens. There were wooden barrels attached precariously with hide strips to the sides of the wagons; seed or grain filled most of them. One was always for water.

At least, they were able to get this far. Tons of rock and mud hadn't buried them alive. Sometimes Sarah wondered if her father would have changed his course. Would he have been tempted by California's gold or the rich farmland of the Dakota Territory?

Several sullen bearded men travelled with them. They didn't drive wagons but rode magnificent tall half-wild horses. Their eyes were cold and penetrating. Sarah kept as far away from them as possible. Obadiah said they carried pistols in their waistbands. In the evenings, they clustered around their own campfire, smoking and talking in muffled tones.

Some in the group were following the Santa Fe Trail, heading for the Great Mountains. Others, like Sarah and Obadiah, were following the Oregon Trail and then, turning north from the North Platte River. Although not as well known as the Oregon, it was fairly well travelled and there was plenty of water and abundant grass along the way for their livestock. At least, that's what they'd been told.

"I ain't goin' to lie none to ya," one of the scouts told Obadiah. "We be comin' into Indian territory soon. Crow an' prob'ly some Sioux or Cheyenne. Ya got yerself a good rifle?"

Obadiah blushed. "No, sir. I don't have a rifle. Someone told us there was a treaty signed in '51 at Fort Laramie and it guaranteed that the government could build roads and military posts."

The old man let out a loud screech, then turned his head, and spit out a stream of brown tobacco juice. "That's what someone told ya, did they? Well, someone oughta tell the Injuns. Son, ya can't stay alive in this har country without a gun." He looked Obadiah over with his tired bloodshot eyes. "What in tarnation are ya doin' out here in the middle of nowhere, anyhow?"

"We're travelling up to western Dakota Territory, sir. I've got relatives up there. They've got a ranch. Our ma and pa were killed, you see."

He shook his head. "They got a ranch, do they? Wal, ya wait right here. I'll round up some guns and ammo for you and yer woman."

Obadiah blushed. "That isn't my woman. Sarah's a friend."

The older man shrugged. "Wal," he said, "might be darn right smart to have an Injun friend along."

Before pulling out the next morning, Sarah and Obadiah discovered two pistols and one rifle on the wagon seat.

They left Independence before the sun was up. For the next several days, all they saw was wasteland.
"I thought this was supposed to be a good trail," Obadiah grumbled. They had stopped for their noon break and the sun was already hot.

"Well," Sarah said, "we're by a river. And, there's grass for the mules. What more do you want?"

He shrugged. "Guess all I want is Frank. That's all."

Sarah patted his arm. "He'll show up. Sooner or later, Frank will join us."

Obadiah looked doubtful.

The days went by quickly. Each day, they covered about fifteen miles.

The army was slowly working at building forts along the way. They would have one almost finished but the Indians would attack, kill the few soldiers and burn the buildings. Sarah wasn't sure whose side she was on. She understood both. This was the Crows' hunting grounds. The buffalo stood and waited for them. This land was sacred. The white people looked at the fertile soil. It would produce good crops. They were eager to begin tilling and planting. The land stretched out for miles. There was water for cattle, hundreds of cattle. Could the Indians and whites share the land? No, she couldn't see them doing that.

In the fall of 1858, the wagon train made its final stop. Winter was closing in. There were over fifty wagons when they left Independence; now, there were only eleven. One group of twenty had stopped along the foothills of the Bighorn Mountains and decided to start a town. There were the makings of a fort close by and they felt safe. Several other wagons had either broken down beyond repair or the occupants had changed their minds and driven off in another direction.

There had been one Indian raid but no one on the wagon train was killed. One farmer's wife panicked and accidentally shot her husband in the leg. That was the only injury. Sarah was thankful that day for the men who travelled on horseback. She might be afraid of them but they were accurate when it came to shooting. Early one morning before dawn, she heard them ride out but they didn't return. One of the farmers said he thought they were heading up to Canada. No one spoke about it but Sarah was sure that they were running from the Law.

"Where do we find your aunt and uncle, Obadiah?" she asked. They had camped beside a river for the night. The rest of the wagons were leaving the next morning for Virginia City.

"All I know is what I heard Ma and Pa talking about. They said we would be living at the Big Bend of Milk River. Milk River runs out from the Missouri, I think. All I remember Pa saying was that it would be easy to find. I guess cause not too many own big ranches out this way."

"Well, so far, we haven't seen any. This is wild unsettled country, Obadiah. Most folks tend to settle on farms and live close to each other."

The young man nodded. "I hope this trip wasn't for nothing, Sarah. I mean, what will we do if we can't find them? It must be two or maybe three years now since we heard from them. My uncle might be dead by now."

"If that's the case, your aunt will need us more than ever. If they had land, I imagine she'd still be on it. Where would she go?"

Obadiah shrugged. "Guess you're right."

The last scout gave them directions before he left for Virginia City.

"If'n they're at the Big Bend, they ain't on no ranch," he said. "That be almost up to Canada." He was a tall lanky man with long black hair, tied back with a thin piece of hide, and was dressed in dirty buckskin. He wore shiny moccasins with most of the beadwork missing and an old army pistol, shoved into his waistband. There were deep lines, spreading out from the corner of his eyes to his ears, from years of squinting at the sun.

"What do you mean?" Obadiah asked.

"What I mean is, there's folks livin' there but they ain't no ranchers."

"Are they farmers?"

"Yer ever har of the Metis?"

Sarah and Obadiah shook their heads.

"Wal, them's the folks that are part Indian and part white."

"You mean like half-breeds?" Obadiah said.

"Them's don' like to be called thet. They got French blood in them. Some got more Indian than French; others, got more French. Them's all called Metis."

"So," Sarah asked, "what do they do?"

"Oh, they got them a village there and they live off the land. Good buffalo hunters." He dug some chewing tobacco out of his pocket. "Them's right nice folk. Love to play music and dance. Have a good time." He shoved some tobacco into his cheek. "Some's that like 'em. Some's that don't."

Sarah turned to Obadiah. "I guess we have no choice. Maybe the folks living there will know where your family settled."

"Yer look like a Metis yerself," he said to Sarah. "Yer got some Indian in yer blood?"

Sarah nodded. "My father was part Abenaki."

"Hmmm. Ain't never heerd of them. This here be mostly Crow country. Course, yer see one Indian, yer see 'em all."

With that, he sat down on his haunches and drew a map in the dirt. It would be four or five days before they would reach Milk River.

The three now travelled alone. They started their day before the sun came up, relinquished the noon stop and camped with barely any light to see by. A fine layer of frost covered the brown grass every morning. They clutched their morning cup of coffee for as long as they could, trying to warm their hands. A few weeks before, brightly coloured leaves covered the trees but now they looked bare and forlorn.

On the fourth day, they came to Milk River. There, nestled in the barren cottonwoods, they spied a group of cabins, built in a circle. In the centre was a long log building.

This was the Metis village. They stopped the wagon and watched for any sign of life. In a few minutes, people began to emerge from their homes. Children stood and stared.

"Well, let's get moving, Obadiah," Sarah said.

"Is this where our auntie lives?" Rosie asked.

"I have no idea but we'll soon find out." Sarah gave the little girl a reassuring smile.

They moved slowly towards a group of people that seemed to grow by the minute. Soon there must have been about forty men, women and children coming to greet them.

"*Bonjour! Bonjour!*" the group called out.

"What if no one speaks English?" Obadiah said.

Sarah held up her hand and waved. "Surely someone will speak English."

They soon discovered that very few spoke any English. It was still quite easy to communicate and before long Rosie was busy playing with a group of girls.

No one had heard of Obadiah's aunt and uncle. There weren't any white settlers close by. During supper, however, one of the younger men started to speak excitedly in French. Yes, he said, he knew where they might have lived. He would take them there tomorrow.

That night, one of the families, insisted that they sleep in a cabin. They had plenty of room.

The cabins were built from cottonwood logs. Clay mixed with buffalo hair filled the cracks between the logs inside. At one end of the room was a fireplace. Packed down dirt made up the floor and skins from buffalo calves covered the windows. Each hide had been worked until it was translucent.

Before they could settle down for the night, the men took out their fiddles and music filled the air. Everyone, young and old, jumped up and danced. It had been a long time since Sarah had seen so many happy carefree people. For a short time, she even forgot about the brother who had abandoned her.

They set out early the next morning, driving behind two Metis men. By late afternoon, the two reigned in their horses. Sarah pulled the wagon up beside them. There, in front of them, stood the remains of a burned out cabin.

Slowly, Sarah and Obadiah got down. They walked over to the ruins. Overgrown tall weeds and grass filled in the shell of the house. Obadiah moved the grass back and forth, searching the ground for anything that might have escaped the fire. Sarah could see the makings of a former corral behind the house. Most of the logs now lay on the ground.

She walked through the area behind the house, wondering if there were any signs of a grave or two. She could see none.

"Sarah," Obadiah suddenly called out. "Come here."

He was holding something in his hand. There were tears in his eyes.

"Look," he said. "I remember this." He held up a small locket. Inside was a picture of a woman. "This is my aunt. My mother had the same picture." He stared down at it. "They were twins."

They made camp there that night.

On the way back the next day, Obadiah was very quiet. Finally, he said, "Do you think we should put up some kind of shelter there for the winter, Sarah? I'm sorry we've led you all this way for nothing. I don't know how I can ever repay you for all that you've done for Rosie and me."

Sarah looked over at Obadiah and Rosie. "What would I have done without you?" she said. "I would be alone now in St. Louis. What kind of life would that be? No, it is I who am grateful to you."

The Metis, however, wouldn't think of them living far away and alone for the winter. They cleaned one of the empty cabins for Sarah and Rosie, and Obadiah moved in with two young men.

It was a mild winter and there was plenty of game to eat. The days went by quickly. Sarah and Rosie learned to speak French and Obadiah fell in love with a pretty Metis girl. In the spring, they were married.

The next winter was not quite as easy. The weather was severe. Some days it was so cold, no one could leave his or her cabin. The meat they had dried or salted was soon gone and there was no game close by. Each day some of the men would go to hunt but seldom came home with anything. Perhaps, a rabbit or two. That was all. Some of the elderly died that winter - some from a fever; others, from starvation.

Sarah stayed with the Metis for the next ten years. Rosie was her family. Sometimes, at night when she couldn't sleep and her stomach ached for food, she would think of Frank. She wondered where he was and if he regretted leaving her. She only wished him well and hoped his belly was full. Perhaps, he and the French girl now had a family. It was quite possible that she was someone's aunt.

There was now much trouble with the Metis people and the government. The Metis were used to travelling freely from, what was now Montana Territory, up to Canada. They would go back and forth. Sometimes, they would follow the buffalo. That would mean a good winter for them. Now, someone wanted to draw a line. A line that would keep American Metis on one side and British Metis, on the other. Some of the hunters who travelled north never returned. Sarah heard the men say that the Northwest Mounted Police had killed them. What was wrong? Why couldn't all men live in peace together? The whites fought the whites, the Indians fought the Indians and they fought each other. Only the Metis did not. The Metis lived in peace. That was what she found.

When Rosie was sixteen, she married. Sarah was alone. Everyone in the camp treated her as if she were family but there was something missing in her life. Obadiah could see she was getting restless.

He came in to her cabin one day while she was sewing.

"One of the men has eyes for you, Sarah. Why don't you marry? He's a good man."

Sarah looked up from her work. Obadiah had grown into such a fine strong young man. She wished he could take his family and move to a more stable environment but she didn't dare say anything. He and Rosie had become Metis.

She laughed.

"Someone has eyes for an old woman? No, that can't be."

"You aren't old, Sarah. You're still a young woman. You're not much older than me."

"I feel old. Almost like I've lived too long already."

"Don't say that." He sat down in the chair, facing her. "What is your dream, Sarah?"

She put down the cloth and sat, thinking. What was her dream?

"I've had only one dream: to live in a valley. Does that sound foolish? A beautiful valley with a river running through. Do you know where such a place exists, Obadiah?"

He smiled. There was love and devotion in his eyes. "If I could," he said, "I would travel the earth searching for such a place for you."

Sarah looked out the open door. The sun was bright and the children laughed and played. Obadiah's little boy was there with them.

"And," she said, "I would like to play a piano again."

"A piano? We have lots of fiddles around here. Why don't you learn to play one of those?"

"No, I would like to have a baby grand piano, like my mother had."

The next winter was one of the harshest they'd had for quite some time. Many in the camp died from starvation. Six hunters went out one day but never returned. A blizzard came up and one of the women discovered their frozen bodies only several hundred feet from the village.

Spring was late too. There were five and six foot snow banks still standing at the end of March. Each day the sun shone but it was bitter cold. Crocuses desperately pushed their tiny faces towards the sun but by morning, they were frozen.

"It's time for me to leave," Sarah told Rosie. "It isn't fair that I eat their food when I'm not one of them."

"But, you are," Rosie argued.

"No, you are. You and Obadiah, but I am still only a visitor."

"Where will you go, Sarah? This is your home."

"I've been listening to the men. There's a place where there is a mission. Judith Basin, it's called. I could teach school there. I'll teach English to the French children. Just like I do here."

"That's why you're needed here." Rosie's eyes filled with tears.

Sarah shook her head. "No, I need to make my own life. I'm more than forty and I haven't settled into my own yet."

"That's because all you've ever done is give." Rosie lowered her head. "Obadiah and I looked to you for everything." She looked up, tears streaming down her face. "I don't think I can survive without you, Auntie Sarah."

Sarah hugged her. "Yes, Rosie, you can. You'll soon have your own family."

Spring finally arrived. As soon as the snow melted, Sarah spent most of the days wandering through the land. Sometimes, she sat by the river watching the water just as she had done years before with her father. What would her life be like if they had never left Portland? Once, she saw a herd of wild horses racing across a barren strip of land and she thought of Levi. They were free like the Abenaki. What would life be like if her husband and children had not died? Would they be living up in Quebec now with the rest of the tribe? At night, she sat out under the starry skies and thought about Frank. Where was he? Was he still alive? If they were still together, where would they be now? Would they have found her valley?

It was mid-May before Sarah was ready to leave. Obadiah insisted on taking her to Judith Basin.

There were only a few out to say good-bye. Rosie stood with her husband's arm around her and tears running down her face.

Obadiah looked at the quiet sleeping village.

"I don't think anyone will be awake before noon," he said, with a grin.

Sarah laughed. The farewell party in Sarah's honour had lasted well into the morning hours. Even in sad times, the Metis smiled through their tears.

"I'm glad. I don't like saying good-bye."

She hugged Rosie and Andre and climbed up beside Obadiah. Before turning the bend in the road, Sarah looked back for the last time. Rosie still stood there. When she saw Sarah looking, she waved. Two people whose lives became so entwined but who might never meet again.

The day was warm and sunny. After the long winter, the horses were happy to set their own pace. Sarah breathed in the fresh clean air and relaxed as the wagon bounced along.

"There is a man," Obadiah spoke up, suddenly, "in Judith Basin. A Metis man. It's said that he was sent by God to help his people." He looked at Sarah. "The Metis need help, Sarah."

"What is it you want me to do, Obadiah?"

"Just talk to him. See if he is as great as everyone says."

"And when I talk to him, what should I say?"

"Tell him about the Metis on Milk River. Tell him that if the government doesn't allow us to trap and hunt across the border, we will all starve to death."

"Do you know what this man's name is?"

"Riel. Louis Riel. He is a Metis from Canada."

"So, why is he here? Why isn't he back in his own country?"

"I believe he had to leave. He is considered an outlaw up there. Louis Montagne told me that some are seeking to kill him."

Sarah sighed. "I don't know if I want to get involved in this, Obadiah. I want to get away from hatred and violence. To live in peace until I die."

Obadiah shook his head. "What is this about dying? You have many years left to live, Sarah. Just because you have lived through so much in such a short time, doesn't mean that you are ready to die. Besides," he reached over and put his hand over hers, "you have to come back and visit your namesake."

"What namesake?"

He laughed. "We are having another baby. This one will be a girl and we're going to call her Sarah Rose. What do you think of that?"

She squeezed his hand. "That is wonderful, Obadiah. I'm so happy for you."

Sarah relaxed and enjoyed the rest of the trip. She thought back to all the land she'd travelled through since leaving the east coast. When she closed her eyes, she could still see the haze of the Blue Mountains, the unending Plains with its tall grass bending in the wind, and the rivers - some wide and wild; others, slow and meandering.

Montana Territory was vast and untamed, with mountains, plains and mighty rivers. There was food and land enough for all: the Indians, the Metis, the farmers and the ranchers. Why would this never be?

It didn't take long for Sarah to settle into her new life. She loved teaching the young Indian children. Soon, they were learning, not only English but French as well. She lived in a small clapboard shack not far from the mission. On the warm evenings, she would roam the countryside, studying nature while softly singing the old Abenaki songs that she remembered.

One day the next spring, there was much excitement at the Mission. The man, Louis Riel, arrived, riding in a Red River cart. Sarah stood in the doorway of her house and watched. This was the man who claimed to have seen visions; the man whom God sent to deliver the Metis. He definitely wasn't a man who stood out in a crowd. She had expected a big man, a man who exuded power. Someone who would turn heads. Instead, this man was thin and looked almost frail of build. His nose was straight and he wore a moustache. He looked French. Sarah's skin was darker. His wife, Marguerite, looked more Indian than white.

Once again, it seemed that Sarah was back living the life of a Metis. Perhaps, she thought, this was her destiny.

Life was good, except there were problems brewing for the Metis people. Sarah would see men coming and going in the night. Riel sometimes spoke of his conquests in Canada and she knew he felt like an outcast. He was now a citizen of the United States but this was not in his heart. His dream was to return and set up his own nation. If there was to be war, so be it.

One quiet Sunday morning in June, 1884, four men rode up to the mission. Sarah heard only from the women afterwards. Louis Riel was going back to Canada. He, his wife, and two small children.

One night around a campfire, Sarah heard the talk about this land in Canada. There was a valley with a river flowing through. No other valley could even compare. It ran through a province called Saskatchewan. Hills, almost the height of mountains, cradled the fast-flowing river below.

"Does this valley have a name?" she wanted to know.

One of the Frenchmen who had come for Riel answered, "Yes.

Oui. It is called the Qu'Appelle Valley. There is a story to it."

That evening, Sarah heard the romantic story of the Qu'Appelle valley. It stirred something within her. Before she fell asleep that night, she pictured herself floating down the river in a canoe and hearing someone call her name. She called out, 'who calls?' but instead of a lover answering, it was Frank. Tears formed. She didn't think of him too often anymore but when she did, it was always painful.

Sarah wasn't concerned with causes. She felt that all men were equal. That didn't mean that she didn't have deep feelings for the Metis people. They seemed so scattered and homeless. If Mr. Riel could help them, she would support him. It wasn't long and everyone was talking about Riel and his escort going back to Canada.

Obadiah and some of the men from Milk River came to see them off.

"This will be it, Sarah," he said. "The Metis will finally have their own land." He looked excited. "Perhaps, our entire village will move up there. And, you will come up and live with us. It will be like living in a new world."

An older man who had been listening, said, "No, young man, it will not be a new world. Riel is a dreamer. He says he is going in peace but there will be no peace. The government will never listen to him. He will be killed. Mark my words."

"No, they will be pleased to have him back to look after his people."

"Ha!" the old Frenchman laughed. "How can they be pleased? They banished him from the country. You think all of a sudden because he wants to take land for himself and the Metis that they will welcome him with open arms?" He snorted. "I don't think so."

"He has God's backing. Isn't that enough?" Obadiah was getting upset.

"God is not concerned with the Metis." With that, the old man stood up and walked away.

"It is going to be good. I know it," Obadiah said. "What do you think, Sarah? You've come to know him now."

"Some men are easy to know. Louis Riel is not one of them, Obadiah. He is a great speaker but some of the things that he says make no sense to me."

"Like what?"

"He sees visions. Sometimes, he compares himself to the Holy Ghost. Other times, he says God has told him that he is like Moses. Moses delivered the Israelites and he will deliver the Metis."

Obadiah shrugged. "So? Who are we to say? Perhaps, that is true."

Sarah smiled. "Perhaps." She reached up and straightened his shirt collar. "I will miss seeing you, Obadiah."

"Why? I will come again in a few months. By then, you will be able to meet Sarah Rose."

"No, I have decided to leave this place."

"Leave? Where will you go?"

"I am going to go to the Qu'Appelle Valley."

He stared at her. "You are going with Louis Riel?"

She shook her head. "No. I'll leave next year. I want to see it before I die."

"Sarah, why do you talk like that? You aren't a hundred years old, you know. You're not much older than Riel."

She nodded. "Yes, I don't think he will live much longer either."

Obadiah put his arms around Sarah. "I'm going to miss you." He let her go. "But, I have a whole year to try to talk you out of it."

Everyone tried to talk Sarah out of her plan to head to Canada but she had made up her mind. She didn't understand what the fuss was all about. Hadn't she travelled all through the United States already? Hadn't she lived through more tragedy than most? Why would this trip be worse? Wasn't the world more civilized now than it was twenty or thirty years ago? Surely, it was. No, she was leaving and she was travelling by herself. No, she did not need an escort. Yes, she would take a rifle with her. Only for hunting.

Early one spring while the sun was only a red glow in the east, Sarah got up and slipped into the woods. Her rig was there; filled with her provisions, ready to go. She had come out the night before in the secret of darkness and made all the preparations. Now all she had to do was give her horse, Molly, a pat on the neck, climb into her light buggy and leave. It would not be an easy trek. She had almost seven hundred miles to travel before reaching her valley.

It was a beautiful spring. One of the loveliest Sarah could ever remember. The sun shone down, warming her back and making the morning dew sparkle like millions of priceless gems. Her excitement seemed to rub off on Molly because Sarah had never seen her mare so full of life. Sometimes, she reined her in so she wouldn't tire out before the long day was over. Each night they camped by a river and Sarah slept under her buggy and watched the stars until her eyelids refused to stay open. Sometimes she sang her Abenaki songs and waited to hear the animals in the forest answer.

She stopped at Fort Benton and spent one night. A Jesuit priest tried to discourage her from continuing.

"It will not come to any good," he said. "There is going to be a great rebellion."

Sarah smiled. "I'm not going there to be part of a rebellion. I'm going to live in peace in the Qu'Appelle valley. Mr. Riel assured me that there was land for me. That's where I'll make my home."

He shook his head. "There will not be land for the taking. The Metis will never win. They will lose everything. Canada has changed since Louis lived there. I hear from travellers as they come south. Now Saskatchewan is filled with the North West Mounted Police. The railway runs right to the mountains. The government has suddenly taken an interest in this god-forsaken land. No, Louis will have many problems."

"But he is so sure he can help the Metis."

"Do you know what he said to me before he left here?"

Sarah shook her head.

"I see the gallows on top of that hill and I am swinging from it."

"He said that?"

"Yes. He knows there will be trouble. Will you still go?"

"Yes. I will go."

"I will give you my blessing."

"Did you give your blessing to Louis Riel?"

"No, I could not. His journey will only meet with tragedy."

"Then, do not give one to me either."

Then next morning, Sarah started out on her journey again. She followed the Missouri River until it started to wind south. At the bend, she turned north until she came to another river, the Souris. She didn't cross the Souris until she came to the Canada-United States border. From there, an Indian hunting party directed her to Fort Ellice. By now, the summer was gone and the scent of autumn filled the air. Farm houses were sparsely spread over the barren land so she travelled from one to another. Each family welcomed her and insisted she take some small portion of food. She knew they could barely spare what they gave.

Fort Ellice was a very small fort. There were only two Mounted Police there but they were expecting four more. It was quite a shock for the men to see a lone woman riding in. It took some time for Sarah to convince them that she was not a local Indian. She was also not a Metis.

"Why are you in Canada?" they asked.

"I have come to live in the Qu'Appelle Valley," she answered.

"Where did you come from? Where were you living?"

"Milk River."

"Then you are Metis."

"No. I happened to be there because I was taking two children back to their relatives. It is a long story."

"Where were you originally from?"

"Portland, Maine."

"So you are an American citizen?"

"I suppose I am."

"Do you think you can just come up into Canada and take land for yourself?"

"Mr. Louis Riel said there was land here."

The men laughed. "I wouldn't listen to anything that man has to say," one of them said.

"What am I to do then? I have come up all this way. I am a woman all by myself."

"You look like an Indian. Indians can come and go across the border as they please."

"I am part Abenaki."

One of the men shrugged. "We'll say you're an Indian. Go and find someplace to live."

"I can live in the Qu'Appelle valley?"

"I don't care where you live, lady. The thing is that as soon as winter hits, you'll either freeze to death or you'll be high-tailing it back down south."

Sarah heard them laughing as she went out the door. That was all right. Let them laugh. They had no idea how much she had already lived through. With a happy heart, she drove in the direction of the valley. Her valley.

The land she drove over was brown with tall wild grass. The wind whipped over the ground making a flapping sound. There wasn't a tree or shrub in sight. Everything looked flat and desolate. Had Riel led her on a wild ride for nothing? Was this his way to fill the land with his followers? There was no fertile valley in sight. There were no rivers as far as she could see. Land, that's all there was. Flat, rolling land filled with dead grass and tumbleweeds. Her heart felt heavy. She'd had only one dream her whole life: to find a valley. A valley with a stream of water running through. A small log cabin to sit in during the cold winter months and a door facing south to feel the sun in the morning. Was that too much to ask?

Molly plugged along. She seemed to feel Sarah's loss. Her mistress had left the reins loose. Suddenly, the little mare quickened her pace. She hadn't had a decent drink of cold water all day. There was the scent of water in the air.

Sarah came out of her spell.

"What's the matter, Molly? You know something I don't?"

The horse started up a high grass-covered mound. At the top, she stopped. Sarah stared out.

They were not standing on an ordinary mound. It seemed almost like the peak of a mountain and down below, far below, was a valley. A hidden valley. A valley whose walls were still covered in lush green trees and at the bottom, there was a river.

Sarah leaned back and laughed.

"There's our home, Molly."

It wasn't easy trying to manoeuvre the buggy down those steep hills. There didn't seem to be any human trail going down. Somewhere along the top of the valley, there was probably a road but Sarah had no idea where it might be or if she would even be able to find it before nightfall. She definitely did not want to camp out in the open for the night. Not with that wind and no protection. She'd had enough of that kind of camping on the trip.

She remembered vividly the plains they'd come through years before. How could she forget? The flat land for miles and miles. However, the land in which she'd driven through in Montana and Saskatchewan had been different. It was the kind of land that filled you with sadness and emptiness. An empty land. Who would want to live on it? Nothing would grow. There was nothing to protect you from the wind. It rushed in against you, almost whipping a person to the ground. There was no food for cattle. Everything appeared grey and dull. At the same time, it was hauntingly beautiful. It stirred up buried emotions.

Here, however, hidden in this vast wilderness was an oasis. The closer she got to the bottom, the more her heart sang. For the first time in her life, she felt at home. This was what she had been dreaming about, waiting for. Here was where she would live and die.

She camped by the river that night and slept under the stars. The moon shone on the water turning the whole valley into a wild fantasyland. A land was so still and wild that she felt like an intruder. The last thing she heard before falling into a deep sleep was the call of the loon.

For the next few weeks, Sarah worked on a shelter. Winter was coming soon and she knew it would be a difficult time. She never met any white people but Indians stopped by now and again to visit. Many of them spoke French. They helped her build a small log house into the side of the hill. She'd crossed through the shallow slow moving river and decided her home would be on the north bank. This way she would escape the cold north wind. Besides, she wanted her door facing the south and the east.

She also dug out a small cave not far away to store her winter food supply. There was plenty of game in the valley and she soon had it filled with dried venison. When the morning air started to nip her skin, she decided it was time to ride back to one of the forts and buy a few supplies. This time, instead of going back to Fort Ellice, she went to Fort Qu'Appelle.

The fort was bustling with farmers, soldiers and Indians. No one paid any mind to Sarah as she quietly went about her business. More than anything else, she didn't want anyone to ask where she lived. She knew her Indian friends would never talk about it to anyone, especially the soldiers.

One of the Metis wives was especially kind and friendly, so Sarah asked, in French, "Have you heard anything about Louis Riel? Is he still alive, do you know?"

"Oh yes, you haven't heard? He is sending a new bill of rights to the government in Ottawa. We will get deeds to our farms and we'll have our own government."

"That sounds wonderful. I have built a cabin in the Qu'Appelle valley. Do you think I will be able to own the land?"

"Yes, you will." She grabbed Sarah's arm. "Come and see my husband. He'll draw up a draft for you. They are all signed already. Then, when the Prime Minister of Canada comes to visit, he will know you have purchased that land."

"Who is the Prime Minister?"

"Oh, his name is Macdonald. Everyone calls him Old Tomorrow because he doesn't make any decisions. So far, he hasn't paid any attention to us but this time he will. I know it."

Sarah left for home with a great joy in her heart. In her bag, she had a deed to her land. The representative for the Metis said that once the government in Ottawa recognized this new bill of rights, then she could begin to make payments on her small homestead. This was not a worry for her because the valley was teeming with wildlife. She would trap during the winter and sell her furs and hides in the spring.

She was also happy because she was able to purchase two glass windows. All the years that she lived at Milk River, she'd never been able to see the outside world clearly. There were some things she missed from her home in Portland. One was definitely windows.

Her biggest worry was Molly. There was no way the horse could live outdoors all winter and there was no time to build a shelter or store up hay. The problem, however, was solved when a group of Metis hunters rode by and offered to winter the horse for her.

"We must all stick together, *Madame*," the leader said. "I see you speak French so you are part of us."

Sarah didn't argue.

When the snow came, Sarah thought she was prepared. She soon realized that no one could have prepared her. In all her life, she had never seen so much snow come down. For two days, she could go no farther than her cave. If she hadn't cleared the snow out to make a path every few hours, she wouldn't have been able to get there either. She was glad she'd listened to the Indian who told her to make her door to swing inside. If she hadn't, she wouldn't have been able to open the door until spring. As it was, every time she opened it, almost half the room filled with snow.

On the third day, the wind came up. It howled and moaned so loudly, she was afraid her cabin would rip apart. Cold air whistled through the cracks between the logs. However, the north wall, built into the side of the hill, was warm. Once again, she was glad she was facing south and not north. Now she couldn't go outside at all. All a person could see through the window was a white world.

On the fourth day, the storm subsided. The sun shone. Sarah opened the door to reveal a six foot wall of hardened snow. It took her two days to dig herself out.

Sarah survived those winter months, alone but not lonely. When she wasn't busy checking her traps and hunting, she was working on hides or reading. Whatever she did, she sang. The only songs she sang were the Abenaki songs.

She thought the snow would never disappear. Much to her surprise, it melted faster than she thought it would. Soon there were patches of green showing and the odd little wild flower showing its face. One warm spring day as she sat outside watching the river, she saw a group of Metis approaching. They brought Molly back, along with a few supplies they thought she might need.

"So, *Monsieur,*" she asked, "what is happening with Mr. Riel? Did the government accept the new bill of rights?"

"Huh!" he said. "They have done nothing. But, Mr. Riel, he has had a sign from heaven. I, myself, saw it. On March 15th, he said that God would draw His Hand over the face of the sun. As soon as he said this, *Madame,* the sun became darkened. I saw this myself. It is not a lie."

Sarah didn't say anything. She had witnessed it too. It was an eclipse of the sun.

It was good to have her horse back. The river was high but there was plenty of fresh green grass along the valley. She and Molly wandered through the valley for miles in one direction and then the other.

It was late in May when Sarah looked up from a hide she'd been working on and saw someone walking along the side of the river. She couldn't see the face. All she could see was the sun shining on a head of long white hair. Her heart pounded. She stood up and waited.

Finally, her brother, Frank, was home.

They laughed in each other's arms. No one asked questions.

"Come," Sarah said. "Come into my cabin. We will have some

coffee." Without thinking, she had spoken in French.

"That sounds good, sister." Frank answered in French.

The days went by, quiet and easy. Without a word from Sarah, Frank set in to fix up the small cabin. It took most of the summer; first, to find enough logs to transport and then to enlarge it. Before the cold winter wind began to blow, he caulked the inside walls and covered them with hide. He built a second narrow bed and divided the one room into two small areas so each would have a semblance of privacy. At their final trip to Fort Qu'Appelle before winter, he acquired a scythe and then worked for hours each day, cutting down the tall wild grass that grew along the hills surrounding the cabin. This he stored in a makeshift lean-to that he'd put together for Molly, Sarah's mare. He was still bringing in hay when the first blizzard hit the valley.

As the first snowflakes started to come down, Sarah called out, "Frank, you'd better finish up now. There's a north wind starting up and the air's turning cold."

Frank threw a fork-full of hay up onto the haystack and yelled back, "Almost finished." He looked up at the dark grey clouds. "It won't be here for a few hours yet, I reckon."

"You don't know this valley. Put Molly in the shed and hurry in."

Within twenty minutes, the wind had turned into a gale, whipping down into the valley like a raging bull, and the gentle virgin snowflakes transformed themselves into a massive world of swirling white. It took all Frank's strength to push the door closed against the wind's fury.

He looked at his sister in amazement. "You've been living here, all alone, dealing with winters like this? This is worse than wintering in Colorado."

Sarah laughed. "You should've seen me the first year. I've learned how to live in this valley and survive. One thing for sure - you don't stay out when the wind starts to blow, the temperature dips down and the snow starts coming down."

He grinned. "You always were a lot smarter than your younger brother."

Sarah blushed. "Here, silly. Let me help you take off that coat. Supper's ready to eat."

They sat together in comfortable silence, listening to the wood crackling in the stove and the cold Saskatchewan wind howling round the corners of the house.

Since the day he'd arrived, Frank hadn't mentioned where he'd been, why his wife was not with him or what had transpired during the past, almost twenty years. Sarah thought that as time went by, he would gradually tell her. Colorado was the first place he'd mentioned. Should she ask or wait until he was ready to tell her himself?

She stopped her knitting for a moment and looked at her brother. Frank was reading a newspaper he'd picked up at the fort. He looked so much older, older than she could have imagined. His once blond hair was now white. There were lines on his face, lines of an old man. Lines that told of hardship and worry. She saw a scar that ran from the edge of one eye down almost to his mouth. How did he get that? Whoever had made it had used a sharp knife. His mouth that could turn so quickly into a smile was now curved the other way. It's true, the smile still came but more slowly. More calculated. It was as if he had to think before he smiled. Guarded. That was the word she wanted. Every word and action was now guarded. She bent her head and went back to her knitting.

Frank glanced up from his paper. He'd read the same articles over many times. Stories about Louis Riel filled the pages. Did Sarah realize the troubles that were brewing? Did she really think she could live here in this valley, on the word of one man? A man whom the government considered a traitor?

He looked at her. Her head was bent over and he could see the grey in her hair. Instead of letting it hang down her back like she did when she was a young girl, she had it pulled tightly back into one long braid. She was still beautiful to him. Still, an Indian princess. Her skin wasn't lined like his was, it was smooth and almond coloured, but she looked old. Her eyes were always tired looking. No matter how much they laughed and sang together, he felt a sadness. She talked too much about dying.

He knew that he was the cause for much of her pain. The joy she had of seeing him again could never outweigh the heartache and worry he'd caused. The scars were buried too deeply. What could he tell her to try to make up for it? Nothing. How could he explain that he'd been so easily seduced by an evil woman? That she'd used him for her own ends? Ends that could have landed him in prison for many years. That when she was finished with him, she tried to kill him? It was something he wanted so badly to forget but every time he looked in a mirror, he was reminded of it. Then, there were the years that he could have searched for Sarah but instead he wasted his time searching for gold. It wasn't easy to face reality but he knew he stayed hidden out of shame. Somehow, he thought, if he could prove to Sarah that his years were profitable, she would forgive him. Would it soften the blow if he came carrying handfuls of gold? He should have known better. Sarah was never like that. Gold held no meaning for her. In the end, he came with nothing. Barely the clothes on his back. Please, God, he would pray at night, I pray that I didn't come back because I had no other place to go. Please, don't let my sister think that. Frank prayed, though he knew no god was listening.

If his sister ever thought that, she never said. She accepted Frank back as if he'd never left. As if the slate were wiped clean. Whatever happened during those years seemed not to bother her. He knew she was waiting for him to tell her if that was what he wished to do.

Spring was in the valley before Frank started to tell her something about his past life. Sarah sat and listened. She didn't make any comment even when he struggled trying to explain why he'd robbed and killed. In self-defence. Always, it had been in self-defence. He felt it necessary to explain but she showed no emotion. Each evening, after they finished their meal and were sitting by the outside firepit, he would try to explain things to her. The more he spoke, the worse it sounded.

"I have no excuse for the life I lived, Sarah," he said, finally.

A slight smile played on her lips. "Why do you feel that you have to excuse yourself to me?"

"Wasn't I the one who said we'd always be together? That I'd look after you?"

Sarah picked up a stick to poke the fire. She pushed the bottom logs up and sparks flew into the air. "No," she said, sadly. "I think I was the one who always said that. It's a foolish thing to say. No one knows what the future holds. We each make our own decisions in life, Frank. You made a wrong one but how were you to know?" She threw another stick of wood on the fire. "I used to wonder if perhaps you had a family and if I was someone's aunt." She gave a little laugh. "However, deep down, I knew your life would be hard. But I knew we'd be together again before I died. I always knew that."

"Sarah, there you go, speaking about dying again. You're not old. We are living in the valley that you were always looking for. We're together, you and me. It was a long journey and it was a very hard journey but we're here now." He smiled at her. "When I'm a hundred, I plan on sitting right here in front of this cabin and looking across the fire at you. Just like we are right now."

"You're a dreamer, Frank Lawdry. I wish that I could believe the same."

"But, you can. Why not, Sarah? You were always the dreamer. Remember when you were a young girl and Mother couldn't keep you in the house? You were always wandering over the hills, picking wild flowers and watching the birds. Or, just sitting and staring at the ocean. Do you remember?"

"I still watch the water. It is the only thing that brings peace to my soul." Her eyes turned toward the river. There were small pieces of ice still floating along, bumping into each other like children at play. "But sometimes I look and see blood running in it."

Frank didn't answer. He looked down at the river too. It was high and moving fast this spring. Trees along its banks were beginning to leaf out. Small dirty patches of snow could still be seen in shady hollows. In two weeks, everything would be green. Then, the hot summer sun would beat down and the warm winds would swoop down, turning the tall wild grass gold. If there were no rains, the grass would quickly become dry and brown. Even then, there was a strange beauty about this place. He knew that this was where he would die too, old and content.

In the second week of May, Frank saddled up Molly and made the trip into Indianhead. They needed some supplies but more importantly, Sarah wanted him to mail a letter to Obadiah. Things were not as wonderful as Obadiah had predicted. She warned him not to come up to Canada with his family. There was still no Metis government nor land settlement.

The sun was settling down in the west, when Sarah saw Frank

approaching from the east. The gunnysack filled with supplies was draped behind the saddle.

"All went well?" she asked. "You mailed the letter?"

He nodded before he swung down and removed the supplies. Sarah dragged the heavy sack to the cabin while Frank took care of Molly. One thing that Sarah appreciated was the care her brother took looking after the horse. Frank might sometimes not have much patience with humans but he always did when it came to horses. Molly had never been treated so well.

Frank came in and stood inside the door. Sarah glanced up.

"If you're waiting to take things to the storage cave, I'm not quite ready," she said. "It will be a few minutes yet."

"Sarah," he said.

She set the can of beans down and looked up.

"What's the matter? Are you all right? You look terrible, Frank."

Indeed he did. His face looked pale in the lamplight and the shadows under his eyes appeared darker than usual. He had started to grow a beard but instead of filling out his face as he'd hoped, it seemed to make it more narrow and bony.

"It's just that you were too late, Sarah."

"What do you mean, I was too late? Too late for what?"

"Too late to warn Obadiah."

"Why? Is he here in Canada? Did you see him?"

He shook his head. "No, he isn't here yet. But, there's word that a group of Metis families are on their way up. They should arrive the day after tomorrow. Sure as anything Obadiah will be with them. Don't you think?"

Sarah was silent for a few moments. Then, she nodded.

"He will. He wrote that he wanted to see you, Frank. It wasn't just that half of them were starving down there; it was mostly that he wanted to see you and have you meet his family."

Frank stared at her.

"After how I treated you and them, leaving you on your own, he still wanted to see me? After the life I led?"

Sarah smiled. "I've never written to him about your life, Frank. All I told him was that you were back. It's up to you to tell him your life story, if you feel fit."

"I'm never going to tell anyone my life story, Sarah. Some things should be told but that is one thing that's best forgotten."

"Then, I'll respect that, brother."

"There's something else I have to tell you."

Frank walked over to the stove and poked the fire. There was a strange look in his eye. Sarah wasn't sure if it was anger or hurt. Perhaps, both.

"What is it? Don't keep anything back. Are you all right?"

"I'm all right. It's Louis Riel, Sarah."

"Louis Riel? What do you mean?" she asked, sharply.

"There's a good chance that he might be hanged."

"What? That can't be. Why?" She dropped into a chair.

Frank walked over and sat opposite her. "They're saying that he's guilty of treason. He and Dumont have been fighting for the Metis. There has been much bloodshed. They're going to have a trial but if he's been found guilty, he'll be hanged."

"They? Who's 'they'?"

"The Canadian government. The Northwest Mounted Police. I don't know. All I know is there's a chance he might be put to death."

"What about his people? What about the Metis people? Who's going to look after them, Frank? Who's going to lead them?"

Frank shrugged. "I guess they'll have to become part of Canada. The Canadian government will have to see to them."

"What about their language? Will they keep their language?"

"What language? French, you mean?"

"Of course, I mean French. Will they be allowed to speak it?"

"I don't see why not. Who can take away your language? No one can."

"Tell that to the Indians, Frank. I've heard the government is forcing them to speak English. Perhaps, they'll do the same to the Metis."

She got up and started fussing with the supplies.

Frank stood up. "Let me do this, Sarah. Make us a cup of tea. I need one after the long ride."

Sarah's face reddened. "I'm sorry. I wasn't thinking. Of course, I'll make some tea. And, some supper."

"Do you want to go, Sarah?"

"Go where? Leave here, you mean?"

He shook his head. "No. I mean, do you want to go to the trial?"

She stared at him. "People can go to it?"

"I don't see why not. Do you want to?"

She shook her head. "No, I think not. I already know the outcome."

"No, you don't, Sarah."

"Yes, we all know the outcome, Frank. *Monsieur* Riel knew it before he came here. It is over now. The Metis have no more power. We will have to find another home."

"Why will you? You aren't Metis."

"No, but they think I am. If they find out that I'm an American, I'll be sent back south of the border. Or, perhaps the government will try to send me to a reservation. I look like an Indian."

"You're talking nonsense. You said yourself, you will die on this land."

She turned to lift the lid on the cook stove and push in a stick of wood.

"If they kill Louis Riel, there will be only trouble. People think he's a saviour. Many will die; perhaps, I will be one of them."

There was no use arguing with Sarah so Frank gathered up the bags of dried apples, beans, flour, sugar, and coffee and took them out to the cave.

He'd enlarged the cave and designed it similar to the one in the Abenaki village. He'd replaced the piece of hide that Sarah had placed over the opening with a large wooden door to keep out any wild animals. Even then, the odd squirrel or prairie dog would find a way in so they stored everything in wooden or tin containers.

They ate their supper in silence. Sarah's thoughts were not only for herself but also for Obadiah and Rosie. What if Rosie had come up to Canada too? Was there no place where they could all live in peace?

"Maybe," Frank said, when they were ready to put the light out for the night, "we should go to California. That's where we were going to go in the first place."

He blew out the light. The room was black. There was no light from the moon.

"No," Sarah said. "I'm too old and tired to travel."

Sarah didn't attend the trial but Frank did. He travelled to Regina and for five days, he sat in the hot stuffy courtroom listening to lawyers try to prove Mr. Riel was not guilty by virtue of insanity. This, however, did not sit well with *Monsieur* Riel. Several times, he disrupted the trial, protesting that he was not insane. At last, Mr. Riel stood up to defend himself. He spoke eloquently about himself, his calling in life and about God. Many women wept as they listened with rapt attention. In one hour and twenty minutes, the jury returned with the verdict.

Frank rode home slowly, dreading the thought of telling Sarah. He would make no comment on his own feelings. Why anyone believed in and blindly followed such a man was inconceivable. He was obviously a rebel against the government. He'd seen men hang for a lot less in Dodge City.

There was a change in Sarah after she heard the news. Now, she kept a loaded rifle by the door. When she went anywhere, she took the gun with her.

"Where are you going, Sarah?"

"Down to the river to bring up water."

"Why are you taking your rifle?"

She gave him a sharp look. "Because I might shoot a fish." Then, she grinned and said, "Or, maybe a white skunk. You know, the kind who tries to run you off your land."

"No one is going to run you off your land. You have papers to show that you own it."

She laughed. "Yes, papers that don't mean anything. Just foolish hopes and dreams, that's all. They are Metis papers, not Canadian government papers."

He tried to reason with her. "Not yet but when they see your intention to stay here, you will have first chance to buy it."

She went out the door, a pail in one hand and a gun in the other. Before she shut the door, she said, "I don't think it will work like that, brother. Wait and you will see."

Two weeks later, Frank was hunting west of the cabin. The deer were plentiful and he'd managed to kill a large buck. It would keep them fed for many weeks. He'd just finished tying a rope around the hind legs and pulling him over a thick tree branch to bleed when he heard the gunshots. Two shots so close to each other, it sounded like one. The resonance thundered and echoed through the valley.

"You'd better not have shot another buck, Sarah Lawdry," he muttered. "I'll have enough work here for a couple of days."

He knew it was hard for Sarah to admit she couldn't gut an

animal or clean a hide like she used to. He watched as she winced with pain each time she had to use her fingers. She tried to hide her swollen knuckles but it was something a person couldn't keep secret forever. She was grateful when he didn't say anything but would appear with a bowl of hot water for her to soak her hands in.

There was silence in the valley after the gunshots. How many had there been? Two? Why would there be two shots? Sarah never used more than one bullet. She never needed more than one. Frank had never known her to miss. She would rather miss a meal than take a chance and injure a fleeing animal.

He continued gutting the buck but he had an uneasy feeling. What if Sarah were trying to send out a warning? There was no reason for her to fire twice in such close succession. The more he thought about it, the more concerned he became. It was less than an hour's ride back. If he didn't go, he'd spend all his time wondering and worrying. He left the warm steaming guts in a heap on the ground, knowing there were animals close by waiting to pounce on it, and he flung the hollowed-out carcass behind the saddle. Molly squirmed at the smell of fresh blood but soon settled down and started to prance when she realized they were heading home.

As he rounded the last bend in the river, Frank looked out towards Sarah's cabin. He could see a thin ribbon of smoke drifting up from the chimney and dissipating gently into the clear blue sky. It was a beautiful day. The valley looked serene and untamed. There was only nature for as far as one could see. He couldn't remember a better summer. The rain came at the right time; the sun shone high in the sky, and the scent of wild clover drifted along with the warm breezes. Each evening he and Sarah would sit outside to watch the deer as they came to drink at the river and listen to the birds as they flitted from tree to tree. They would sit for hours in silence until the moon shone down and then, in unison, they would get up and ready themselves for the night.

He knew that this was what Sarah had been searching for. He was happy for her. Why couldn't he have had such a dream? But now he would find contentment. All that mattered was making Sarah happy.

The closer he got to the cabin, the more nervous Molly became.

"What's the matter, girl? You should be used to that old dead deer on your back by now."

Frank held the reins tight as Molly neighed and jerked her head.

"Easy, Molly, easy. What is there, a wild cat hiding in the bush?"

He held her close to the gravelled shore where the ground was flatter. If there were a wild animal ready to pounce, Molly would be on solid ground and his shot would be more accurate.

He was so focused on his surroundings and trying to control his horse that he failed to look up until he was almost at the doorstep.

"Sarah," he screamed. "Sarah, what's wrong?"

He jumped down and ran to his sister. She lay crumpled in a heap, her face to the ground, her rifle clutched in one hand. A sickly dread consumed his body; a dread so fierce he couldn't breathe. He gasped for air like a drowning man. Before turning her body over, he knew. He knew his sister was dead. Blood still oozed out of the wound between her shoulder blades. He removed the rifle from her grasp and gently placed her on her back. Her black unseeing eyes stared back at him. He could see no pain, only resignation.

"Oh, Sarah," he whispered. "I'm so sorry." Tears of sorrow that Frank had sworn he would never shed again, ran down his face. "If only I'd come right away, you might be alive." He sobbed as he threw himself over her body. Time stood still for Frank Lawdry. He cried until there was nothing left in him. No one could imagine the emptiness. He sat up and cradled Sarah's head in his lap.

"We never got to say good-bye, Sarah. This is the second time. But, this time, you left without saying it. You left me without saying good-bye." He rocked his sister, his face buried in her hair.

Frank didn't know how long he stayed like this. The sun went down and the moon came up. Finally, he carried her into the cabin and laid her on the bed. Sarah's blood covered his hands and shirt. He went down to the river and sang the dead song. The Abenaki song.

The next morning, three Metis hunters came by. They were uncouth men but never passed by Sarah's place without seeing if she needed anything. She'd made it clear that she wouldn't tolerate drunkenness, smoking, or foul language and they complied.

Frank met them outside.

"You've come too late," he said. "Perhaps, if you'd been here yesterday, you could have tracked down the person who murdered my sister."

The three men sat in their saddles, staring at him. He still wore the same blood-caked clothes.

"What do you mean, murdered?" Pierre, one who had helped Sarah build a cabin when she first arrived in the valley, spoke in French.

"Yesterday," Frank replied, in French. "I was hunting. While I was down the river, I heard two shots. I didn't think anything of it. I thought Sarah had probably shot an animal. I came home to find her, dead on the ground, a bullet through her chest."

"Did you find any tracks?"

Frank shook his head. "I didn't look."

Two of the men turned their horses and started slowly walking along the river, their eyes to the ground.

Pierre said, "Have you buried her?"

Frank shook his head, again.

The big Metis got down from his horse. He walked over to Frank and crushed him in his arms. Frank sobbed as the man gently patted his back. After several minutes, Pierre pulled away and said, "We will help you. Sarah was our friend. You are our friend. We will get the man who did this."

He led Frank into the house and sat him in a chair in front of the stove. In a few minutes, he had a fire roaring and a pot boiling to make coffee.

"Now," he said, "I will go to see Sarah."

He took off his hat, repeated the only prayer he knew and crossed himself, as he stood by Sarah's bed.

The two men sat at the small wooden table, drinking coffee. The other men had been gone less than an hour when the door opened and they came in.

"Aw, *Monsieur,*" one said, "you do not have to worry about who killed your sister. We have found him."

Frank jumped up. "You found him? How? Who did this?"

One of the men smiled, revealing a row of yellow teeth. "Your sister, she is a good shot too. The man lies in a clump of trees, not far from here. He bled to death."

"Who?" Pierre stood up. "Who is this man? Do you know him?"

"We do not need to know him. He is wearing a uniform."

"A soldier?" Frank asked. "Why would one of the soldiers kill

Sarah?"

The young man shook his head. "No, not a soldier. A Northwest Mounted Policeman. That is who shot your sister."

Frank turned to Pierre. "What do we do? Whom will we go to? Can we go to the police for help?"

"No. We will do nothing. We will bury your sister. We will let the police find their own man. We will do nothing."

Frank stared at him. "We'll just leave him there?"

Pierre smiled. "Yes, my brother. We'll let the birds eat his flesh and the animals have a feast."

"But won't someone come looking for him? Will they say Sarah murdered him? Or, perhaps, one of us?"

"Don't worry. We will make sure no one gets too close. Now, where do you think Sarah would like to be buried?"

Frank chose a place where there was a curve in the river.

"Here," he said. "Sarah can see everything: the sun coming up in the east and the sun setting. She can see the deer that come down to drink, the birds that nest in those trees and whoever is coming downstream or upstream." He stood and looked up and down the river. "She'll like it here."

One of the men, said, "You talk like an Indian but you don't look like one."

Frank nodded. "Yes," he said. "I am from the Abenaki tribe. My sister was married to a very important man. Levi was his name. My great-grandfather was married to Black Swan. Her father was Wougwses."

"I thought your sister was a Metis. That's what everyone said."

"No, she was Indian."

"Well," Andre said, "if she was an Indian and you're an Indian, they won't take you off this land. Did you know that?"

Frank shook his head. "I can't stay here. Louis Riel is going to be hung. His execution date is September the 18th. That is not too far away. The Canadian government will then take all this land."

Andre grunted. "Riel has good lawyers. There are more hearings, I am told. Besides, they will take land only from the Metis. If you are an Indian, you will be able to stay. Watch and see. There is enough trouble brewing. They won't want to take on all the Metis and the Indians. Too many have already been killed. The Indians will band together."

"My first thought was that I should be as far away from here as possible." He looked over to where the two men were beginning to dig the grave. "But, it would be wrong to leave Sarah here, alone in her valley." When he looked up, there were tears in his eyes. "I won't make the mistake of leaving her again."

Pierre nodded. "It is good if you stay." He took Frank's arm. "Let's bring your sister. My brother, Martin, can say a few words. He was going to be a priest once. That was before Germaine became pregnant."

Before the men left, Pierre asked Frank, "If you are an Indian, what is your name? You must have an Indian name."

"My name is Winnipesaukee."

"What does it mean?"

"It has no meaning. It is only a name."

When I opened my eyes, the sun was shining high above. The back of my neck was wet with sweat. I couldn't remember falling asleep. It was probably more like passin' out, I would think. Slowly, I sat up and looked around. It appeared that I was all alone. All I could hear was the sound of the river and a fly buzzin' round my head. I stood up and stretched.

"Mr. Winnipesaukee," I called out.

There was no answer, except for an ol' crow, cawing in some tree. I sat down on the big rock that had served as a chair for me the night before. It was then that I noticed a piece of paper, held down by a stone, and flappin' in the wind. I picked it up and read it. There were only three words: Be back soon. 'Course, since I had no idea when he'd written it, I didn't know when it might be fulfilled. In any case, I thought it best to wait awhile before traipsing off to my car. Especially, since I didn't get a chance to say thank you for his supper and more importantly, his story.

There was one thing I was goin' to do before he got back and if I planned on doing it, I'd better get crackin'. I mean, I'd hate to get caught snoopin' in his cabin and then have him catchin' me. I was sure if I waited, he wouldn't mind if I had a look but somehow, I wanted to be all alone in that place. After all, it was Sarah's cabin. I took one last look down the path before going to the door.

The inside was dark and cool and it took a few moments for my eyes to adjust. It was just as I'd pictured in my mind. The room was still divided into two areas. Frank's (although I had a hard time thinkin' of him as that) bed was along the wall on my left. It was easy to tell it was his, seein' that it was all messy lookin'. There was an ancient cook stove, some shelves filled with dishes and such, and an old table with two rickety chairs. There was a faded picture in a wooden frame on the wall above his bed so I walked over to have a look. There were three people in the picture: two men and one woman. It was one of those old pictures like my granny had on her dresser. The kind where everyone looks kind of sad and mean-looking. I took the picture down and went over to the window so's I could have a better look. The woman I knew right off was Sarah. She sure did look more Abenaki than white. I stared back at those sad black eyes. It was hard to imagine the one man was Mr. Winnipesaukee but I knew that's who it had to be. I guess that was because now his face was covered over with wrinkles and beard. But one thing was for sure; he was jus' as tall now as he was then. He towered over his sister and his friend. There was a signature in the corner of the picture. Sort of an autograph, I guess.

Louis Riel.

I slipped the picture frame back on the nail and turned to leave. Somehow, a great sadness had come over me. I gave the room one last look. To my amazement, there was something I hadn't noticed before.

To my right, at the end of Sarah's bed, tucked into the corner, piled high with papers, magazines, and clothes sat a baby grand piano.

The End.

www.ingramcontent.com/pod-product-compliance
Lightning Source LLC
Chambersburg PA
CBHW07081518062618062618
46818CB00001B/270